I0700521

EVAN CHRONIS

ZEPHYR

For my family

Prologue

July 18, 2025
Jamaica, Queens, New York City

ANTHONY SANTINO tapped his foot and awaited an explanation.

Abdul winced as he reached for the worn leather briefcase that his wife had bought for his thirty-fifth birthday. He was forty-five. Once gilded and shiny, the buckles had since been clouded over by a foreign gunk.

"Here is your invoice," Abdul began. "Please contact me if you would have any further wish—"

"Put that back."

Abdul blinked. "I'm sorry?"

Without hesitation, Anthony grasped the trout by its tail and flung it over the window pass, his toe rounding at the end of the movement like a golfer following his swing. The fish landed with a sickening *crunch* beside the dish sink. Abdul watched, horrified, as Anthony reached into his pocket and gingerly unfoiled a Nicorette square. "This charr was just flown in this morning! Do you know how hard it was for me to find this thing outside of season?"

Anthony chomped down, cracking the gum's faintly ammonic crust. "That *thing* smells like a French whorehouse."

Abdul fumed. He thought to tell him, *You are shameful. I will not do business with a shameful man.* Had the fool known he had once served in his Majesty's Royal Guard, he might have bowed or kneeled rather than sneering in his direction. His eyes were incapable of meeting his, focusing on his eyebrows instead.

But Abdul smothered his pride, briefly imagining his income without the classy restaurant boosting his sales, his child without toys or things. "As you wish, Chef. Next Wednesday, then, I will see you." He buckled his briefcase and bowed slightly. "I will do better next time—*sir*."

Anthony raised his voice as Abdul escaped through the kitchen's swing doors. "Excuse me. Aren't you forgetting something?"

Abdul turned, aghast. The chef was smiling stupidly toward where the dead trout lay, a slick of tread grime and fryer grease besmirching its once brilliant scales. Anger bubbled in Abdul's chest. He thought to turn and defend his pride. It would be simple violence, and justified. The chef had the look of a man who was granted success. He'd never learned how to earn things. He would not offer much resistance.

No, Abdul reminded himself. *To cause harm is to injure oneself.* He inhaled slowly. *It is not for you to pass judgment onto others. God sees with eyes unblinded.*

When he exhaled, the redness had dissipated, and his palms relaxed. He would save the commissions from the disgraceful chef's subsequent order to buy himself a new suitcase, yes, or perhaps a new video game for his son. He was obsessed with the things, his wife had told him over the home phone he still paid for, for old times' sake. *Yes, the old times.* He sighed, eying the fish as he approached, its fear-shocked eye agape, staring at him, judging him.

Old times. Those had been the good times, times he now wished for. He wished for many things. He wished he would have remained faithful. He wished he had seen her unhappiness before it was too late. He wished he had spoken with her before she filed the divorce papers and forced his hand in signing them. He wished he would have spent the money on a proper lawyer, a Jew, perhaps, and fought harder to keep his son. He wished his son was of an age where he could fly from godforsaken El Paso alone and see him without his mother's consent. He wished he did not have to bow before such arrogant men just to pay the rent for his lonely two-bedroom, which he kept for his pride's sake. He reminded himself that his hard work would pay off when his son came to visit in eight weeks' time.

Abdul sighed heavily and bent over, gripping the trout by the gills and holding it as far as he could from his silk jacket—his most valued garment, purchased eight years ago from the Nordstrom Rack. He strained against the fish's dead weight, twisted his neck, and bowed toward Anthony. The chef nodded back, grinning, chomping, as Abdul exited through the swinging doors, his back arched stiffly as if to retain some dignity.

Once the fishmonger was out of sight, Anthony turned to his fry-man in training, Ernesto, who was gazing at him with apprehension and some fear. Anthony gave him a stiff nod. Ernesto nodded quickly as if to agree on some unspoken matter and turned back to his work. He raised his voice with some reluctance, his hands never stopping their work, quickly spooning ovals of meat suspended in bechamel and dusting them with flour: "Chef, what go wrong with the trout?"

Anthony flicked his chin toward the clock hanging above the window pass. *8:38.* "The camel jockey was late." By six minutes, to be exact; the confrontation had taken another two. He noticed a lapse in Ernesto's spooning technique and snapped his fingers. "*Más suave.* They're not gonna run from you, chef."

"Sí, Chef." Ernesto tucked his chin and resumed his work, his hands moving with trained precision.

◆

His delivery van needed a fresh coat of paint. Rust marked it in spots he had once thought rust was alien to; the orange-brown rot had crept from the undercarriage all the way to the van's roof. It did not matter. Neither Ferraro brother placed much importance on appearance. They were men of function and not form, and if their business functioned well with minimal superficial intervention, then that was optimal.

Abdul closed the door behind him, opened it again, then swung it shut harder so the latch caught. The engine responded to a certain jostle of the ignition, which he had perfected to a science.

It took him just over a half hour to reach Jamaica of Queens. He thought to stop at an electronics store obnoxiously advertising its *GOING OUT OF BUSINESS!* sale and purchase something for his son, before realizing his rent was due at the end of the week. He sighed. It would have to wait. He might have asked his landlord to take pity on him and allow him an extension, but he had asked the same of him last month. He feared overstretching his goodwill.

The façade of Ferraro Brothers Fishery was in a similar state of dishevelment as its delivery vans. Its sign was visibly tinted by the sort of moist, chilled air that emanates naturally in the presence of fish and other crustaceous organisms.

Abdul parked the emptied delivery van in a non-assigned spot on 186th and Jamaica Avenue. It was a Friday. The eldest brother Ferraro still lauded his ability to recognize the date and adjust his parking behavior accordingly—a skill that didn't require much from Abdul but had a disproportionate impact on the functionality of Ferraro Brothers Fishery. Bulk shipments arrived early on Saturdays, and so the receiving dock where the vans normally sat parked would be occupied most of the morning. Having one less vehicle clogging up the back alley meant more space and less room for error on the delivery trucks' part. Abdul had recognized the need for more space and began parking across the street on his own. When he asked why other sales representatives hadn't started parking elsewhere, Al Ferraro had slipped him a twenty and slurred, "Listen Abdo: the others ain't worth a shit." Abdul did not agree with him, but he didn't disagree either.

A neon-lit outstretched palm prevented anyone from fording Jamaica Avenue. *WAIT*, chanted the tiny voice hidden inside the crosswalk's cable box. He calmly awaited the white-silhouetted walking man to flash onto the sign.

Abdul's eyes wandered from the hand-painted and fish-rotten sign above the fishery to the sky above. The day was humid and gusty, mired by hot winds that denied the clouds any rest. He squinted at the perfect white popcorn balls slowly creeping above him until the sun suddenly lost its blinding might.

Abdul's heart slowed. He gazed up as the heavens drifted and swirled, then suddenly became very still. He forgot the feeling in his palms and floated away from his mortal shell, watching through a lens undeterred by fear or doubt or anxiety. The clouds had started to shed parts of themselves. Long, skinny fingers of nimbus sighed down from the mother cloud like moving stalagmites. He became totally transfixed when the ghost fingers began to curl and form letters. The letters coalesced, first forming words, then entire sentences, though they belonged to a language Abdul did not know. It need not matter. The message was made clear by its author, who'd chosen Abdul as his scribe.

The sound of a woodpecker hammering away at a steel drum pulled Abdul from his vision. He looked up, still partially dazed, and realized the crosswalk had changed over. He swallowed, feeling as though his tongue were stuck in his throat, and forced his numb legs to proceed across Jamaica Avenue.

"*Gah!*" A pale-gold sedan sped across the intersection. Abdul flailed his arms in front of him, just barely managing to avoid falling underneath the wheels. The driver blared his horn and sped off.

Abdul watched the car disappear, adrenaline still raging through his veins. He glanced around to see if anyone else had witnessed the blatant offense and caught all or some of the miscreant's license plate. He saw no one. He wetted his tongue and glanced up at the sky before cautiously crossing the street.

◆

Abdul entered his place of work, still in a daze. The workers had already emptied the premises, save middle-son Johnny Ferraro cooped up in his office. Abdul felt as though he were floating. His floating feet took him to the packing floor without his express consent, where the bottoms of his shoes instantly became coated with a pungent mélange of melted ice, blood, and fish guts.

He was standing, staring remotely at one of the filleting stations, trying to uncover the meaning behind the vision God had shown him when the door of the nearest bathroom swung open abruptly. A cutter fully garbed in his apron and rubber boots stumbled out from inside. Abdul did not recognize him. The Ferraro brothers gutted employees almost as efficiently as they did fish. They had mastered the art of replacing departing employees (which typically included drug-involved youth and no-call-no-shows). The turnover was constant, yet the business somehow continued to be profitable, which was a testament to Abdul's sales acumen; he was the Ferraros' top salesman, approaching eight consecutive years now. He preferred to think of it as his human acumen.

The boy was muttering to himself. His hands crept up to his scalp and he began tugging at his hair, lightly at first, then violently. He seemed not to notice Abdul staring. The boy was dark-complected and of a small stature. He was experimenting with a thin beard that'd begun to creep past his cheeks. Just a boy, really.

The boy stood, muttering and tugging before his hands moved over his mouth. His body jerked suddenly. The boy was sick almost instantly; he did not even bother rushing toward one of the countless dump bins filled with skin and bones and guts nearby. The vile substance covered his apron and splattered onto his rubber boots. He seemed indifferent to it. Drool fell from his mouth, and his eyes were black marbles, stuck in one unremarkable spot on the floor.

Abdul rushed to the boy's aid, who was crouched with his head between his knees, panting. "Let me help you from this thing," he said, pinching at the collar of his apron. The boy showed no indication whether he had heard him, but he allowed Abdul to untie the soiled apron from his waist regardless.

Abdul guided the boy to a plastic chair by the cutting floor's exit, where workers gathered to shoot the shit during their lunch breaks. The boy seemed to have regained some awareness. He shrugged away from him as they came to the break area.

"Water? Something?" Abdul asked. The boy shook his head. Abdul asked if he was okay. The boy shook his head.

"My brother's dead."

Abdul observed the boy's face carefully. There was a small quiver caught in his lip, though he fought to prevent any tears from falling. "I'm sorry. I once had a brother, too."

The boy sniffed. "I think it might be my fault." He pinched his nose. "I could've done something to stop it."

Abdul grasped the boy by the shoulder. "Nothing is under our control. The only comfort we can take from this is knowing that it is God's will." The boy did not seem comforted in the slightest. Abdul frowned. "Do you believe in God?"

The boy shied away from him. "No. Not anymore." He blinked. "I can't remember the last time I went to church ..."

"God does not care whether you visit his place of veneration; only that you believe in him in your heart. If your faith needs restoring, then look no further. A car almost ran me over, just now, outside. But before I stepped into the crosswalk, I *saw* it. Look at me." The boy did. "I would not be standing before you if I had not seen God's light. It was God who saved me. I know it. I know it to be true." He smiled. "What more proof of his existence do you require?"

He thought about what the man had said. "Then I guess I do." They sat in silence for a while, Abdul's hand planted firmly on his shoulder until the boy began to cry. Tears dripped down his face, joining the cold water filling the treads of his boots.

He let the boy wipe his tears away before asking where his parents were. "At the hospital. I think ... I don't know."

"You should go then. But first, pray with me."

He did not wait for the boy to reply. *God writes our destiny,* Abdul thought as he took the boy's hand in his own. "It is not for us to question God's actions. All we can do is heed his word and know it is pure."

Part I

It would be absurd if we did not understand both angels and devils, since we invented them.
– John Steinbeck

I

No. 21 Month 7, oooi P.F.
Pittsburgh, Pennsylvania, United States of America

HIS FATHER'S men came at sundown. They raided his bedroom and installed a spongey material that blocked August's screams from entering. Adam could not sleep afterward. It was somehow more disturbing hearing her suffering muffled rather than outright.

After the men left, Adam crept from his room down the hall to the spare bedroom serving as his mother's ward. He sat cross-legged by the dimly lit door frame and listened to the sharp gasps escaping from the room. The noise made his insides hurt.

After a long and blissful stretch of silence, Adam peeked through the door. He was surprised to see his father inside, kneeling beside her, his head resting on her abdomen. Adam saw the weathering on his face. He looked frail, even beside his mother, whose face was stained with a permanent grimace. An emerging beard darkened his cheeks. Adam could not recall seeing his father anything but clean-shaven.

Adam tucked his knees to his chest and dozed off until she again awakened him. The sun had risen while he was asleep, which didn't feel right to him. Mom was warmth. When she was gone, the sun should've gone too. Adam evaded the sunlight and crept back to his soundproof box in case his father's men returned.

◆

Abdul tried his earnest to preoccupy Adam. His preferred method of distraction was games and sports, whereas his colleague, a bleak professor turned corporate counsel named Santero, much preferred the quiet contemplation that comes with lectures and readings. But their efforts did very little to distract Adam.

"We cannot push him too hard," Abdul told Santero in the late hours of the second night while Adam was supposed to be asleep. Neither was attuned to Adam's constant eavesdropping, his ear pressed up against the crack beneath his bedroom door.

"Yes, but the Chief doesn't want him knowing."

"The Chief is not with us now. Let him be with his wife while she is still alive. Adam is young, not *stupid.* His mother is dying. Throwing books at him will not change this."

"He's only nine," Santero reputed.

"Yes! Nine years old! He will not be a child forever." Abdul paused to exhale. "August will be gone soon. We cannot coddle him as she did."

Did? Adam wanted to leave the room and attack Abdul for his words. Even then, however, he knew that he was speaking truth. He bit his lip to hold back the tears threatening to escape him.

"You're right. Of course, you're right ... but do you realize how significant of a change this will be? It could toughen him—or destroy him. We are responsible for guiding him through this." The one-time professor dipped his voice before adding, "Just don't forget who our employer is."

"I'm not likely to."

Their assessment was correct; Adam knew his mother was sick. He knew she would not get better. He knew his brother was still inside her.

He had yet to overhear any news of his brother.

◆

For three nights, Adam pretended. He sat cross-legged in his room and pretended to be asleep. He pretended he was naïve to his mother's suffering. He pretended he was somewhere else. He pretended his life was a movie. All his pretending did nothing to quiet his mother.

On the third night, Adam again snuck away to his mother's doorstep. He had yet to see his father, apart from that brief glimpse two nights ago. He supposed this meant he'd never left her side; neither to use the restroom nor to comfort his firstborn son.

As Adam sat guarding the bedroom, there came a loud knock at the front door. He heard the guards posted outside have a brief exchange with the visitor. Suddenly, footsteps came echoing down the hall.

Adam slid on all fours into the small closet next to his mother's sick room. The weighed-down Oxfords *clack*ed down the hall until they arrived at his mother's door. The intruder knocked softly on the door. It quickly opened to a crack. *"Quiet, man!"* his father whispered sharply from inside.

Adam peeked through the slit in the closet at the visitor's shoes. They were Oxfords, battered and worn at the toes. Flimsy blue pants flowed down his legs and stopped just above his shoelaces. Adam thought they looked like the pants a doctor or dentist might wear.

The men spoke in hushed tones. *"No!"* his father whispered urgently. The doctor or dentist spoke urgently into the crack in the door, inspiring a prolonged silence. Adam waited until a tired and hoarse version of his father finally replied.

"Then it's settled," the Chief said firmly. "Use whatever means necessary."

The doctor must've nodded. He entered the delivery room silently, his feet trading places with George's. And then Adam heard a noise. Unbeknownst to Adam, it was the first and only time he would ever hear it. The noise came from his father. It *sounded* like he was crying, though Adam doubted it at first. Such a sound couldn't have come from George Crombie— *Chief* George Crombie. It wasn't until the sound swelled that Adam knew it was real. Sobs reverberated from George's chest, shaking his lungs into submission. Adam thought he heard him whispering some silent prayer or mantra, the same words over and over like he was warding off the devil. Then, just as suddenly as it had started, the noise stopped, cut out from existence. The Chief's gleaming shoes flashed across the doorway and disappeared into the foyer.

Adam poked his head out of the closet. He heard his father giving orders to the men who stood guard at the front door. Adam crawled out from his hiding place and slid noiselessly to his room. He froze outside the door. A blood-curdling moan emerged from the delivery room. Adam was nauseous. He wanted to run back down the hall, throw open the door, and attack the man hurting his mother, but he knew they would easily overpower him. She sobbed. Next came tense commands from the doctor: "Deep breaths, August!"

Adam decided he didn't care if the man was bigger than him. He took a step toward his mother until he heard his father's voice coming from the foyer: "How is he ...?"

The accented voice that replied was Abdul's. "Good. He's sleeping again."

"That's not what I meant. I mean, does he know?"

Abdul paused before responding. "He might need some time to process—"

"No. I'll see him now."

Adam's hands went cold. He fled to his room and searched frantically for a hiding spot, a hidden passageway, an invisibility cloak—something to help him evade his father. But he knew he would find nothing. He wished he was sitting with his mother at that moment, proudly showcasing his latest enfant-garde sketch in his art book while she sat sipping her bitter morning ritual. He wished he was sitting at the kitchen island, his legs dangling from one of the four barstool-height chairs, watching her craft some elaborate pastry she was set on mastering. He wished he could see her smile. "*You're going to be such a good big brother someday,*" she'd say, caressing his cheek. He would even take being grounded. Anything but ...

His father knocked, but Adam felt his presence before. The Chief was too *big* to not expect. George Crombie entered wordlessly.

Adam struggled to recognize his father. He appeared to be in a daze. His eyes, usually calm and sharp like a still pond, darted anxiously from left to right. He'd shaved recently and left a rash on his neck from the razor. Adam had never seen that look on him either.

The Chief caught Adam's stare and smiled toothlessly. Adam sat on the edge of his bed, petrified as his father advanced on him. George stepped over Adam's half-collected drawing kit, his colored pencils and half-dried paintbrushes and liquid chalk pens poking out from its hinges. He lowered himself with a sigh as Adam's bed sank at his behest. Adam watched his feet sway above the ground. His father's presence erased his mother from his thoughts, replacing her with anxiety. "Do you know where you come from, Adam?"

"Why are you letting them kill Mom?" Adam blurted, surprised by the severity of his own words.

The Chief inhaled sharply and loosened his collar. His shoulders twitched as if they wanted to shed his wrinkled jacket. He had never seen his father in wrinkled clothes. "I would never do anything to harm your mother." The hand closest to Adam began to tremble.

Adam's lip quivered. He bit down and wiped his nose with the back of his palm and waited for his father to speak. But the Chief said nothing until a sudden, soft rain began to patter against the bedroom window. The *thump*ing seemed to bring him back to reality.

"There are *people* down there, Adam. They live buried up to their chests in water, in seclusion, terrified of getting sick from each other ...

And yet, they still believe in us." The Chief shook his head incredulously. Adam was not sure whether he was speaking to him or himself. "We cannot keep them safe, Adam. But we can make them *feel* safe. Do you understand?" Adam nodded and wiped his nose, his original question left unanswered. "They believe in us because we're *strong*. *We* are the ones who do the protecting." The Chief placed his hand on Adam's shoulder. "We have to be *strong*. Do you understand now, Adam?" Adam nodded slowly, unsure of what he was agreeing to.

Someone knocked politely. "Come in." Abdul entered, his tan skin gone pale. Adam listened for any noise coming from his mother's room as the door swung open; either the soundproofing was serving its purpose or his mother had gone to sleep.

"Chief," Abdul said stiffly, noticing the dried tears on Adam's cheeks. George nodded sharply. Abdul acknowledged Adam a moment longer than he would have liked, then winced and turned his attention to the floor. "It may be best if we speak alone, sir."

"No. Go on. I'm listening."

Abdul winced again. He said a silent prayer before realizing his duty. He folded his arms behind his waist and relayed the information as he'd been told to do so—factually.

"Mrs. Crombie died just moments ago. After inducing labor, Dr. Alvarez identified a postpartum hemorrhage. Despite his efforts, he was unable to stop the ... the blood ..." He cleared his throat with a polite *Excuse me*, as if he were delivering a press release and not telling a boy his mother was dead. "Cause of death was determined as ek—" The word choked him. "*Exsanguination*. She did not respond to resuscitation."

The Chief nodded robotically. His hand had stopped shaking. "And my son?"

Abdul's eyelashes fluttered and then went back down to the floor. "Stillborn, sir."

The Chief released Adam. Abdul bowed slightly and dismissed himself. And then the room was silent.

Abdul's words didn't quite translate to Adam. Time itself seemed to come to a standstill. The only thing that moved was the rain, a steady beat outside his window.

The Chief rose then, avoiding his son's eyes. "Within every tragedy there is opportunity," he announced before leaving.

II

No. 8 Month 3, 0017 P.F.
Mustang Base #8, Capital District, New American Colonies

TYLER'S EYES crossed as he watched the smoke drift from his lips. The radio was doling out an old Elvis track that no one aside from Brooks knew the words to (he made it known by treating them to a somewhat respectable impression of the King, simultaneously crooning and throwing half-hearted karate kicks). Just as he was belching out the second chorus, the radio turned to fuzz and garbles.

"Piece a shit!" Brooks sputtered, pounding the thing with the flat of his palm. The signal scrambled momentarily, and the King briefly returned before dying a third time. They joked about someday patenting Brooks's hands because of their seemingly magical signal-boosting effect on the old radio; the thing absorbed beating after beating yet always came back to life. He smacked it once more, to no avail. It seemed the abuse had finally cumulated past a certain point. Tyler sighed and swiped meagerly at the clumps of cigarette ash collecting on his chest.

"I'm tired of fixin' that thing," Brooks muttered. "Bet them boys up in the Ninth Quad got themselves a good setup—wireless, subwoofers, all that jazz."

Crunch nodded. "Listen to all the damn music you want with one of them."

"Try hitting it again," Ed chimed in.

Brooks spat. "Boys ain't even left the Ninth. Probly still green as grass," he growled.

"Do you guys ever stop bitching?" Tyler hummed beneath his cigarette.

Brooks gave him the finger in reply and packed his cheek with Skoal from the tin he kept scrunched up in his pocket. Anytime Tyler or Ed had a ciggy, Brooks would take to lecturing them on the "cancer inducin'" effects' of such modes of nicotine absorption. "This right here," he'd declare, tapping the cylinder at his thigh, "is the new world's medicine."

"More like dipshit," Ed would dispute, making the other soldiers snicker. And so the cycle continued, until one day the remark bothered Brooks enough for him to throw Ed to the ground and administer a sternum rub that brought tears to his eyes. That made the others snicker more. Frankly, no one in their battalion (Brooks included) could give a shit about the substantial health risk. Hell, Tyler would've welcomed cancer with open arms. He figured he might as well sunbathe while he chain-smoked, just to improve his odds. Say *Fuck you* to the universe, *Fuck you* to existence.

And then he would exhale, and think to himself, *Fuck that.*

They did their earnest to keep themselves occupied, and if casual dependencies helped them through another day, then so be it. Not that they didn't also have to make sacrifices; Tyler had to give up the needle for his job's sake. H and soldiering did not go hand in hand; being around deadly weaponry and at risk of nodding off was neither responsible nor wise (at least in the view of his superiors). Ed quit smoking reefer, more for lack of a veritable supply than anything. Booze actually suited their profession quite well, it being portable, potable, and not strictly illicit. Technically, their consumption did not void the sanctity of their enlistment. Most importantly, alcohol aided

Tyler in throttling his memory—somewhat. The past was painful. So were hangovers, albeit to a lesser degree.

Tyler covered his head with his elbow to drown out the banter. Being sober made it difficult. So did their volume. "Ey, Haj!" Brooks jeered at him. Tyler twitched his elbow in response. "Member the day I found you? Shape that you were in?" he mentioned for the thousandth time. He poked Tyler's ribcage. "Look at 'im now! Spry fucker."

"Shut up," he grumbled, and for once, Brooks obeyed. Tyler did not want to think about that day. He did not want to think, period. He was fantasizing about his patrol shift later that night. Having to watch meant not having to think. A fearsome anxiety grasped Tyler whenever he didn't have a patrol shift to slog through, or any errands to run for one of their commanding officers. Booze helped him through those eventless stretches.

He drank to such effect as often as his body permitted him. Sometimes the alcohol would only further immerse him in his memories, memories from before God decided to fuck over the entire world. It was amazing how much he took for granted in those days, him and everyone else. The little things, like being able to take a shit and simply flush it away to some unknown abyss. Or going for a walk without having to pretend not to notice the constant smell of rotten fish and sewage. Or pointing at a Christmas tree and having a seasonal employee saw away at its trunk, then strap it to the roof of your car. Or having roads.

His squad mates resumed their discourse, but Tyler did not notice. His mind was racing now, thinking of ways not to think. The universe was unmoved by his wishes. He brainstormed ways to become an indifferent mortal shell until his brain finally surrendered.

He dreamed he was at the beach, toes wriggling in the sand, seagulls fighting for leftover picnic scraps.

◆

He and his brother used to love going to the beach.

The memories were short-lived, in truth. Their family vacations in Monmouth Beach had only lasted two summers at most. He couldn't remember exactly why they'd stopped going, though he suspected it'd had something (or everything) to do with their mother's drinking or their father's struggling business. A bit of both was the most likely culprit.

The memories served as ideal placeholders he could turn to whenever his past came calling. Those summers came before his mother ever started her worrisome habit and while their father was still making an active effort to spend time with his family. Tyler had been too young to remember much else besides the khaki-colored sand and the shadows of the seagulls falling over him. Nonetheless, they were idyllic memories, free of pain, free of hardship. The memories became even more precious to him after his brother died.

May 19, 2024

Lori blinked wearily and reached again for her glass. "So, Aaron, do you know what kind of doctor you want to be?"

Tyler's brother picked at his fingernails. He was always picking at his fingernails, Tyler recalled. *Click*, followed by a pause, then another *click*. And so on. "Primary care, probably. I don't wanna be on call the rest of my life."

Lori swallowed her beer, an accoutrement. She frowned, almost naturally. Even the densest of foundations could not disguise the deep wrinkles attributed to her abusive misuse. "But wouldn't you make more money as a surgeon, or a researcher ... What do they call cancer doctors?"

"Cancer doctors."

"Oh. Well *I* think, I mean, you've always been so shy and awkward, have you thought about ..."

Tyler had always had a short fuse. The worst of this anger came out whenever his mother handed out her trademark subcutaneous insults. Though he never physically expressed any resentment, he was terrible at hiding it. Always had been; his eyes darkened, and he ground his teeth to the point that his molars had collapsed inward. He could almost hear his blood boil. He remembered his uncle laughing at him once when he was young, on his birthday, when the wind blew out his candles before he could blow them out ceremoniously. Rather than sob or snivel, he became irate, chewing his molars and clenching his fists, standing from his chair and fighting tears. His uncle had laughed. "*You look just like your father when you get upset,*" he goaded him, which had only made Tyler angrier, and his dark eyes darker. That only caused his uncle to laugh harder.

Tyler searched for any hint of the same rage in his brother's eyes as their mother grasped for unfamiliar words to slur. The brothers were of one and the same shade, equally enraptured by their father's dark-of-hair-and-eyes genes. But Aaron's eyes were wider than his, calmer. More open to gratitude.

Tyler scanned his brother's eyes, but they showed none of the same narrow fury that his exuded. He had escaped into his smartphone, and their mother had not seemed to notice. *Smart move*, he noted.

"Hup—excuse me. All I'm saying is, there're a lot of shitty family doctors out there. I had this one ..." Lori paused to drink and rehearse the ending to her oft-repeated tirade.

A familiar lump formed in the back of Tyler's throat. "So you're saying he'll be a shitty doctor?"

"Just lemme finish my story." Lori turned to Aaron; surely Aaron would listen. But he had vanished into a clip from his favorite

YouTuber, *donkeyhotay*. Her husband feigned interest at her side, a rerun of *Nightline* capturing his attention.

Lori found her own meaning in the situation. She spoke to Aaron as if neither Tyler nor her husband were in the room (in a way, the latter was not). "I had this doctor, Dr. Ramos, and honest to God, he tried to kill me with Xanax and shit ... Do you remember, I dunno, ten years ago, I was in so much pain, my back was hurting so bad I couldn't sleep ..." Aaron nodded absently to signal *Yes*, he remembered. *All of it*, Tyler was sure of it.

The bottle came with the baby. On February 14, 2005, Lori Stahl (soon to be Haji) was involved in a major car accident on the Hempstead Turnpike, near Bennett and Fulton. The inciting driver was a hungover college student who veered from the opposite lane and struck her head-on. The boy, who was texting his girlfriend to say he was on his way to meet her for Valentine's Day breakfast, suffered permanent brain damage and remained confined to a wheelchair until he died of the flu in 2025. Tyler Haji was born on May 21, 2005.

Fortunately, Tyler survived the accident unharmed (though he [allegedly] went quiet inside his mother's womb for about a week after, which terrified Lori and her soon-to-be husband). Lori's Pontiac G6 did not fare nearly as well. It was very, very dead after.

As for Lori? Lori survived, but not without having something taken from her. She spent three months mostly awake. Her doctor tried to comfort her, citing that her insomnia was "normal" and attributed to her "nerves." He prescribed her rest (which she could not do) and lorazepam. The combination was ineffective. She delivered Tyler to this world with just three hours of sleep spread across three days. Once Tyler was out, she supplemented her sleep regimen with the bottle, and Lori slept for the first time in ninety-seven days. She'd slept like a baby ever since.

School was their day job. They reported for duty from precisely 8:18 AM to 3:30 PM. It wasn't until after they retired that they realized how grateful they should've been for the structure school provided them. Every morning, Aaron would nudge Tyler awake and pour him a bowl of Cocoa Puffs while he yawned and stared idly at *Spongebob* on mute. After work, they would proceed to whatever after-school endeavors were on offer at the time. Whenever band, football, or detention were not in season, the brothers would arrive home only to find their mother lifeless on the couch, lights and blinds closed, reruns of *The Young and the Restless* filling the house's empty void. They'd tiptoe to the basement to play video games and avoid waking her and invoking her deadened wrath.

Tyler remembered. Not the accident, but the cereal, the afternoon mummification; he remembered and wondered whether he'd been marked or somehow traumatized along the way. Maybe he was just soft. Or, perhaps his memory itself was the issue.

Maybe there was a way to delete his memory.

Tyler decided to test his theory. He copied his father's practiced blocking mechanism and watched his mother speak without actually hearing her. He watched his mother drink from her favorite glass, a Stella goblet with its edge permanently stained by her lipstick. The glass had only ever known one fluid: Miller Lite. He watched her beady eyes lose and regain focus on the wooden tabletop, desperate, as if analyzing the skinny wooden grains would somehow restore the euphoria of her first drink.

He watched her suddenly stand, as if she had been programmed to do so precisely at that moment. He watched her set both hands on the dining table to support herself and spin toward the fridge. Lori had a peculiar habit of rotating her beer in the freezer. Whenever her glass bypassed its halfway point (as it had just now), she'd retreat to the kitchen, place a can horizontally in the freezer drawer, and set a timer on the microwave for seven minutes and thirty-three seconds to remind her to fetch it before it exploded. When she'd finished her routine, Lori sat back down and switched to the stemmed glass. Her nights were an intricate dance of dueling glasses. *A dance of damage,* Tyler thought remotely.

Tyler's theory failed. As he watched her dance to the liquid's cadence, he realized just how alone she was. He wanted to feel sorry for her, really, truly. But he could not. The shadow of his pride obscured his empathy. *After all, you tried to help her,* his ego whispered to him. *More than once. Don't you remember?*

Yes, I do.

The most recent occurrence was the most severe; *I'm your son and I care about you.* He'd forgotten the rest of it since, willingly or not. The words had seemed to come not from him but from some other soft-spoken voice. *I'm your son, and I care about you,* he'd begun ...

Tyler had seen enough. He stood to go to bed. "Goodnight," he mumbled to no one in particular, a polite courtesy. "Remember to turn off the TV, please," he added, directed toward his mother. The night before, Lori had passed out before remembering to turn off the television, and *Real Housewives* had practically shaken the walls until morning.

"I never leave the TV on," Lori defended.

"Just turn it off," Joe Haji grunted, having returned to the land of the living. Lori drank to that.

"Night," Tyler reiterated, sauntering off to saner, lonelier environs. *What kind of son doesn't love his mother?* Tyler wondered as he hobbled away to the room he and his brother had once shared. He hated himself for the love he did not feel.

◆

It was not hope or opportunity that drove Tyler away from home; it was anger. Every hatchling must eventually leave its mother's nest. But a bird that rages at its own mother's presence? They tend to leave suddenly—and rarely return.

He told his father he'd gotten accepted to NYU. Joe was proud; he wanted his son to do more than run a glorified bodega. Go to school, get a job, claim benefits. Push paper, eat lunch, marinate in traffic. Earn punch card rewards. *Congratulations! You've earned a free bagel!*

It was a lie. Had Tyler applied to begin with, they would have rejected him. While he scored a 1350 on his SAT, he had slagged his way through high school, unlike Aaron. Tyler considered B's to be A's, because getting a B required zero effort from him. But an A? Ooph.

Grades aside, Tyler had no intentions of attending an institute of higher learning. He had no intentions at all, in fact, other than to forget 113 Madison Avenue.

Wake up, Coffee Mate, screen time. Wait to drink, drink, pass out. So went his mother's daily routine. *Wash, rinse, dry, repeat.* Tyler found himself slowly unraveling, caught in an endless time loop of his parents' shared misery. Each night granted him another opportunity to watch his mother get drunk and his father pretend to care. He worked for his father during the day, working the register at the 7-Eleven that Joe had franchised to replace his old bodega. There was nothing there for Tyler. He trusted they knew that just as well as Tyler did; the signs were more than apparent.

He briefly weighed joining the Air Force, but he knew his father would not condone his son becoming a soldier. The news sold a story of the world being a dangerous place, and Joe Haji bought it wholesale. *Iranian nuclear arms, China's rising military state, thuggish oligarchies, communistic oppressors, terrorism, domestic and abroad.* As a boy, Joe's own father had taken him away to America, away from a place tattered by war and famine and chaos. He would not condone his son revisiting the same place his father had helped him escape; never.

And so Tyler headed off to college.

Lori had already passed out the night Tyler left. Shame ate at him as he packed his things silently in the night and left before the sun rose. *What kind of son doesn't love his mother?* he thought as he struggled silently with his disheveled bag.

Tyler found a second-floor studio from a Mexican woman looking to fill the space her brother had died in. He paid her cash. His only neighbors on the same floor were a swinger couple whose sexual escapades only occasionally involved hosting orgies. He called his father once a week to let him know how school was going. According to Joe, Tyler was doing well in his requisite coursework and really liked his Psych 101 professor.

Tyler worked four days a week for three Italian brothers in Queens who offered to train him gutting fish. He got high and watched TV or played video games the rest of the time. He spent what he earned. It was a simple life, one he could hide behind.

July 18, 2025

Tyler answered not because he knew the number but because he was expecting a call; his weed dealer was running a Halloween special. "Yo."

But it was not Kevin, who in reality had already liquidated his special supply; it was a woman. "Am I speaking to Tyler Haji?"

"Speaking." Tyler frowned. He hoped he wouldn't have to go to the dispensary; he only had a hundred bucks to work with.

"Tyler, do you mind me asking where you are?"

Tyler stared at his boots. They were coated with an invisible layer of omega-3s and fish guts. "Work. Mind me asking who this is?"

"My name's Angela, and I'm a nurse practitioner at Hackensack Meridian JFK University Medical Center. Are you sitting down?"

Aaron Haji died of a heroin overdose, which made no sense because Aaron Haji had never *done* heroin. The thought was inconceivable. He was the only member of the Haji family to abstain from extracerebral stimulation. Tyler smoked his first joint at fourteen and hadn't stopped since; Dad regularly had a glass of scotch before bed, and Mom, well ...

Aaron? His first time drinking alcohol was with Tyler, a forty of King Cobra. Foam came spewing from his mouth like a human beer faucet when he took his first pull. That was the last time Tyler saw Aaron explore the wide world of recreational substances, controlled or otherwise. Whenever Tyler offered him a puff from his bowl or to split a beer, he just smiled and shook his head, *No thanks.*

"What?" Tyler shouted from the toilet.

"I'm so sorry," the nurse replied numbly. "Your parents are in the mortuary now. I can give you the hospital address if you'd like to meet them."

A wave of nausea rushed over him. He tried swallowing, but there was some sort of blockage in his throat. "What the fuck did you just say?" Tyler croaked, but it came out different. He didn't like the way it came out; *Whathefuckdijoujusay?* He felt his chest and leaned against the tank, his knees splaying in each direction, panting for air. The same sentence kept ringing in his ears: *How the fuck didn't you know?*

The nurse did very little to try to calm him. This was for the best. Tyler *was* calm. He was just confused. "What?" was all he could ask. *What? What? What?* He could not tell whether he was repeating the question out loud or if it was echoing in his mind.

When the nurse did not answer, he began to cry. He felt the hot tears slide down his chin and watched them drip neatly on his boots' oily skin. *How the fuck didn't you know? How the fuck didn't you know?*

He stayed like that for a while, stooped over his knees, sobbing until his tear ducts finally gave out. He gathered his pants to his knees and retied his apron around his waist.

Even in this most grievous of times, Tyler did not neglect to wash his hands. The brain can be programmed in shocking ways. He gazed emptily at his reflection in the mirror as he scrubbed beneath his nails, hearing the same sentence over and over. The brain can be programmed in shocking ways.

July 20, 2025

Aaron hid his addiction well. This is because he was an experienced addict, and, as such, was capable of maintaining a veil of normalcy.

Tyler and his father (tailed by a Xanax-induced version of his mother) had not sought out his brother's heroin kit once they were entrusted the keys to his apartment. It simply stumbled across their laps while they were searching for a suit jacket to decorate his corpse in.

They found it hidden on the top shelf of his closet. He kept his supplies in a brown leather briefcase that his father had bought him as a graduation gift. It contained syringes and lighters, spoons, a rubber exercise loop, a bottle of antiseptic solution, laxatives, and other stuff.

Tyler gazed at the leatherbound thing, amazed. How could his brother, the "shy" and "awkward" one, *Aaron*, for chrissakes, have been so ... dedicated? "Should we call the cops?" he asked nervously.

Joe said nothing. He took the briefcase, took the lift downstairs, and walked it to the nearest dumpster.

The funeral was held two days after the pathologist concluded that Aaron Haji had expired of a routine heroin dose tainted with fentanyl. When the finicky ordeal of men shaking hands and women making teary-eyed remarks was over, Tyler's father sat him down and asked him to come home until things went "back to normal." Lori lay with her face buried in a pillow, alone in a dark room. It was the lone occasion that Tyler's pride did not reject such behavior.

Tyler never considered that his father might ask such a thing. His mind was still preoccupied with trying to unearth what had justified Aaron's deplorable hobby. "What for?" He hadn't sanctioned the words; they just *came*.

His father's eyebrows tilted sharply. "What do you mean 'what for'?" And then his face flattened. His eyes fluttered toward the room where his wife lay, lifeless, and he quickly realized he did not have a good answer to his question. Tyler returned to Lorena's flat the next day and found himself in the same aimless position as before, though he now owned a black suit and a profound sense of self-loathing.

◆

There are high barriers of entry to becoming a heroin addict. To acquaint oneself with Harry, the Dragon, Smack, or however you refer to God's most pristine creation, two things are required: a disregard for one's personal health/safety, and an In.

Tyler's In was anonymous. He came home late from work one day, still covered in the day's blood and guts. He'd taken to working sixteen-hour shifts, what the rest of the crew called "chummin' it," because once the fish came in contact with your skin long enough, the smell was stuck there permanently. Tyler didn't care. He could go home smelling like a shipyard every day. What he couldn't do was stop thinking about his brother. His goal was to arrive home every day so exhausted that he could not think anymore. It had been mostly working lately.

In his state of exhaustion, he almost missed the note that was slid under his door:

Your brother's plug:

117 15th Street #406, Garden City
Ask for Chesty.

Curiously, Tyler felt calm and collected as he gently folded the torn sheet of notebook paper and left it on the cheap end table where he left his keys and wallet. His mind turned immediately to the logistics of violence. He did not own a gun. He'd only ever shot twice, once visiting his grandfather while he'd still lived, a *Don't Tread on Me* type who lived in rural Virginia, and again with a whitetail-crazy neighbor they had in Jersey named Dan. He'd found both times that he was a poor shot, the explosion within the rifle surprising him no matter how hard he tried to hold steady.

A knife was undoubtedly more feasible to obtain and use. The fishery where he worked was in no shortage of sharp and sinister-looking cutlery. Even so, he had never been trained to wield one against anything still moving, much less a person. And besides, the guy would probably be strapped—what kind of heroin dealer wouldn't be?

Despite his trepidations, he forced himself to trudge back out the door, still in his work clothes, armed with little more than the flimsy note.

◆

He knocked and asked for Chesty.

The first thing Chesty noticed about the kid was that he seemed *itchy*, out of place. Chesty typically avoided asking his clients unwarranted questions. His philosophy had always been to find out the *why* later, and only when it came naturally. But Chesty knew this type: the type that was leaving one vice for another.

Chesty was smoking a cigarette when he let him in, the window open to let in the hot and muggy summer air. "First time?" Tyler nodded.

The second thing Chesty noticed about the kid was that he smelled fishier than a Catholic jeweler. Chesty patted his shoulder, resisting the urge to plug his nose in revulsion. "Nothing to worry about. This stuff is as clean as it gets; that's for damn sure." *Is that what Aaron thought?* Tyler raged. Yet he did nothing. "Ain't no shame in it either. Stuff gets a bad rap is all."

Tyler nodded absentmindedly, remembering the promise he'd made to himself before coming. He was already editing his initial mission statement. He knew instantly that his affiliation with his brother's killer would not be limited to one encounter.

He began telling Tyler how he'd arrived in his position (the apartment was shockingly nice for a heroin dealer, Tyler confessed). His eyes darted about the room as he vaguely listened to Chesty's tale. He noticed a red enameled pack of cigarettes on his kitchen table that read *Chesterfield* in diagonal font. *He's a fucking hipster,* he thought. *A hipster killed your brother.*

Chesty began using after graduating with a 4.0 ("Damn near it") from the Air Force Academy. This was part of an effort to please his folks. They apparently were not pleased enough. They kindly informed Chester that his next ambition was to become a JAG, or "Whatever they call those snake fuckers in camo." Chesty vehemently opposed this career track, much to his stalwart father's dissatisfaction. He told his father (a proud veteran himself) that if he wanted to send one of his sons to die in some war, he should try Armie [his brother] instead. Chesty opted to pay back his tuition rather than fulfill his contract. After discovering that he was drowning in debt, he very consciously decided to become an addict. His career had flowered from there.

His story affected Tyler deeply. He let his grand illusions of revenge give way to the twin allures of escape and self-harm. He wondered how his brother had navigated the process. How had Aaron even scored H to begin with? Had he been told the same story? Had he bought it too?

"First time's on the house." Chesty held out his hand. Tyler shook it, and suddenly forgot his thirst for vengeance. It'd been replaced by a sense of harmony, the likes of which he'd never felt before.

Chesty began gathering his supplies; a blue exercise band, a syringe, a spoon. He lit the burner on his stove. "Wait," Tyler stammered. Chesty looked up from his cigarette, a bored expression awash over him. "Can I take it with me?"

Chesty frowned at him, cigarette dangling from his mouth, the spoon still hovering over the open flame. "You know how?" he asked doubtingly. Tyler nodded. He turned off the gas. "All yours, buddy."

Tyler stuffed the little baggie inside his pocket and made for the door. He turned his head before he went and asked whether he made deliveries, for any future purchases.

"Depends whereabouts," Chesty responded, easing his elbow against the doorpost.

"I live in Hempstead. There's a Carvel next door."

Chesty smiled toothlessly, his dart wriggling out between his snake-like lips. "Right on. My girl lives in those whereabouts. You got my number?" He didn't, so he gave it to him.

"Right on," he muttered, tucking his iPhone back into his pocket. "Second time ain't free though. But you already knew that, didn't you?" Chesty said, smiling. Tyler nodded.

◆

Chesty began making deliveries to Tyler's apartment, due in large part to the bulk quantities he bought in. He quickly became accustomed to Chesty's sleaze remarks and scumbag smiles. More often than not, he would wrinkle his nose at the fishy smell in Tyler's apartment. It smelled like fish even after he stopped showing up to work at Ferraro

Brothers Fishery. That was the price he paid for chummin' it. In little to no time, Tyler had exhausted all the money he had saved chummin' it on heroin he did not use.

Each time he called Chesty for another shipment, he'd devised a new way of ridding him from the world. He'd smoke a joint with him on the roof and push him off; he'd stab him as soon as he walked in, roll him up in a carpet and dump him off the Turnpike, like a character from *The Sopranos*; he'd buy or borrow a gun and make him sit on his couch and confess to killing his brother. And then he would shoot him, and the world would be that much better off.

He followed up on none of his fantasies. Chesty's visits always led to the same outcome: another nose wrinkle, another snide comment, and another two-grand worth of scag buried underneath Tyler's couch cushion. The more time he spent with him, the more he wavered on wanting to murder him. In the meantime, Tyler began seeing a girl on the fifth floor—one of Chesty's "best customers," he once bragged to him, ever the sleaze. "This route's a big money maker for me."

From their first encounter in the building's laundry room ("*Tyler*," he'd introduced himself while shaking her hand lamely), Allison omitted her addiction from Tyler. But their eyes spelled out what their lips refused to tell: they both had an In. It was more than either of them shared in common with the rest of the world, even if Tyler's addiction was a ruse.

The first time they got high together (not on heroin, which Tyler was only interested in buying, not doing) they wound up fucking on the floor in Tyler's barely furnished living room. If he still smelled like fish from his chummin' days, she did not seem to mind. The practice eventually moved to Allison's apartment, too. She kept her heroin in her entertainment stand, but Tyler was not interested in knowing that. It was that unsaid commonality that interested him, that shared, universal truth: the hungry stare, the sorted schedules. Yearning for escape.

They had chemistry—that much Tyler was sure of. Allison was older than him and into deviant acts in (or out of) the bedroom, like roleplaying and bondage. Shockingly, despite her familiarity with downers, Allison was unacquainted with reefer, which Tyler took great joy in introducing her to. Their chemistry had germinated from there. But it died long before it could take root.

He learned she had a kid the hard way, knocking on her door with a joint he'd rolled for them to share. She worked nights waitressing at a chain sushi restaurant, and her apartment was adorned with random Japanese knickknacks and anime posters. Tyler came over on his days off (which he began taking more and more of), and she was usually there alone in the mornings, drinking coffee and performing requisite house duties, like dusting her knickknacks in her underwear.

Just before he knocked that morning, he heard the cries of an upset child. She was swaddling the kid when she answered, plugging a pacifier into his mouth before opening the door. She'd call him later, she told him as the infant bumbled at her chest, and Tyler turned bashful and left. He suspected that their relationship had just come to an end. He did not yet understand that this was a blessing in disguise.

October 2025

Under normal circumstances, the virus would have been merely catastrophic—which it was. Under abnormal circumstances, however, the virus would have been apocalyptic. Which it was.

The first symptom was a nagging headache, which most shrugged off, allowing the germ to spread. Next came the chills; then, diarrhea. The fever traded off with the runs. Both came and went and came, then came and went again, and again, until the former eventually outmaneuvered the latter. Most died in states of delusion, which was viewed as a blessing by those who contracted the virus and lived to stay inside their apartments another day.

Tyler suffered only a few short months of celibacy after his and Allison's implicit separation, which was considered lucky by most standards. Many virgins died as they had lived: virgins. Lots of non-virgins died, too.

Shortly into the pandemic, Chesty stopped coming around, but by then, Tyler's heroin stash had grown large enough to kill a horse; or, perhaps more apt, an entire stagecoach team. *Why let it all go to waste?* a voice in Tyler's head suggested to him more than once. *You never know. It might help you.*

"Fuck off," Tyler told the voice under his breath. He went back to counting the number of birds he could see outside his window.

This was just one of the imagined dialogues Tyler began having with himself.

Tyler ventured out for groceries just once, early on. His bulging cart included copious amounts of peanut butter for fat, Gatorade and Wonder Bread for carbohydrates, and the occasional morsel from a beef jerky stockpile to up his protein. He self-prescribed Burnett's vodka for his waking anxiety. He left his TV on, though it did him no good.

Tyler only witnessed two deaths, both of which amounted to a pedestrian collapsing on the street and never getting back up. Mostly people just disappeared. Death became the sort of thing left up to assumption; lights left on, water running, phone calls unanswered. Although legally someone could not be considered *Deceased* until after their body was recovered, most preferred making the simple assumption that a person's disappearance signified their death. Things were better off that way: that they were simply gone, disappeared. It made things less painful. And besides, venturing out to confirm something that could simply be assumed was dangerous.

The streets suddenly became empty corridors populated only by jittery Wall Street types and joggers desperate for their dopamine fix. They later refilled with masked and unmasked protestors shouting about freedoms and injustices. The ensuing spike in cases (and deaths) drained the streets once more. The only constants were the degenerates who went outside to smoke. After the supermarkets shuttered, they were joined by people hunting on their balconies or fire escapes; one could catch a pigeon if they were quick enough and roast a squab for supper that night. The truly desperate baited mousetraps, hoping to ensnare a wandering rat.

The city quickly became too short-staffed to excavate the large swaths of unoccupied dirt needed to amiably bury the bodies. And so the city became awash with the acrid and traumatizing smell of human ash. The virus did not discriminate—healthy and frail, young and old, poor and famous. All suffered the same fate, celebrities and housewives and celebrity housewives included. The swinger couple that lived next door to Tyler went away on an extended sex retreat or something. Whatever it was didn't matter. The only lifesaving attribute was luck— genetic luck.

Curiously, even as humanity fought and eventually lost to the virus, the televisions remained steady; *If it bleeds, it leads.* Night after night, grim-faced reporters wearing masks would somberly report the day's tidings:

10.01.2025 *Over ninety thousand cases in New York City alone ...*

10.03.2025 *Initial findings suggest negligence by the White House, the president since defending his actions ...*

10.05.2025 *Martial law taking effect immediately at midnight ...*

10.07.2025 *The estimated death toll in America has risen to almost 150,000, making ALIN-12, commonly referred to as "El Tubo," the deadliest virus since the Spanish flu ...*

10.09.2025 *... a major explosion near the border of Russian-backed Belarus and Ukraine. The incident reportedly occurred near a* nuclear power facility. Belarusian investigators have yet to determine the cause of the explosion. Russian state media released a statement this morning, blaming the incident on rebel vigilantes. The Kremlin has since stated they would authorize "appropriate intervention strategies" to "properly" investigate the incident …

10.10.2025 *Riots in Dallas, protests in the capital …*

10.15.2025 *The vice president swore in the oath of office from a remote location today, assuring Americans at home and abroad that the virus is under control. The president also revealed the promising discovery that immune, virus-carrying individuals would be required to submit blood samples starting …*

10.19.2025 *With an estimated one in three Americans carrying the virus—*cough*—excuse me—and over 2.8 million Americans dead, ahem … excuse me …*

10.20.2025 *Good evening, fellow Americans. Fellow patriots— workers, essential and nonessential. Today we find ourselves at a turning point in our nation's history. The unprecedented virus known as "El Tubo" has robbed many Americans of their lives. But the United States government is committed to fighting and defeating this virus. We ask for your cooperation as we work to do so: wear your mask, avoid crowds, and do everything you can to care for your health. Lastly, and it goes without saying, the United States government and its armed forces disavow the insurgent uprisings in the following states:*

Arizona,

California,

Florida,

Georgia,

Idaho,

Illinois,

Kentucky,

Louisiana,
Michigan,
Montana,
Nevada,
New York,
New Hampshire,
Oklahoma,
Oregon,
Rhode Island,
Tennessee,
Texas,
Vermont,
and Wyoming.

The United States pledges to take forceful action against all dissenters of freedom. No matter what ridiculous claims are made against our democracy, know that America and our institutions are built to endure this greatest of tragedies.

Within three weeks, approximately 4.2 million Americans were dead—or simply gone, unaccounted for, vanished from existence. "El Tubo," as the people took to calling it was as close to perfect as a virus could strive for. It forcefully ejected itself from its hosts, coating hands, lips, and all available surfaces with particulate. Once it was pegged somewhere, it stayed, until someone else picked it up and spread it elsewhere. Approximately four out of every ten of those infected died. Approximately one out of every one hundred of everyone died.

America provided the perfect set of conditions by the virus's own sinister standards. The country's expansive network of passenger airlines allowed it to spread across a geographically vast area in little to no time. The virus made short work of the overweight and shorter work of the obese, and both were in surplus. Yet most integral to the virus's success was its socially divided, unprepared, and undisciplined population. Basic preventative strategies became political talking points; mask up or not, quarantine or reopen, rest or exercise the brain/body.

In other words, things were normal.

◆

"Kick 'im."

"You do it," Ed muttered.

"You know how many times I've had to kick 'im?"

"Fine. Shoot him, then."

"Fine."

Brooks bent over and snapped in Tyler's ear. Tyler swatted at the noise and covered his eyes with his elbow. "The fuck?"

"Get up."

"Fuck off. It's Sunday."

"Not no more it ain't." Brooks hacked up a loogie. Tyler quickly uncovered his eyes and flinched. His spittle went flying over their makeshift encampment's low retaining wall.

Tyler propped up on his elbow and lit a cigarette. "What the fuck's so important? It's Sunday. Look around." Tyler swept his hand across the barren, swampy capital. Although the flood had receded significantly in the twenty years since its onset, its impact was still apparent. Faux rivers and lakes still dribbled and lapped up against concrete and earth alike, and the land itself was permanently transformed. A thousand Atlantides were buried along the shores where surfers and beachcombers once ruled, lost forever to the flood. "And it's *Sunday.*"

Brooks sucked his lip. "Normally, I'd be obliged to agree." He frowned at their bulky comms radio. "The Letterman called. Says it's time to get goin'."

Tyler frowned. "Thought we were stationed here till summer."

"Exactly what I said," murmured Ed.

"We ain't goin' far," said Brooks.

"Where?"

"Somewhere fuuuuun."

"Just say where."

"*South.*"

"How far?"

"Just a few miles."

"Mount Vernon," Crunch clarified, exhausted by Brooks's bullshit.

Tyler crossed his legs and exhaled. *Mount Vernon?* The name was familiar. "What's there?"

"Probably nothing. But we go where the storm falls," Crunch grunted. *Our Amphibious Force is comprised of dedicated men and women who live and fight by our founding principle: We Go Where the Storm Falls.* So went one of the Colonies' many over-produced, masculinity-fueled commercials praising their valor.

"My ass," Ed swaggered. "You can't even go to the beach without freaking the fuck out. Neurotic-ass."

"What was that?"

Brooks corralled them with a sharp *Ey!* People tended to listen when Brooks spoke. "Letterman says a few migrants been seen crossin' there lately. Place is above flood level, I guess. Probably just stoppin' to rest there on their way south."

"Again, what's that have to do with us?" Tyler flicked his cigarette, agitated. "Last I checked, camping wasn't illegal."

"*Show me your paypahs!*" Ed shouted in an angry German accent, extending his palm for effect. "Better start practicing now, Haj."

Brooks pretended Ed hadn't spoken. "Shouldn't be nothin' too crazy." He sucked his teeth. "Besides, y'all ain't got no say in this here predicament. What the Letterman says goes."

"Fuck him," Tyler scowled, though he knew Brooks was right. The Letterman was their superior, even though they only saw each other when they were on base—which was rare. Tyler once made the mistake of asking him to transfer him to an administrative division. The Letterman had laughed in his face. *You're made for soldiering, Private, not paper pushing.* The old man did not tolerate weakness. He belonged to a different class of men, one that only arises in times of war and/or poverty. He was small and wiry, but tougher than old wood. He was the only man Tyler had ever met who'd contracted the virus, been hospitalized, put on a ventilator, and survived the ordeal. The virus took something from him though, hardening his voice (which he claimed was once angelic) until it resembled something like gravel and ice stirred in a whiskey glass. *You're made for soldiering, Private.*

Tyler went along with it. That was his way of doing things; duck your head, follow the path. He hadn't strayed from any path since enlisting, which he could no longer recall why he did in the first place. Patriotism had nothing to do with it. It'd been a natural decision; Brooks had saved him from the flood, and *he* was a soldier, and the world was fucked. His brother was dead, along with the rest of his family. So he'd signed the papers, naturally.

He looked at the others' cots and saw they had already packed up their shit. He sighed, swigged from his flask, and began lacing up his boots.

III

No. 4 Month 3, 0016 P.F.
Pittsburgh, Appalachia, New American Colonies

"YOU STILL don't know what makes us tick." George Crombie paused to finish chewing. "I thought you might've learned a thing or two from your seat at the board," he continued, staring down his son like prey. "But you haven't." Adam gazed at his untouched plate, avoiding his father's eyes until he returned to his dinner of leathery mutton.

More often than not, Adam dined opposite the Chief, not his father. His father had once been a cheery man, quick to laugh and quirky in an endearing way. But that man no longer lived. He had perished alongside the woman he loved.

George's steak knife did not stray from its smooth glide. "Things aren't as simple as you'd like to think. You can't just show up and delegate roles. It takes more than that to run this company. It takes *vigilance.*" The Chief was not one to lose his temper. It had the effect of making the prospect of him losing it all the more petrifying.

Adam had only casually mentioned his inevitable succession. His father's harsh reaction amused him somewhat, given that was the only intended outcome for him; at least, George claimed as much.

Granted, George had no clue his only son was preparing to abandon him. Only Adam was privy to that. Had he known, he might've begged on his knees for him to stay and passed on his title then and there. But he need not know that which would destroy him.

Adam resisted the smug grin tugging at his lips and kept his composure. He wanted to stand up and call him a fool, then laugh hysterically at the confused look on his father's face. But he did not. Instead, he nodded and sipped the black wine in front of him. "You're right. I was wrong to bring that up. I'm sorry."

George chewed mindfully, the muscles in his jaws working like pistons. "Don't apologize; *listen.*"

♦

The Chief felt some things were more pertinent than others in his son's development. Physical training was important, yes; Abdul made sure that Adam could handle himself as needed. More pertinent to George, however, was mental strength—self-discipline, willpower, the capacity to learn.

The Chief considered failure in certain departments to be indicative of a lack of mental acuity. Diplomacy was one of them. Adam was constantly being enrolled in diplomatic exercises, which the Chief dubbed "essential." But the Chief never seemed satisfied with his son's results.

Adam remembered one occasion in particular. The simulation had revolved around a castle under siege. Winter rations were nearly empty, and the townspeople would soon starve. The soldier class was outnumbered and starving alongside them. Abdul provided him three choices: "A, surrender your arms and allow the invading force into the city; B, mount a counterattack against the enemy; or C, reduce rations further and pray for an early spring."

Adam considered the repercussions of each response before providing his answer. *The only chance of survival is escape.* "We should surrender the castle to the invaders. When they cross the gates, we escort the king and his family to safety through a hidden escape. That way, the bloodline survives." He felt confident in his answer. His father's words were seared into his memory: *Nothing lasts forever, Adam. The day I'm gone will be the day you become Chief. You have to be ready for it.*

"No," Abdul growled, his thick brogue barely evident in his tone. "The answer is sitting right in front of you. Try again." Adam sat, his grayish eyes darting over the glass figurines spread over the backlit stratagem board. Abdul circled the table. "War is not a game. No enemy or ally can be relied upon in war." He stood calmly with his hands folded at the waist. "Tell me when you've found the answer."

Adam closed his eyes and envisioned the figurines moving in his favor, forming a path to victory. When he opened his eyes, the board had not changed. He bowed his head in defeat. Abdul shook his head. "You cannot restrict yourself to one path. Choosing one path in war is lethal. If you choose from a list, you are dead. If you choose nothing, you are dead. Your enemy has the offensive advantage, but you have something which he does not. That is your strength. Use it." Adam chewed his lip.

Abdul never revealed the answer to him; he scowled and told him he would never become Chief if his ineptness endured. Abdul's words did not cut him, though; his father's did. The Chief revealed the correct answer over dinner that night. He paused long enough to chew his food and clear his throat. "There is no *we*. There's only *you*, Adam."

Adam's tests endured until he turned eighteen and became eligible to succeed his father. That marked an end to his formal education. Now he had a say in company matters, a seat on its board. As such, his actions carried consequences. The pair ate in silence from then on. On the rare occasion they feigned at interaction, it almost always concerned company matters: politics, production, profit margins, or otherwise.

◆

"Forget it," the Chief said abruptly. "There are more important matters to discuss." He chewed, processing his words before they came, as he always did. "I spoke with Ides yesterday. He says they've hit a fresh vein."

Adam leaned onto his cheek, playing with his food as a child might. "More blood for the taking, I guess," he muttered. The Chief entertained another bite and paused. His fork hit his porcelain with a *clink*.

"You do know where we conduct our mining operations? Or have you opted to forget that as well?"

"Some desert shithole," Adam muttered. As usual, George did not entertain his son's malice.

"Nevada, to be precise. If you recall from your schooling, that *desert shithole* remains the largest mining operation in North America, which means they're heavily sought after. Were it not for our drone patrols and the good Mr. Ides, the mines would likely have fallen over to the Alliance by now. Were that the case, we wouldn't be able to harvest the gold and lithium needed to produce Loops. And were *that* the case, you might not be so privileged as to speak so disrespectfully to your father."

Adam flinched despite the great length of mahogany between them. George had scarcely laid a finger on Adam since his mother passed, to show affection or otherwise. As to the latter, sharp words and icy stares were more than sufficient. He deflected the sharp words and emptied what remained of his glass. "Then I guess we should be grateful for the good Mr. Ides," he said, bravely trying a piece of the mutton. Just as he'd expected: grisly.

The Chief left the snide comment unanswered. He sipped measuredly from his wine glass, though it levied only water. He scarcely drank while he dined, preferring to savor alcohol's effects alone and undisturbed by other stimuli.

"There was something I wanted to ask about. In private," Adam said, veiling the wine's influence over his voice.

"Yes?" Few spoke without the Chief's consent.

"Do you remember where you and Mom first met?"

George's grip on his steak knife tightened. "Why do you ask?"

Why am I asking about my dead mother? Adam cleared his throat. "Well, you've never said."

George eyed his plate. "At a bakery. Why do you ask," he repeated flatly.

"I was wondering what happened to the place."

"The flood ruined it." His knife hand had not yet relaxed. "Why do you ask?"

No. You did. Adam paused to take a bite of blandness; the Chief always ate plainly, opting for longevity over flavor. "No reason," he said as he chewed. They finished their meal to the *clink* of silverware meeting ceramic.

His father suddenly broke the silence. "It was a small place. The bakery. But it was hers. She used to shovel and salt the sidewalks in the winter. She'd shovel the whole block by herself. Neighbors too ..." George's eyes glazed over, lost, his coal-colored irises gleaming in the candlelight.

Snow. Adam mostly remembered snow from films. He had only spent a short time living on the surface. His memories of life above ground were blurred and fuzzy, like wavering dreams. He sometimes dreamt of the moon's soft celestial glow, but never of the sun's harsh rays. He could not recall the feeling of the sun warming his skin. His brain seemed to dodge the memories, as if recalling them back might invite him back to the surface.

The Chief blinked at his half-finished meal as if he'd suddenly awoken from a dream. His normal, steely gaze returned just as quickly as it had gone. "The past is what holds us back," he grumbled, sipping from his glass.

Adam looked down at his untouched meal and stood to leave. "Well, good night," he declared, replacing his chair gently.

♦

Adam did not know his city. Not like a true resident. Certainly not like his father; he knew and saw everything. Long before the Subterranean became an overcrowded, constant rat-race to the top (or bottom, depending on how one saw it), United company men had mounted security cameras on nearly every street corner. The unblinking things aggregated raw data from faces, behaviors, and average and not-so-average conversations. If a certain area lacked coverage, there was almost certainly a police officer posted somewhere along the block, and if not, a man dressed in inconspicuous business formal.

Adam's only ventures outside of his posh living situation were to the glitzy, protected confines of the Business District. He knew nothing of the poverty on the surface or in the Subterranean's furthermost corners (though the media [at the Chief's behest] vehemently denied any such poverty existed in the first place). Although Adam could make assumptions about what life was like in such forlorn places, he'd never see (much less experience) the wet, shame-filled existences that the people living there must have endured. Yet, for some unspoken reason, Adam felt a need to understand their reality. He longed to experience something other than his noble upbringing.

But he'd never come close to touching them. Not as the Chief's son, or *Pittsburgh's Next*, as the media was fond of heralding him. He'd been deemed too precious to visit such places. Ironically, many of the same people bound to such gutters likely idolized him. It was not unbeknownst to yinzers to display the Crombies' likenesses in their kitchens in framed portraits. Citizens both privileged and not believed they owed their lives to the Crombies. Mostly they were indebted to George, whether they lived in scaffolded housing on the surface or were afforded property underground. Adam's face sometimes joined George's over mantlepieces and impromptu altars, though his was nowhere near as ubiquitous. Adam had realized long ago that he'd always be second to his father.

Adam hated the fact that he could not know his people. He did not desire the life of fancy adornment he'd been born into. He wanted to disappear, to escape, perhaps to the earth's surface, perhaps not. But he knew that his father's associates would never allow such a thing to occur. They surrounded him, corporate rats, wolves of the oligarchy keen on his every movement, all vying for his favor. He did not have the means to evade those whose sole purpose was to analyze him.

It was not until the sixty-first day of Year 16 Post-Flood that hope came to him. Hope came in a package that could only be delivered by air.

◆

The Pole was not friendly to most aviary species. The path leading to Adam's living quarters was rife with hot air ducts, spinning generators, and perilous exhaust fans, which helped to sustain the Subterranean's controlled climate—none of which were conducive to winged travel.

Adam lay atop a richly woven rug, his bare chest heaving lightly, elbow partially obscuring his face. His stomach growled. He'd left his abridged supper still hungry, though he was too proud to admit it. He scowled beneath his arm.

His dwellings were built primarily with security in mind. There were no windows to look out from, no gingerly placed family photographs. An abundance of furniture and drapery, ottomans, and fireplaces designed to make the space feel warm and snuggly masked the room's coldness. Its only entrance/escape was a set of great mahogany doors inlaid with an ornate panorama of Pittsburgh and its encompassing hillside. He often left the doors open to let in cool air from the underground corridors. He tried to capture what little life could be harvested underground.

The sudden entrance of a bird madly flapping its wings startled Adam. He reacted instantaneously, his reflexes fine-tuned by his years of training with Abdul, and snatched at the airborne threat like a cat pouncing onto its supper.

His fingers swiped air. Adam looked down, perplexed, unsure how the intruder had evaded him. He slowly shifted his focus on his assailant. It was a gray carrier pigeon. The bird fluttered onto the ledge of a wood-and-velvet sofa and looked at him with its neck cocked. Adam stalked forward, his hand outstretched.

The pigeon brilled sharply. It stood poking its tiny leg out, balancing on one foot as if to say, *See?* Adam paused and noted a small strip of fabric tied about its ankle. "Huh," he remarked aloud. The pigeon stopped its flustered I-have-to-pee dance and hopped onto the couch's cushion, spreading its arms like a toddler waiting to be picked up. Adam smirked and tugged gently at the slip around the bird's ankle. The bird stayed put, staring ahead.

The silk tie was blank, save a small insignia on its tail end—a fox standing on its hind legs. Adam rubbed his fingers along the ribbon's edge and felt a slight bump. He squinted; there was a chip of some sort, stitched precisely into the fabric itself. He brought the silk tie to his teeth to tear it loose, and the pigeon cried out, piercing his ears. "Dirty bird," he muttered, glaring at his companion. It stared back idly, twitching its neck.

Adam furrowed his brow. A small, metallic rectangle gleamed on the side of the pigeon's head. Adam leaned closer, perplexed. Someone had installed a tiny implant of some sort just above where its ear would have been, if pigeons had ears. He tapped the side of his head. "Here?" The bird chirped lightly in agreement, poking its neck out.

The chip fit perfectly into the microscopic fitting, the ribbon dangling down from the pigeon's temple like a tiny bow. A blue light glowed on the implant's side. The bird sat back and folded its wings as if to get comfortable.

After a pause, a robotic voice emitted from the device: *DATE: February 28, 2042 (EASTERN FORMAT: No. 18 Month 2, 0016 Post-Flood). TIME: 9:00 AM Pacific Time (EASTERN FORMAT: 9:00).*

The bird sat frozen in stasis as the tape switched over. A woman's voice cut through the room's dead quiet. "Hello?" she asked once to verify the recording. "Sorry for the subtlety. I hope this dumb bird gets to you. You're a hard man to find, Adam; I'm sure you know that by now." The woman cleared her throat before resuming. "You're not who you think you are, Adam." Adam arched his brow.

"You are the heir to something far greater than your father's capitalist scheme. Your mother wasn't just some Midwest gal who baked bread for a living. Her father—your grandfather—born Vasilis Milo, went on to adopt the name Bill Edenson. Father of the West, Bill Edenson. You are Bill's only surviving relative, Adam. Which makes you our new Father."

Adam smirked. It was a well-produced ruse, to say the least—most likely an internet troll trying to embarrass someone of such high rank. He'd only ever heard stories about the Father of the West, which came from scrupulous sources at best. They were most often recanted by drunkards about the Business District, regaling their hippie pasts in pursuit of some western dream. Some of them claimed to have followed Father Bill from the humble beginnings of his movement, and to have witnessed him perform miracles in front of crowds that stretched beyond the horizon.

The woman continued blathering, with Adam only half listening. "I'm only telling you this because of how essential you are to us. *All* of us; *you* will unite us, Adam. *You* are the Untold. Your place is here, in the West." The pigeon occupied most of his attention. Adam poked at a wing, feeling for some slip-up in its animatronic engineering, and found nothing of the sort. The thing appeared to be made from one-hundred percent organic material, which was impossible. Adam frowned.

"Bill left Pittsburgh at a young age. He never returned; fate took him elsewhere. The West needed a prophet, someone young and strong and caring, and Bill was just that. He answered the call. He had to make sacrifices, though. He left a daughter behind; your mother to be exact, August. I don't think he ever expected to see her again." The woman paused. "He would've saved her, had he known."

"That's enough," Adam muttered, reaching to shut off the birdy boombox.

"You did everything you could to stop it, Adam."

His hands stopped short of the pigeon's neck.

"I promise you don't know me—and I wasn't there that night, so stop guessing. I'm sorry about what happened to her. I'm sorry about what you've gone through. But you *have* to trust me when I say I'm telling you the truth." Adam sat quietly, staring at his reflection in the gleaming gem on his forefinger. "The Chief knows about it. He's kept it hidden from you all these years. Otherwise, he would lose his only heir; the Crombie name would die with him. Your father is jealous of you, Adam. *That's* why he hasn't told you. And even though I don't have any evidence, I think he resents the fact that your name is more powerful than his. August didn't want you to know either; she hardly knew Bill herself." Adam flinched. Few people dared speak his mother's name, in the Chief's presence or otherwise. There were few better ways to invoke his wrath. Unless, of course, that was your aim. "But her father—*our* Father—*had* to leave her, to serve a greater purpose."

Adam suddenly recalled his father's deadpan voice from dinner that night: *Why do you ask?* Did he suspect Adam had somehow uncovered the truth? Maybe he was worried he would lose him if he found out.

Maybe he was right.

"Only three people besides you and me know your secret. Bill designed it that way on purpose. One works closely to your father. He will assist your escape, albeit from afar. The other lives in the West, someone who Father Bill himself confided in; he's the one who told me. And the third is George. The public, you, and George's closest allies have all been led to believe that you come from his blood." *Why do you ask?* "But now you know the truth. You are your mother's son." *Why do you ask?* "We've been waiting for you ever since Bill left us. You are the Untold—our New Father."

A muted *bonk* sounded from the instrument before Adam could fully process her words. The woman spoke in a hurry. "You can't tell anyone. It would put you in danger. These messages will be our only way of communicating going forward. Don't worry about Samantha; she's programmed to return to my location." Adam eyed the frozen bird quizzically. He'd thought of it as a "he" up until then. "If she's made it this far, she'll be fine."

"It could be months before we have the proper support in place to bring you home. When the time comes, you'll be the first to know. Remember, you can't tell anybody." The audio emitted a second *bonk.* "Shit; start preparing for the journey now—mentally, physically. Know that you are being constantly monitored. You are still your father's most important asset." The woman shuffled with her microphone before leaving him with her parting wish: "Believe nothing your father or your government tell you. They're liars. Remember these words: Water Is Life. To fear water is to fear life. To live in fear is to live in denial. We deny f—"

MEMORY FULL, the tape's robotic secretary stated.

Samantha suddenly stood, twisting her neck as if to relieve some stiffness caused by the device. Adam reclined and teased the animal with his finger. The drama had exhausted him. "Water Is Life," he hummed aloud. Samantha hopped onto his chest and lifted her leg.

Adam plucked the ribbon from her headpiece and fastened it to her leg. She left the couch and floated in the air momentarily. Then she flapped her wings and fled out the mahogany doors, up and into the inner valves of the Subterranean's steel heart.

◆

Adam had ample time to ponder his escape.

He prepared physically by performing vigorous calisthenics precisely between 2:00 and 4:00 AM, the only hours he knew he was not being monitored. He heard once every ninety days or so from his fixer. The messages were brief, simple rehashes of the same story; the prophecy remained unchanged. Still, it helped knowing that Samantha's enigmatic master had not forgotten him. Each time the bird visited made the next few months somewhat more tolerable.

Adam often speculated who his supporter was within his father's organization. He was desperate for someone other than a pigeon to confide in. Could it be Santero, the wizened old professor who'd been in the Chief's service longer than anyone? Somebody embedded in the Chief's security detail? Or perhaps one of the other board members, the flock of political leeches who had been clinging to George's coattails since Adam could remember? The most inconspicuous (and therefore logical) choice would've been one of the many cooks, porters, and unassuming maids who pruned after them. He searched them for any hint of recognition, a private nod, a wink, or a surreptitious hand gesture. If any of them were a covert agent, they were too skilled (or terrified) to confirm. The mystery drove him mad.

He had his sights set on it being his former teacher. Though his relationship with Abdul had changed markedly over the years, the roots of their bond were still planted firmly. After his mother's death, Adam saw more of Abdul than he did Chief. He hated him at first, though he'd hated almost everything then. Pain and failure dominated their time spent together. Abdul oversaw Adam's training, which was designed to make him a successful Chief when it came time to take on his father's mantle. He taught utterly without mercy, at the Chief's behest. Adam often left capoeira instruction covered with welts and dark bruises where Abdul had *whap*ped him with a makeshift wooden dowel. Each mark served as a reminder of a lapse in his form, large or small. He used to cry in private after each lesson, sometimes from the pain but more often from frustration and loneliness. Abdul overheard his sobbing and pitied him. Yet he never afforded him any cheap victories; Adam's progress was to speak for itself.

His education had always been the utmost of George's concerns. It was not adequate for the next Chief to equal his predecessor; he was expected to go above and beyond every hurdle placed before him, and to carry United with him on that journey. The pressure was immense, yet his teacher was there for him at each stage. When Adam felt anxious about going home to his father's shadow, it was Abdul who comforted him. When he yearned to explore the world outside the confines of the Subterranean, it was Abdul who accompanied him. When Adam caught a sharp elbow during a brawl in a packed Business District pub, it was Abdul who stitched his bloodied chin back together.

Whenever Adam strayed from the path, Abdul was there to set him straight. He counted him as something his father had never been to him: a friend. Adam asked just once if he'd ever had a family of his own. His eyes had darkened. "I have seen many tragedies," he said gravely, and Adam hadn't dared question him since. He supposed that made them family then, since neither of them had ever had a real one.

The relationship changed again once Adam grew old enough to take his father's place. After his eighteenth birthday, George determined that Adam's learning had slowed. He had grown too comfortable with his teacher, he alleged. The Chief acted quickly, awarding what remained of Adam's education to Santero to realize. Abdul was asked to return to his role as Chief Security Officer (CSO), organizing George's protection and accompanying him on his daily exploits. Adam rarely saw or heard from his former teacher after, besides at board meetings, which Adam suddenly became beholden to; he was a man grown, by definition.

Yet he knew his hopes were likely misplaced. Abdul could not be his fixer; he had been gone some six months "on business" in the Capital District. Or so George claimed. Adam had begun to suspect he might never return from his trip. Never had he spent such a long time away from the board, for business or leisure.

Despite his anxiety, he forced himself to share his secret with no one. His suspicions were only that—hopeful guesses, a way to remove himself from his angst. And besides, past loyalties were subject to change. This was one of the first lessons he was taught.

No. 4 Month 3, 0016 P.F.

Adam entered his quarters and sniffled. One most always felt cold beneath so many layers of earth. He removed his shoes and collared shirt and donned a loose-fitting knit to combat the chill.

Beating wings disrupted the stale air.

His heart skipped a beat. Six months had passed since Samantha's last visit. He skidded into his airy living space and found the bird silently waiting for him atop his coffee table. Adam knelt and showed his wrist.

The bird hopped obediently onto his palm and pointed her beak up like a show dog. Adam gently unfastened the white ribbon tied around her ankle; a paper scroll slipped out from her foot and fluttered to the floor.

Samantha cooed atop the coffee table as Adam plucked up the tiny note. He gently unfurled it, careful not to crease its tiny corners, and held it between his fingers. He squinted at the first line: *5AM, tomorrow. Check sink.*

His eyes widened. He began reading faster. *REST. Long road ahead.* Oriented vertically underneath was a miniature set of directions and coordinates: *GCS 2 B.D. 40.421° N 80.0005° W 133.2%/mast. Courtyard w rusted gate.* The scroll culminated with an image of a dancing fox and the same farewell all her messages ended with: *Water Is Life.*

Adam stowed the paper in his pocket before turning his attention to Samantha. She cocked her head at him. The pigeon stood docile as Adam gently fiddled with the device on her head. She chattered but remained still. Adam worked at the headpiece until its bulk fell into his palm, leaving just a tiny input for wiring on the bird's neck.

Samantha's eyes widened immediately. She fled, scratching the delicate skin on Adam's palm. He clutched the wound as the once-intelligent avian now flew about the room in a panic. The bird beat its wings against the closed mahogany doors before settling, pecking at the floor for dirt or crumbs.

Adam stood and unlatched the door. The pigeon flew down the steel corridor from where it came, operating only on its basic instinct. Adam watched the creature rise and escape, past the layers of earth and toward freedom.

Interlude

February 12, 1941–October 31, 1991
Birth

JOHN MILO carried a certain disdain for leather goods. It was his one instant agitator—a pet peeve, one might say. Whether for fashion or furnishing, leather was strictly forbidden from his home. He scowled unintentionally at men and women alike who wore boots or jackets of bovine origin. His hatred was not spurred by the primitive source of the material itself. Nor was it because he considered it to be unreliable or uncomfortable. In fact, he longed for the days he could see without feeling disdain.

Bill knew better than to complain after he pleaded for a leather mitt to use in Little League and got a synthetic one instead. At first, he mistook it for frugalness—and John Milo was a frugal man. Yet the artificial glove had only been slightly less expensive than the leather one sitting on display. Glove shopping became an annual ritual from which Bill came to expect the same result: confusion.

Unbeknownst to Bill, cost had nothing to do with John's distaste for the material.

◆

John Milo turned eleven on February 12, 1941. He was not home when the men in leather burned down his house; he was out playing soccer with his schoolmates. His older cousin came to fetch him in the middle of the match. At first, John challenged his summons; they'd just tied the game and gone into penalties. As such, his presence was warranted. It took miming threats from John's mother to convince him otherwise; just one vicious *whack* from one of her slippers could convince a serial poacher that poaching should be punishable by death.

The gated terrace his father built with his own hands had melted down to nothing by the time John arrived. The house's foundation was still intact, but the flames ruined everything they touched, charring the stone facade and super-heating the tall glass windows until they exploded. One of the shards went flying into John's younger brother Paul's left eye. After some coercion, Paul opted to wear a patch over the scarred tissue in public, though he claimed he could still detect light through the ruined organ. John never questioned his brother's assertions. Paul abandoned the eye patch as soon as smaller children began confronting him with rudimentary questions ranging from "Can I wear it?" to "Did you used to be a pirate?"

Even after they extinguished the flames with water and time, the house stood strong as ever. John's father and two uncles had built the home themselves: poured the foundation, covered the walls in asbestos, and layered the roof that made it strong. In other words, they ensured the lot would never again be empty. It is for this reason that the house remains standing to this day, albeit vacant in a mostly deserted village.

John's mother was most affected by the soldiers' botched arson. Although they failed to penetrate the thick stone masonry her husband had shaped, they did erase the earthen history planted in her garden. All that remained of the lettuces and pole beans and tomatoes lining the front of the property after the leather men had their way was ash.

Losing the garden was devastating; it was the only thing that kept her distracted while her husband was off fighting in the hills. She took comfort from the fact that the flames did not touch their cellar, where wine, vinegar, and other precious goods were stowed for year-round use. The woodburning oven that made their home the neighborhood's unofficial bakery also survived. It was charred on the outside, just like the house and the goods it produced. She baked Paul fresh loaves of bread laced with butter and honey while the doctors worked on his eye, which brought her some joy.

When spring came, John's mother planted a new garden. When her husband finally returned from the mountains that summer, skinny from constant retreat and ambush, she showed him the fresh mounds of soil she had tilled by herself. She replanted the few seeds she'd salvaged from the charred mess of the last garden, though they grew to be lesser in stature than their mature predecessors.

John's father looked upon the misshapen earthen mounds and cried. He cursed the men in leather, and that image stayed in John's mind long after he'd left home.

January 1945–February 14, 1946

The soldiers stayed and made the town's grade school their base of command until their war machine began to show signs of deterioration and powers greater than they ordered them elsewhere. Some obeyed their superiors and pursued their new objectives; others saw that defeat was imminent and stowed across the sea to avoid jurisdiction for their actions. Those with ranks too low to invoke the courts' fury went home to their mothers. Where the soldiers went didn't matter to John. They had already forced their ill will. They drove his father away for a year. They burnt his mother's garden and ruined his brother's eye. What more could they take?

The family finally felt at ease once the men were gone. Their father repainted the house with the help of his sons. They then cleaned their orchard of thrush so that they might harvest apples later that fall.

Things were calm for a time. But the papers spoke of a different tale unfolding in the capital: mass protests, failed coups, and twin ideologies that consumed people and turned them into radicals. The dissent still felt too far from the village to affect them until one day, while John and his friends were playing ball, a younger boy from the neighborhood came to them, crying. "They took my dad last night," the boy said in tears. The older boys frowned and took the boy by the shoulder and asked what he meant. But the boy just cried until his mother came with black shadows underneath her eyes and screamed at the boy to get inside. That night, John recounted what had happened as they sat eating dinner. His father turned red in the face and warned John not to talk about such things.

There was fresh violence in other parts of the country. Brother turned against brother. Men young and old hunted each other through the mountains. The new sickness had yet to infect their village, but John's parents sensed it coming.

By then, John had grown tall and lean and reached the age where girls and risk become more appealing than the sport of childhood. He'd begun to hang around a new group of friends, boys who wore jeans and high-top sneakers from America. Their fathers often gathered at taverns to argue for or against their government. The occasional brawl would ensue, fortunately with no serious harm ever occurring. John's father did not want his son involved with such people. He started keeping a close eye on his son.

One day, while John, Paul, and his father were digging fresh channels for their cherry trees to drink from, John asked his father why he was not upset by the police officers who'd set a curfew and begun patrolling the streets at night. "There have been worse times," his father said without pause. John bit his tongue and kept digging.

The following week, their father announced he was going away on business. He left John and Paul in charge of the fields. The boys split the work their father would do in a day while their mother took care of the house and their sister attended school. The farm kept running.

One night while the patriarchless group sat eating dinner, a loud knock sounded at the door. Their mother smoothed her dress and calmly addressed the policeman waiting outside. They exchanged words, and she invited the officer inside to join them. He politely declined before excusing himself with a tip of his visor. She returned to the table pale-faced and quiet and ate very little.

Their father returned three nights hence, another startling knock in the night. Where the officer had only carried a pistol, he wore a shotgun at his shoulder and a large envelope tucked in his jacket. He sat down eagerly for supper, and the family ate together for the last time.

◆

Their father shook them awake before sunrise. He told his sons to gather their things and to be quick about it. They did so without questioning him and came to the kitchen clothed and ready. Their mother sat restlessly at the kitchen table in her nightgown. She saw her sons and knew that they were still just boys. She began to cry softly. Paul tried comforting her, telling her not to cry. He assumed they were simply headed south again to work the harvest in another town.

But the eldest son recognized the finality of their farewell. John knew the change they were undergoing would be permanent. He'd gathered as much from his friends' increasingly rebellious thoughts. He mirrored his father, kept a smooth face, and embraced his mother before they left under cover of morning.

◆

Their father was not a dramatic man. He told his sons plainly that he would be turning back once they arrived in the next town. After that, they would be on their own.

He handed John an envelope—the same one he'd come home with the night before—as they bumped along in the old wagon and told him he was responsible for keeping his brother safe. Inside, he explained, were the savings and papers required to get them on board the ship that would take them to America. John swallowed his fear and nodded. Paul began to sniffle until their father glanced at him sharply.

The driver stopped as soon as they'd arrived at the next town. Their father handed the man some coins, offered his thanks, and made John and Paul do the same. Then he shook their hands with his iron grip, staring proudly into their eyes, and embraced them, a ceremony which neither John nor Paul could recall ever having occurred. He handed John a folded parcel with seeds from the garden that he'd kept safe in a little drawer in the wine cellar and instructed them to board the next train bound north. Then he climbed back beside the driver and left, turning up the valley without glancing back.

March 1, 1946

Lady Liberty met the brothers with her cold stare. They did not notice the warning in her stone frown. She saw them and thought, *You are imports. You are not welcome.* Not until they proved themselves worthy of her benevolence.

The brothers worked as painters, bricklayers, and cooks and still received the same look. Two years into their arrival, Paul met a fellow countryman at the factory where he assembled television sets for a time—transformer, resistor, vacuum tubes, screen, housing, in that order. The man told him about a company that paid men equal wages indiscriminate of their color, be they Anglo-Saxon, Italian, Negro, or periwinkle. Effort was the only determinant of pay. Paul asked urgently what borough the company was located in. The man laughed at him. "No borough, my friend; you'll have to go to Pittsburgh if you want to work there."

That night, Paul told his brother the exciting news. They packed their few belongings and by morning had left New York.

September 27, 1948

The bus wound west through hills and valleys that reminded them of home. It saddened them to think of their parents and sister, whose faces were blurring with each passing day.

The first sign they saw directing them toward Pittsburgh was the smoke emanating from the city's mills. They followed the chimney's trail until they landed at the United Steel Company's contracting office with all their belongings in hand. The manager briefly explained some terms before offering them their contracts, which they each signed very deliberately. The manager then shook their hands and welcomed them to the United family. He handed them some documents explaining their employee benefits, along with membership cards for a union where many of the steelworkers congregated.

They excelled through their first days sweating in the mills. They were relieved when they saw their first checks with their names written on them; the man in New York had delivered on his word. They pledged not to waste their recent fortune and threw their union cards in the trash.

English snuck up on them both, most notably Paul, whose accent all but disappeared. They befriended their fellow steelworkers and met girls who later became their wives. After five years in the mills, they took their budding families together on vacation to Niagara Falls. They lived tired but comfortably for a long while and steadily grew independent of each other. But they never forgot where they came from. Blood was an eternal bond.

Though they were grateful for the lives their jobs afforded them, living and breathing steel day and night was by no means a flawless way to live. Each time the union workers went on strike they were asked to work sixteen-hour shifts—which they did, since they were the only men willing to do so. The mills become so understaffed that, rather than go home to their own beds, the Milos began sleeping in cots outside the blast furnaces. Their wives gradually grew accustomed to their absence and sought each other's company in their stead, drinking coffee together in the morning and delivering their husbands dinner come afternoon.

In 1966 the American President Johnson visited the mills. He shook hands with many union men while they enjoyed their allotted one-hour lunch breaks. Neither John nor Paul got the chance to shake Mr. Johnson's hand. They were too busy doing the stoking and casting and cooling while the others posed for pictures.

When the workers struck for the third time that year, the brothers went to their plant supervisor's office to hand in their gear. The secretary told them when they arrived that Mr. Carroll was in a meeting and asked if they would like to schedule an appointment instead. John told the secretary they would wait.

They sat in the small waiting room in their grimy work clothes until, eventually, a man in a crisp, tailored black suit exited the office. He caught their stares and paused to shake both their soot-covered hands. The man asked for their names. "Keep up the good work," he said, smiling apprehensively as he quickly excused himself. Had either brother known the man was Ezra Crombie, they might have stayed on and worked. But neither one recognized the president and CEO of the company they had spent more than a decade working for. Instead, they went into the office and made their peace with their shift supervisor. The man didn't seem bothered much. He stared absently out at the paused steel mill, no longer emitting smoke from its chimneys.

July 1960

Two years before their departure from United, John and Paul invested in a small tract of land west of the city. It was there that they planted the seeds their father gave to them. Row upon row of young apple and pear trees dotted the small parcel.

One day into his unemployment, John decided to take his wife to spend the afternoon at the orchard. He merged onto the interstate that eventually grazed the outer edge of the property, only to find temporary warning signs and orange traffic cones blocking their path. He frowned and turned around the way from which they'd come.

As John grew increasingly flustered (and lost) trying to find an alternate path, they passed by a car dealership. The dealership lay on the city's outskirts and boasted foreign beauties that John could only dream of being able to afford: Mercedes and BMWs, Audis and Porches. Excited at the prospect of playing the part of a rich man for the afternoon, they decided to explore the lot further.

When they peeked inside the glass showroom, John saw a man unfold a briefcase filled with stack upon stack of pale-green dollars. John's jaw dropped. He later recalled the experience to Paul. "*This* is where the money in America is!" he said enthusiastically. "Jewelry, cars, luxury."

The brothers came to an agreement in little to no time. They called the man who'd sold them the farm and bought the acreage next to it, taking out loans against their wives' wishes. Next, John drafted a letter to the General Motor Company of Detroit, requesting an application for him and his brother to become certified automobile dealers. They signed the letter mutually, *Milo Brothers Auto.*

A week later, a man from Detroit arrived without warning to meet with them. The brothers gave the man a tour of their land parcel, which was located within sight of the interstate. The man left with a contract bearing both brothers' signatures, and Milo Brothers Auto was established seven days later.

September 1970

In 1970 their father took ill. John immediately contacted his travel agent in New York (a friend of his cousin's) and purchased two standard tickets: one for him, one for his wife Julie, and none for their son (whom they named to honor John's father), because the airlines still considered children as luggage in those days. He went knowing beforehand that he was going to see him for what would likely be the last time.

He asked Paul to join them, but he declined. He would go on his own later, he explained; their father would be disappointed if they abandoned their growing business just to see a graying old man. John thanked him, vowing to do the same for him later.

His cousin greeted them at the airport. The embracing was awkward and forced by relation initially, but any shyness dissipated as soon as they escaped the capital and began driving through the mountains. Words from his language that John had not forgotten but merely locked away for later use slowly returned to him as he traded jokes and stories with his cousin. They laughed as the pine trees whizzed past them. The scenery reminded John of the morning his father smuggled him and his brother to America. He smiled at the memory while Bill bumbled on Julie's lap in the back seat, his eyes soft and sad.

John found his father sick but unchanged when they finally arrived in the hometown. His back was stiffer and his hair whiter since they'd last met in 1966, when he came to Pittsburgh to remark on their lives and their wives. Whatever cancer was eating away at him, he did not let affect him. He ate, drank, and worked with the same thirst as usual.

He cried when he met his grandson, the first time John had seen the phenomenon since the men in leather razed his mother's garden.

John's father weighed his grandson by the armpits in spite of his cancer, kissing his foot and talking baby talk to him. He asked John if the boy was baptized. John shook his head.

The following day they dipped Bill in holy water, and that evening John's mother cooked for them and all the attendees, a second family that'd sprouted during John's absence. They ate and drank through that night and each night after until it came time for John to leave once again.

1983-December 1988

Bill inherited his father's tall, broad stature, but his slight and handsome features resembled those of his grandfather. He took from his mother's side his hazel eyes, long, dark eyelashes, and little else.

Bill was well-liked at school—unanimously so. He was friendly and topical with all his classmates, irrespective of popularity, race, or status. He had no close friends but no close enemies either. Bill was a natural athlete, yet he was humble. He took no credit, even when it was deserved. "That Billy Milo's a good kid," his classmates' parents would declare after meeting him—often in front of their own children.

Although Bill possessed the tools for creative endeavors, John and Julie discouraged him from utilizing them. Despite their pride in his academic and athletic accomplishments, Bill's parents sheltered him from the arts, which inherently carry risk. They encouraged him to take part only in activities they deemed *sensible.* Joining the basketball team was sensible, as was delivering newspapers or detailing cars at the dealership. Opening a savings account was sensible. College was sensible. Being safe was sensible.

Bill stuck to what was sensible until he graduated and realized he only knew how to do sensible things. He'd neglected to find something he enjoyed, a passion that carried risk. Bill's parents encouraged him to continue his studies, a sensible enough decision. He was a high achiever, and his father had earned the resources for him to attend any school he wished.

But Bill had no desire to study, work, retire and die. The narrative felt overstated, a cookie-cutter formula for middling success. He feared being trapped inside that narrative.

Bill revealed his plans for his future late one evening while sitting around the kitchen table. His father was furious, which confused him at first; he'd chosen a sensible enough pursuit. John recounted aloud how hard he'd worked to provide him the resources to succeed in life and repeated things about Bill's privilege that he already knew. Bill listened idly and finally understood why his father was so averse to insensible doings. It was regret for always having acted so sensibly himself. He stood from the table without his father's blessing.

On December 30, 1988, Bill enlisted in the Marine Corps.

September 9, 1990

The constant desert storm pitched salt and sand everywhere. The fine dust coated Bill's clothes, boots, rifle, and lungs, even though he was inside a Humvee near as often as he was not. The particles left a gritty ocean taste in his mouth that he could still taste as the helicopter transported him to the military hospital.

Bill remembered the flight home, but not the moment the floor of the Humvee was shredded to bits beneath him. He remembered not being able to hear anything but a faint and high-pitched buzz. He remembered tasting the blood that'd dripped from his nose into his mouth. He remembered being pulled from the vehicle's smoking hull and dragged through the sand by the back of his vest. He remembered the trail of blood that followed him and asking himself, *Is that mine?* He remembered staring up at a beautiful sky plagued by smoke. He remembered reading the lips of the medic who'd ridden in the second truck, feeding him reassuring lines like "Hang on, Mimi" and "They're almost here, Mimi." He remembered his comrades' nickname for him, *Mimi,* the same name one of his childhood friends used to call his grandmother. He remembered seeing but not hearing the chopper blades before being scooped up like an owl snatching prey. But most of all, he remembered the taste of the salt-sand grit on his tongue.

His last memory was the shock of the hospital lights. Then his body fell into liquid and stayed that way for a long time.

December 12, 1990

When he awoke, a nurse with platinum blonde hair was in the room with him. She faced away from him, tidying up the room. Bill said nothing. He watched her work until her ears perked and she spun around; she must have noticed a shift in his vitals.

She initially looked at him with a blank expression on her face. "You're awake?" Bill nodded. Then her eyes widened, and she covered her mouth with both hands and ran from the room.

Bill remembered his name—Bill. He remembered his parents' names—John, Julie. He remembered his squad mates' names— Miguel, Sturgill, and Harry, their nickname for Cpl. Clayton Eastwood, who didn't much resemble the actor or Dirty Harry at all. He remembered his social security number and the capital of New York. It was Albany, not New York. Yet he remembered nothing of the accident. He did not remember how he'd arrived at a hospital in Germany. He did not remember his exact injuries until his doctor listed them to him: *Multiple fractures to the skull. Blast-induced traumatic brain injury (likely severe). Multiple inoperable embedded shrapnel fragments (potentially toxic). Third-degree burns along the right calf (posterior) and bottom of foot. Fractured left radius and humerus. TM rupture and middle ear damage (likely permanent).* "To sum it up," the doctor began, "you're a lucky man, Sergeant Milo."

The fractures, burns, and lacerations would heal with time, but the injury to his soul worried him. He felt different. Almost fractional, like part of him was still stuck in the tarry muck where he'd spent so long. The doctor laughed when he asked him if this was what shell shock felt like. "Maybe, back when we still called it that," he said, his tired smile slowly receding to a tired, straight line.

His brain was kind enough to communicate to his body that life was to be postponed for those three months. Bones fused and tissue regenerated while he slept. His muscles became somewhat atrophied, but not to the extent of crippling him.

He began therapy in a wheelchair, practicing stiffening his ankles, calves, and then thighs, and eventually worked his way upright into a walker. He only needed its assistance for about a week. A nurse came into his room one afternoon and found him standing in his gown, his pencilly calves shaking under his own weight. "Mr. Milo!" she shouted, rushing to catch his imminent fall. But Bill stood tall.

Winter–Summer 1991

The captain promised he would not regret it if he chose to resume his service. Wounded soldiers gained the utmost respect from their counterparts, he explained as Bill worked at balancing a tennis ball on top of his foot. They would make him an officer if he so wished, instantaneously making his counterparts his inferiors. The thought made Bill uncomfortable; weren't the men risking future mutilation braver than those who'd already faced it?

Bill told the captain he needed some time to think about it. "Of course. Take your time. Enjoy your health now that you have it." He clasped him on the shoulder, and the tennis ball rolled out of the room. "You deserve it, soldier."

◆

Bill decided to do some traveling while he weighed his future and enjoyed his restored health. He inquired the hospital employees on places to go. One of his nurses recommended a small alpine town near Austria for its receptiveness toward foreign folk and general lack of crowds. His activities after his doctor declared him fit for discharge mostly amounted to skiing, eating, and drinking in line with local taste.

They met at the drafty ski lodge Bill was staying at. It lay directly beneath the mountain's crest and was said to be two degrees colder than the rest of the town at all times. This was attributed to a fierce wind that howled down the mountain's face and directly upon the rustic inn.

She managed the lodge on the owner's behalf, a local real estate tycoon who'd retired away to the Alps. It mostly sat empty outside peak season. She spent most of her time tending to the property, which drowned beneath flowers in the spring and snow in the winter. She liked to sing while she worked in words that Bill couldn't understand. She spoke perfect English, having gone to school alongside affluent British and American children whose parents' jobs had brought them to Vienna. Both her parents had died recently. She had no siblings.

Her hair was light and straight and fell just past her shoulders. She had a perfect nose, Bill thought immediately upon seeing her first, narrow at the bridge and ending in a lovely button shape. She was slight of figure and short of stature, yet her walk commanded the eyes of anyone nearby. When she caught the wavering eye of some potential suitor (of which there were plenty) she judged them with that crippling steel gaze, those blue-smoke eyes. Most men never dared another glance. They felt bitter afterward, yet rarely spoke anything of it. Bill did not look away but smiled when she directed this gaze toward him. He smiled the way one does when they have fallen in love and abandoned their apprehension. He told her in plain speak, *I think you're lovely and I'd like to spend some time with you.* Sharing their time quickly became preferable to spending it apart.

September 28, 1991

He gazed into his daughter's steel-blue eyes and wasn't sure who looked more afraid.

He'd never been afraid at any point during his deployment. There had never been enough time for fear to take root. More often than not, he'd been *excited,* the adrenaline and epinephrine pulsating through his veins at a chaotic rhythm. He'd been co-responsible for the lives of his comrades, a terrifying proposition in and of itself. But that's what he'd signed up for. They were brothers in arms, delegated to the same chaotic reality, trained to have each other's backs. It made it easy, knowing he was not alone.

When he saw his daughter's face, he realized what the war had taken from him. He could not contend with the unknown, the void, the maybe. The realization was clear, crystalline. And terrifying.

October 20, 1991

Shortly after his daughter was born, Bill received a letter formally inviting him to resume his service stateside. When he had finished reading it, he folded it neatly into thirds and began drafting his reply.

He and the mother of his child calmly discussed their futures together. They entertained the prospect of monogamous accord and concluded it was not feasible. They were equally pragmatic souls, if not fearful of commitment. Inevitable forces prevented them from staying together; commitment to duty on one hand and a thirst to explore on the other. And fear.

But a child should not suffer the consequences of poor planning on its parents' part; they shared that feeling, too. Bill knew he would have to face the problem head-on. So did she.

And so, she kissed her daughter one last kiss time, her steel-gray eyes meeting hers, and gave her up to her love, who flew her across the sea to put in the care of older, wiser hands.

October 31, 1991

It was Halloween when John and Julie Milo met their nameless granddaughter. Solo travelers, couples, and freshly reunited families milled about the airport, some in stiff business get-ups and others in costume: Ferris Bueller, He-Man, each member of Mystery Incorporated (save Scooby), and countless vampires, werewolves, ghosts, and ghouls.

Their son *stood* differently. They almost did not recognize the tall, broad-shouldered man who strode out from the little feeder-hole called ARRIVALS. Bill carried his daughter in one hand and his suitcase in the other. He seemed to handle both weights with great ease.

The oak dining room table where they'd gathered all those years was unchanged, along with the rest of the house Bill grew up in. They ate dinner in relative silence, making polite, cold small talk while pretending to ignore the storm of questions hanging above them. But Bill did not give the past its due time.

After the initial shock of reunion passed, Bill quietly asked his parents to raise his daughter with a resounding lack of somberness. They did not agree immediately. "Why don't you stay?" his father implored. "You can live here until you get a job. It's easy here for veterans to find work."

"There's no job here," Bill said simply.

John gripped the table with his left hand, his neck bulging at the rut in his jaw. "Why don't you stay?" Now he was pleading. Bill stared at him blankly.

"Because there are people who still need me."

John stood from the table. He did not raise his voice often, but he did then. "*She* needs you!"

She, Bill thought. He felt the sting of what John had truly meant to say: *What kind of father abandons his own daughter?* He blinked wearily and looked down at her. She was silent in her carrier, which had been her mother's parting gift to her. For a moment, he wished he was still with her. Then he reminded himself why he'd come this far and stood from the table to leave before the sting widened into a gap in his heart.

He stayed the night in a motel and called the nearest Marine recruiter in the morning, asking for someone to help him to his next destination.

November 1, 1991–

The girl peered out from her crib with an unnatural calmness. John and Julie saw a stranger at first, with light hair and eyes that came from a mother who was alien to them. But that quickly changed.

They named her August, after Julie's mother. August rarely raised a fuss but loved to laugh, especially after John discovered her fondness for "Old MacDonald Had a Farm." She was raised in equal part by her grandparents and her deep and loving extended family: aunts, uncles, cousins, and various other family members whose relations were harder to pin down, plus her grandparents' exuberant and dependable collection of neighbors and friends. It took a village.

August became the shining light in their otherwise fading life. Neither of them felt their true age; their granddaughter seemed to attribute a certain youthfulness to them. August grew up to be beautiful, just like her mother, a living question mark who never fully escaped the backs of their minds.

Yet all the joy August brought them was not enough to erase the price they'd paid for their right to love her, for her joy brought pain too. And the pain only grew sharper the more she took after her father.

IV

November 29, 2015–January 2, 2016
Pittsburgh, Pennsylvania, United States of America

AUGUST KNEW her grandfather like a dog-eared book. She could see whether he felt tired, frustrated, or ecstatic (which he often was) just from the seen in his eyes. And vice versa; John could detect when August felt uncomfortable, irritated, or otherwise. Like a dog scenting a trail. This was a testament to their fondness for each other.

John insisted on making her breakfast every morning throughout her school years, despite his rapid-fire work schedule and his wife's constant bemoaning over the messes he left. Not sugared cereal dumped into a bowl; bacon and eggs (fried in said grease), pancakes, and, if he was feeling illustrious, crepes filled with Julie's homemade jam. He reserved weekends for her as well. Friday nights were movie night at the AMC Waterfront 22, with ice cream from Cold Stone Creamery afterward.

John Milo was a good parent despite the fact that he was not August's father. He was a good parent because he was a good man, and vice versa. It was John whom August confided her secrets to, John whom August went to whenever joy or gloom was bothering her. She did not go to him seeking economic resources. What she sought from him instead was advice; conflicting jobs, plans for the future, struggles with her boyfriend at the time (which usually upset John; hilarity ensued), and more singular oddities, like a dream that was bothering her. Though John's advice was not always perfect, he put forth his best effort in guiding her, which was ultimately what mattered to her. He gave his honest opinion no matter the situation or how his words might affect August. August learned to appreciate his candidness.

If there was one negative that came from John's love for his granddaughter, it was the regret it placed on him for not offering the same to his son. The one time Bill went to him for advice, John had failed him. He told him that his dreams were impractical and were therefore not worth pursuing. And his son's response was to fight in a war that wasn't his.

August went to college and studied industrial engineering on her grandfather's advice, which proved to be a sensible enough pursuit. She graduated and worked the beginner jobs most engineers get upon graduating. From that moment on, August lived in fear. The thought of the rest of her life playing out dedicated to the same empty-feeling pursuit was terrifying. Passionless work. Work trapped behind a desk. Work that she disliked and therefore became work.

August went to her grandfather for advice, per usual. As she vented her frustrations and expressed her dream of opening a bake shop, John's first instinct was to guide her toward the sensible thing: keep her job for another couple of years until she found a new one. And save, save, save so that she could later marry and have children, and a house, and a dog, and a 401(k).

But he rejected that instinct. It was that instinct, to steer rather than guide, that had driven his son away from him. He was old and wise enough to recognize the same reaction creeping up on him then. Or perhaps he was not wise but weak, an old man terrified of repeating past mistakes.

So, John embraced his granddaughter and told her to do whatever made her happy. And August cried, because it was the best piece of advice she'd ever received.

◆

August was the sole baker, cashier, janitor, general repairwoman, and proprietor of Steel City Sweets. Her days began at 4:00 AM. Her first duty opening the bakery in the morning was to start the ovens. Then she began preparing the next day's menu while that day's confections were proofing. She baked until 6:30 AM, then swept, mopped, polished, and set up the coffee station so she could open for business at 7:00 AM sharp.

August sold out often and often early. She closed at 6:00 PM at the very latest. August tasted all her confections to ensure their quality and trueness. Any malformed batches she reserved and donated to friends or family. The nature of her work and a blessed metabolism kept her figure slight, despite her high sugar absorption. The time August spent kneading and flipping and molding and shaping dough made her shoulders and forearms unnaturally strong for a woman. She was consistently tired, but that was fine by her. Her work was fulfilling, and so it was not really work but life. Her customers were kind and generous for the most part. Most faces were familiar, and the small TIPS jar by the register was typically full by the end of each day. August did not get much sleep, but what she did get was good. It felt deserved.

◆

On a cold and wet day in November (the kind where snow falls but merely collects into a thick slush on the street), August was late closing and stayed at the shop past six. She was packing up leftover kolaches to drop off at one of her regular's front stoops when a man walked in through the front door, which had a bell at the top that went *ding*! His shoes were caked in the November slush. He swore lightly and stomped out his Oxfords before entering, generously trying and failing to avoid making a mess of the shop. "Hello," said August, trying to sound jovial despite her exhaustion. "There's not much left, but feel free to look."

The man smiled politely and gazed disinterestedly at the remainders of August's display case. She glanced past him at the nasty weather outside. He'd likely come inside in search of shelter from the storm. Still, this was Pittsburgh. One was expected, better yet, *obliged* to be able to handle a bit of cold weather. If not, well, they should join the other snowbirds and "take a hike" to Florida. Her father was fond of saying this.

The man smiled handsomely at her. August crossed her arms instinctively. He wore a mustache and goatee that made him look older than he probably was. He was tall, over six feet, with broad shoulders and a heavy, proud chest. "I'm sorry. I don't mean to sound rude—I just saw your sign and it made me laugh."

August frowned. "Sorry, I don't get it," she replied, perhaps a bit more stiffly than intended (confrontation was not one of her strong suits). The man laughed, which only angered her further.

"I didn't mean to offend you. I meant 'cause our businesses bear a lot in common, the whole 'steel' theme and all ..." The man paused, went, *Hmm,* and became oddly contemplative. August laughed nervously, not knowing what else to do before the man snapped out of his frame of mind. "Sorry, I don't mean to keep you. I'll have a coffee. And the rest of, uh ..." He waggled his finger at the half-packed kolaches. "Those."

August gave the man a tight-lipped smile. After she had boxed the rest of the pastries, she turned to fetch his coffee and found the burner empty. She heard her father's stiff voice before she complained to herself: *Never shortchange the people, the people* meaning *customers* in John's half grasp of the English language. "Coffee'll be a sec," she said plainly.

"If it's a hassle ..."

"It's not a hassle." She poured the grounds and started the machine.

The man frowned. "At least let me buy you a cup. To pay for the pot."

"Trust me, I'll take care of it," August wised back. She was not at all being sarcastic—her caffeine consumption had become increasingly disconcerting of late. The man smirked, withdrew his wallet, and deposited a twenty into the recently emptied tip jar. August watched from the corner of her eye. *Thank those that are good to you.* "That's very kind," August remarked.

The man gave a courteous nod and asked whether August took custom orders. "Of course," she replied. The man explained he wanted to order a cake for his grandmother.

"She's turning a hundred years old this January. Incredible; sometimes I think I'll be lucky to make it halfway there," he said, looking down disconcertedly and grabbing his belly for effect. August snorted (a noise that she hated and hid as best she could), blushed, and said she could put together whatever he wanted. The man asked if she would join him ("How about we sit down and I'll buy you a coffee and we can talk things over?" was the way he framed it) so he could explain his idea for the cake. August agreed.

The topic of cakes was not discussed until much later. The man spoke lightheartedly and was easy to talk to. Before she knew it, August was chuckling alongside him at his childhood memories of his grandmother, which mostly concluded with her threatening to spank him over some mischief he'd incurred as a boy. He paused at one point to sample one of August's kolaches and from thereon did little else but marvel at her "quaint little place."

August laughed at his stories without thinking to share any of her own. She'd never been good at engaging in unstructured conversations. It was part of the reason she'd opened the shop in the first place; she counted her customers as her friends (and vice versa), if only because she was good at making conversation while engaging in the economic façade of so-many dollars for so-many sweets. Before the shop, she had struggled to make friends; the shop gave people a reason to seek her out.

She found herself uncharacteristically sharing one of her grandfather's numerous exploits. She recalled one of his stories set in the eighties (back when he and Julie still ran the dealership) that featured a customer (purportedly from South Africa) who'd offered to pay for his Mustang in diamonds. After his jeweler examined the jewels and labeled them "flawless," John agreed. All was good and fair until the gentleman swapped out the diamonds with zirconia stand-ins before the exchange. Her shoulders began to relax after the man corroborated a similar story involving his uncle; "Must've been in fashion." They continued to share laughs and stories until long after dark, the coffee maker's bright orange HOT indicator the only thing illuminating the coffee bar.

When she finally glanced at the clock, she saw it was almost nine. The man saw her alarm and was beside himself with apologies. He scrambled to fill out a form with the date of his grandmother's birthday (January 2) as well as the size and shape and filling of the cake, then scheduled a date and time to pick it up. August checked the details twice over. She asked her gracious new customer if he would like a reminder slip for his order. "Please."

August stood to fetch him a slip, but the man raised his hand. August sat back down. She hadn't been ordered to, but she felt compelled to. He dug into his wallet and pulled out a worn business card he had buried inside. "Here." He set it facedown for August to write on.

August picked up the card and instinctually flipped it over—not because she was prying for information, but because she had a tendency to fidget with things and place them in a way that pleased her visually. In doing so, she glimpsed the name printed on the card's face. It caught her eye for two seconds longer than it should have. Centered alone and in bold print read, **GEORGE A. CROMBIE.**

August's stomach turned. George A. Crombie. President of United Steel Company, George A. Crombie. The man in control of the global steel trade, George A. Crombie. Casually stopping by her shitty little bakery, George A. Crombie. **GEORGE A. CROMBIE,** sitting across from you. Whoop-dee-fucking-doo, August.

She immediately felt embarrassed for not recognizing United's heir apparent. She suddenly became conscious of whether her face had turned beet-red, which made her face turn beet-red. Crombie scratched his forehead casually and pretended not to notice. August pressed down on the card to write down ...

She blinked and tried to recall what date and price they'd agreed upon.

◆

August hit the couch with a resounding *sigh* and flipped on the TV to consume her nightly news and noir (the pinot variety). Instead of relaxation, she found George A. Crombie. She sat up, suddenly awake as Lester Holt's voice filled her living room:

—allege that your company stole already patented technology in order to develop new United products. What do you say to those accusations?

Crombie smiled, just as he had smiled at her a mere two hours ago. There was a little sadness to that smile. *They're true,* George replied simply.

August sat up fully and turned up the volume. They showed Mr. Holt's shock on the screen. *Erm, I'm sorry, Mr. Crombie, but why do you say that?* George sighed and clasped his hands together.

I don't think many people listening fully realize that United Steel is the backbone of America. Some might laugh at that; our city, Pittsburgh, has undergone significant changes since my great-great-grandfather built this company from nothing in the middle of Appalachia. But the fact remains that steel is essential. Without United, Americans would not have access to the same jobs, housing, and infrastructure as they do today. Yes, times have been hard as of late. The tech sector has slowly overtaken industrialism over the past twenty-odd years. But we're a strong company, and an even stronger country. United is America; we built the very foundation it stands on. And if we collapse, so does this country. They showed Holt squinting at him. *I hope that answers your question, Lester. We here at United are doing all we can to keep America strong. That includes my uncle, myself, and the rest of the executive board. And, most important of all, our workers. They have been here for you every step of the way, and I will use whatever means necessary to support them.*

◆

August spent the next day (and the better part of the next night) at the shop, hoping that Crombie might *ding* through the door. She obsessed over his logic. What benefit was there to confessing to breaking federal law on national TV? And doing so *willingly?* She tried coming up with a way to ask him without sounding too forthright; *So, George, just wanted to ask, um, why is it that you fessed up to patent infringement? Asking for a friend.*

But the front door never went *ding.* For the next month, August stayed past close, regardless of whether she had anything left to sell. She did not see or hear from George Crombie in person or online. Sometimes on those long, lonely nights, she would research the ongoing lawsuits against George, scanning online newsfeeds for any mention of his name. But he had vanished from the public sphere.

Poof—one day he was there, the next he was gone, as if cut out from existence.

The weather worsened and the days shortened, and George A. Crombie crawled further into August's thoughts. She even mentioned the lawsuit to her grandfather while they sat eating baked ham and wild greens (an odd combination that somehow worked) on Christmas Eve. John's face became locked in concentration: "I worked for Ezra Crombie for fifteen years, and not once did I ever hear anything about fraud. I know they had the charity fund they put some of the money into, but the rest of it ... who knows? I don't know what's going on there now that Alfie's in charge, but back then, they were *good* to us. They treated us fair, no matter where we were from ..." His voice trailed off. August pretended to be content with the answer.

August spent New Year's Eve with her grandparents, and her great-aunt, and her children, and *their* children, whom she referred to as "cousins" for lack of a proper designation, but her singular focus was cake—George's, specifically. She studied his order form for seemingly the hundredth time while she prepared vasilopita and panettone for the New Year's crowd:

> *3-tiered round vanilla. Strawberry layers, buttercream frosting, <u>NO</u> ganache. Fresh strawberries on edges—*out of season?**
>
> *Message: "To My First Love—Happy Birthday!" (in script please)*
>
> *Pickup: 1/02/2016 @ <u>6:00 PM</u>*

The order wound through her brain like ticker tape even as she sat surrounded by family counting down the "New Year" (they were celebrating the ball dropping at nine instead of midnight, for the sake of the little ones' guaranteed participation and their orderly sleep schedule). August didn't join the choir of nieces and nephews and great-aunts twice-removed and all the rest of them raising a toast to the

New Year. "Happy New Year!" They blew out a numbered candle that read 2016 and eagerly began slicing the marble cake (a product of Steel City Sweets, of course) it'd sat upon. *A hundred years* was all August could think.

The shop was closed on New Year's Day, but August spent her day working on the Crombie Cake anyway. She sliced and macerated strawberries for the fringe garnish he'd requested, creamed butter, sugar, and eggs together to aerate the cake, then baked and molded and frosted and sculpted until she'd finally finished the Goddamn Thing. She was not put at ease, however; the day of reckoning was yet to come. That night while she sat poking at a slice of prime rib that John accidentally overcooked (a New Year's tradition), her only thought was George's scheduled visit the following afternoon.

◆

August woke at her usual hour to brush her teeth and assemble her hair into a rat's nest. She hadn't slept well. Her anxiety over the Cake (plus one or two too many glasses of wine to help combat the anxiety it exuded) was the cause. She wondered who would show up; the warm gentleman she'd met two months ago or the man with the steely voice from the interview. The chance of it being the latter only made her more anxious.

She found her car frozen, a regular occurrence in Pittsburgh during the winter. She scraped her windshield awkwardly against her thick bundle of coat, gloves, and scarf. The shop would be frozen too, until she fired the ovens.

A small inlet behind the shop provided just enough space for August to park her car and receive the truck that delivered flour, eggs, sugar, and whatever else she might need to keep the shop up and running the rest of the week. Her commute took her in front of the shop before parking, and she typically glanced over the facade as she drove by, for no reason other than to ensure it had not burned down during her brief absence. One misfortunate morning during her first month open, someone had tossed a brick through the window and raided the shop for cash or other rewards. They came away empty-handed (she was not in the habit of stowing cash there), aside from some stale cookies she was gladly willing to part with.

That morning, an unidentifiable bulk of human wrapped in a parka sat shivering beneath the shop's veranda. August sucked her lip. She hadn't been very sympathetic to the homeless prior to opening the shop, but her opinions had since changed; *she* had changed. It made her sad to see humanity like that, misshapen lumps bundled in mismatching down and flannel just to keep warm. It wasn't the first time she'd caught someone sheltered beneath the awning. They usually fled once August turned the lights on.

The clock on her car read 4:58 AM, which meant it was 4:41 AM actual time. August yawned and braced for the cold before shuffling hurriedly to unlock the back door. She rubbed her hands together and flipped on the shop's main convection oven, then passed through the swing door that separated the dough room from the front and turned on the lights. She retreated to the dough room before the down-on-their-luck noticed the lights and fled. She hated bearing witness to what was undoubtedly an embarrassing moment for the person.

August turned to head back through the dough room until she heard a *tap* on the glass. She spun unwisely and bumped her head on the swing door. "Ouch," she said robotically, rubbing her forehead. Then she looked out the window. George A. Crombie was peering in through the glass door, a gloved hand shielding his eyes.

August almost turned back to the ovens to pretend she hadn't seen him. Instead, she forced herself an inhale, smiled, and went to unlatch the front door.

"*Jesus*, it's cold. Thanks for saving me." August smiled and nodded like a moron while trying to ignore her mounting panic attack. "Happy New Year, by the way."

She'd never seen Crombie in anything but a suit and tie, in person or otherwise. His parka was shedding feathers along the bottom. "2016 already ... Time flies." He placed his hands on his hips and arched his lower back, *oomph*ing in relief. "How many years have you been in business now?"

"Three," August answered, trying to hide her nerves. "I opened in October, though, so four, technically."

"Oh."

He neglected to acknowledge his earliness, so August meekly said, "Sorry if I'm a little late opening up," which George insisted was not the case. He promptly sat in one of the bistro chairs scattered about the front as August fled to the dough room.

When the door swung shut, August bent over and inhaled deeply. *Just get him out. Tell him you're closed. The oven's broke.* But then he would just have to come back later. *He couldn't have just come at close like we agreed,* she grumbled to herself. Then she noted the wall clock in the dough room, which showed 6:12 AM, and nearly smacked herself. "Around six, if it's not your busy time." George had said it with a wry smile when they arranged the order. *Stupid,* August thought to herself then. She hadn't even bothered to ask whether he meant morning or afternoon. She'd taken him at face value and wrote down *PM* instead.

A *clang*ing noise behind her made her jump. "Sorry!" yelled Crombie from the other room. August crouched and peeked through the window pass to see what had occurred. Crombie was attempting to operate the espresso machine. He looked remarkably confused; he'd dropped a foaming cup, and it'd *clang*ed on the floor. August felt sick. "Sorry. Was curious."

"I'll take care of it," August said, clanging through the swing door. She tamped grounds into the lever and switched open the valve. The machine gave a resounding *groan* before shuttering. This made August very upset.

"Shit," Crombie muttered. He vowed to pay for any damages, then smirked. "Normal coffee will do."

August managed to laugh through her distress. "Don't worry about it. Coffeemaker's in the dough room—in the back. I'll go put a pot on."

"Dough room'?"

August smiled facetiously. "Oh, it's nothing special."

"Mind if I see it?"

"Not at all."

Crombie loomed behind her as she led him through the door and put the coffee on. When she turned, Crombie was admiring the main oven. "It's *huge.*"

August bobbed her head. "Yup." George stayed and watched as she gathered her cake pans and baking trays and floured them with the same flicking motion she'd learned watching her grandmother. She tried and failed to remember what confections she'd prepared in advance the day before. George seemed oddly fascinated, like a kid in a toy store.

The coffee machine *beep*ed. Porcelain *clink*ed as Crombie carried her mug over. August accepted graciously and burned her tongue. She wanted to scream and pull her hair out by the roots, but she hid that feeling with a smile instead.

She'd spent countless hours brainstorming how she would circle the conversation back to *60 Minutes* on the date Crombie would come to pick up his cake. She would finally understand whatever hidden logic had inspired his confession. But now that he was standing in front of her, she felt like a rabbit hiding in a shallow hole while a wolf poked its head in, snarling and snapping at her.

"Why did you admit on national news that you stole patents from other companies?" August refrained from hitting herself. *How eloquent of you, August.*

Crombie looked pleasantly shocked. He swirled his coffee, grinning to himself. "Would you prefer to hear the truth? Or the bullshit?"

"I'm sorry ... I didn't mean ..."

Crombie sipped his coffee and smiled facetiously. "Because I felt like it."

"Oh." August looked at her clogs. She started over. "So, is your entire family celebrating your grandmother tonight?"

"Whoops, almost forgot." He leaned against the wall. Flour coated his arm without his knowing. "Just me and her, actually. My father and grandfather have both passed. No siblings. My Uncle and I are all that's left."

August snorted again. George looked somewhat offended. "Sorry," she murmured. "It's just that your cake is very big for two people."

"Is it?" George frowned. "Guess I was just trying to impress an expert at her craft."

"Well, I wouldn't call myself an expert, but ..."

"No. I think your work is very beautiful." He seemed unable to accept humble denial.

"Thank you," August said plainly.

Crombie checked his watch and sighed. "Well, I'd better get out of here. Before my boss gets mad at me." August smiled. "How much do I owe you?"

August gasped. Her fingers went tingly as she dashed out to the front display. George frowned after her. "Is something wrong?"

No Cake.

A siren began ringing in her head. August grabbed her hair. *FUCK. FUCK. SHIT!* She'd brought the Cake home overnight in her mania, staying up late to pluck strawberry slices with tweezers and dip their top halves in white chocolate. The Cake was still languishing inside her garage fridge. *No Cake.*

"Are you okay?" George asked from the swing door, sounding genuinely concerned. August leaned heavily against one of the café tables.

"I, ah ... I forgot the cake at home," she confessed in her state of crisis.

Crombie's shoulders shook with laughter. *He looks like a lumberjack,* August thought passively in her panic. She went for her keys (which were not in her pocket at all) and paused. The oven would be practically blazing by now. "I'm so sorr—"

"Shit. Now I *really* have to go," Crombie muttered at his watch. He forced down the rest of his coffee and declared he would have someone pick it up "*when it's ready.*"

"Wait—I handle deliveries," August said without knowing what she was saying. "I can bring it to your grandmother, or drop it off at your ..."

"She lives in Florida," he added casually. "But if you insist, you could swing by the airport tonight. My flight's at six." August hesitated. "Forget it. I'll just have someone come pick it up."

"No!" August blurted. "I can do that."

Crombie scratched his beard. "It'd be easier on the both of us ... But I understand where you're coming from. *Customer satisfaction guaranteed!* He smiled, then nodded curtly. "I'll have someone meet you at the terminal."

August continued apologizing, while George insisted there was nothing to apologize for. He paused before returning to the frigid cold and asked for her name. August gave it to him. He beamed and shook her hand gently. "Nice to meet you, August. Would you like to have dinner tomorrow night?"

August nodded. She did not consider the implications of this nod. George smiled and left without having introduced himself in turn.

◆

August was not in the right frame of mind to bake after George A. Crombie left. She sold out of what little she had left over from the New Year early and was home by three. She planned on leaving extra early for the airport in case there was any traffic or an accident en-route. She'd embarrassed herself enough already.

August dressed in a flurry. She briefly considered her sparse collection of makeup and scowled, opting to pull her hair into a ponytail instead. She tugged her parka over her shoulders and headed to the airport, remembering to remember the Cake.

There was an overwhelming flow of return flights, people concluding the holiday travel grind and reconvening with their ice-ridden vehicles. August buttoned her coat up to her chin, secured the Cake under her arm, and walked past shivering couples arguing over where they'd parked the week before.

August was unsure who or what she was supposed to be looking for. She saw no sign bearing her name until she walked to the next terminal. A short, wiry man wearing a suit and round, gold-rimmed glasses waited beside Terminal B's main entrance. He held up a sign that simply read CAKE. The man looked about the space critically, as if it was unworthy of his presence.

"Hi," said August, peeking over at him. He jumped and looked up at her in surprise. "Hello. I brought Mr. Crombie's order." The man frowned at her. "The cake?" August clarified unnecessarily.

"Oh. Yes, I've been waiting." The man adjusted his spectacles and cleared his throat. "Did you bring any ice?"

Ice? "No. I mean, I didn't think ..."

"Ah," the man replied, frowning, an apparently permanent fixture.

"Um. Can I help any other way?"

"Well, is there any other way to keep it cold?"

Why yes, actually. August put on a phony smile. She hoped he saw it was disingenuous. She patted the box. "*Actually,* the box is insulated. It'll be just right by the time Mrs. Crombie gets it; it's been chilling since last night."

The man raised an eyebrow quizzically. "*Mrs.* Crombie?"

August frowned. "Mr. Crombie's grandmother? That's who the cake's for. The one who lives in Florida."

The man put a finger to his lips and hummed while looking toward the ceiling. "Hmmm ..."

August chewed her lip. "Uh, *Ms.* Crombie? He mentioned that his grandfather had passed away, so ..."

"Oh, I see." The dweeby man exhaled. "*Madame* Crombie passed away last year. Were you not informed?"

August hesitated. The man waited expectedly. She mirrored her prior smile. "Anyways, here's Mr. Crombie's order. Tell him I'm sorry for the delay."

The man nodded. "No apologies are necessary." He accepted the cake, set it down lightly, and promptly withdrew a wad of cash from his pocket. He began counting off hundred-dollar bills until he reached ten. He looked at her, confounded. "Will this be enough?"

August faltered. "Uh—like, a tenth of that. Here, I brought the receipt ..." She reached for her wallet.

The man shook his head and raised his hand. He split the money, stuffed one half back into his pocket, and gave the other to her. He turned away with the Cake under his arm before she could protest. "*Bonne nuit,* Miss Milo," he called over his shoulder.

August watched him go as the money unfolded limply in her hand. *Miss Milo.* Funny; she didn't recall giving George her last name.

V

THERE ARE *times in which gravity ceases to exist. The Earth stops turning. The world holds its breath.*

"Madame."

It's in times like these that bravery speaks volumes. It's in times like these that the strong distinguish themselves from the weak.

This Perseverance Day, we remember those who succumbed to ALIN-12's—

"Madame Secretary."

This Perseverance Day, we ~~remember~~ honor those who succumbed to ALIN-12's unimaginable—

"Madame Secretary. You have a visitor."

"Who is it?" Naomi asked, irritated.

"He said he's here on behalf of—"

"I don't have time to talk to representatives. Tell them if their boss would like to discuss security matters, they can speak to me directly."

"Ma'am ... Madame ... he said he's here on behalf of George A. Crombie. *Chief* George Carn—"

Naomi set down her gilded fountain pen. "Yes. Of course. Why didn't you say that? Send him in." She saw hesitance in the intern's eyes. "Now," she commanded, accentuating the word with her red-stained lips. The boy turned shakily to retrieve the United ambassador.

Her visitor announced himself with a light knock. A second later, the door clicked open, and the Chief's ambassador stepped through graciously. The man was not physically intimidating, but he carried a certain air of sophistication. He inspected Naomi's office as he introduced himself. "Madame Secretary, thank you for seeing me. The Chief sends his apologies for not being here personally, but he has been unable to travel of late due to chronic fatigue." He avoided Naomi's eyes, who stood to greet him.

Fatigue. She'd already been briefed on Crombie's recent struggles with "*mental and physical exhaustion attributed to fatigue.*" But even MARS's internal spies in Pittsburgh lacked sufficient access to determine what was actually ailing him. The Chief had the means to force his privacy, as desired.

"I'm sorry to hear that. Please send the Chief my best wishes." Naomi extended her courtesy. The man accepted reluctantly, his hands cling-wrapped by thin leather gloves. "I'm equally pleased to meet you, Mr. ...?"

"Vesper," said Vesper, reverting his eyes to the floor.

He straightened his rimless glasses and set down his briefcase before taking a seat opposite her. The briefcase hit the floor with a heavy *thud.* Naomi's eyes flicked toward his luggage. "Mr. Vesper, how can MARS Group be of service to you?"

Vesper crossed his legs at the knee and spoke with a frown that seemed to be glued to his bald face. "First and foremost, my client wants to ensure that this conversation is being held off the record." Naomi hid her smirk; *on the record* was in direct conflict with her line of work.

"Of course. I value my privacy too." She nodded at the ceiling. "The building we're in is a physical air gap. No outside signal or transmission is permitted entry unless we've approved it. Rest assured, this conversation will remain between us."

Vesper nodded approvingly and bent over for his briefcase. He fiddled with its latches and selected a thick computer and a cigar from its contents. He rolled the latter between his fingers. "May I?"

"Go ahead." Vesper fetched a butane torch from his breast pocket and worked the cigar until it burned neatly enough to satisfy him. He opened the laptop and began typing away, the cigar plugged in his mouth like he'd left the frame of a spaghetti western.

Naomi sniffed and waited for him to speak. Vesper ignored her, absorbed by what was on his screen. *If he gets his, then I can have mine.* She reached under her desk and opened a drawer for the near-empty prescription bottle inside. She pinched one of the tiny capsules between acrylic nails and swallowed it dry.

When she looked up, she found herself sitting opposite a black screen. Vesper had stood and replaced it in his own seat. Naomi stared at her reflection on the screen as Vesper stood casually at the machine's side, admiring his cigar. She glanced at him awkwardly before he finally acknowledged her. "I'll retrieve my things once you're finished." Vesper slid his glasses up his nose and bowed slightly. "It was a pleasure, Madame Secretary." He exited abruptly, a dissipating plume of smoke the only proof of his existence.

The screen illuminated with a ringing symbol as soon as the door shut behind him, as if it'd been waiting for him to leave all along. Naomi corrected her posture and chased her bangs away with her fingertips.

When the screen refreshed, she was met, expectedly, with George A. Crombie. *Fatigue,* the claim was not without merit. He certainly looked the part; his face was naturally square and full, but he appeared gaunt nonetheless, his eyes red and veined in the blue light of his monitor's screen. He frowned and brought his face closer to his webcam, muttering unintelligibly until his audio finally synced. "Yes?

Hello? Yes?" he asked, glancing down at his keyboard as he brought a glass full of dark essence to his lips.

Naomi cleared her throat. "I can hear you, Mr. Crombie. My name is Naomi Cieslinski. I'm glad we finally get the chance to meet, even if it's not in person."

"Zelensky? Is that what you said? Hello?" She repeated herself. The Chief's eyebrows curled farther inward. He broke it down syllable by syllable. "Shis-lin-ski. *Cieslinski.* Right. Well, I hope you understand how big of shoes you're stepping into, Miss Sheel— Cieslinski. Your predecessor, Mr. Boseman, was very good at his job." He grasped his chest and exhaled hot air. "Very good."

Naomi tried to hide her grimace. *He's drunk.* "My predecessor kept things well-organized. I'm grateful for that."

Crombie laughed, a wheezy, genuine sound. His shoulders shook from the contractions. "Yes. Although Mr. Boseman did not last long in his position, he certainly accomplished a great deal during his tenure. We may never see such artistry put on display again. Like that time he ignored the terrorist attacks against my workers in Indiana—I can assure you that some faulty generator did not cause those explosions. Oh, and we must not forget about the time that dam was seized in Virginia—Acadians, if I remember correctly. That one was not my construction—though it certainly could have been." The Chief smirked, toying with his beard. "But yes, Mr. Boseman left the Group in such *stellar* organization; I cannot deny him that."

Naomi swallowed. "I won't comment any further on my predecessor's actions. But what I can say is—"

"That he was a good fucking manager. I understand. I've managed people, *thousands* of them, mind you, every waking moment of every single day for the past forty-five years. It's not as complicated as it seems. Now, Miss ... Er ..." He snapped his fingers. "Right; *Cieslinski.* Tell me: You are aware of the change underway in the West, yes?"

Naomi smiled thinly. *You only have to tell him as much as he already knows,* she reminded herself. *Unless he knows more than you do,* another voice suggested. She spoke calmly. "I am. I've been told that the threat is negligible. The nearest Rite our agents have infiltrated was in Columbus—some twenty-something year-olds doing a poor imitation of the Frog way of life. Too young and dumb to know any better."

"*Frog.*" George sat, weighing his beard.

Naomi frowned. "Yes?"

"Most people your age shy from using such words." George chuckled and savored his drink. "That is precisely why I called for this meeting today. I've been told you're taking a more, ah, hands-on approach to running the Group; less bullshit, so to speak." Naomi shifted uncomfortably in her seat. "Still, this threat your people have deemed negligible has the potential to sweep east to the Atlantic." Naomi was dubious, but all that showed was a tiny inward fold of her brow. "And we can both agree that it is not in our best interest to allow a califate of radicals to capsize us. That would be bad for business. I intend for this supposedly 'great' nation of ours to endure, despite its innumerable flaws." Crombie ingested his drink. "I have a favor to ask of you, Miss Cieslinski."

She folded her hands. "Well, I am obligated to hear all inquiries from those with a seat at the Anti-Terror Committee. Go on, Chief."

George smiled. "The floor is mine. You came from nothing. I'm understanding that correctly, yes? You used to be a—"

"Yes, I was a waitress before the flood. And after for a while." Naomi shrunk into her chair. She preferred only to share what sparing details of her past were pertinent to the situation.

"Before'? Really? And here I had already mistaken you for a floodling. I wouldn't've placed you a day over twenty-five," George said easily. *He's certainly not lacking in charm,* Naomi thought as she thanked him politely. "Waitress, eh? Plenty money in it, but not much room for growth. I get the sense you saw that, didn't you?" George nodded in self-affirmation. "I respect that. Instead of merely continuing to exist, you chose to reinvent yourself. Most people are terrified by the thought of reinvention. It's doubly true of the rich and famous; we simply *pretend* to reinvent ourselves."

Big men demand big respect, Naomi thought to herself. "With all due respect, Chief Crombie, I beg to differ. You completely transformed your business model after the flood. Not many other people were flexible enough to do that." *Or stupid enough,* she quietly asserted. She'd heard the Subterranean had cost upwards of fifty *billion* dollars to construct. She knew that at one point George had been worth about a hundred billion of them, so it was not outrageous to say he was half-buried in his own ambitions.

"Ha—please. Save your charms for someone your age. I reinvented nothing. I came fifth in the lineage of slightly ass-wipish, privileged Crombies whose fortunes already awaited them. My only hope is that I have acted slightly *less* ass-wipish Chief than my father or uncle, and that my son is a shade less so. Yet the fact cannot be disputed; all of us have feasted off the same ancestral privilege. So was the case with me, and so will be the case with my son." George sighed before he finished. "But what's done is done. First, we must address the task at hand ..."

"Of course." *Big men demand big respect,* she reminded herself. *And offer bigger rewards.* She toiled with her pen.

She saw hesitation on Crombie's face for the first time since the meeting's start. He licked his lips. "I would like to employ the Group's services. Specifically, its security forces."

A sour taste formed in her mouth. *He's crazy. A schizoid.* George shook his head as though he could read her thoughts. "I understand your apprehension. MARS Group has served the Colonies and the Colonies alone since its inception—but I'm afraid this matter is urgent. I can no longer trust the people surrounding me, save my own son. So that's why I'm reaching out to you." *Or a cokehead,* she thought, adding to her list of suspicions.

"I see." Naomi shifted uncomfortably. "Why would you want to do such a thing?" she asked simply.

"To strike first at our common enemy."

"I'm sorry? Who is that?"

"*What.*" Crombie rubbed his beard. "It's not 'who' that is threatening us, per say ... it is *what*; lies, deceit, fake promises of sanctity and 'spiritual reawakening' ..."

Naomi frowned. "I can't help you if you continue to speak so vaguely, Mr. Crombie. If you would like to employ the Group's services, then—"

"*Change is not always warm and cozy, but it is very often necessary.* Do you know whose words those are?" Naomi shook her head. "Bill Edenson. The same man who created this mess in the first place. You can't say he was wrong, though." He lingered over his drink. "*That* is the threat, Miss Cieslinski."

"Bill's been dead almost a decade," Naomi said calmly.

"But his legacy lives on. And we are *weak.* The Colonies lack hope, and that is something that, dead or alive, Father Bill excelled at fabricating." George licked his lips. "Before we go any further, I have to ask you something: can I trust you to keep a secret?"

She smiled confidently, as she'd practiced in front of a mirror so many times. "You can trust me."

George interlaced his fingers. "Good."

◆

Naomi rapped her nails on her desk. Her eyes moved to the laptop's insignia, which was etched permanently below the screen: UT, the T shaped like a bull's horns. The *U* stood for United, and the *T* for Technologies. She briefly glanced at the Loop strapped around her own wrist, knowing the same branding was inscribed somewhere on its strap.

George continued his tirade. "There is a woman they call 'the fox.' She is rumored to convert and escort anyone blind enough to believe her message West. I have lost almost a thousand of my people already—my former Chief Security Officer among them. *One thousand.* They abandoned me after everything I built for them ... I gave them new lives away from the flood. Away from fear." He shook his head. "It must stop." Naomi stared at the laptop's insignia before recollecting herself.

"It's more significant than I'd thought," she admitted. She already knew some of what George was explaining to her—but some of it she had not. "Have you considered using your own company's resources?" she mentioned, the logo again capturing her attention. George smiled, though it did not appear joyous. His seemed sadder than most.

"I am. At this very moment, I'm afraid. We make more than Loops and computers, you know. Your, ah, *association's* primary concern is security, is it not?" Naomi nodded. "Then surely you know what else we make. Our surveillance technology is second to none. But unfortunately, machinery cannot completely predict behavior; not subtle behavior, at least. Yes, it can be used to create propaganda, monitor profiles, spread dissidence, etcetera; but these strategies have a low ceiling. And sometimes, they only create more dissent." George's glass was nearly empty. "What I need is men. Men who will weed out any Alliance sympathizers and command a presence in my city. Most importantly, I need men whose allegiance cannot be questioned." He poured himself a fresh drink. "I've heard good things about your Internal Military Police. Are the good things they say true?"

Naomi nodded. "Our agents are as impressive as they say. Most are ex-military, and the rest were police or paramedics before." There was no need to specify before *what.* "Floodlings are barred entry, so most have prior combat experience. I've seen their training firsthand.

It's no walk in the park." She briefly recalled watching two men engage in a knife defense drill on the beach during high tide, when the water and the sand conjoin to create a soupy mess. By the time a victor was crowned, only the whites of their eyes were not covered in the sand soup.

"Is that so?" George scratched his chin. "How many do you have currently stationed in Pittsburgh?"

"Two hundred and ten," Naomi responded automatically. She prided herself on knowing the Group's ledgers like the back of her hand.

Crombie nodded in agreement, as if he'd already known the numbers, and hers checked out. "I see. Well, I'd like to see that number quadrupled."

Naomi paused. "That would be ... challenging."

"Yes. But you are used to challenges; how else would you have reached your current office? From waitress to Madame Secretary?" George grinned.

Naomi maintained a neutral expression. "You're too kind, Chief Crombie."

"Please; George."

Naomi felt her face flush. "*George.* You're too kind. But what I mean is, it won't be easy to find that many officers. I would either have to source them from less-than-stellar recruiting pools or receive emergency authorization to increase our intake capacity. And I am not willing to do the former." The Group's high standards did not allow for a lapse in the quality of its mercenaries.

"You bring up good points," George muttered. "As to the latter ... Well, an emergency authorization requires a unanimous decision from—"

"The Anti-Terror Committee."

Crombie seemed content. "Seeing as I hold a seat on the Committee, it very well may be possible." George smiled meekly and sipped heartily. "I'll think on it. For now, let's discuss what's most pressing. How many men can you send me in the next month?"

"Did I mention the outstanding organization Secretary Boseman left the Group in?" George laughed heartily, and Naomi grinned. But behind the smile was a reminder to herself: *Now's not the time for apprehension.*

She opened a drawer in her desk and unfolded a large ledger she had within. She pretended to skim over the document, which was unnecessary, because she already knew the exact numbers. "I have about fifty standing ready in the C.D. Another thirty will graduate from their training by the end of the month ... and I can spare maybe another fifty from the other major polities." In truth, she had twice as many men at the waiting, but the Chief need not know that. *No need to get greedy now.* "But it won't be easy. And before I commit to anything, I need to know ..."

"Of course. You want to know, 'What's in it for me?'"

Naomi stopped in her tracks. It was precisely what she'd meant to ask, if in less precise terms. According to her position, she was compelled to pursue the Group's interests, and the Group's interests only. But she had yet to hear any rewards for her cooperation—yet. George continued, "It's a good question. An *honest* question. You will be rewarded for your work, rest assured. I will shower MARS Group with technology, steel, money—whatever you wish, so long as I have my men." He lingered over his drink. "Believe me when I say this threat is *very* real ... *Change is not always warm and cozy* ..." He fought an itch in his throat and scratched it with another drink. "The choice is yours."

He might be mad, Naomi thought to herself. But he didn't seem a step slow for an allegedly fatigued and assuredly drunk man.

She did not let her voice falter. "One hundred and thirty officers before the end of the month."

George smiled and offered a small toast. "Good. They should have all the training you mentioned—surveillance, detainment, interrogation, and whatever else it entails. Restrict it to current or former military. They should be familiar with conducting tactical operations. I will proportion them throughout our sectors as I see fit. I also want agents performing constant surveillance on my bore train network—regular old desk jockeys will do, just as long as they can read a screen and follow orders."

Naomi's head was spinning. She blinked and realized she had forgotten to take her medicine. It wasn't a problem she often had; the call had grasped her full attention. "I can make that work," she muttered, resisting the temptation of yawning. "But excuse me, Chief Crombie—"

"*George.*"

"Right. My only concern is ... well, I'm not quite sure whether what you're asking is legal, strictly speaking."

George chuckled. "Of course. Everything is legal, Naomi. This is America, after all. Here, we *interpret* the law. And besides, this conversation never took place." George's tone softened. "Earn my trust, and you'll be in good standing for the rest of your career—no matter who your boss is."

Naomi nodded and smiled her best before the screen turned blank. "Of course, George."

◆

Naomi opened her desk drawer and swallowed two of the capsules she kept tucked next to the small .32 she kept in case of emergency (nowhere in the Capital District was entirely crime-free, her lofty office in the Tenth Quadrant included). She scrounged around inside the bottle and counted. *Five left.* It would last another day, maybe two. She sighed in quiet relief and went to pen a few more words before she went to fetch Vesper.

This Perseverance Day, we honor the brave men and women who were made victims to that greatest of tragedies. It is thanks to them that we today enjoy a society free of pain and suffering. It is thanks to them that I, a proud daughter of the New American Colonies, continue to live in a society undeterred by chaos.

This day serves as a valuable lesson to all Colonists who value a safe and orderly society: without unity, we are fragile. And a fragile society is a weak one.

God bless, and God bless the New American Colonies.

Naomi Cieslinski
Secretary of MARS Security Group

VI

YOU'RE NOT *old enough to know the different types of rain: the slow and sullen tears, background noise, fast and vicious shards. Or, for those less poetically inclined, Flood Advisories Category 1 through 5 …*

Tell me, Adam: How will you lead this company if you have not yet braved the storm?

Adam awoke with his father's words still echoing in his mind. He'd barely slept. The room recognized his waking and adopted a soft yellow hue. He wandered groggily to the bathroom, feigning an early-morning limp convincingly.

Rather than relieve himself, he knelt to inspect his sink. He found a set of barber's shears and a bootlegged Loop duct-taped underneath. He strapped on the Loop, ripped the shears away, and inspected himself in the mirror.

Moments later, he was hacking off his dark locks, the strands tumbling about his shoulders like wisps of smoke. When his hair met his ears, he stopped and admired his work. The hollows beneath his cheekbones appeared just as sunken in. Frowning, he shaved and took a long shower, wary that both could be his last.

The room filled with steam and the smell of soap. Adam let the water turn his skin pink and wrinkly. He smiled at the sudden uncertainty his life had taken on. There was not a great deal Adam had ever been uncertain about. His future had always been laid out, factual: *You are the heir to the industrial backbone of this country. Because of you, man stands above the flood.* As a child, he'd dared challenge such notions. *Then why do people live on the surface?* he remembered asking Santero once. *Because they were born there*, the professor replied. Someone of his status should not be concerned with such trifles.

The choice to stay was still in play. Staying would mean a life of relative comfort and stability, one with preordained access to wealth beyond imagining. But staying also meant signing his life away to a story with no end: expand the family's wealth, propagate, manipulate, repeat. Continue the Crombie legacy, like his father before him. Ensure the ink never went dry. And why not? He was the last of his kind, George's only child (to the best of his and the public's knowledge).

But it was too late to reverse course. He had not made his decision in haste. He'd spent nigh on a year preparing—judging the distance from the nest, plotting how to dodge each branch below. Making himself ready for flight.

Adam shut off the water and briefly sat in the steam before drying off. He normally dressed elegantly in clothes designed to make him look noble. He opted instead for a waffle-knit long-sleeve and worn denim. The garments made him look common. *Good*, he thought.

◆

Adam walked hurriedly down the steel gateway. Error in the coming hours would be fatal. They would not afford him a second chance. Once the plot was uncovered, it would be over, dead in the water—perhaps him with it.

The gusty pass led to his personal bore train car. His father's surveillance network gazed down at him. He did not bother concealing his face. The men tasked with watching him would be notified the second he departed; it was not like him to make such an early morning trip to the Business District.

The bore train's access slid shut behind him, and the car gently came into motion. The fluorescent lights lining the tunnel blurred as Adam catapulted to his destination. Adam tapped his feet anxiously. He hated his father's earth-digging trains. The normal passenger trains were loud and uncomfortable; his personal car was only slightly less so. George took great pride in his machines, despite their abrasive nature and the fact that they were not his invention. His uncle and predecessor Chief Alfie, whose life's work was bringing cheap, universal public transport to Pittsburgh, had overseen their development. The system went online just after he died of a chronic wasting disease. The newly incumbent Chief George made it a point to revamp its infrastructure, investing in underground economic hubs built adjacent to the pre-dug bore train stations; thus, the Subterranean was born. Only then was Alfie's grandiose tax-funded vision hailed as a success. The Chief afforded credit to his uncle (at least what credit he felt he deserved) by planting a colossal bronze statue bearing his likeness in Grand Central Station. Still, Adam believed he secretly detested Alfie for coming up with the idea before he did.

The *hum* beneath Adam's feet slowed. The cabin lights lit gently. *NEXT STATION—GRAND CENTRAL STATION*, hummed a familiar robotic voice over the intercom. Adam fit a surgical mask over his nose before he stood to exit the platform.

The ring of mighty Romanesque columns lining Grand Central Station dwarfed all those who passed beneath them. Beyond the marble fencing, the city underground lay, waiting. It was a confounding mess of makeshift side streets and alleys, each leading to a distinct neighborhood or hidden borough.

An air of doubt clouded over the skyless city. This was in large part attributed to its quasi-medieval construction, all stone, plywood, and thatch. A small but significant number of the ninety-eight million Americans who perished by the flood's hand were skilled carpenters; a smaller but equally significant portion were steelworkers. The ensuing shortage of skilled workers led to a decidedly DIY approach to building a new home. Things only worsened when United Steel (the company responsible for digging out the city and hoisting up the Pole in the first place) made a "strategic decision" to abandon its 150-year practice of forging steel and instead shift its focus to producing Loops and other impressible technology. Its new, production-focused subsidiary, dubbed United Technologies, would be headquartered in the Subterranean itself.

The instability was tangible. The city swayed without any wind to sway it, and its residents were never at ease. Adam felt it too and wondered whether the people's collective anxiety was a product of their environment or their personalities—though one had to have a certain propensity for disarray to abandon life on the surface and seek shelter underground to begin with. But one most certainly changed once they'd forgotten the life-stowing properties of the sun's rays.

Adam passed beneath the columns and joined the mess of tired souls on their commutes throughout the Subterranean. The crossing was enameled in gray-veined marble, designed to hide dust and grime from the thousands of treads that passed through on a given day. Chief Alfie towered over them at the main platform's center, his face sculpted to a hard, stern edge. Adam's footsteps merged with those of his suited-and-tied companions, each passerby indistinguishable from the other, marching penguins in suits, faces hidden behind masks. Adam felt out of place, despite his anonymous guise. If he were to suddenly reveal his identity, every passing soul would likely pause what they were doing to bow their heads or rush to snap a photo. Or spit at him. Sometimes they did both.

But the suits were too stricken with the Station's hectic energy to afford Adam a second glance. An electronic buzz filled the air, voices chatting into signal-boosted Loops that sucked in satellite beams through the layers of earth above.

A billboard of a seductive, neon-lit dancing woman inexplicably linked to a hot dog stand caught Adam's attention. The advertisement seemed to have worked to a tee; a long line extended from the order window, mostly listless men suckered by a womanly figure and a need for protein. As Adam watched the sign flash, he felt the hollow stare of a man beside him wearing sunglasses. He stood two shoulders to his left, awaiting his turn to scan through a metal turnstile. He reverted his eyes when he caught Adam's stare, feigning interest in the neon sign and shuffling forward as the line progressed. Adam's fixer's voice looped in his brain like a recorded message: *Know that you are being constantly monitored.*

Adam pushed through the crowd and veered right, away from the Station's center. He hurried toward a row of tented food stalls, where a gruff-voiced fishmonger was proudly advertising his wares: "Ocean fish, pole-caught! Bright-eyed and fresh!"

The sound and smell of oil over flame enveloped the alleyway, hungry eyes darting back and forth between wafts of smoke. Adam walked past an ornamented palm-reading booth and glanced over his shoulder. The man in sunglasses was pushing his way through the crowd, mirroring his path.

Adam quickly passed an older Asian man sitting on a curb, smoking a cigarette. He glared warily at Adam, noticing his attire's crisp, unfaded lines. Most of the people working in the little alleyway lived there, too.

Adam checked behind him for the man once again, but the smoke and asthma emitting from the stalls obscured his vision. He felt more necks chasing after him and worried that perhaps his clothes had little to do with what was bringing him such unwanted attention. Something besides his cleanliness distinguished him; perhaps it was his perfect posture, or an invisible royal aura that traveled with him.

Adam stopped and swore at the sound of Oxfords clacking.

He veered quickly into a tent filled with spices. A man checking over his wares turned to the noise, the owner presumably. Adam looked hesitantly at him. The man stared back blankly with almond eyes pinched at the corners. Adam removed his mask and reached into his pocket. He presented a heavy metal coin to the shopkeeper. His eyes widened. "Please help," Adam said in broken Farsi.

The man dipped his head. "Your Highness," he sputtered and immediately began ushering Adam away from the entrance. Behind the shop's small counter, the flooring shifted to wooden planks. The shopkeeper pressed his heel into the edge of one of the panels, lifting the opposite corner from its place. He wriggled his hand through the gap and removed it, revealing a wooden set of stairs that descended into a cellar-like space. "Down. Go," he instructed. Adam descended into the darkness as the shopkeeper replaced the floorboard above him.

Adam stepped blindly down the wooden stairs, patting the cool clay walls with his palms. The perfume of hashish was suddenly overpowering. Adam heard the shopkeeper's feet move toward the store's entrance above him. "I only serve paying customers," he heard him say with a thick accent.

"I'm looking for a person," a stern voice replied. "Tall with dark hair. Wearing a brown jacket. Wearing a mask."

The shopkeeper cursed in his mother tongue. "Many such people! You must go now. I have business to attend to."

"Ah," replied the monotonic voice.

"Yes," the store owner replied without a stutter. A long silence; Adam inhaled.

"We'll be back," the intruder commented before his footsteps reversed, announcing his departure.

Adam leaned against the stacks of tightly wrapped contraband for what felt like an eternity before the panel lifted again from the same spot, spilling dim light into the cellar. "It's good," the shopkeeper called down.

Adam climbed the stairs and quickly scanned the room. A fat man sat reclining against a thick-padded cushion on the floor, smoking a cigar wetly. He was balding and wore rings on various fingers. "Kos nagu," the man muttered when he saw him. Adam recognized the expression from his Farsi lessons with Abdul all those years ago: *Holy shit.* The fat man rolled onto his feet to offer Adam his hand. He pulled Adam into a sloppy embrace.

The shopkeeper nodded knowingly as his associate conveyed what an honor and privilege it was to be in his presence. The shopkeeper offered the coin back to Adam. "I am grateful for you," he said.

Adam shook his head. "No. For my thanks," he translated sloppily. The shopkeeper licked his lips and bowed deeply. Adam slipped his mask back above his nose. "Khoda hafez," he said before exiting briskly; *God be with you.*

Adam heard the fat man exclaim as he left. "Silence!" the shopkeeper warned him in Farsi. "You are not made special by this. We are all indebted to His Grace."

◆

The alleyway fed into a string of boutique shops and restaurants adorned with gaudy modern facades, frequented mainly by women in dazzling dresses and men in ironic hats sipping cocktails over brunch.

The affluence eventually reverted, and the road led Adam to the Station's south gate. He scanned the counterfeit Loop at one of the gate's turnstiles. An electronic panel on the post flashed green and displayed a smiling green emoji as the gate *clack*ed open: *Welcome, GRANT HARRIS, to—BUSINESS DISTRICT; GCS SOUTH GATE.*

The Business District sprawled before him, neon billboards reflecting blue against his pupils. Familiar advertisements from various for-profit organizations flashed before his eyes: pre-flood conglomerates like Coca-Cola and Nike, niche manufacturers of highly specialized tech such as HUD lenses and home cryochambers, makeup companies claiming their products' "melanin-boosting" properties, pharmaceutical companies pushing the latest mind-numbing happiness solvent, and, of course, the company that would one day be Adam's: *United*, omnipresent, ubiquitous, everywhere. A commercial for the latest entry in United Tech's Loop lineup ran on one screen, featuring everyone from celebrity athletes to composers touting the new wearable. Every few minutes, the screens would synchronize, and the mayor (a puppet piece known to frequent the Business District's bars and brothels) would appear with his phony smile and pulled-back skin. "Pittsburgh! Above or below, wet or dry, we work for *you!*" his voice boomed before submitting to the constant stream of ads.

Hawkers and buskers lined both the District's glitziest and most porous areas. Adam passed a sitting man wearing a neural implant of some sort. A swath of speakers lay about him, emanating mediocre electronic music live from his thoughts. The man didn't flinch when Adam brushed past him. He stared forward with fluttering, muted eyes.

Adam was familiar with the area; he'd often gallivanted about the District as a teenager. The tightly clustered buildings allowed him to mask his precise movements. It was impossible to cover *every* corner of the Subterranean with surveillance, the Business District in particular. It was an urban spiderweb with secret debaucheries spun in every corner. Hidden penthouses, basement taverns, brothels where one could smoke fine, illicit substances, "health clinics" peddling designer drugs, family-owned restaurants specializing in cuisines thousands of miles from the Colonies—Chinese, Polish, and Ethiopian, among countless others. Monocled ex-coal brokers and prostitutes walked the same streets. They were each other's equal, in unitary pursuit of the same carnal delights.

Adam headed west, toward the Pole. One could spot it from almost anywhere—the Business District, the Banks, and beyond, even from the furthest of the Subterranean's outer slums. Inside the massive structure were the Chief and Adam's living arrangements, as well as several United Tech offices, a surveillance center, and the bulk of the Subterranean's power grid. It spoke of the Pole's immenseness. It was necessary, to prevent the earth hanging overhead from burying them all alive.

Adam pulled the slip from his pocket. *GCS 2 B.D. 40.421° N, 80.0005° W 133.2%/mast. Courtyard w rusted gate.* He'd followed the instructions to a tee and found no such gate before him. Adam sat at a flimsy wooden bench in the plaza and crossed his legs. A pair of children ran about the square, kicking a patched soccer ball between them. An ancient man sat across from him, his wrinkled eyes folded shut. He tapped his cane on the pavement occasionally, as if to remind those around him he was still alive.

Adam craned his neck to juxtapose his location. A dotted circle tattooed onto the Pole's foundation marked its 180-degree point. Santero had once referred to it as the Bullseye.

Adam's judgment was correct; this was the place. *Maybe she made a mistake.* He hung his head back and sighed. *Or maybe she doesn't exist.* He'd gone almost four hours on foot already. The soreness in his calves was already betraying him, though the worst part was knowing that there was more in store. For twelve months, he had forced himself awake in the middle of the night to do push-ups and burpees in the dark. *No sudden drops in weight. They can't suspect a thing,* his fixer told him in one of her messages. *Wear loose clothing. Don't overeat, but don't undereat either.* Still, his exercises had not taken adrenaline or endurance into account. He winced and massaged his calves.

Adam's ears suddenly perked. A distant horn sounded off from near the Pole's center. An identical sound occurred thirty seconds later, this one closer. The noise relayed out toward the Subterranean's outer edges. A woman hollered from an open balcony. "*Niños!*" The children whined and paused before slowly resuming their game, testing their mother's authority.

The old man stood up shakily and began dragging himself home with his cane. Sirens echoed off to the south, growing increasingly distant until Adam could not hear them at all. A few ticks later, there was a loud *clank,* and the lights dimmed.

"*¡A la casa! ¡Ahora!*" shouted the mother, her tone dangerous this time. The children scooped up their ball and trotted past Adam, quietly bemoaning their play being cut short. Adam felt his face in his palms and pressed in on his eye sockets. He would have to find an alleyway to hunker down in and find the gated courtyard early the next morning. He forced himself to his feet before he was caught outside after lights-out and escorted to jail.

He paused; the old man had dropped a crinkled pamphlet where he had sat. Adam frowned and checked to see whether he was still moseying down the sidewalk he'd left by, but there was no sign of him.

Adam bent over to pick it up. Its cover was adorned with checkerboard advertisements for mid-end real estate. He flipped it over and paused. A marking on the pamphlet's back caught his eye; neatly sketched in gray pencil was a fox dancing on its hind legs.

Adam began scouring each page, arching his back as if to ward off any eavesdroppers. Apart from the pencil etching, the pamphlet only seemed to contain coupons for a myriad of local businesses: *Clogged Pipes? Call Peter the Piper and Take Back Your Plumbing! (724) 131-2940.*

He leafed through the pamphlet dejectedly until his finger caught on something. He squinted; a page near the end was neatly perforated, almost impossible to spot unless one was given reason to look. Adam separated the page in two, careful not to tear or crinkle the paper. There was an address scribbled on the page's interior with a simple instruction: *74 Sicily Dr. (G) Wait until lights-out.*

Adam grinned to himself as the lights dimmed then vanished.

VII

No. 9 Month 3, 0017 P.F.
Mount Vernon, Capital District, New American Colonies

THE MEN marched single file, not unlike baby ducklings tailing their mother. In this case, Brooks was Mama Goose.

A dense layer of clouds rolled east overhead, accumulating a strong, gusting wind that whistled through the pines. "Gonna rain," Crunch stated bearishly. They were well above the flood, an abnormal pleasure for the common amphitrooper. *No matter the circumstance, we answer the call with the single greatest weapon the world has ever known: the fighting spirit of our Troopers.* At least that was how the commercials sold it. In reality, most of their daily endeavors could be summed up as slogging through shit-tinted water to make pointless repairs to decades-old infrastructure. They were grateful whenever the opportunity to staunch some puny revolution in New Hampshire or West Virginia or wherever arose. At least that was engaging.

Tyler was not so enthusiastic about their mission. Scouting was a tepid duty that necessitated long stretches of time spent alone, thinking, remembering. *"Fucking Frogs,"* he complained under his breath.

They marched on in silence, passing beneath a buzzing, aromatic canopy of oak and pine. The trees drank from a previously sought-after reservoir of flood water and had grown to at least a hundred feet. *At least it's peaceful,* Tyler noted.

Close thunder announced the approach of rain. Thunder was fine by Tyler. He did not much care for rain, though; not since the flood. Few people did, except Brooks, who made smart-ass remarks whenever it started raining. "Hey-o!" he exclaimed then. "Been waiting since '25 for a storm like this 'un!" He stuck out his tongue and began collecting droplets like a pelican sifting whitebait in its beak. Tyler watched him hop and dance along the trail and pretended to laugh with the others.

But Tyler saw fear in Brooks's eyes when it rained. Maybe it brought back memories of the first days of the flood. Brooks was one of the lucky few who'd managed to escape the city—which Tyler supposed he ought to have been grateful for, even though seventeen years had passed and Brooks still refused to explain what brought him into his apartment that day. Brooks shared many stories, but none about how he'd survived. The scarce details Tyler knew from Brooks's personal life had nothing to do with the flood. Most of them were *one-time-I-got-drunk-and* tales of mischief, or memories of crabbing with his father as a child.

Crunch was just a kid when the flood landed, making him a floodling by virtue, if not by definition. Very little distinguished him from those born after the flood, apart from a few spliced memories running around his parents' ice cream parlor in Savannah. Surviving as a child had toughened Crunch seemingly to the point of emotionlessness. Or stoicism was the reason he'd survived to begin with.

Ed was the oldest of the bunch. He had plenty of pre-flood stories to share—too many. Ed was like a vintage bottle of wine found in some damp cellar; suited for assholes, not laymen. Nevertheless, Tyler enjoyed most of his tales, even some of the more gruesome ones, like seeing couples jump from the Twin Towers as a teenager, or those from his brief bout of homelessness during the '08 recession. It was not unknown for Ed to throw in a certain amount of bullshit, too. "I knew the guy who got the first case of Tubo in New York. He was a chef too—I told you guys I owned a food truck, right?" Crunch groaned audibly. "I used to see the guy out at bars every once in a while. I heard they wouldn't even let anyone see the poor shitter in the hospital. Guy probably died all alone."

Tyler chewed his lip. He couldn't tell if Ed was fucking with them or if he genuinely didn't remember the forty-eight thousand other times he'd recounted the same story. "You sure about that, Edy?" he probed.

Ed frowned. "Course I am. Haven't I told you—"

"Nah, I meant, you sure he didn't catch it from fucking you?" The others snickered while Ed's face turned red.

"On my mother's grave—you can look that shit up, man. I'm telling you." Thankfully, the others joined him in calling out Ed's bullshit before his ego got too inflated.

How they each viewed the world's end didn't matter to Tyler. Everyone maintained their own opinion on what happened. The Colonies cited the flood as an ongoing health crisis, while the Western Alliance viewed water—*all* water—as a sacred gift. Made sense, when all you knew was drought, Tyler supposed. Even so, Tyler didn't subscribe to either notion. In fact, he rarely thought about water at all. It was the change that bothered him—the sudden loss of innocence, being forced to grow up before his time was due. Yet he'd known it was coming. It was inevitable. You're a kid until one day you're suddenly not. The flood had simply sped things along.

The rain had started to come down on them. It fell in sheets, flicking at them sideways in the wind, moving so fast it cut through the pine needles and created a fine mist in the air. It would've felt cold to most. Not to them. To them, wet was just wet. Fear was the greater concern.

Tyler brought up the rear. He reached for his flask and kept his head down, following Crunch's bootsteps and trying to avoid putting much thought into it.

◆

America was still mourning when it started raining.

On October 20 it rained exceptionally, burying the streets of Manhattan under seven inches of water. On October 21, the torrent continued. Basements and ground-floor apartments were flooded. It drizzled on the twenty-third, twenty-fourth, and twenty-fifth. The flood seemed to drink the rain and grow stronger.

Some said that abnormal weather patterns were commonplace throughout Earth's history. Others viewed it as evidence of a greater truth. Stanley Cusack, Associate Professor at the Columbia University Earth Institute and longtime member of the American Meteorological Society, sent the following Tweet on October 25:

Republicans: "climate change is bullshit"

October 2025:

Professor Cusack died in his sleep on October 29.

Some feared the rain would never end. A priest successfully abducted two Andean bear cubs from the Queens Zoo. Unbeknownst to Father Huber, both were male. He succumbed to the virus on the twenty-eighth. Others insisted God would soon intervene. He would save him, because why wouldn't He? Their faith was their savior, but their faith did not save them.

Some believed the Illuminati had funded the creation of a giant weather machine capable of toppling the U.S. government. Others insisted that it was not a machine, but a rain-producing gas emitted from jet engines. Some blamed the Israelis. Others blamed Hezbollah. Some owned umbrellas. Others didn't. Everyone got wet.

It did not rain on the October 26, but the clouds brought a fierce wind that carried the water to places it had not yet visited. The great climate debate fell into deadlock. The virus did not.

The sun finally returned on the twenty-seventh. The deniers claimed victory over their counterparts. Regardless of their opinion, people flocked outdoors. Some took walks, despite reports that the virus thrived in standing water; their craving for sunlight blocked better judgment. Some got sick and died. Others didn't, so to them it was worth it.

Few understood then that they would soon yearn for the days when the virus was only catastrophic.

October 27, 2025

It was time for some fresh air, Tyler Haji had decided. *Why?* "Because *fuck* living," he whispered to himself, and not for the first time—because what was life when living meant living the rest of your life trapped in seclusion? He wouldn't let the apocalypse stop him; it was time to turn a new leaf.

Tyler swung his stiff legs off the couch and smoked a bowl before making his coffee. He picked up the phone to try checking in with his parents again. No one answered, but then again, it was only eleven, and Mom was probably still passed out from the night before. He refused to consider the more likely scenario: that Mom and Dad would never wake up or answer the phone again. *You could've gone and seen them, at least.* The voice was but the faintest whisper, though he heard it regardless. He pretended he hadn't.

They'd shut off his cable a month ago, and he'd never been much of a reader, so he opened the big bay window (the sole luxury in Tyler's month-to-month studio) and climbed out onto the fire escape to enjoy his coffee in the great outdoors.

Tyler leaned out onto the rail in his boxers and mesh Deron Williams jersey and hugged his coffee to his chest. It was chilly. The cold breeze flapped beneath his boxers and toyed with his bits. Tyler did not mind the cold; a little fresh air was in order. He looked out beyond the alley and moved his arm reactively to shield his eyes, spilling coffee onto his toes. He flicked his foot out, annoyed. The sun seemed to exude a radiance the likes of which Tyler had never seen before. He briefly felt embarrassed; he'd turned vampiric over the course of the increasingly depressing past week, in which it had rained like it was monsoon season day and night. It didn't help his cause that his hip bones suddenly ached from pressing up against the fire escape.

When his eyes had recovered, he moved his elbow from his eyes and stared out blankly. It was not just a light-sensitivity issue that was behind the overwhelming brightness. An unperturbed pool of water covered the streets below, augmenting the sunlight tenfold.

Tyler watched the lack of traffic until his coffee went cold, then climbed back inside.

He checked his phone for the cause of the neighborhood's waterlogged state. He tried Googling *hempstead flash flood updates* to no avail. The Wi-Fi had been down (along with all of Long Island's, he presumed) the past three days, and even if he'd had a fresh tank of data, most links you clicked on just redirected you to the CDC's official website.

An outdated calendar notification alerted his phone that he was supposed to work on October 27, but considering Hempstead was under about two feet of water, he thought it safe to assume that his boss would not be expecting him. He'd taken on a roofing gig since he quit gutting fish, though he was yet to finish his training. He briefly envisioned himself scampering about some storm-damaged roof while his boss, Carl, sporting his pedo-stache and whiskey breath, screamed at him and his coworkers like some sadistic cattle driver. He wondered if he should call about his employment status.

Tyler threw on some sweatpants over his boxers and stuffed a dime bag in his pocket. He sauntered up three flights of steps to see what Allison was up to. He inhaled shakily, dreading what it might mean if his knock went unanswered.

He knocked and fidgeted nervously outside the door. "Who is it?" She sounded hurried.

"Special delivery," Tyler replied.

After a pause, the deadbolt sounded, and Allison's lively, blue eyes peeked from behind the door chain. She lifted her eyebrows suspiciously. Tyler grinned stupidly and jiggled the sack of stale bud. She unlatched the door and gestured him in silently, turning to the kitchen with a cigarette in hand. "Coffee?" she asked.

"Only if it's Irish."

"Ha-ha." Allison kept no booze at her place. She claimed to be allergic to it, which Tyler had initially poked fun at: *Let me guess: it makes you feel dizzy and confident?* She'd just rolled her eyes at him.

They sat on the couch sipping their coffees, Tyler's spiked with sugar and Allison's with cream. The ceiling fan circulated humid air uselessly. After a while, she put her hand on Tyler's shoulder. "How're you holding up?" she asked sincerely.

Tyler blinked. He'd forgotten about the weed. He began fumbling in his pocket, only for Allison to clout him on the cheek, leaving a stinging red mark. "What the hell!" Tyler gaped and saw tears streaming down her cheeks.

"What?" he asked dumbly. Allison burrowed her face into the couch. Tyler sat awkwardly, unsure how to react. He patted her feebly on the back. After a moment, Allison collected herself and sat up, sniffling. She reached for her coffee.

"Johnny came and took Hugo last week," she explained, her voice hoarse. "He said he was gonna take him for a drive and watch him over the weekend, so I said okay. But he never called, and now I can't call him back or go out, and—I don't know what to do. I don't know if my baby's okay." She covered her face with her hands. "I'm his mother, for fuck's sake. He could be sick, or ..." She began sobbing into her hands, her fingers softening her cries.

Tyler frowned into his mug.

◆

He didn't decide to help Allison out of sound principles. In truth, he hadn't stopped thinking about her since their brief stint together came to its unceremonious end. Although their relationship had been nothing more than a means to sexual fulfillment, the inevitable sense of dominion that plagues men had wormed its way into his brain anyway.

Tyler assumed her cause for worry was unwarranted. He figured the kid was fine and that Johnny (who he vaguely recalled her mentioning being on parole for possession with intent) was probably just trying to pull Allison's strings and got sidetracked by the flood. So, he agreed to take her to Johnny's place in Queens Village.

A submarine, much less Allison's '08 Impala, would have struggled to make it to Queens. Tyler thought about knocking on the neighbors' doors on the off chance someone owned a kayak. They tried two doors and twice were answered by echoes.

They managed to outfit themselves pretty well with makeshift gear from their apartments. Allison suggested they use Hefty bags as makeshift overalls to keep their legs dry. Tyler yanked out both their shower rods to use as pokers to test the street below them, and Allison had an off-putting number of bandanas hanging from her dresser, which they tied over their faces to thwart the sewer smell that filled the streets. They looked like alien cleaning maids by the time they were finished.

They descended the stairwell together, their steps echoing off the concrete walls. A murky pool extended from the building's double doors to the foot of the stairs. "Ready?" Tyler asked. Allison nodded, her eyes wide and agitated.

They waded through the busted vestibule onto the sidewalk. Tyler retched immediately; a vulture might've turned its nose at the reek outside. They made eye contact then, borrowing strength from one another, their eyes stinging from the fumes. *The things we do for love,* Tyler sighed.

◆

They were almost in Queens, splashing along the Hempstead Turnpike when Allison shrieked and pointed at the meridian.

"What's wrong?"

"D-don't you see it?"

Tyler frowned and looked toward the center line and saw a floating object. It appeared to be a garbage sack somebody had thrown from their fire escape. He tugged Allison along, her hand trembling in his. "C'mon, it's fine."

They trudged through another half block of waste before Tyler recognized what the blob thing was. The man wore a gray T-shirt that read *Don't Tread on Me.* He lay face-up, staring at the sky, his body pinned by an electrical box. The decay behind his skin had caused his neck and hands to go purple. His exposed belly had black veins crawling along its surface, as though someone had pumped him full of helium just before he died. Tyler stared his eyes forward and held his breath, counting up, *One, two, three ...*

"I think I'm gonna be sick," Allison mumbled.

The back of Tyler's throat began to itch. "Please don't."

"Saying that doesn't help." Allison swallowed heavily. "Oh, God— I need some air." She began hyperventilating. Tyler grabbed her arm and led them forward blindly. Allison trembled under his arm and turned to face the building, guiding them along. They walked, waving their shower rods in front of them till Tyler counted to fifty, and it was safe to look up again.

Their Hefty waders held up surprisingly well to the water; only a few drops from their splashing feet thwarted the triple-bagged plastic. The streets were utterly devoid of human life. A radio would occasionally echo from the open window of a looming apartment, signaling the gaze of some onlooker. A modest number of people scuttled in and out from fire escapes, ashing cigarettes into the water below and doing little else to occupy themselves. One woman sat in a lawn chair, reading a magazine in only her underwear and a pair of Ray-Bans. When Tyler and Allison approached, the woman stood and shouted angrily in what sounded like Russian. Tyler waved; she screamed at them as they waded past before promptly sitting down again to enjoy her literature.

They waded for another blissfully uneventful half-hour before Allison paused. "This is it," she muttered, staring at a brown brick building across the street.

"You sure?" Tyler asked. He frowned. He had visited the same apartments before; just a few short weeks ago, in fact.

She squinted at him. "Of course I am." Allison headed across the street, Tyler following reluctantly. He kept his eyes focused on the fifth-floor window.

Tyler had to wedge the heavy mahogany door open with his shower rod to let some water in so they could enter. The building's dilapidated foyer smelled of moldy wallpaper. Allison threw off her Hefty attire and started up the stairs two at a time. Tyler hesitated. He yanked the shower rod out from the doorframe, gripped it tightly, and ran after her. He knew what floor.

Allison was listening intently through unit *501*'s entry when Tyler caught up. She cupped her hand over Tyler's mouth to snuff his gasping and touched a finger to her lips with the other. Tyler swallowed and nodded, painfully cognizant of the bloomy pheromones she exhumed. They crept up on either side of the door and listened.

"Johnny," whose real name would never replace the cigarette-pseudonym in Tyler's mind, had either held on to an old radio antenna or his cable had somehow survived the maelstrom; a muffled buzz emitted from a speaker behind the thin walls. Not music—voices.

Tyler swallowed and waved for Allison's attention. He made a knocking motion with his fist. She nodded. He knocked twice and waited. No response.

Tyler shrugged and knocked again, this time louder. Again, nothing. He looked at Allison helplessly. *"Now what?"* he mouthed silently. *You're not built for this, man. You think you are, but ...*

Allison chewed her lip and knocked softly on the door. "John?" she called softly. She knocked again. "John," this time more sternly. Only the radio's unfaltering voice.

Tyler stepped back and pointed at the door with the heel of his foot. Allison shook her head.

A noise came from inside the apartment. It was the sort of noise that suddenly stirs something in one's primordial synapses; the sound of a crying child. Allison's eyes widened with motherly instinct. She looked at Tyler, then at the door. "Do it." Tyler hesitated. "For my baby," she said before he could refute it. Tyler nodded and squared up to the door reluctantly. He kicked once, cracking the frame, then again, splintering the wood around the lock. The door shuddered open.

Tyler crouched with the shower rod clutched between his fists. He scanned the familiar dingy living room. Dust motes sat suspended in midair. A radio with a long antenna tinted the room green-blue. Tyler flashed his palm to Allison and crept toward the hallway.

And then she was ahead of him, charging down the hallway with a pocketknife arched high above her head. She began swinging open each door, screaming, "I'll kill you, son-of-a-bitch!" until she opened the door at the hall's end and gasped. The knife landed softly on the carpet.

Allison rushed for the baby carrier, which sat atop an unadorned queen-size mattress. She scooped up the little package within, sending an empty formula bottle clattering to the floor. The child's cries ceased instantly. "You're okay," she hummed.

A body lay slumped against one of two nightstands framing the bed. Though he struggled at first to recognize him, fate presumed it was "Johnny." He tried forcing his gaze away but couldn't help but look. The carpet underneath was crusty with dried blood. The cosmetic work had evidently occurred before his death. Chesty's lenders had deliberately sliced both his eyelids open in cruel, red *X*s. They'd done the opposite with his lips and sewn them shut with crude nylon stitches. A few had torn incidentally during the torture, suggesting he'd tried raising a protest.

The pack of cigarettes peeking out from the man's pocket erased any of Tyler's misgivings. The red lettering spoke truths that his stitched lips could no longer. Tyler forced himself to turn away.

Allison wobbled to the door and left quietly with little Hugo clutched to her chest. Tyler shadowed her. Neither of them paid any mind to the man talking on the radio's emergency loop:

Attention, New York Metropolitan residents: The NYPD has ordered all citizens to seek shelter in the nearest elevated space if they have not already. Safety officials recommend taking the following precautions while taking shelter: Ensure reliable access to clean water and food. Avoid unnecessary risk to yourself to rescue lost pets or possessions. Avoid contact with failing or compromised electric wiring. Due to increased volume, the NYPD and New York City Fire Department kindly ask all citizens to avoid calling for emergency assistance unless absolutely necessary. If you suspect you have been exposed to ALIN-12, please dial 911, and the next available operator will be with you. Thank you.

No. 9 Month 3, 0017 P.F.

They arrived at the small, dilapidated mansion (to the extent which one can be small) two hours into their involuntary slog. Only then did Tyler remember why the name rang a bell.

Mildew and vines covered the once-glistening exterior of Washington's summer home. Most of the glass-paned windows were broken, allowing nature to creep into its innumerable halls, libraries, and fumoirs. The notion of entering the home and exploring its contents was pervasive, but Crunch shut down any such action. "The Letterman wouldn't approve. It's disrespectful to the Founding Fathers," he precautioned. Brooks snickered, but remained quiet. He rarely rebelled against the Letterman's orders, despite his insistence otherwise. Brooks was the only one to have ever actually soldiered alongside the Letterman. Back then, he was known as First Lieutenant James Lowry, like the salt. His nickname, based on his uncanny resemblance to the late-night television host of yore, was only adopted after he'd earned the rank Captain. They were practically twins, from his impressive white beard to his rimless oval glasses. The Letterman's only distinguishing factor was his pitch-black skin. He'd been the Letterman ever since.

After establishing a perimeter, they set about surveying the land in pairs. It made sense that the area had (allegedly) become a traffic hub for Frogs headed that way. The Potomac drained into the Atlantic just beyond the manor's massive back porch. Any Westerners looking to supplant themselves out East could've easily floated down the bloated river channels from Cleveland or Detroit. The thought of traveling by water terrified most Colonists. Citizens sought the high ground just to keep away from the flood. In extreme cases, they dug themselves underground or lived on scaffoldings—which was understandable, Tyler supposed, if you'd lived through both ALIN and the flood.

Even those who'd grown up accustomed to the flood were terrified. Floodlings tended to be more sensitive about their proximity to water than their older peers. They'd been preconditioned from birth to avoid the stuff; most were fed folk tales and nursery rhymes about monsters who lived in the water, and all were taught that the flood carried the plague (this was a key part of the Colonies' standardized education). On one of many duty and joy-free Sundays, Ed and Brooks asked Crunch whether he'd like to try his hand at fishing. He agreed, albeit after some "light" mockery ("bedwetting gimp" was Ed's exact insult). Crunch remained deathly pale for the outing's entirety. But when Brooks intentionally rocked their raft and sent Crunch reeling into the water, you might've thought it was acid. He splashed and clawed to the edge of the raft like a cat being given a bath while Ed and Brooks guffawed above. He was quiet and traumatized on the trip back.

Tyler knew their fear was not warranted. The flood had receded substantially from its peak levels, though the Colonies would not formally declare it. But none of that mattered. None of it mattered, so long as that fear was still in place. The government had been working on a slippery slope, first implementing travel restrictions, then social interaction guidelines, and then daily Flood Advisories. *Go to work, go to the store, then go home. Watch our news, eat dinner, then go to bed. Just be safe. And afraid; be very afraid.* It was too late to reverse course now.

That same fear had inspired countless people—young and old, rich and poor, all desperate for something *pure*—to go west. West, where drought and desert were aplenty, and water scarce—but at least it was dry. And *safe*. Even if Bill Edenson had never started spinning his magic yarn, they would've left anyways. Fear was the stressor that'd motivated them to escape, like the body rejecting a cadaver ligament.

Bill had always seemed like a bullshit artist to Tyler. But at least it provided an alternative; an opportunity to be *not* afraid, and be reborn as someone (or something? Tyler was genuinely not sure) less scared. He occasionally wondered what his life would have been like had he joined one of the hippie caravans instead of enlisting. He was still young after the flood, still flexible. And so what if the Kool-Aid they drank was bullshit? At least it tasted good.

But fear had gotten a hold of him. Fear of change, fear of commitment. He could've lived a relatively quiet life in the West, free of fear. Yet there he was, masquerading his misery as dedicating his life to service.

Whoever they served did not reward them for their efforts. Military grunts like Tyler and co. were expendable. They were supposed to get their feet wet.

◆

A ring of buildings encompassed the property, each labeled with a faded museum placard explaining their purpose at the time of its construction. The one Brooks chose as their base of operations had, according to the sign, once been G-Dub's horse stable. It had fallen into disuse since and was missing planks from its siding, as well as a section of its roof. Even so, it offered ample space for them to spread apart, and more than enough cover to keep them dry. It was more than what they were used to. "Make yourselves cozy," Brooks declared upon swinging open the unlatched barn door.

Tyler sniffed the air. There was still a hint of barnyard smell from its former inhabitants. Hay was neatly stacked in the stalls where the horses had once slept. There were scalable rafters on either side of the center aisle. One of the upper windows was busted, though they could easily board it shut with any of the dense wood planks lying about.

"Didn't you hear what I said?" Crunch said, agitated. "If the Letterman finds out we're staying on the Founders' property—"

"Finds out *what?* That we disturbed the goddamn horse spirits?" Crunch opened his mouth to protest before Brooks shut him down. "Go build a fuckin' cabin then, Honest Abe. We'll be nice, dry, 'n' cozy in here." That stifled any further protest from Crunch. They got to setting up their home for the unforeseeable future.

When Brooks was satisfied with his troop's progress, they laid their wet clothes out to dry in the stable and sauntered over to the manor's raised patio. The rain cut off as soon as they'd settled, as if the heavens had decided they were deserving of some dryness. They sprawled out, passing around a bottle of wine of untold age Ed had recovered in one of the stock buildings and admiring the sun's disappearing act in their baselayers. The setting sun glinted off the Potomac's south-running choppy waters and was quietly dazzling. Brooks opened his flask and offered it to his squadron. They passed it around, a healthy sip each. Tyler abstained. He maintained his own supply, what little good it did him. The booze hadn't been doing the trick lately; the memories came rushing back just as often as they didn't.

They stumbled back to the stable as soon as their fatigue had settled on them, buzzed and exhausted. Ed undid his bedroll and patted it down. Brooks clicked his tongue. "Fraid you're on first. Seniority rules." Ed didn't protest; better to be somewhat inebriated while out on patrol than not at all.

Tyler considered joining him. He felt bad for Ed and wasn't tired (he rarely was). Ultimately, he decided against risking having to hear another one of Ed's tall tales. "I'll take next," he announced to unanimous approval via grunt and nod. Tyler lay down and began making swirling patterns in the dusty ground below.

◆

Tyler stayed up throughout most of Ed's shift. The stable was quiet apart from the Potomac rushing outside, teeming with fish, crabs, and any nocturnal beasts that came to its edges to hydrate. Perhaps a Frog was floating by on its waters, too, plotting a swift end to the enemy fascist regime. Or maybe there was nothing at all to bother them— nothing but the wind and the water and the hidden sound doers of the night.

Tyler shut his eyes for half an hour. His breathing evened, his heart slowed, and his hearing steeped, but his mind still raced. He assumed Ed would wake him whenever he decided to retire prematurely from his patrol, which always occurred. It didn't bother Tyler. In fact, he had given him permission to do so if he was on deck. "I don't need much sleep," he'd explained vaguely.

Thirty minutes came and went, and there was still no sign of Ed. Tyler perked his ears and heard Brooks and Crunch both soundly asleep. He slid quietly from his sleeping bag, pulled on his coat and boots, and crept out the barnyard door.

Tyler felt for the square of stale Chesterfields packed alongside the flask of whiskey in his chest pocket. He emptied the latter, then sparked a cigarette, his lighter briefly cutting through the inky night. Clouds rode the wind above head, blocking any celestial bodies from sight.

He finished checking the cluster of buildings to the manor's left and looped back around to the start of Vernon's circular drive. Tyler stamped his cigarette in the wet, half-wild grass. He reached for another and shook at the pack's barren contents, tossing it into the brush, agitated. The wind picked up and lashed through the thin, burlappy undershirt he'd been commissioned. He would make Ed fetch his coat when he showed face.

A pair of squirrels chattered loudly somewhere off in the woods leading up to the mansion. Tyler considered calling out for Ed. *Maybe he came the other way around*, he thought. He turned to loop back to the stable in case they had just missed each other.

"*Tyler.*"

Tyler jumped at the sound of Ed's voice. "Yeah," he called back.

"*Tyler.*"

Tyler spun in a half-circle, checking over his shoulder simultaneously. He'd heard Ed clearly this time; it'd come from just around the corner of the next small building. He walked toward him. "I got it from here. Soon as you grab my threads, that is."

"*Tyler.*"

Tyler frowned. The same pair of squirrels chattered behind him. He slowed his gait and rounded the corner to the spot where Ed should've stood.

In his place sat a walkie-talkie.

Tyler did not feel the bullet's sting. He was already running when the first gunshot rang out. The sniper's bullet grazed his ribcage and blew a chunk out of the concrete building behind him. A second shot whizzed past Tyler's ear as he sprinted toward the stable.

Brooks and Crunch burst through the barn doors with their rifles pressed up against their cheeks. Brooks moved toward the back of the estate while Crunch took cover behind the nearest hut. Tyler veered off his path away from the stable. A familiar-sounding rifle *bang*ed in the distance, which Tyler judged as Brooks covering him from the high-sloping manor. He crossed the lawn and slid behind one of the hut buildings.

The sounds of gunfire and men screaming at each other. Sounds of agony. Crunch shouting for cover; Brooks opening fire. Tyler heard them all, but vaguely, as if he were trapped in a liquid dream.

Tyler made his move then, veering toward the barn to retrieve his rifle. He sprinted past two buildings one in line with the other before stopping in his tracks. A man stood in his way. He was at full draw, his fingers hinged around the bowstring's apex. It was aimed precisely at his chest.

He loosed just as Tyler thought to himself, *Duck.* He bit his tongue as his chest hit the hard-packed dirt and tasted blood but felt nothing. The shaft drove into the Colonial-era hut behind him with a *thud.*

A wild thing took control of him. He rose, and instead of retreating, he snarled like a dog, zagging toward the source of the death-shot. He huffed and saw the glint of the second arrow being knocked, its broadhead shining in the moonlight some twenty yards away. The archer took his time, tracking Tyler's movements; calm, accurate. When he was ten yards downrange, the archer loosed.

Tyler dove. The broadhead cut through the hem of his jacket, searing past his armpit as he rolled. The arrow shaft disappeared into the earth beneath him as Tyler bounced up and fell onto the smaller man, toppling him to the ground. He slammed his fist into the archer's face and missed his eye as he'd intended, striking him in the jaw instead. The man grabbed for Tyler's collar, but Tyler flung his arms away. He arched his fist back again. His knuckles came away bloody, the cuff of his jacket speckled by beads of spit and tooth and blood. Tyler hit him once, then twice more, and eased off him. The archer gargled meekly on the ground.

Tyler lay panting, listening to the chaos of gunfire and shouting. He heard voices coming from the circle drive, so he rolled onto his feet and ran away from them, past the time-elapsed estate and toward the Potomac. There were torches ablaze on the manor's back patio, where men were dumping bodies into the varicose river. He heard two heavy splashes.

Tyler turned down the embankment and followed the river's current east. He ran until he could not anymore, scrambling from left to right in the wet sand until he realized he was trapped, surrounded by water or torches on all sides. No escape.

He gritted his teeth and scrambled into the river.

The tepid liquid felt cool to him. He waded until the water touched his chest and dove beneath its surface. Within moments of his first stroke, a barrage of ammunition spun through the frigid ink. One grazed his shoulder as he pushed downstream. Bubbles escaped his mouth. He paddled until his lungs threatened to explode, then paddled some more. He only submerged when he felt blackness creeping into his vision. He lingered beneath the surface, fighting the urge to take loud, gaping breaths that might expose him.

When the black spots had cleared from his vision, he wiped the murky water from his eyes and blinked. The crosscurrent had been stronger than he'd expected; it'd swept him half a mile or so downstream to the opposite shore. The Frogs swept the shore beneath the first president's manse, their torches flickering in the darkness.

The water carried him further downstream until he felt his feet scrape up against the river's muddy bottom. He crawled up the beach quietly, his endorphins silencing the burning in his armpit. He'd come out lucky; the bullet had just grazed him.

What'd you think? The voice was as much his as it was real. *Be honest with me.*

"You're dead," Tyler growled as he stumbled into the woods. The cold had yet to set in.

Interlude

1992–September 2009
Revelation

EXCERPT FROM *a letter addressed to Captain Paul G. Kaminski, dated November 2, 1991:*

> *While it remains my undying wish to defend the United States and all it stands for, respectfully, I have decided to decline any offer of further service with the United States Marine Corps. I feel that I can best serve my country and my family at this time as a member of the civilian population.*

> *Sincerely,*
> *Bill Milo*

◆

Bill received numerous medals, none of which were of great importance to him. He was honorably discharged.

Whereas guilt and trauma make most men sheltered and serious, Bill's made him looser in the shoulders, and fluid with his talk and movements. He had no specific plans for civilian life. All he knew was that he wanted to meet people and hear their stories, and preserve those learnings.

He tended grapevines in the Salinas Valley for a time, just as his father and grandfather had done, albeit in a different time and place. He met all the people he could. He learned a few words of Spanish until the season ended and his new-made friends left to work elsewhere.

So Bill headed to Los Angeles, with no express purpose other than to absorb all he could. He tended bar for some time, meeting and serving and learning from as many people as he could, until one of his regulars (who seemed to spend more afternoons sipping Aperol spritzes at Bill's bar than at home with his wife and children) revealed he was a producer at a major studio. He told Bill he had "leading man energy," and promised to introduce him to an agent friend of his. "Sure," Bill replied. He never met the man.

Bill took well to the spoken word. He avoided the acting classes, networking opportunities, agents, and PA positions adored by young, parent-supported L.A. transplants. Instead, he learned by watching his peers and auditioning for roles in tiny productions.

He struck gold early when a director attending an independent production of *A Midsummer Night's Dream*, in which Bill played the role of Oberon, took notice of Bill's uncanny ability to deliver monologues. After the show ended, he approached Bill and cast him as the lead in a small production that went on to be acclaimed by newspapers and online critics. Bill did not push for fame after. One night while he was unchaining his bike after a rehearsal, a journalist snuck up on him. "Excuse me, are you Bill Milo?"

"Wrong guy," Bill said. He rode off to his apartment and left the next day.

Bill went north to San Francisco and beyond. He certified as an EMT then fought fires for two years, learning to play the guitar in his off time. It felt more comfortable in his hands than a rifle ever had. He began to sing alongside his pick, which helped him remember his lover's voice. They were nothing but good thoughts.

The owner of several bars and restaurants overheard him playing on his porch one day and hired him to play almost nightly gigs across his establishments. He met more people. *Billy Milo? I know 'im. Nice fella!* was a quote oft heard and said. People boasted of his brave acts in the field for him. He earned a reputation for plunging into houses near collapse to rescue his trapped comrades. He received permanent gratitude and friendship from every man he saved, and firm handshakes from strangers at the grocery store.

Bill left for Seattle, where he learned how to fish for salmon and trout and dig for scallops along the Pacific shoreline. He played his guitar and sang and thought of his father's aversion toward things that he did not consider sensible. They were nothing but good thoughts. He took a bus south to Denver and discovered a penchant for making things, cabinets, chairs, wooden spoons, and anything else people would ask for. He took his strings with him and played them when he could. He met all the people a man could.

Bill's network grew exponentially. In addition to his writing, he maintained a handwritten resume with a detailed list of references from his friends and former employers. It was a habit more than anything. Every man needs routine and ritual to govern his life.

Bill lived alone but was never lonely. His sex life was healthy, even for a man who acted impulsively. He was not cruel. As a matter of fact, Bill brought joy. But something was offering him resistance. He felt like he wore a chain at the ankle but could not see what was attached to its end.

By the time he landed in Colorado, he carried thirteen journals with him, each filled to the brim with his fine print—and a fourteenth was in progress. He knew exactly what words lay on each page: names, numbers, addresses, and the transcribed lives of the countless people he'd met over the years. Bill humbly neglected to include anything about himself. The notebooks were self-censored, modest logs of his travels.

He was so busy studying how other people grew and lived that he forgot how to do so himself.

September 2009

West of downtown Colorado Springs is a picturesque tract of land known as the Garden of the Gods. Whoever named it was good at naming things. Upon finding a good vantage point, one is struck by a magnificent valley of verdant thrush and marble crags. It appears as though God or the gods planted each rock and blade of grass intentionally.

Bill often visited the Garden in between work. He found he felt more whole when he left than when he came. On one such afternoon, he departed very early on foot with just a thermos of coffee and a bag of granola with him—and, as always, his notebook. The seventeenth.

He stopped when his legs grew tired, splaying his long legs out in front of him and posturing back on one elbow. He wrote freely in the morning dusk:

In the Garden of the Gods lays a fruit invisible to most men. In the Garden, all life was brought by a higher being. Only those keen of eye and open in their hearts may see the slight intentions sown by him.

The sun crested above the horizon. Bill basked in its warm glow and suddenly thought of his parents and sister. He hadn't spoken to any of them in a very long time. It made him sad to wonder about his family. They felt more distant to him than anyone he'd met since he'd escaped that meaningless, oil-induced war.

"Don't it ever make ye feel sad, lookin' out and not seein' a thing to nail ye to one spot?"

The sudden voice startled Bill; his only company had been the rocks and pines. He turned to face his encroacher. Before he could do so, someone tapped him on the opposite shoulder. Bill jolted at the touch and discovered a small, bearded man sitting next to him. "Sorry. I didn't hear you coming off the trail." Bill smiled, glad to share the view with someone else. "Guess I'm not the only one who knows about this spot."

The man's eyes crinkled. His thick lips parted, revealing brilliant white, gapped teeth. He shook Bill's hand and introduced himself, though later Bill could not recall his name. He could not discern his accent, only that it was somehow different from others, and very old.

"Pleased to meet you," Bill found himself saying without any context as to why he was saying it. He blinked and offered him his half-empty thermos. "Coffee?"

The old man looked down and sighed. "Thanks, but I can't have caffeine in me no more. Doctor says it's no good for me ticker." He tapped his chest. "Says the walking's good for it, though."

Bill nodded and twisted the cap back on. He did not mind the man's company. He seemed as friendly as anyone else he'd met on his travels. When he asked the man what he did for a living, he responded vaguely, only saying that his work was important and necessitated frequent travel.

The old man's words morphed into one long string of sounds as Bill sat pondering his own work, his lifelong journey to discover the thing tied around his ankle. He listened absently as the old man recalled a story about God's love. The story went that God had prepared a great flood to test mankind's proclivity for love. He predicted that man would respond to God's loving wrath with fear, mistaking His gift for death instead of what it truly was—life. "Water brings life. Look around ye; water fed those trees, carved those rocks. If it weren't for water, this place wouldn't exist. Just 'cause it brings death sometime don't make it all bad. There's plenty good in it." He waved his hand. "Listen to me. Talkin' in circles, I am. Right he were, that Nietzsche lad. But what's the point when yer health goes bad? That only thing matters." And then he said nothing.

Bill smiled politely and sipped his coffee. The Garden seemed to glow with an ethereal, warming light. "What's ye name, son?" the man asked.

Bill did not remove his eyes from the light. "Bill. I'm named after my grandpa. He grew apples." Bill chuckled and sipped from his mug. "It's funny. I've never even planted a seed, you know."

The man rubbed his chin thoughtfully. "Way you speak it, might be fulfilling."

Planting seeds. Bill nodded. "It could be ... The only question is, what type of seed? And where to plant them?" He looked up at the man warily. "Who will plant them?"

The man slurped loudly from Bill's thermos. A line of coffee dribbled down his chin. He looked into Bill's eyes and patted his shoulder. "Why, who else?"

"But ..." Bill looked at the ground and frowned. He felt as though he'd forgotten to ask the man something, something *important.* "When will I know when to start?"

The old man chuckled. "Just wait for the first drop. You'll know then."

Part II

My, I'll bet you monsters lead innnteresting lives.
– Bugs Bunny

VIII

No. 19 Month 4, 0017 P.F.
Pittsburgh (Subterranean), Appalachia, New American Colonies

A BARELY legible note slid underneath the doorframe: *Visitor. Came in from the blackout.* Isabel knocked twice, quickly, in reply. The messenger's feet shuffled to allow their guest inside.

Two men briefly chattered at the front door, followed by a sharp *Shhh!* Isabel crossed her legs in her chair and sighed. "Royalty," she scoffed aloud. *Must be nice.*

An ambling, three-pronged gait that could only belong to Charles moseyed up the half flight of stairs, followed by a faster, more youthful stride. He banged on the door with his cane. "Ey, hun? 'Bout done in there? Got any soap I could borrow?"

"Just a second." Isabel leaned back and stretched her arms, relieving the tightness in her back before rising. She limped over to meet the man who was to be their savior.

◆

A familiar old man greeted Adam upon knocking on the front door of 74 Sicily Drive. The intense sleepiness he'd exuded at the plaza was gone and replaced by a crinkle-eyed awareness. He arched his eyebrow at Adam in soft alarm and *hushed* him with his fingers. "How'd you wind up out here so late past dark? Is the South Bend train running late again?" He'd arrived mostly by luck, navigating the darkness cautiously, flattening himself against brick and wooden facades until he stumbled across the sign that read SICILY DRIVE.

"I'm here to see the dancing fox," Adam began before the old man yanked him inside with shocking strength. He swung Adam into the foyer and slammed the door shut behind him all in one fluid motion.

"We're happy to host you for the night, but once lights are back on, you'll have to be on your way. My wife and I go out for breakfast in Saint Anthony Square every morning, you see." He released his grip on Adam and winked. Adam frowned.

"I was told ..."

The old man drew a finger to his lips and hissed sharply. "Keep it to a whisper now. My wife's asleep *down the hall.*" He emphasized the latter part by nudging his head sharply behind him. The old man scrunched his lips in frustration. "C'mon, then. Let me show you the guest room." The old man leaned on his cane and motioned Adam to follow him. Judging by his strength, Adam doubted it was necessary.

The old man led him up a half flight of stairs separating the sunken-in basement from the upstairs hallway. "Hold on. Lemme grab you some stuff so you can warsh up tonight." He banged his cane harshly against a door and asked whoever was inside for soap. There was a muted reply. The old man guided him toward the door as a butler would.

It opened abruptly to a dark-haired woman with shadows under her eyes. She judged Adam from head to toe, then scoffed and rolled her eyes. He looked back to the old man for reassurance; he smiled and bowed slightly before turning down the hall. The woman stepped aside and shut the door behind them. "Thanks, hun," the old man mumbled before the lights shut off in the hall.

Adam quickly surveyed the dimly illuminated space. A large bookcase spanned the wall directly across from him. A reading area was arranged at the room's center, two old armchairs sitting catty-corner to a glass-topped coffee table. In the far corner was a cracked leather reclining seat with a matching wheeled stool, like a museum display of a 1940s dentist's office. Old furniture and various odds and ends filled the spaces in between: a fox pelt hanging above a small fireplace, a glass display case lined with old bobbleheads, and an ornate secretary lined with old records. One was playing, filling the room with a soft, jazzy croon Adam couldn't quite place. The walls were covered with haphazard, glued-in-place soundproofing, emphasizing the music's dominance.

The woman began rummaging manically through an old wooden trunk. It was filled with the sorts of things one throws into a junk drawer, not knowing how else to designate it: product manuals, plastic sleeves containing screws and bits of metal, an antenna to an old television set. When she was satisfied with her search, she faced Adam and demonstrated a starfish stance. Adam copied her. She held up a small metal brick resembling a chalkboard eraser and flipped a switch on its side. The machine hummed quietly as she ran it over Adam's arm and legs. When she dragged the device across his neck, it emitted a soft *bonk*.

Adam grew annoyed. He flopped his arms down. "I'm here to meet the fox."

The woman clicked her tongue and wagged her finger. She pointed for Adam to sit in the reclining chair. Adam shook his head. "What is this?" She pointed again, more crossly this time, and sat on the wheeled stool, which reacted with an unpleasant squeal. Adam reluctantly eased into the recliner and closed his eyes momentarily. They snapped open at a pinch at his neck. Adam glanced to his left. The woman held a scalpel pinched between her fingers. A medical kit lay at her feet.

Adam jerked away instinctively. "The fuck—what are you doing!"

The woman calmly displayed her hands before him. "Do you want to meet the fox or not?" she asked.

Adam gritted his teeth. *You're an idiot, Adam. A gullible idiot. What were the odds that the dancing fox was even legitimate? Or real?* She and the entire conspiracy could just as easily be a figment of his imagination. Perhaps now he was strapped to a chair in a sanatorium, and this was just his rotted brain's way of processing reality. He almost laughed as the blade pricked his skin. *Too late now.*

The woman dabbed at the small incision with a piece of cotton soaked in alcohol. She leaned away and placed the blade between her thighs to fetch a new instrument from the kit; a terrifying, pen-like object lit on one end by plasmatic energy. Adam jerked away, but the woman eased his shoulder forward until he felt a gentle tug behind his skin. The pressure intensified until it emerged painlessly from the incision. When the woman leaned back, a bloodied metallic slug had attached itself to the pen-shaped device.

The woman set down her tools and claimed a bottle of antiseptic and an adhesive gauze pad. Adam blinked. "What the hell was that?" he asked, wincing as she dumped rubbing alcohol on the small incision. The woman ignored his question and finished cleaning the wound. Content with her work, she reclaimed her stool and stared at him with her legs crossed, like an art collector appraising a painting. He met her gaze and offered his hand instinctually. "Adam Crombie." The woman stared at his palm and made no move to offer hers.

"Crombie. Old name," she muttered.

Adam folded his elbows onto his knees and looked around the room warily. He stared at the device she'd removed from him and lowered his voice to a whisper. "Are you the dancing fox?"

Isabel covered her mouth and giggled, revealing a glimpse of a smile that, until then, Adam had assumed did not exist. The smile quickly faded. "I prefer Isabel." She waved her hand toward the extracted metal. "It's called a geobug. Tracks everything from your movement to your pulse to the vibrations in your vocal cords. Picks up outside noise too. I guess the Chief doesn't like when other people play with his toys ... They plugged the thing in pretty deep."

Adam grimaced. *Pretty deep* was a neat way of putting it. He frowned. "Then they probably know I'm here." He looked around the room in silent alarm. "We should go."

Isabel scratched her chin dismissively. "To be honest, I'm surprised they let you make it this far. Could be that your daddy doesn't want the media finding out you're gone. Or maybe he thinks you're gonna change your mind and come home," she added starkly. Adam clenched his jaw. "You're still an asset to him, for now." Isabel calmly observed Adam's eyes. She noted their hazel color, identical to Father Bill's. "I guess I should call you Father now, huh," she said, looking at him strangely.

Adam shifted uncomfortably. "I prefer Adam."

She nodded and looked down at the bug. "Did you know you were being watched?" she asked openly.

"Not like that."

Isabel sighed. "Most people bleed out in two minutes when they try to yank those things out. I guess that was his idea of insurance."

"I know why he did it," Adam clarified. Isabel straightened a bit on her stool. "I know exactly what he wants from me."

He looks just like the Father, Isabel thought incredulously.

◆

"Careful out there. Lights don't come on for another two hours," the old man warned them before they left out the house's back door. Isabel bowed lightly, thanked him, and told him she'd be back sooner rather than later.

Adam was used to the lantern hue of the Subterranean after lights-out, albeit from above. In his teens, he had often escaped to a scant ledge that jutted out from the Pole to look out over the city at night. Without the lights' sunlike glow, the only thing keeping the city from drowning in eternal darkness were the jury-rigged (and often illegal) lamps and bulbs that residents installed to ward off any would-be squatters or robbers.

Navigating the dusk itself was a whole different story. Adam had to mind his feet carefully for fear of twisting an ankle, yet he still managed to trip on several real-or-imagined hitches along the paved streets. Isabel scampered along the paths with no concern, as if she'd been born and raised in darkness.

They encountered no one else braving the night, save a few down-on-their-lucks seeking shelter in alley dens unbeknownst to most housed residents. The housed tended to dodge the streets after lights-out for fear of being detained by the city's night police, who trolled along looking to pick up ne'er-do-wells and vagrants. It was a miracle he'd made it to the fox's den to begin with, Adam reflected.

They navigated the eerie quiet, sneaking through inky alleyways and downtrodden neighborhoods until they reached a plaza filled with various shut-down small businesses. An abandoned garage door sat partially open to the square. Isabel led them into the refuge and sealed the door behind them. "We'll wait here until lights come back on." Adam nodded.

They had not yet endured a minute of awkward silence, sharing the garage's cold concrete floor before a shuttering noise came from outside. A mechanical pulse followed it, echoing one, two, three times. The gap between the garage and the concrete flooring suddenly illuminated.

Isabel glanced at her Loop: *4:28.* The lights did not come on until 5:30 AM. The only exception to this rule was in "*circumstances deemed dire or urgent by the Chief himself.*"

The day's proceedings had been deemed as such.

Confused feet shuffled awake in the co-op houses above the garage. The Subterranean speakers temporarily paused the fake ambient noise they played at all times for an emergency address. The first three notes of "Hail to the Chief" played noisily outside the garage. Adam grimaced, anticipating his father's voice before it came:

This is your Chief, George A. Crombie. I apologize for the sudden lights-on procedure. However, this announcement concerns an urgent security matter. Your full attention, please:

Two rebel vigilantes broke into the home of an elderly man and assaulted him early this morning. The suspects, Alexandra Ramos, mid-twenties, and a male accomplice who has yet to be identified, were last seen escaping 74 Sicily Drive around three o'clock this morning. My apologies, viewers; the following images obtained from the crime screen are graphic:

"Oh my gawd!" a woman living above cried.

For listeners' convenience, the images on your screens show the deceased victim alongside sketch portraits of Ramos and her associate. We ask that all residents, especially those residing near the Business District, New Little Italy, and the surrounding neighborhoods, take extreme precaution when leaving their homes, and consider staying in until police apprehend the suspects.

Authorities are tracking the vigilantes as I speak. While safety remains our top priority, you can help our search without putting yourself in harm's way. If you have seen any suspicious activity or have additional information regarding the suspects, we ask that you immediately contact your local Patrol Office via the SubCity Loop applet. Any information that leads to the successful capture or arrest of one or both suspects will be eligible for meaningful compensation.

Thank you for your attention. God bless Pittsburgh, and God bless the New American Colonies.

The anthem repeated, signaling the broadcast's end. Muffled applause and curses rained down from above:

"Fuckin' animals …"

"They'll find 'em. Don't you worry."

"It's too early for this shit."

"I hope they hunt that little bitch down."

Isabel swore under her breath. "Anyone could recognize us now." Her voice was shaky. "Do you have access to any private bore train channels?"

Adam shook his head. "The only line that runs this late comes from South Bend. We won't make it."

Isabel bit her lip. "Then I guess we're stuck."

Adam was quiet. He'd come this far, only to have the hounds set on him. They had his scent, and the moment he braved the crossing, they would be upon him. *Stupid,* he thought of himself. Doubt came creeping back: *It's not too late. You can stay. There are just as many people who need your help here …*

The doubt suddenly cleared from his mind. He had an idea. "You know, a river runs through this city …"

Isabel nodded and sighed. She knew where the sewers ran.

◆

The garage contained two sets of ancient mechanic's coveralls that'd once belonged to Fusek's Discount Tire. The since-shuttered company mascot, a winking cartoon duck holding a wrench, was embroidered on the chest pocket. They shook the dust off the suits and slipped them on alongside matching baseball caps. Adam towed along an empty toolbox for appearance's sake. They waited awkwardly in the eerily lit garage until their Loops read 6:12 AM.

They exited abruptly into the plaza and followed the nearest hub road, joining the area's early-to-rise, blue-collar workers. Knoxville was their destination. Crossing through the District was their only means of arrival without boarding a train.

Their dirt-green uniforms blended perfectly with the diverse assortment of costumes that populated the District. Businessmen wearing expensive leather shoes and custom suits; obnoxious street hawkers; shift workers sneaking in cigarette breaks; vagrants too accustomed to nervous passersby and free handouts to act modestly; and everywhere, flashing billboards. Isabel watched a monogamous couple of cartoon bears play with toilet paper on one screen. She found herself staring at her own face on another. The message beneath her picture, taken from the ID card from her old alias, read: *HAVE YOU SEEN THIS PERSON? IF SO, CALL 789-123.* She quickly dropped her gaze from the screen and tucked the bill of her cap.

Adam steered them toward the same vendor-lined street he'd escaped by the day before. Stools occupied by hungry working-class lined each side of the alleyway. They reached the alley's end and confronted the familiar, swirling traffic of Grand Central Station. Adam huffed; uniformed police were stopping passersby at various checkpoints. He watched a couple being frisked by the ticket scanners. They showed their Loops and the officers shook their heads, demanding to see physical IDs. They gave the officers huffy looks before they were allowed to pass.

Isabel tugged Adam underneath one of the vendor carts. "We should split up. Less of a chance we'll get spotted."

Adam shook his head. "No. I came to you for a reason."

"It's the only way."

The cart's owner noticed them and shook a soup spoon at them threateningly. He complained loudly enough so his customers would overhear: "Si quieren comer, ¡comen! ¡Merodear no!" The man gestured toward a sign posted to the back of his stall. "Look the sign!" NO LOITERING, the sign read in prominent bold.

Isabel shoved Adam away and began apologizing to the man in fluid Spanish. She glanced back at him before he started off alone.

Adam made a beeline for the metal turnstiles ahead, rubbing his Loop anxiously. An officer wearing a mask warned him on approach. "Sir!" He pretended not to hear and walked a few paces farther until the man repeated himself. "Sir, please—hey!"

Adam bumped his Loop down onto the reader. Its automated voice greeted him: *Welcome, GRANT HARRIS, to— KNOXVILLE; GCS SOUTH GATE.* His pursuer overheard the tone and let him pass without further protest. Adam passed beneath the gate's stone arches and didn't look back.

◆

Knoxville was easy to spot; a dingy-looking wooden sign welcomed Adam to *Knoxville—Pittsburgh's First Paradise!*

The town the sign tried to make light of was a slum, one of many in the underlying region the people had named the Banks. The neighborhood was constituted of the same cheap plywood from which they had built it. Contractors during the Construction Period capitalized early on their involvement in the Subterranean's construction. The first inbound citizens from the surface set about building their homes in Knoxville as soon as their new mortgages were approved. They paid thrice the rate to have wood and appliances lowered in by crane. The contractors held a monopoly on building materials, so they could charge ludicrous prices for what was little more than plywood. Still, the tiny homes they built were preferable to the barely standing waterlogged huts they had lived in on the surface.

They used the resources at their disposal to found the very first Subterranean polity. By the time the Pole was finished, the township of Knoxville had already been operating for some eight months. They'd formed their own micro-economy and were thriving, for the time being. That all changed as soon as a few powerful real estate magnates took notice.

They planned to construct the Business District just outside of Knoxville. Their reasoning: to add to Knoxville's "already thriving" community whilst simultaneously "heightening economic opportunity" in the newly minted underground city. This was seen as a blessing by the middle-class workers (miners, the overwhelming majority of them) who lived there. They were offered double what they had paid for their lots and quickly sold off their assets while the striking price was high. Those that had sold themselves either moved to newly constructed rental units in the District or returned to the surface. Others stayed, eager to open new businesses and capitalize on the affluent incoming population. With half the town bought outright, the District's visionaries demolished homes to dig a channel, which they promised would bring "clean energy" to Knoxville and the surrounding area. This was a lie.

Shortly after, the channel was redirected south in order to "better serve taxpayers." What this meant was that it became a river of human excrement draining from the District all the way to the Wall's southernmost point. From there, waste was pumped up to the surface and removed. Meanwhile, business in the District was a-boomin'. The corporate wheel kept churning.

This channel was Adam and Isabel's intended escape route.

Adam swung the phony toolbox at his side like a counterweight to his stride. A pair of vagrant boys clutching flimsy leaves of corn came to bother him as he made his way along Knoxville's crummy Riverwalk. They showed off their wares with boundless enthusiasm. Adam regretted not being able to give them anything without risking his confidentiality. They took no note of his persona, however, and eventually gave up to find someone more receptive to their soliciting.

Houses of tin and plywood lined the channel on either side, a dystopian Venice. A few old bodies perched on their balconies, sipping from coffee mugs or smoking cigarettes. The Subterranean's mechanical rumblings echoed from the Wall nearby. The noise there was not only perceivable when the lights or air cycle were on but *always*. Knoxvillers had long grown accustomed to the steady racket, or had simply stopped caring.

The neighborhood became increasingly sparse as Adam neared the Wall. He gazed up at its outer workings, surprised by his sudden awe at his father's grand infrastructure.

"Drop the box. Hands straight in the air, stay facing away from me. Down on your knees, one at a time."

Adam set down the toolbox and slowly lifted his arms. He had not noticed the officer on his tail, who had followed him all the way from the Station. He closed his eyes and waited for him to approach.

He would have one chance.

◆

Isabel scowled at her Loop. She'd opted for the long route into Knoxville, winding through an adjacent Banks neighborhood in a bid to dodge the town's notorious main road entirely. Knoxville's ungainly reputation preceded itself; few women were rash enough to risk walking alone there.

Isabel was one such woman.

Her frown deepened. She'd taken a wrong turn along the way and landed herself back at Knoxville's main gate. *Stupid*, she thought to herself. Precision was integral to her job, and in the rare scenario that precision evaded her, it angered her to no end. She hurried along at an even greater rate, fearing Adam was waiting for her alone at the channel's drainage point. Men who walked alone underwent similar scrutiny as their female counterparts. Knoxville did not discriminate.

The channel snaked south toward the Wall. It was an ugly thing bordered by twin cement barriers riddled with crude graffiti. Isabel followed the rows of apartment homes overlooking the river, many of which were seemingly abandoned. She kept her hands tucked beneath the folds of her jacket, in case the silence was suddenly upended.

The first sign of human life she encountered was not some vagrant with bad intentions who jumped out at her seemingly from nowhere. Instead, it was a man walking ahead of her. He disappeared around a gentle curve in the road.

Isabel jogged along the pavement until she spotted him again. When she did, her heart jumped. The man wore full body armor, and moved with a sense of purpose atypical of a standard patrolman on duty. Isabel moved to a jog, keeping her shoulder glued to the apartments' ongoing brick facade. The officer suddenly diverted his path across the road to the river's barrier.

Isabel veered off toward the river to see past the buildings' curve. She looked in front of the officer to see what he was chasing.

The man was carrying a toolbox.

◆

The darkness crept inward from the corners of Adam's vision, like a vignette on a poorly designed camera lens. "You're lucky you're your daddy's boy," the officer snarled from beneath his visor as the blood flow to Adam's brain was put on pause. He'd clawed at the officer's eyes to no avail, his face shielded by a tactical helmet. His voice sounded tinny and faint, like the sound effect used in war films after a mortar shell bursts. Adam feared the vein in his forehead might explode before he passed out.

There was no begging, no pleading for mercy. No resignation of loyalty to the Chief. No vowing to forget the encounter and allow Adam to escape. No crying for his mother. No consideration was given to the man with the wife and newborn child beneath the helm. Isabel aimed the handgun through the crease between the officer's helmet and body armor and fired once.

The officer's weight collapsed forward all at once and rolled to one side of where Adam lay, sputtering for air. He coughed feebly as his brain resumed its normal oxygen intake and the ringing in his ears eased. When he came to his senses, he propped onto his knees and gazed beside him, where the officer lay in an unmoving heap. Adam moved his eyes up to Isabel. She was calmly returning a tacky-gripped pistol to her waistband. A fine red mist coated her jacket sleeve.

"Get up."

◆

They dumped the officer's body over the barrier in tandem, then dropped down themselves.

At some point, a little girl playing in the street above spotted them walking below and began following them like a stray begging for food. She skipped behind them noisily, her feet clad in foam flip-flops near falling apart. Isabel tensed at her presence, but Adam walked forward with indifference. The Wall loomed ever-larger above, beckoning toward freedom; beckoning west.

The little girl began singing a lyricless tune, the sort of thing a child resorts to alleviate their boredom. She followed them until they reached the channel's drainage point. They found the cavernous hole where waste was shuttled up to the surface restricted by steel bars.

Adam swallowed and looked to Isabel for answers. She just stared at her boots blankly. There were rust-colored splotches where the officer's blood had splattered on the matte leather.

Adam turned and found the little girl making waves in the channel with the bottom of her sandal. He approached her and eased onto his bottom next to her. "Hi." The girl ignored him, focusing her attention instead on the ripple in the rust-colored water. "We need to get to the surface. Do you know how to get up from here?" The girl did not address him. She swept her foot eerily through the water.

"We'll figure something else out." Isabel tugged at his shoulder and made her way toward the channel's nearest exit point. Adam sighed and started after her.

"Wait!" the girl shouted abruptly. "I know a way."

Adam whirled around against Isabel's wishes. He shrugged away from her and kneeled to meet her eye level. "What's your name?" he asked the girl curiously. She looked down nervously at her outfit, an oversized basketball jersey that met the hem of her shorts. "It's okay. We're good people."

"Myrah," the girl responded, still watching her toes.

"Myrah, do you think you could show us?"

"Yessir, Mr. Chief Crombie!" Myrah answered feverishly. She squinted at Adam. "You have to promise, though. You can't tell anyone about it. It's *secret.*"

Adam smiled slightly and touched his finger to his lips. Myrah turned and fled up the staircase out of the channel. Her feet pattered down a cobblestone street along the omnipresent Wall. They stumbled behind her, their feet slipping on the cobblestone.

"Daddy!" Myrah shouted up ahead, aiming her voice toward a second-story balcony. A heavyset man wearing a robe and slippers slipped past a curtain covering the screen door, scratching his beard.

"What is it, sweetheart?" the man grumbled between a loose cigarette.

"Daddy, come down! Hurry!"

The bearded man moved his attention past his cigarette and saw Adam and Isabel walking doggedly. The cigarette fell from his lips before he hustled back inside and hammered down the steps.

◆

"We built it so we could get stuff they don't ship on the main Knoxville freights: booze, fruits, vegetables, that sort of thing. We avoid import fees that way. Lotta folks around here can barely afford to keep the lights on, much less keep their kids fed. So, they come to me. Got to if you wanna survive out here." Miguel toyed with his cigarette nervously. "I charge locals at cost. The only profit I bring comes from out-of-town clients." He looked at Adam uncertainly. "I figured you'd understand where I'm coming from, Mr. Crombie."

Adam craned his neck at the line of LED lights illuminating the illicit cargo tunnel and tugged on the gruesome cable supporting the lift's platform. "I think what you've done here is beautiful," he said hoarsely. Miguel patted his daughter's head.

"Run home and grab some water for Mr. Crombie." He glanced toward Isabel in the near pitch black. "And Miss ..."

"Maria."

His nod went unnoticed in the tunnel's dark. "And tell your mother everything's fine." Myrah lingered, staring at Adam. "Go," Miguel warned. Myrah nodded and ran off.

When his daughter was gone, Miguel's tone darkened. "Mr. Crombie, I don't mean any disrespect, but ... I heard about what happened back there. Whole neighborhood knows already—what's left of it, at least. Things are rough around here—bodies get dumped here pretty often—but wasn't that guy night police ...?"

Isabel moved to shoot down his querying; Adam raised his palm. "You've been more than generous. You deserve to know." Miguel shifted his weight in the tight space. "I'm leaving Pittsburgh. That officer was from the capital. He was sent to stop me." Adam lowered his voice, despite being encrusted within the Wall. "There's a change coming. It's a revolution, I think, a society that recognizes it's only as strong as its weakest link. Where *everyone* is on equal footing. Places like Knoxville are worthless to people like my father. I'm going west to fix that. To bring us *together*, instead of driving us further apart. It's our only way forward."

Miguel said nothing. He extinguished his cigarette, their only previous source of light. The three sat alone in the darkness until Myrah reentered with a tote filled with bottled water and granola bars. She presented the package to her father, who smiled down at her. Adam leaned into Miguel's ear.

"Be careful with what I told you; no one can know about it until the right time comes." He grasped his shoulder. "You'll know when."

Miguel handed over the care package and smiled warily. "You're a good man, Mr. Crombie." He gestured Adam to the platform.

Isabel did not join him. She forced a folded envelope into his fist instead. "It'll get you where you need to go." She paused. "This is where I'm needed most." Adam nodded.

Adam rose on the steel platform and watched Myrah wave goodbye enthusiastically. He waved back, watching her grow smaller and smaller until she disappeared from sight entirely. The crisp scent of fresh air closed in on him.

◆

Miguel kissed the crown of his daughter's head and shoved a fistful of coins in her palms. "Why don't you run up to the market and get some strawberries? For your little brother's birthday." Myrah nodded eagerly and ran off to fulfill her latest errand. Miguel smiled at the light skip in her stride until she veered down a side street and disappeared. He frowned at the cracked Loop hugging his wrist before beginning the short walk to their rickety home.

It was a long time waiting.

IX

No. 4 Month 2, 0017 P.F.
An undisclosed location in Appalachia

THE DOGS howled as they picked up his scent, their voices echoing down and through the valley. Abdul applied pressure to the wound on his side and wiped his bloodiness onto some leaves. He turned east, away from the setting sun. *Let your dogs track me back to Pittsburgh,* he sneered. Abdul had experience at his arm. If one of those youths or their hounds caught up to him, he would show them the deadly accuracy that comes with age and repetition. He hiked downhill, away from the babbling.

The valley gradually descended into a flood basin, one of those dreadful things most Colonists cited as a threat to their society. *Water ruined everything: our mines, our roads, our people.* Abdul pitied them. From his perspective, their fear was warranted. God's first flood had inspired dread from those who were not even made witness to it. Why would His most recent, which they were made to endure, not do the same?

But Abdul was not like them. He did not fear God's judgment. Instead, he learned to embrace it. What harm could a return to watery chaos do to him? If anything, it was proof of God's domain—a thing of comfort.

Still, he was not totally blind to the flood's devastating impact. It *did* change everything; the land, the country, and, most prominently, life as it was known. Even the Chief suffered a tinge from the most severe virus the flood carried: fear. It was apparent in his actions. In a matter of months, the flood wiped away more than a century of the United Steel Company's history operating on the Earth's surface. It was a sign, Abdul warned George shortly into his tenure as Chief Security Officer—an open invitation to diversify their business. But the Chief was resolute. "*Then we'll go where the flood cannot.*"

He was righteous in his own way, Abdul supposed. Some evils were necessary to arrange for a brighter future. And it was not just evils George committed. He had invested in Abdul when he was at his lowest; one moment he was sleeping in a flood-filled gutter in Newark, questioning his faith to no end. The next, he was being helped into the back of a Mercedes, where Chief George Crombie himself sat, his legs crossed leisurely. "You were the head of the Crown Prince's counterintelligence program. Is that right?" Abdul had nodded, huddled amongst what possessions he'd dragged with him through the flood. He need not hide his past allegiances any longer. His Majesty was likely dead alongside the countless millions of students and salarymen, housewives and gig workers, movie stars, and professional athletes who had perished. "How interested would you be in taking on a similar role?" George had smiled sheepishly. "Albeit for a comparatively impoverished client." He still often wondered how George had tracked him down.

Abdul had nothing at the time; even his faith had abandoned him, it had seemed. George put him on the path toward retribution. But that did not erase the sins George committed. No man was impervious to God's judgment.

They dug underground first. They escaped the surface in droves, abandoning God's light to grasp at some misinformed dream that lay below the earth. The scaffoldings came after, once the water had receded from certain parts of the city. Suddenly, one could move above *or* below the flood—granted, they had the capital to do so. "This is unnatural," Abdul had warned him early on. But George did not listen.

"Natural or not, it's necessary. You of all people should know that, Abdul."

Those were necessary evils, George felt. Abdul recognized the sentiment. He too committed evils for a future, albeit one antithetical to the one George pursued.

The boy's eyes captured Abdul's attention even before he learned where his destiny truly lay. He could almost see them now, so many years past. He'd presided over his entire upbringing, from the moment his mother died bringing his brother into the world on. They had burned into his memory; wide and fearful at first, growing calmer and more relaxed with each passing lesson. Language and mathematics, history and philosophy, culinary and martial arts—his education was all-encompassing, and brutal at its core. But not once did Adam show any sign of defeat, nor of his father's thirst to control things and people. Those defiant eyes reminded him of something; some inherent truth he'd been shown years prior. But he could not discern what it was.

He watched his student closely, trying to remember. There were obvious things. Adam was always markedly intelligent for his age, not just academically but emotionally. He was a serious child, quiet but honest with himself and with others, save his father. He often put others ahead of himself, the greatest and most dangerous virtue a person can have. Adam was equally content learning to care for a potted plant as he was reciting the various gestures of good faith in differing cultures. More confounding than anything, Adam possessed none of the Chief's zealous pursuit to leave a greater mark than his predecessors. Had the difference merely come from his mother's side, Abdul wondered? Or was there something more? Something else hiding behind those eyes?

And then, suddenly, as if God had *thwack*ed him on the head with a stick, he realized why God had spared him. God had invented a flood to wipe away half of mankind, thrown Abdul into George's service, and saved him from death countless times just so he could grasp one idea: Adam. Mohammed was no more the last prophet than Jesus was the last savior. God had shown him that day in Jamaica, Queens that to say so was not heresy; it was *rectitude*. God was good. God cared for his children. God had seen the division coming to this world, and he had acted in advance. There would be another prophet, one who would mend the rift separating east from west. And though he would be born in the east, his destiny would take him west.

God guided Abdul every step of the way. But it was not until Abdul saw the resiliency in Adam's eyes that he was able to decode His message. Only then did Abdul realize his duty. It was to serve the prophet and no one else. It was God's will.

God sent a fox to aid Abdul in fulfilling Adam's destiny. He'd avoided contacting the fox since leaving Pittsburgh. He feared their communications being intercepted and Adam's truth being revealed prematurely. Instead, he'd simply performed what actions he knew were necessary from afar. Abdul understood the risk of his treason. He knew there was risk involved in compromising the Subterranean's surveillance system. He knew there was risk involved in smuggling Adam west. He knew there was risk involved in betraying George. He'd seen the risks and acted anyway. He was willing to suffer whatever consequences his treason wrought; life on the run, cold winter nights. Speak little, think much. Hunt for your food, be hunted. Be moving—always moving. Be a vigilante.

He did what was necessary.

◆

Abdul greeted the basin's edge and dug a small ditch in the soft mud. He quickly memorized his coordinates before burying his GeoLoop inside and marking the spot with a twig. Any smart-enabled equipment attached to him would lead the dogs (canine or otherwise) directly to him.

He removed his clothing and stuffed it alongside the rest of his belongings into a waterproof skin. He tied the bundle around his waist before sliding noiselessly into the freshly thawed green water. His mind knew to override the shock to his nervous system. His thoughts turned instead to his most pressing needs: water, shelter, and a smokeless heat source. *Survival.* Survival was all he'd ever known. He'd spent his childhood trapped in a godforsaken country where bombs fell in place of rain, and most of his adulthood trapped in a country that neither welcomed nor valued him. His years under George had been good by comparison, idyllic considering what they had all suffered, but still a lie. He knew his true purpose lay elsewhere. He envisioned himself West, serving the Untold amongst the smell of orange blossoms and the ocean, things he hadn't smelled since those years he'd survived as a boy.

Abdul emerged from the opposite side of the basin, leaving his fear-minded pursuers without a trail to follow. He wiped the water from his skin and slipped on his dry clothes.

He heard the drone before he spotted it. It made a horizontal pass across the gorge, expertly maneuvering through trees and gnarled branches. Abdul fixated on its glowing spider eyes and calmly prepared himself for what was coming. He began climbing to higher ground, indifferent to the drone's incessant *buzz.* His blood pumped through his legs and was reinvigorating. It was a good feeling, like he was young again.

A meadow awash with moonlight crowned the basin's edge. Abdul sat cross-legged in the meadow's center and unpacked the last morsel of honeycomb he'd harvested. *This would not be such a horrible last meal,* he reflected as he chewed. The stars winked at him until a patch of clouds the same shade as the night rolled in, blocking their vision.

A twig snapped to his rear. Abdul's neck twitched. Red lasers danced through the foliage behind him. He snorted and calmly slid his knife from its sheath.

The men stalked the woods in their carbon helms like aliens trying to ward out the planet's toxic air. Abdul scoffed. They were blind. They took the drone's sight for granted, neglecting to see what only the eyes could behold. While they toyed with their monitors, Abdul had been busy learning their watch patterns and the *crunch* of their boots.

He let them pass before he struck. His blade slid smoothly underneath the rear man's armpit, flashing in the moonlight as it sunk into his chest. Abdul gently laid the dying man in some leaves before sliding his gloves off his fingers.

The remaining trio *crunch*ed up ahead before they found Abdul's abandoned encampment. One of them paused and touched his earpiece. "Call."

"Simmons, do you—"

The smart rifle immediately registered the glove's imprint. He fired three times. Each round passed cleanly through the empty spaces between the soldiers' helmets and shoulders. The last man had just raised the barrel of his rifle before he fell. Abdul watched from behind a tree until their convulsions seized. When they did, he began foraging them for necessities.

He realized his mistake two moments late.

The first dog was not so wise as to approach silently. It snarled viciously as it bounded towards him on its sinewy legs, granting Abdul a moment to prepare. He did what was necessary, dropping to one knee and extending his forearm as bait. The dog leaped from two meters away with all its weight behind it. Abdul caught its maw with his elbow and fell backward, absorbing its momentum. He rolled as he fell, sliding to the dog's back and clamping his opposite arm underneath its jaw. The dog snapped at his fingers, barely missing them before Abdul jerked his elbows to one side. The dog went limp instantly.

Abdul came to his feet and inspected the controlled damage to his forearm. He grimaced. Its jaws had touched bone. Blood came gushing from the holes it'd left in him. He'd come out lucky; many years had passed since he'd studied how to defend himself from such beasts.

The second was wise enough to stalk from behind while the first was still attacking him. Unlike its brother first, it approached soundlessly, seeming to have learned from its sibling's rash ways. It clamped onto Abdul's hamstring rather than his bait-arm.

Abdul fell forward, landing on his mashed forearm. The dog latched onto his rear, shaking its maw triumphantly, shredding the flesh further. He tried kicking at it with his opposite foot to no avail.

He flipped onto his back, screaming as the dog pulled away from him. It was only momentary. Before Abdul could react, it had clamped down again, this time onto his knee.

Abdul thrashed on the forest floor, the dog twisting and snarling until he finally landed a flailing heel into its ribs. It yelped and released him momentarily. Abdul scooted backward, creating enough separation so that he could aim a kick into its snout the next time it came leaping at him. It did, snapping for his groin, but his strike landed. The dog yelped again, but was undeterred. Abdul slid back again.

This time when it came, he had freed his knife from its sheath. The hound came leaping for his throat as Abdul thrust the blade up desperately, hoping, praying that it stuck. It did.

Abdul shoved the dog's weight off him and staggered to his feet, crouching to listen for a third sibling. It never came. He paid no mind to the dying dog's whines as he limped over to one of the dead soldiers and emptied his pack onto the grass. He rummaged through the stash of MREs, hydration packs, nylon rope, and personal heirlooms until he found what he was looking for. He clenched his jaw before plunging the syringe into the mangled tissue on his leg, crying out in agony regardless. The burning instantly eased. He repeated the same for his arm, the pain no less than the first.

When he felt sufficiently numbed, Abdul cautiously removed his bloodied pants and packed both wounds with gauze soaked in alcohol. He winced at the dulled sting and smiled despite his agony. *It is a beautiful thing, knowing God has a plan for us,* he thought tranquilly as blood ran over his fingers.

He finished dressing his wounds and pulled on the tallest of the soldiers' fatigues. He combined the leftovers of their canteens into one and immediately began moving through the trees before his wounds dried. He gazed up as he walked, past the dense canopy above. The stars had reemerged. He closed his eyes and said a prayer, not for his safety but for another's.

X

THE FIRST man brought the liquor.

Tyler knew better than to oblige him. He knew it was not sustainable; any future supply would be unavailable to him so long as he was in the hills. But he gave in to the temptation of escape, temporary as it was. He needed to forget, and the more he drank, the more he was apt to forget. It became a simple equation of volume versus strength; how much you could carry versus how much you could handle. Tyler usually opted for the stronger stuff, though he feared it, too. He had his reasons. Its advantages? Well, it was portable, and shelf stable. But liquor had its own detrimental effects. For one, it beckoned Tyler to make drunkenness a permanent rather than temporary condition.

He heard him before he saw him. The distant but loud *clank*s made it seem like there were several travelers approaching. As the *clank*s drew closer, however, a throaty, almost antique-sounding voice joined the tin chorus.

The man might have been a star in a world unencumbered by plague and flood. He did not stay long on any one tune in particular. His style shifted every so often, from flawless imitations of instantly recognizable tracks to melancholic jazz ballads to experimental slides and slaps. His fingers seemed to move at their own behest, constantly adapting to the *clanks* and *dings* from the tin chimes strung to his jacket. Each step he took produced a unique sound, a product of both his gait and the terrain he traveled. He rarely paused to rest or look down at his feet; he seemed to have a built-in radar that detected every nary root and snag along the trail. Through hill and valley, ascent and descent, his feet churned, his fingers fretted, and his hand strummed.

He was performing a rendition of "Rocky Raccoon" when they first crossed paths. His voice was high and raspy, with a hint of a Southern drawl that was not at all unpleasant. It was only upon becoming properly acquaintanced ("Headed west?" Tyler asked once they drew within shouting distance. The man responded with a toothy grin. "Sure thing!") that Tyler learned firsthand the origin of the rasp in the man's throat.

Tyler slowly sipped the music man's moonshine, admiring its burn. He gazed into the campfire, quietly bemoaning how much he enjoyed the liquor's sting.

October 27, 2025

Tyler felt sick. The going had been easy. The excitement of the mission (plus a few months' worth of pent-up sexual desire) helped him see past the unbearable stench of death and decay beneath them. Coming back was significantly more difficult. Every splashing footstep seemed to drain his battery another percentage. Meanwhile, Allison couldn't have been more jovial. Even trudging through flash-flooded neighborhoods, she couldn't help but smile, looking down at her Hugo asleep in her arms. Tyler was grateful she was too preoccupied with Hugo to notice his patheticness.

And then suddenly, by God or Whoever's grace, they arrived. In his foggy state, he'd neglected to realize that they'd turned onto his street. He muttered a silent *Thanks* and hurried toward their building.

"I'm gonna run and put Hugo to sleep," Allison said, her eyes stained red by the fumes and exhaustion. "Meet you downstairs?" Tyler nodded doggedly and smiled. She hurried up the shoddy steps, Tyler's eyes lingering on her ass for a second.

He took off his filthy attire outside his apartment. He didn't want to make a mess of the place; things were looking up for the first time in months. He walked into his apartment wearing only his boxers and undershirt, his other clothes piled in a heap outside. He doubted the clutter would bother anyone; he doubted there was anyone left to be bothered. And besides, he wouldn't be needing clothes soon. He grinned to himself.

There was a man in his apartment.

Oh, was the first thought that crossed his mind. He must've left the entrance open when they'd left. He hadn't bothered locking up; the building was vacant, and the potential of contracting the virus should've scared off any opportunists foolish enough to think his shitty studio contained anything of value.

The intruder looked like a weasel; short with a cinched back, neck craned to peer through the cumbersome gas mask he wore over his face. He wore an oversized rain shell that billowed past his hips, hiding his size. He turned around quickly at the sound of the door opening.

"What are you doing here?" he asked, his voice muffled by his mask. Tyler could tell he was afraid by the way he stood, all hunched over and stiff.

"I live here." Tyler suddenly wished he still had the shower rod in his hands—and that he'd kept his pants on. "I don't have anything—"

"Shut the fuck up." The intruder's voice cracked midway through the sentence, and Tyler thought *Oh* again, and realized it was a woman. She must've realized her mistake. She took a step away from him, her neck snapping toward the window that opened to the fire escape. Tyler smiled and raised his hands in a bargaining motion. He took a step towards her.

"Listen—"

He had only meant to warn her. *How the fuck didn't she know?* His night was going so well. Justice had been served on a cold platter to his brother's killer, and he was squarely positioned to fuck his girlfriend—*ex*-girlfriend—shortly after discovering his body. Trespasser or not, he didn't want to ruin his night by having to hit a woman.

Through all his flaws (and hers), Joe Haji never laid a finger on his wife. *"Only weak men hit their wives,"* he'd preached to his sons. That did not stop him from verbally demoralizing Lori for her more worrisome habits. *"Just shut up. You're trashed,"* Joe would grumble whenever Lori was well into another of her drunken rants. But the seed had taken root, and Tyler hesitated at the thought of having to hit a woman. He never anticipated that this hesitancy would be his demise.

He didn't get close enough to infect her with the virus (which was her greatest fear), much less hit her. In one smooth blur, she reached underneath her parka and drew her revolver. The clack of the hammer locking in its back position seemed to merge with the ear-shattering *bang* that came soon after. Before the flood put an end to quick-draw sharpshooting contests, Nastassia Cortez had been a two-time New York state champion. But Tyler Haji never learned Nastassia's name, much less the numerous titles she'd won.

"Fuck," was all the woman could manage. She leaped over Tyler's body mere seconds after he'd collapsed, flinging the front door open and flying down the stairs, skipping the last flight entirely.

Tyler gasped and stood. His trembling fingers tried staunching the blood that'd already soaked through his ratty undershirt to no avail. He swiped a bloody hand through his hair and tried to think of what to do. He could think of nothing but trying to plug the newly formed hole in his shoulder with a bath towel. He spasmed at the sudden pain that choked him when he touched the white linen to his shoulder. He pushed into it anyways and screamed. Black spots dotted his vision as he slid down the wall to the floor. He stayed there for a while, staring at his bloodied hands incredulously.

◆

The music man became suddenly shy as soon as they stopped to make camp. Tyler was grateful for that. The man had the switching eyes of the sort of person who rarely spoke with others. They'd nervously maneuvered the boundaries of social interaction in real-time. The man eagerly poured Tyler another tin cup's worth of his deadly hooch. Tyler should've objected; he'd already let the man's desperate kindness go too far. But he was good and buzzed now, feeling better than he had any right to, given the circumstances.

The night was bitter, but the fire and the hooch kept him warm. Tyler watched the man rotate the two squirrels he had shot over the flame. He worked the spit idly with one hand, caressing his boxed instrument's neck with the other as grease flared up against the fire.

Tyler sipped the firewater and tried to maintain a clear head. Up to now, he'd revealed nothing about himself. *Keep it that way,* he reminded himself. He was getting drunk with a mountain busker for a *reason.* Just like his mother drank—it was all for a *reason.*

The man grinned at his spinning prizes. "Best there is. Appalachia's always got the best squirrel."

Tyler nodded as if the man had a point. *Making new friends, are we, Tyler?* He had yet to be accustomed to the geographically variable quality in squirrel flesh. But he had to admit, the roasting rodents smelled otherworldly. *Remember what you're here for,* Tyler reminded himself grimly.

The man gripped the spit with a stained rag and transferred the sizzling squirrels to a soot-worn frying pan, quartering them on the same surface. He beckoned Tyler to the fire and set the skillet down in the brush for the two of them to share. "Yer welcome to however much you like," he said before he set about devouring his portion, sucking the grease off his fingers like Cheeto dust. Tyler attacked his supper with only slightly lesser enthusiasm. The meat tore cleanly from the bone and tasted like greasy chicken. He reached for more.

◆

"Tyler?"

His eyes opened to her voice. It'd come from outside the front door, but it could have just as well been an angel.

"Yeah," he called back, wincing.

"Where're your clothes?" Allison giggled. Tyler smiled feebly. It was a cute noise, her laugh. He'd thought about it often since they'd stopped seeing each other. It was not long before Allison realized the door was unlatched and let herself in.

"I thought it came from outside," was all she could manage as her eyes gaped at the bloody mess. She crawled over to Tyler, sat on her haunches, and tried to move the bath towel from his shoulder. Tyler shook his head. "Let me help," she sniffled.

"Stop, I can't—" His throat had gone so dry the words stopped there. She stood quickly and went to the sink before remembering the boil order that'd been put in place almost two weeks prior. She opened the fridge and found nothing potable. The water was outside, collecting in a Dutch oven that used to be his brother's. But Allison did not know that.

She closed the fridge and started crying. She sank to the floor and sat like that for a while. Tyler closed his eyes, the blood rushing to his ears, deafening him.

Allison suddenly flung the hair from her eyes. A wild-eyed look had replaced the tears. "Where's your stash?" she asked urgently.

Tyler blinked. He had forgotten he was posing as a heroin addict in his pain. "It's gone."

"You're lying." With that, Allison stood and began flinging open drawers and cabinets at random, sweeping the few glass and silver wares Tyler owned off the shelves and onto the floor. "Johnny told me you were his best customer!" she yelled, her face flushed an uncomely shade of red. Tyler sat quietly as she whirled manically about his kitchen, searching.

"Is that why you asked for my help?" he asked slowly, after watching her for some time.

The rage seemed to dissipate almost immediately from Allison's body. In a matter of seconds, she became a new person. She slid to her knees and touched Tyler's cheek softly. Tyler flinched. *You're a junkie,* he realized, far too late. *How the fuck didn't you know, Tyler?*

"No," Allison crooned. "I just wanna help." She grasped his hand and smiled. He knew then it was all fake, her and her phony facade.

"I don't want your help," Tyler croaked.

Her face morphed once again, her eyes sharpening into python slits. She leaned in close: "Tell me."

He understood then that she would not leave until she found it. "Couch cushion." She bounced to her feet and flung the cushions from the second-hand thing Tyler never sat on. The cushions seemed to float momentarily before landing on the tile floor with soft *poofs*.

Allison huffed and felt inside the couch's crevices. "There's not shit!" she exclaimed.

There's no way. Tyler made the mistake of trying to shake his head; his shoulder exploded with agony. He clenched his jaw and closed his eyes, tears welling in their creases. He stared into the backs of his eyelids until the fireworks of color in his vision faded. "You used it all, didn't you? You're a *junkie*. I should've known."

"I've never used."

"What?" Allison glared at him suspiciously.

"I just buy it." He suddenly recalled the intruder, the way she'd turned away when he walked in through the front door, her rain shell billowing out past her knees. It had been as if to conceal something. He smiled, closed his eyes, and let his head hit the cheap plaster wall with a soft *thump*. "She took it." The look of dismay that swept across Allison's face almost made Tyler laugh aloud.

Hugo began crying some three floors up; the walls were thin enough and the crisis severe enough that his voice was faintly audible. Allison glanced at the ceiling before shifting her focus to Tyler. "Do you want me to help?" she asked softly. Any note of affection she'd hinted at that afternoon or during their two-month stint as lovers was all a sham, Tyler realized. All he could see standing before him now was a coiled serpent, sampling the air with its forked tongue.

"No," Tyler said. He was feeling dizzy now.

"Good. Then I'll help." With that, she fled, leaving Tyler alone in the dark, his fingers forming a crust and sticking to the rusted bath towel.

He wasn't sure how long she was gone, but his apartment was freezing when she returned. The only borrowed light came from the moon's glow shining through the fire escape window; most of the city lights had gone dark.

She was carrying a needle.

Tyler didn't feel the pinprick in his bicep. He did feel the immediate wave of nausea that worked its way up from his chest. His vision suddenly blurred, and the room trembled at first and then shook. Dead sound filled the space above him, like he was drowning at the bottom of a swimming pool. Allison leaned down and pecked him on the cheek, but he didn't feel that either. His hand fell away from the oozing hole in his shoulder, the half-dried linen detaching from the wound painlessly. He slowly slid down the wall until he lay on the tile in a cold, senseless heap. The question reverberated through his skull: *How didn't you know? How the fuck didn't you know, Tyler?*

She wished him luck before leaving him for the darkness to swallow. Tyler did not hear her words, only the sorrow in her voice. It almost sounded genuine.

◆

They cleaned every ounce of meat off the bones, the air eerily absent of any noise aside from their chewing and the fire crackling. Tyler was still hungry when he finished.

The music man tooled with his pack and pulled out a pipe. He took his time filling it with tobacco. "Where ya from?" he asked slowly. He seemed to struggle to put the words together, as if his brain had surrendered to the logic of guitar chords and seclusion. Tyler wiped his fingers on his pants.

"East." *Technically true,* he noted.

The music man processed this. "Whatchyew do fer a livin'?"

Tyler yawned. "I work for United. Procurement." He pretended not to notice the man's confusion. "I buy raw materials. The stuff they use to make stuff."

"What kinda stuff?"

"Do we make?" The penniless busker nodded. "Everything. From Loops to shitty furniture to steel beams ... the Crombies make it all."

"Y'mean, you *know* George Crombie?" the man asked, lighting a match to the bowl of his pipe.

"Not personally. I just work for him," Tyler lied measuredly.

The man puffed three perfect rings of smoke from his lips, neglecting to ask why it was he was caught in the middle of nowhere, alone. The smoke rings traveled away from the fire, dissipating before they reached the treeline. He suddenly hooted and slapped his knee. This reaction confused Tyler. "Shoot. That reminds me; met this gal on the road, 'bout, I dunno, few months back. Anywho, she was all in a hurry, talkin' bout the Chief and some man they call the prophet. Er, somethin' like that. She handed me this paper an' told me to show anybody else I seen. Lady talked kinda funny ..."

The man unzipped a pocket in his cargo pants and fumbled around until his fingers caught on a slip of paper. He blushed, suddenly embarrassed. "Never learned to read or nothin'. Was hopin' you could spell 'er out for me." He offered Tyler the note. He blinked and held it up to the fire's dancing light:

DEAR READER, BE YOU WESTERNER, OUTSIDER, OR NEW COLONIST:
THE CLAIMS BY THE DESPOT EASTERN GOVERNMENT REGARDING THE DEATH OF THE WAY ARE <u>FALSE</u>. THE GRANDSON OF FATHER OF THE WEST BILL EDENSON IS <u>ALIVE</u>. SOON HE WILL LEGITIMIZE CLAIM AS NEW FATHER OF THE WEST, SHEPHARD OF THE GREAT FLOOD, LEADER OF THE AMERICAS, THE UNTOLD. WE WILL NO LONGER TOLERATE THE LIES AND PROPAGANDA OF THE SWINE GOVERNMENT OF THE NEW AMERICAN COLONIES AND ITS COCONSPIRATORS.
THE ALLIANCE WELCOMES <u>ALL</u>. WE CHERISH WATER, WHICH IS THE FOUNDATION OF ALL LIFE.
WITHOUT WATER THERE IS NO LIFE.
WATER IS LIFE.

Tyler folded the piece of paper back up and rubbed the smoke from his eyes. The music man stared at him as if he were some magi. "Whassit say?"

Tyler shook his head. "Nothing. Just some road that's closed off cuz of a mudslide."

"Oh." He looked down sadly and tucked his hands back into his pockets, his fingers jumbling imaginary chords. Tyler tossed the paper into the fire. He watched the man fiddle in his pocket.

"What else you got in there?" *Making new friends, are we, Tyler?* he sneered quietly. The man looked abashed and pointed at his hip. "Yep. In there."

To Tyler's astonishment, the man pulled out a gleaming GeoLoop from his pocket. He held it up to the firelight and admired its gleam. "Found it in dem hills over yonder. Wish I knew how it worked."

Tyler gaped at the military tech. The man had stored a ten-thousand dollar piece of equipment in his pocket like a pack of chewing gum. "Can I see it? I'm pretty good with those things," he offered.

"Sure," the man said gloomily. "Ain't like I can read it."

Tyler wiped some crust off the screen's surface and pressed the power button. The GeoLoop's OLED face lit up blue and emitted an abrupt tune. The man flinched at the sound, knocking the pair of tongs suspended over the spit into the coals. He plucked them out with no concern for burning himself.

Tyler waited for the Loop to establish a connection. He frowned when it did; the map showed he'd gone a mere forty miles from Mt. Vernon. He'd felt each mile tenfold, his thighs and calves burning with a soreness that was neither sweet nor welcome.

"Give it back." The music man held out his hand expectedly. Tyler shrugged and tossed it over the fire. The man slipped the gem around his wrist and admired it briefly before his gaze shifted forward. He concentrated very deliberately on the ground before suddenly grinning and snapping his fingers. "Thas it! Y'know, that gal tol' me somethin' else kinda funny. Said the capital was gonna burn." He made a wheezy sound resembling a laugh. "Said George Crombie's gonna burn it all up and make a new one. Gonna move everyone down to the Sub-tur-ay-nee-um."

"Huh," Tyler replied.

"Huh, yeah. Musta thought I was some dope."

Tyler thanked the man for the food and the hooch. He looked at Tyler sadly. "Yew headed out?"

"No choice, I'm afraid." Tyler clutched a stone lying next to him and lunged over the fire, diving on top of the man in a wild struggle. He had him pinned initially, but the music man writhed like an animal and flipped him off him. He rolled on top of him before he could react and arched a fist high above his head, roaring and swinging down savagely onto Tyler's eye. His head *thump*ed against the forest floor. The stone went clattering from his fist into the dirt.

"*I'll kill yew!*" the music man screamed. He scrambled off him and scampered over to where his pack lay.

Tyler recovered and dove onto his back, snapping his guitar's neck beneath them. He cried out briefly to lament his most prized possession, worth twice as much to him as the gem-like thing strapped about his wrist. But that moment was all Tyler needed.

Tyler wrapped his forearm around the music man's throat and clutched blindly in the dirt next to him. He found another jagged stone and released his forearm, driving the stone's point into the back of the man's skull. His forehead hit the ground violently. He moaned and began clawing away, blood dripping past his ears, his fingernails chipping against bits of rock. Tyler stood, arched back, and swung down a second time. This time, the stone stayed in place.

Tyler fell to his knees to catch his breath. His chest heaved. The dead leaves below him were a blur. He flopped his neck back to look up at the stars and shut his right eye. Faint slivers of light shone through the opposite organ. He laughed up at the trees, a faint croak.

Apart from the cicadas' song and the branches' groans, the forest did not respond.

Tyler staggered to his feet and kicked dirt over the fire's embers. He rummaged through the dead man's bulging pack. He found a molded piece of hardtack, a reused Ziploc filled with chestnuts, his tobacco pouch, and what remained of the tin hooch jug, which he downed in one gulp. The clear vitriol burned in his throat as he went to undo the GeoLoop from the dead man's wrist. Tyler strapped it onto his own and staggered into the woods, drunk and half-blind.

XI

January 3, 2016

Pittsburgh, Pennsylvania, United States of America

1:39 AM.

August's eyes snapped open immediately, the angry red digits of her alarm clock staring at her. She'd trained herself not to linger in that puddle between sleep and wakefulness, for fear that she would fall asleep and the shop would not open. The phone was ringing. She kept a landline on her nightstand for old time's sake—a tradition passed down by her grandparents, which made it "the" phone, not "hers." She kept "her" phone on mute and free of social media—though she contributed to a fairly active group text thread with some of her college friends (those who still cared to maintain their past connections; the grand majority had removed themselves from their past ties, which was fine. There were plenty of good reasons to forget about human beings you once shared bonds with: careers, moves, marriages, and more.).

She answered with a subtle groan from being freshly awakened. "Yes?" she asked before she was barraged with lines of hysteria.

All August could extract from Julie's frantic monologue was, "Your grandfather's gone crazy and won't listen." August quickly wrapped herself in her parka and drove as fast as she dared to Bloomfield.

Julie answered the door in her robe, talking loudly to her sister on the phone. "Jeanie, I'll talk to you later." John sat in his chair, staring at his fist.

"Pa?" August breathed quietly to herself.

August's mother hung up and then pointed to the hole in the wall. "I just heard a *bang,* and when I came out your grandfather was punching the wall, so I said, 'John, what the hell are you doing?' And he just *stood* there. And now he won't talk; he just sits there. So, first thing I thought to do was call—"

"Why the fuck wouldn't you call 911?" August snapped. She immediately regretted her words. Tears welled in her grandmother's eyes, and she covered her mouth with her hand. "I'm sorry." August quickly went to kneel beside her grandfather—at a safe distance. "Papa?" John scanned August's face with wet eyes.

"Maria?" he asked. And August's heart sank because that was her aunt's name, and she'd been dead for a decade.

◆

August asked the paramedics to keep their distance because she did not know how John would react to them initially. The hole he put in the house's insulation confirmed that his strength had not been lost with his mental acuity. She did not want him landing in court as well as the hospital. This did not inspire confidence from the operator on the phone. They made a brief note to the ambulance dispatch: *Patient potentially aggressive.*

August's message was not handed down the proper chain of command. Shortly after she called, an ambulance came screaming around the block. She sighed and waited outside to greet the paramedics before they incurred any further damage.

"We need to assess the situation inside, ma'am," they said upon arrival. August snapped and jabbed a finger at the young man's chest.

"I don't need you to tell me the situation." The kid swallowed, and *yes, ma'am*ed. They left the stretcher outside.

The hospital grunts edged through the kitchen to where John sat in the living room. He looked at them with a confounded expression, like he was trying to decipher friends whose faces he had not seen since childhood. The younger-looking of the two kneeled and began gently taking his vitals, asking him rudimentary questions such as, "Can you hear me all right, Mr. Milo?" and, "How are you feeling, Mr. Milo?" John nodded to the first question and said *Fine* to the second.

They asked if they could speak to his wife. John frowned. "My wife ..." he mumbled. His eyes scanned the air for some answer hidden there.

"I'm right here!" Julie cried from the kitchen, where she was making coffees for the *gentlemen*, as she'd so graciously coined them upon opening her home to them. John turned to her voice but did not speak. He seemed powerless to connect the auditory cue with its significance.

The EMTs resumed their schedule and asked August if the patient had ever had a stroke. "No," she replied. They briefly deliberated, and the older of the two asked to speak with August and her mother alone. They agreed and ducked into the kitchen while Doogie Howser stayed and engaged in a one-sided conversation with John.

The older one explained that the safest course of action was to admit John so that they could run further tests. Given that he couldn't remember her name, August agreed. Julie felt differently. She pinched her forehead and signed the cross. "The man hasn't been to the emergency room his whole life. Chrissakes, why the hell should he go now?"

"It's just some tests, Ma." Julie remained stubborn until they finally got her on board by promising to have him home before dinner the next day.

The paramedics seemed relieved until Julie presented one additional condition, that John did not go in the ambulance. "He won't be comfortable," she reasoned, which was only half the truth. The other half was her anticipating John's future begrudging over having to pay the ambulance bill. The paramedics decided against insisting otherwise and followed August to UPMC Hospital.

◆

"August? What time is it?"

August was yawning when he said her name. It ended as a sigh of relief. "It's late, Papa," she replied.

"Oh my God!" Julie cried from the back seat. She wrapped her arms around him from the back seat.

John learned what'd happened on the way there.

"They're just gonna run some tests," August explained. John knew better than to protest the decision. He'd already lost the reins of the situation—and his mind. He watched the streetlights pass by in silence until they arrived at UPMC Shadyside.

John exited the car calmly and thanked both paramedics as they entered the emergency department. They bowed their chins but raised their eyebrows at his sudden reinvigoration.

August described the abrupt end of John's symptoms to the ER physician, and they were rerouted to a normal examination room, where they again recorded John's measurements. John had a running joke with his granddaughter in which he bragged about his stellar numbers, despite his overall lack of concern for diet or fitness. He waved his hand with gusto when the nurse read his blood pressure aloud. August managed a smile despite her restlessness.

The doctor smiled through tired eyes of her own and explained that since John had no prior medical issues, they would merely perform the routine scans and tests first. "Just to make sure nothing serious is going on," she explained. All three Milos nodded in uncanny agreement.

The doctor asked if John would be comfortable spending the night in one of their outpatient rooms.

"We live a few blocks over," Julie began. John cut her off with a chopping motion.

"Yes, that's fine. Just as long as we do the tests first thing in the morning; I got a hot date tomorrow." He winked at August slyly. Julie's expression remained unchanged (tired and worried), but she slapped her husband on the arm, as was customary. The doctor smiled slightly as she jotted down her last notes.

Two hospital grunts began preparing a room down the hall. Even though it was three in the morning, John would be up at six o'clock sharp, like always, whether the doctors were ready for him or not. August asked if he wanted her to stay.

"No." John understood how businesses failed: inconsistency. Without her, the bakery would be forced to close for a day. Maybe a new customer would try to walk in and find the door locked. The idea was unfathomable. "No, honey. I'll be okay. Your mom will be here." Julie Milo had gone about setting up her own lodging outside of John's room. She'd "found" a few extra bed pillows from an adjacent room and used them to fashion a chair and coffee table into a waiting-room cot of sorts.

"Call me," August said to him seriously.

Rather than return home, August went straight to the shop, where she promptly passed out with her head rested against a sack of flour. She dreamt she was at an ornate ball in which she wore a silver dress with thin shoulder straps. The evening was at its end, and she was dancing with a strapping young doctor who looked like Doogie Howser when the sound of someone trying to get in through the front door woke her abruptly.

◆

Business was slow after she hurriedly opened the shop, her eyes ringed by black shadows and her hair still ruffled by sleep. The door *clink*ed just twice after noon. People were starting their New Year's diets after gorging through the holidays.

At 3:15 PM, her grandfather walked in with his normal gusto. "You never called," August started before she saw the bouquet he was carrying. "Crazy old man. Did you forget how flowers work? *You're*the one who's supposed to be getting the flowers."

John smiled coyly and shrugged. "I don't know where they come from. They were in my room when I woke up." He pointed at a tag on one of the stems. "Any clue who this is?" he asked seriously. August squinted.

To health and happiness.

   - George

August trained her face. "Huh. I don't know anyone named George ... You?" John chuckled.

"Oh, yes. Many."

He sat in the light from the store window and began explaining the process behind the scans and blood tests. August listened distantly. "Then the nurse took some blood and they do some more scans. Then they ask me some questions, and ..."

John's voice faded into the backdrop. She couldn't go out to dinner as promised, not anymore. Maybe never again. She could get the same phone call from her mother, only this time she would be too busy eating Lobster Thermidor with George Crombie to answer. The thought was horrifying.

And then there were the flowers.

"Your grandma slept the whole time," John added jokingly. He could not resist bringing her into the fold, no matter how illogical it was doing so.

John asked if August had plans for the night. "Nothing, really," she squeaked, omitting any mention of George Crombie. John left behind some pamphlets he'd taken from the office, though the information within seemed irrelevant to John's sudden mental collapse. A customer could've, in theory, walked in at any moment, so John bade her adieu for the time being. "I'll call you in the morning," August reasserted.

The door did not *clink* once after John departed. August stayed and worked anyway. She had some leftovers from her New Year's display that she was determined to revitalize. She'd been thinking of buying an ice cream machine secondhand, maybe finding some help and getting an old-fashioned ice cream cart up and running for the summer. She was already shooting off ideas for flavors she could make from whatever didn't sell at the shop; the pistachio panettone that had lingered in her display was too dry now to eat on its own, but she thought she could make it into a badass ice cream mix-in.

August stayed well after the sun quit shining through the front display. She swept, mopped, and sifted flour so she wouldn't have to do it in the morning. She made syrup for halva. And candied and roasted pecans. And made lemon crème filling. Time melted as she worked. The clock ticked past six, then seven, and approached eight.

She was wiping down, feeling accomplished, when she heard an attempted *clink* at the locked front door. She jumped at the sound and realized she'd forgotten to turn the lights off out front after locking up. August rushed out to see if it was a regular. It was.

George Crombie stood doing calf raises in the cold. He was back in his usual suit-and-tie and carrying a reusable shopping bag that looked awkward hanging by his side. When he spotted August coming to the door, his eyes brightened. Partly relieved, partly anxious, August opened the door to let him in. "Brrr. Thanks."

August smiled. *Just another customer.* She pretended she was speaking with one of her regulars, like Mr. Bennett, recreational cat espouser and her next-door neighbor. "How was the cake?"

"Lovely.' She sends her compliments to the chef. Or is it baker? Head baker? Anyhow, thank you for bringing it all that way; you very much made her evening."

"You're very much welcome."

He stood somewhat awkwardly, guarding the bag at his hip. "Is your father feeling better?"

August reddened. "Yes. My grandpa. Um, thank you for asking ... and for the flowers. They're beautiful. He's fine, though, really. He's seen worse."

"*Grandfather*, my mistake." Crombie set down the bag gently. "Are you married?" he asked without hesitation.

"Um." Her cheeks flushed. She laughed nervously and flopped her arms. "Nope. Never have been."

George smiled sheepishly. "I had to put it out there. You'd still like to have dinner with me, then?"

Is now really the time for this? she thought incredulously. She was ready to say no and go home and sleep. But then she saw his nerves: his thumb absently picking at his middle finger, his toe lifting and falling underneath his shoe, his eyes unsure where to look. He seemed almost desperate for her to say *Yes.* It was as if her little cake shop was the only thing tethering him to some normalcy.

"Sure," August said. "You pick the date."

Crombie toed the bag beside him. It responded with a gentle *clink.* "How about now?"

August scratched her nose and stained it with flour. *"Here?"*

◆

"Sorry if I packed light. I figured it'd be better than going out, with all that you're going through."

Better it was; light, it was not. They ate more than well, dining like Parisians transported to the Rust Belt: a bottle of burgundy, a baguette, country ham, pimento cheese, and a tomato-cucumber salad dressed in olive oil. August was still coated in a fine dust of flour and leftover grog from the late night at the hospital. And hungry. She could have easily cleared what they set out on the small circular cafe table without George's contribution.

They neglected any mention of romance over dinner and instead shared stories starring their loved ones. August laughed at a Christmas dinner gone awry that ended with George's father and uncle wrestling bare-chested in the living room. For some unspoken reason, she could think of nothing to share but one of the few stories she'd been told about her father. Even though she'd only ever seen photographs of him as a boy, she'd always pictured him as a younger version of her grandfather. The sparse details she knew of him came from John, though she'd stopped asking about him early after seeing the sadness that mentioning him inspired.

Before she could stop herself, she was conveying everything she knew about him: "When my dad was a kid, he tried climbing our neighbor's terrace to pick roses for this girl he had a crush on. I guess it was Valentine's Day or something ... Anyways, he made it all the way to the top before he fell and landed in the bushes. He was covered in cuts, but he never cried about it. He climbed back up, made a nice bouquet, and took it home. When my grandpa asked how he got all cut up, he goes," she acted out a sigh. "*The things we do for love.*" George guffawed. "My grandpa still laughs about it."

"Is your father still around?" George asked gently.

"No. I hear he's doing fine, though." She complimented the wine. He understood she was evading the topic. He let it happen.

"I'm glad you like it. I bought it at Kroger; super rare vintage."

Though her knowledge of oenology was limited, she recognized the bottle—Chambertin 2005. It was far from a fifteen-dollar bottle. *Multiply that by ten.* She paused. *Maybe more ...*

◆

"I'm still not sure why Pitt accepted me. I was a shit student."

August rolled her eyes. "I don't buy it."

"No, really. I couldn't long divide, much less reflect on Freudian values. Still can't."

"Me neither."

"See? We're not *that* dumb, though, are we?"

August shrugged and smiled. "I dunno; you tell me."

George laughed. "Seriously. I place a lot of faith in street-smarts. God knows you have it—look what you've made for yourself. This place was *empty* before. That's *crazy*."

August performed the prerequisite blushing and *oh, stop*ping. He was right, though; the only tenants occupying the space before her had been a ragtag group of pests and vermin. It had been left up to her to drive them out before setting up shop. Most things were left up to her. Her lack of a payroll attested to it.

George patted his belly and mentioned *almost* not having enough room for dessert; he was still stuffed from overindulging his grandmother's birthday cake, he explained. Regardless, he pulled a syrup-soaked walnut cake from the bottom of the grocery bag. "My grandmother doesn't know how to receive a gift," he said. It was still warm. August pretended not to notice.

Crombie didn't attempt to explain how he'd learned of John's sudden hospital admission. He never delved into details about his own family, omitting them deliberately or incidentally from his dialogue. He made no further mention of his grandmother, aside from her comments on the cake. From what August gathered during her preliminary internet research, his entire family was either deceased or had intentionally severed their connections to the family. His exclusions did not bother August; she had spent the past thirty-six hours stressing over her grandfather's well-being, and now all she craved was escape from the issue of family.

After the last drop of the wine was poured, George told August that she was beautiful. Normally she would have taken this as a banal plea for gratification. Not with George. When he said it, it sounded true. Whatever George Crombie said felt true, whether he could prove it or not.

August blushed and thanked him. She let it happen.

◆

Dinner with George Crombie never quite ended. It extended into that night and many nights after. She was engrossed by him, though in a strange way. She felt as though she'd been convinced of it.

After George finally made his move, August began staying over at his lofty apartment. He'd adorned his walls with paintings from artists he admired. And books; two bookcases filled with the things stood front and center in the living room, framing the fireplace that'd been gutted to comply with HUD protocols. There were no family photos, no framed diplomas, no framed posters or travel souvenir doodads. Everything that was not ancient was brand-new and worked efficiently. Everything smelled of lavender. August learned that was George's smell, and she quickly grew accustomed to it. She was a part of his life now.

He didn't only take care of her. George had John introduced to a new doctor, a man who specialized in the brain and memory. John was put on a new medication yet to be made available to the public, and his condition remained stable for several years longer than the other doctors forecasted. When John asked where August had found Dr. Alvarez, and how come they never billed him after his visits, August simply shrugged. "Sounds like they're just making things easy for you, Pa." That's just how George was: he made things easy.

The shop continued to operate, occasionally with August at its helm. George stepped in and found her good help, something which had evaded her in the past. At first, she came in every day to ensure things were being done up to her standards and the place hadn't burned down in her absence—they were, of course, and it had not. Soon she was there some of the time, taking part in some of the kneading and shaping and doing the bookkeeping. Her visits became rarer and rarer as time went on. Steel City Sweets ran smoothly with or without her. They even expanded, adding an ice cream parlor where kids got a free scoop for every A or B (and sometimes even C's; admittedly, the rule was poorly enforced) on their report cards. August was proud despite her noninvolvement. Her original vision for the shop remained intact. The goods were classic and lovingly made, and Farideh attracted as many (if not more) customers as she ever had— and was a more talented baker on top of it. August became involved mostly with George. She loved him. And she was his treasure.

January 2, 2020

It was understood from the onset that their marriage would produce children. The Crombie legacy would endure. This did not bother August; she had always wanted children. How their last name might predefine them did not matter to her.

"We could adopt," August mentioned gently once while they sat sharing tea. They'd been trying for a while with no luck. "He'd still be your son." George blew on his tea and sighed.

"I know. I just ... I want him to come from *us.*"

The results followed soon after: "Given the genetic factors at play, I would gently recommend in vitro fertilization as a suitable alternative to adoption."

Only after the doctor finished explaining did she realize there were tears silently streaming down her cheeks. Her husband came to her side and held her, his chin casting a shadow over her. "I know," was all he could say. He kept repeating it: *I know. I know.* What else was there to say?

September 9, 2020

August was confused when she looked down at her son for the first time. She'd never been able to form a solid image of her father's face. The only pictures she'd ever found in her grandparents' nooks and crannies (which she had searched without permission) showed him as a child. They had helped her form a blurry image of what her father *ought* to look like, but there was nothing solid to it; nothing backed by memory. Yet she saw him then, eyes shut, crying and reaching for her breast, as if her infantile memories of him had been waiting till that moment to come flooding back.

It was as if Bill had been born again.

August smiled broadly because it was her son, and she already loved him more than anything else in the world. But she needed time to process the immediate resemblance—and to question her sanity. She gave her son over to her husband, who was smiling and weeping simultaneously. She watched George from what felt like a great distance. *He doesn't know,* she thought remotely. He nuzzled their son's face close to his and said his first sentence to him, something that made the nurse smile and laugh. *How could he?*

And then came John's turn. August carefully scrutinized his sun-spotted face to see whether he saw what she did. He was still sharp.

Still him—for now. That was how Alzheimer's worked, as far as she understood.

Her grandfather was overcome by emotion. His blue eyes sparkled with tears. But her senses told her they were tears of joy, the joy of meeting his great-grandchild, and that he had been born healthy and red-faced and crying. He did not see what August did.

George excitedly took his son back into his canopy and rocked him back and forth. The baby was quiet and his eyes still closed, but George was confident they would be brown-black, the same color as his. "You're gonna be my little buddy, Adam. You know that?" George stooped down and nuzzled him with his broad nose.

Looking down, he saw the future.

Interlude

Winter–October 2025 (*Exact dates disputed)
Enlightenment

BILL PLODDED west, searching until the land stopped and the ocean started. He stayed a few weeks in the small beachside resort town he landed in, but the stillness quickly grew stale. Something was eating at him. It weighed him down; like an invisible ball at the end of the chain. He headed east and then south, dragging the weight behind him, not knowing when, where, or if his travels would end.

Somebody had warned him it would rain. It'd rained plenty in the years since that day in the garden when the man told him his truth. But he knew his ankle would not be free of its burden until his rain fell. It'd rained plenty in the years since, but never the way the man had described. Each rain brought with it disappointment. It was maddening, and he felt the ball and chain growing tighter.

So, Bill decided to move to the desert. That was as good a place as any to wait for that rain. It rained very little there, so he wouldn't be disappointed as often.

◆

El Paso favors dry over wet. Dust covers everything. The wind howls in from the desert mountains and brings with it a cloud of dust that hangs over the city. There is little moisture to give the dust any heft.

The dry specks float freely, covering most places and things. Few people seem to mind, since we view dirt differently from dust. There is a lack of respect for dirty things. Dirt hints at misuse and neglect, whereas dust signifies age and maturation. Dirt carries consequences. Dirt must be cleaned, whereas dust can be swept away.

Winter in El Paso means very little other than at night things freeze before they get warm again. This change in centigrade creates some moisture via condensation, presenting a real problem for obsessive-compulsives who prefer their office buildings gleaming. When things get wet, they get dirty. To wash away the dirt, more water is required. In a city with no rain to wash the dirt from the sides of office buildings, the only way to dispose of it is via manual labor.

This was Bill's job.

Bill learned to watch the wind and predict how it would change. A powerful enough gust would shake and rattle the metal carriage he stood on until it eased. Early in his career, he would cling onto the rails like an old woman braving stairs, terrified of falling even if he was just three floors up. He only grew confident with time and practice, learning to adjust his weight based on the wind.

Bill lived in a loft unit above an old woman from New York who'd moved to El Paso to escape the cold and to be closer to her granddaughter. She mainly talked about two things: mule deer and her grandson. Both were primarily discussed over the phone, with the mornings dedicated to deer and the afternoons to her grandson. "Sabes el ciervo mulo?" she asked him once. "You know mule deer?" Bill had shrugged. The old lady smirked at this, as if she had access to some hidden knowledge that Bill was not privy to, which was true. The next day Bill found a permanently stained plastic Tupperware levying a red substance at his doorstep, still warm from the hours spent braising in the oven. He tasted it and immediately understood Lorena's obsession with mule deer.

When spring ended and there were not so many windows to clean, Bill began hunting mule deer with Lorena's son-in-law, Francisco. Francisco knew even more about the animals than his mother-in-law but was more reserved about it. When Bill revealed he had tried and savored Lorena's stew, Francisco laughed and promised he had yet to taste the real thing. After sampling his first piece of tenderloin from an animal harvested by his own hand, Bill understood what Francisco had meant.

Bill's new hobby began to overshadow his principal work cleaning high-rises. Up there, the sun tanned you then reddened you and eventually filled you with cancer. Bill developed peeling spots on his arms and neck that no amount of SPF 150 could prevent. Eating beef jerky alone suspended hundreds of feet in the air no longer appealed to him the same way, not after having learnt to hunt the plains. Luckily, Bill did not have to work squeegeeing buildings much longer.

◆

ALIN-12 (which had yet to become recognized as its more common designation, El Tubo) came to El Paso in the summer of 2025. Where, who, or what the virus's first iteration came from was beyond anyone's knowing. Rumors circulated regardless: *I heard it came from a lab. Who knows what's going on in those bases out in the desert? No, a guy brought it here. He was on a flight from Australia or some shit. Probably fucked a kangaroo, or a wallaby, or somethin'.* At the cafe Bill frequented, he heard even wilder theories thrown around. *They say everyone's gonna get this ALIN shit. And if ya don't, the government'll force-feed it to ya in a vaccine.* Doña Lorena resisted rumors that it came from sick mule deer.

What El Paso lacks in moisture it makes up for in its people. It is not a tall city, though Bill knew the parts that were. El Paso sprawls. People are friendly. There are few social rules to abide by. Two languages are spoken (sometimes in combination with each other) with mostly pride and little animosity. Neighborly accord is guaranteed, given you perform the prerequisite tasks: take out the trash. Keep the yard looking nice. Wave hello. Stop over for a beer every once in a while.

Amiability, alongside a superfluous border, a bustling airport that made frequent exchanges with JFK International, and a less-than-modern public health system made El Paso a desert petri dish.

Contracting the virus was popular. El Paso did not take well to animosity or coldness. Men shook hands. Workers shared spaces. Babies were kissed, and events were held. Life went on, until it didn't; the law of diminishing returns.

The virus affected some more than others. It became deadlier the older and fatter its target was. Silent bets based on one's prior health scores were wagered, a forecast of one's odds of survival. Even deaths from old age or tragedy became subject to scrutiny: Lo tuvo? *Did he have it?* Sí. Lo tuvo. *Sure did.*

The virus's notoriety spread from there, alongside its alpha variant. Everyone knew someone who'd *presumably* had it, but it was seldom confirmed by a test. The easiest test was seeing whether or not they were dead. Or worse, dying. The results spoke for themselves.

El Tubo remained high in the public consciousness, a byproduct of its around-the-clock news coverage. Whether you were a leftist, a rightist, or a the-virus-was-invented-by-a-world-order-of-celebrity-occultists-ist, there was content made to suit you. Bill was indifferent. The coffee shop he frequented showed the news, but he was not sure what channel. He listened (he had no choice in that matter), but rarely watched. Oddly, they'd affixed a ticker with the nation's death toll on the bottom of the screen. It went up every minute or so.

Bill watched traffic in the city dwindle from hectic to light to nonexistent from his perch in the sky. By mid-September, the buses had halted service. Any pedestrians running about were either suicidal or had obligatory errands to run. Only the grocery stores remained busy. Busier than ever, in fact; stocking shelves became dangerous work. Many employees got it and then had it. *Lo tuvieron.*

The suits who worked in the tall buildings Bill cleaned all left. Not long after, the real estate tycoons who managed the high-rises voided their contract with Bill's boss, who was kind enough to inform Bill that he was being laid off in person, which he appreciated.

Whether he worked or not made no difference to him. Bill hadn't signed on for the money in the first place. He didn't try offering his services elsewhere. He'd come to the desert with a set intention.

◆

The National Guard arrived shortly into Bill's unemployment, purportedly to facilitate new ALIN-12 testing sites. What began as a calm and friendly city quickly devolved into one plagued by violence. Citizens lined the streets in protest of the government-run treatment centers, which denied the city's undocumented. *¡No hay justicia, no hay paz!* Bill walked amongst them. The marchers overestimated the Guard's capacity for empathy, and many left the ensuing riots battered and broken. That only enraged them further. Teenage boys with lean shoulders and cocky struts threw bricks at the soldiers. They started fires and cornered officers and robbed them of their equipment. Some were beaten in turn for their actions. Others worse. The virus was indifferent.

◆

It was a Friday, and the city was at odds with itself, but more importantly, it was a beautiful day.

Bill decided to extend his walk. He walked alone. Occasionally he passed a wandering beggar, confused by their sudden solitude, or a young Guardsman nervously patrolling a street corner.

Copia Drive was home to mostly semi-suburban, blue-collar folk. It was where Francisco and Lorena's daughter lived. Bill had visited many times while helping transport their successes in deer hunting. He walked along the street slowly, eerily devoid of children shouting or basketballs bouncing, until a loud *bang* caught his attention. It came from a house with a lawn dominated by a huge overgrown oak.

Bill jostled over and pressed himself against the trunk. He watched a small squadron of riot police officers ram down the house's front door and enter with their rifles raised. A child screamed shrilly inside.

They made it a quick job. Within forty-five seconds, the soldiers wearing face shields had the family of three detained. The soldiers pushed them into a waiting van, using long, metal prods that locked around each detainee's handcuffs. When the mother cried out for her son in Spanish, the officer detaining her *click*ed a button on her leash. Her back spasmed in reaction to the voltage. They prodded the family into the back of the van before fleeing.

Bill watched the truck pull away, angry and confused by the violence. Anger came unnaturally to him. But he was becoming more and more familiar with the feeling of late. He was a little angry when his boss told him he was no longer considered an "essential" worker. He was furious when he saw armed forces beating down women during the protests. And he was most upset now. *One nation, under God, indivisible, with liberty and justice for all,* Bill recalled as he sulked home.

•

An idling vehicle sat parked on the street above Bill's small bungalow-style home. It was an unmarked white transport van with the windows pained over. Bill eyed it as he turned up the driveway, peering over his shoulder.

As he climbed the half stair to the bungalow, he heard sniffles coming from the boxed-in patio. It was Lorena. She sat alone, wiping her nose with a paper towel, muttering prayers. Bill leaned over the retaining wall. "What's wrong?" Lorena did not speak. She hid her eyes underneath the webbing of her palm. "What happened?"

Bill hopped down into the patio and touched her wrist despite the social pressure against doing so. Lorena flinched at his touch. "Francisco. He get sick. Se murió."

Bill was quiet. He sat down and held Lorena's hand. They stayed like that for a while, Bill hearing her prayers.

Bill asked quietly if her daughter was safe. Lorena nodded. "She go to the desert con el pequen. They staying with a friend." Bill asked if she needed anything, food, medicine. She shook her head, sniffling. He would bring her something regardless. He would go hunting tomorrow in honor of his friend.

Bill told Lorena to stay strong. He left her to mourn alone in the dry heat, scampering out of her stoop. He noticed the white cargo van still parked on the street, the engine struggling in the dry heat. Bill was climbing the stairs to his front door when the engine died. He paused and glanced behind him.

A Caucasian man wearing sunglasses and cargo pants stood outside the van watching Bill, a boxy mask strapped over his face. Bill waved. The man stared back at him from behind a cheap-looking pair of wraparound sunglasses. Bill slowly opened the front door and shut it behind him. He peeked warily out the glass.

The man turned and wiggled his finger toward the truck. Two similarly dressed men exited. They formed a line and walked hurriedly to the back of the house.

An alarm sounded in Bill's mind. He remembered the mother being detained earlier. *My boy!* she had screamed. *He's not sick!* Bill had heard about people who'd gotten sick and were not seen afterward. They simply vanished. Where to, no one knew.

The backs of those trucks. That was where.

Bill stalked his living room, adorned by a TV, a La-Z-Boy, and a locked trunk. He unlatched the box and retrieved from it a Winchester twelve-gauge and a carton of slugs.

The men knocked loudly on Lorena's back door. They did not announce themselves. Bill watched from the kitchen window above. The first man pointed toward the corner of the house. The recipient of the command, a thinner and younger clone of the others, nodded. A third man, heavy and bearded, stayed behind with the first while the younger one shimmied along the house's siding.

Bill padded to the front window and watched the young one clear the house's corner, pistol raised. He hesitated before dropping into the lowered patio. Bill twisted the front doorknob after him, slowly. There was no squeak or hydraulic action from the doorstop. He quietly descended the wooden stairs, carrying the shotgun in his fist like a baton.

Bill dropped into the patio, wearing only his socks. The boy left the sliding door open behind him. He watched him inspect Lorena's kitchen. Bill silently prayed she was hiding in her bedroom.

The boy cried out in surprise when Bill kicked his legs out from underneath him. The two went sprawling to the floor, Bill underneath. He wrenched the shotgun beneath the boy's chin. He grasped at the barrel crushing his trachea, his pistol *clink*ing against it, steel on steel. Bill wrapped his ankles inside the boy's calves and yanked the shotgun's barrel upward. The boy's head snapped back and stayed that way.

Bill slid into the living area and lay behind Lorena's plain brown couch. The back door burst open, the big man leading. Bill let him walk toward the kitchen. His superior entered shortly after. The big man said, "Christ." That drew his CO's attention.

Bill rose and unleashed a slug into the first man's skull. His body crumpled to the floor. Bill pumped the twelve-gauge again. The big man had yet to turn from the boy's body. Bill did not let him turn around.

And then all was quiet.

◆

DO YOU KNOW THE VIGILANTE KNOWN AS THE "PIG HUNTER"?
IF SO, CALL THIS NUMBER:
(915) 453-8475
¿CONOCES EL VIGILANTE CONOCIDO COMO EL "CAZAPUERCOS"?
SI ES ASÍ, LLAMA A ESTE NUMERO:
(915) 453-8475

◆

Bill walked. He walked during the day. He walked at night. He changed clothes and slept. He woke up, brushed his teeth, showered, and slept. He walked.

He listened on his walks. He would listen and he would act. But one man cannot aspire to protect an entire city. It takes a village.

The riots only intensified as more and more people went missing without explanation. Night after night, citizens from El Paso and

Juárez filled the streets. What they were protesting changed. At first, it was the virus; *What is it? Who or what made it? We demand to know.* Versions of the same story. Then it became the social climate; *Why can't we leave our homes? No work. No money. No food.* Versions of the same story. Last and loudest were the disappearances; *Where's my father, mother, son, daughter, cousin, best friend, _____?* Fill in the blank. Versions of the same story.

The police became more and more liberal with their use of force as the protests devolved into riots. The resistance's doctrine shifted yet again; *Why are you so cruel? You are corrupt.*

To label war as "unrest" is a dangerous mischaracterization. The timid stay home in times of unrest. In times of war, those who would otherwise flee or hide instead take up arms.

In El Paso, war was conducted. The young, the old, the brave, and the untried all marched as one. At night, arcing tracer rounds drew red comet tails in the sky. There were no active city lights to obscure their luminance. Only the gunfire and the stars and the snake-like band of lights that ran along the border stirred in the night.

Masks were worn. Masks were burned. The death toll climbed.

Colds, coughs, fevers. Necks swelled. The death toll climbed.

People died. Many people died. The bodies they burned. The ash fell like rain. One story: a never-ending tragedy.

It had yet to rain.

October 2025

They looted the supermarkets either as a precedent or as a result of the declining food supply. Bill didn't take his piece. He was always hunting. He forbade his followers from partaking either. They would earn their keep and grow, harvest, and preserve their own food.

Bill was always hunting. More men in sunglasses rolled by Lorena's house in their vans. They found it empty. Lorena, her daughter, and young Raul were staying about ten miles east of town, close to the border, where they were left alone. Perhaps the men came searching for answers. Perhaps they were just following orders. Bill did not care. Each one he hunted was replaced by a duplicate.

Bill was always hunting.

The desert suited Lorena, and she scoffed at the perceived challenge of feeding her family there. Her knowledge of the land and what grew there was a cornucopia. She filled the table with stewed cactus and coñejo and tortillas. Bill brought venison. No one was hungry.

Bill taught the other men to hunt just as Francisco had taught him. They called each other "neighbor" even though they lived miles apart from each other in trailer homes or cottages that stood out against the desert.

His protegees learned quickly: how to pick a deer out from the rocks and shadows. How to stalk in, always from above. How to move against the wind. How the deer will fall. An animal is no good if its bones are all broken.

On days the men went out (including Al Steersman, who was seventy-six), they would eat together afterward. They could harvest three, four, or sometimes five in a day's work. Their yields would sustain their cohort for three days or so. There was Lorena and her family, Alejandra with her husband, Israel, and their son, David, Jon Torrez, and his nephew, Kyle, and Amy Wu. Then there were the Steersmans, an older ex-pat couple who left Juárez as soon as the virus began to spread. And last, there was Bill himself.

They became more than a family because their commitment to each other was not obligated by blood. Though Bill never acknowledged that he was their leader, he was. His followers often went to him for counsel; *What's happening? What will happen?* Bill only answered with what he thought was or would happen. But that was enough. Bill's thoughts gradually became truths.

◆

Bill shot an animal, cleaned it, and decided to take it back to Lorena's. He rucked it in from seven miles out. It was not debilitating; the mule deer were small, and Bill was big.

When he arrived, he found the group waiting for him. The sun was nearly set, and the cold desert night loomed over them. They were gathered around a fire, some in folding chairs, some bundled up in blankets, a few in the bed of Al's blue pickup. Scattered amongst them in the sand were their most important belongings: suitcases, cans of gasoline, rifles, crucifixes, sealed crates, lanterns, photo albums, bundles of firewood, children's toys, and more things. The troop watched Bill approach with the animal slung loosely over his shoulders.

When Bill drew near, he saw a surprising look in their eyes: anticipation. There was more to it, however. It was admiration; watery eyes looking at someone who provided answers. Like a mother seeing her child for the first time, or that grown child watching their favorite ballplayer lumber to the mound.

Bill set down the animal and placed his hands on his hips. "Hello, everybody."

The group turned to Lorena. She approached Bill and hugged him. She was crying. "Bill, we wanna go from here. It's not safe."

He held Lorena and looked around at the group that had become more than a family. The men leaned on their rifles while the women sat. Not far off, Raul and the other children shouted and chased after a soccer ball. *They* were the answer. They would free him from his shackles; no more ball and chain.

Bill squatted down and patted the dry ground. The mountains loomed overhead, gray rain clouds hanging above. He swiped his hand in the dirt and felt a drop of rain hit his neck. *Just wait for the first drop. You'll know then.*

Bill gazed up at the clouds. Lightning danced somewhere within. A storm was coming, riding the wind from the mountains. He plugged his thumbs into the belt loops of his jeans and smiled.

"Then we'll go."

The group of survivors straightened at his simple solution. They stirred from their seats and began wondering aloud where they would go. Bill already knew which direction.

The storm rolled over them. A flash of lighting signaled the start of the rain. It fell in sheets, hydrating the unaccustomed desert, immediately forming a slurry of dust and water underneath Bill's boots.

No one sought dryness or comfort. Bill's followers gathered around him and raised their arms toward the sky. He closed his eyes and let the water clean out his tear ducts. It felt wonderful. He felt pure, nourished, and loved. Reborn. He would lead his village north then west—always west.

XII

SKYRAIL FINALIZED Adam's trafficking. Illinois, Kansas, Colorado, Utah—they ditched one polity for the next every few hours. Appalachia, the Midwest, the Great Plains, then the West itself, all of it one sliding panorama of hill and river, mountain and desert.

The journey took just shy of twenty-four hours to complete. Adam slept intermittently, snacking on chocolate-covered cashews and salted crisps upon waking before he would inevitably pass out again. The entire train car was at his disposal, a far cry from his father's cold, windowless earth-boring boxes.

SkyRail was designed to exhilarate the passenger. The siding on each train car was floor-to-ceiling glass, allowing one to absorb the flowing scenery as it whizzed past. Las Vegas woke Adam with violent enthusiasm, brilliant lights and fireworks illuminating the train's interior red, green, and purple. He sat up in his plushy reclining chair and gazed at the convulsing lights until the city's irradiant glow submitted to the vast desert.

The sun rose unexpectedly over the desert horizon about an hour later. A presentable waiter wearing a SkyRail uniform entered and presented a metal dish to him: "Poached salmon with a quiche of spinach, potato, and chevre. Enjoy," the waiter said succinctly. Adam almost stopped the waiter to ask him what LA was like, but he feared muddying his first impressions of the city with someone else's point of view; better to judge it for himself. He knew it would take some time before his new home truly felt like one. He had eaten his fair share of anti-West propaganda. Even though his father was open with him about it being all puffery, still, deeply supplanted in his subconscious was fear, even *revulsion* of the allegedly God-hating, anarchic culture of the West. "Frog" had unwillingly become a tool in his vocabulary.

Adam enjoyed his breakfast slowly, peering out the window into the brightening sky. He briefly wondered whether he would repeat the trip, albeit on a train headed in the opposite direction. LA, not time, would tell.

◆

LA was a different beast from Vegas. LA was invisible. It revealed itself gradually. It made Adam anxious, watching out the window, waiting. First, there was nothing but desert. Then came a dribbling of homes, a smattering. Next came a difficult-to-discern barrage of towns, incorporated places, and villages. Last, finally, came a city replete with skyscrapers and busy streets, as was customary.

The conductor announced their arrival via intercom. *Welcome to beautiful and sunny Los Angeles! We ask that all passengers present a verifiable form of identification before deboarding. Enjoy your stay, and thank you for traveling with SkyRail: Here for you, there for you! … ¡Bienvenidos a …*

Neither set of escalators was running, so Adam had to climb the dusty marble stairs leading out of the cave-like depot. He shielded his eyes from the brilliant afternoon rays as he emerged.

The sun warmed his skin, but different from the UV lamps in the Subterranean. This felt real, *alive.* He removed his cotton sweatshirt to soak in the feeling.

The station was empty, save a few commuters waiting on benches, mindlessly checking their Loops. Adam took out the lone sheet of paper left inside the envelope Isabel had thrust at him before he left. It'd contained his tickets and other documents needed to board the train. He reread the message sprawled over the paper and crumpled it back into his pocket.

A grand fountain recycled water at the station's center, and the fine mist it produced drew a silhouette around its base. The fountains no longer ran in Pittsburgh; certainly not above ground. They'd only collected rain since the flood. Two homeless women were lounging in the mist's path. *Never neglect disaster*, Adam thought, one of Bill Edenson's tenets from *Sympathies*. Adam studied his grandpa's writings from his quarters in Pittsburgh while preparing for the journey. It'd been difficult for him to secure the forbidden texts; difficult, but not impossible. His excursions to the Business District as a teenager were not all in vain. For example, he learned that the man who kept bar at Dowery Street Saloon also dealt in contraband from time to time, contraband such as (but certainly not limited to) Western scripture. He'd given Adam an odd smile when he requested the book.

Adam stuffed his hands into his pockets as he passed by. The women more closely resembled female hunter-gatherers transported from prehistoric times than they did common vagrants. They were dressed in dusty leather and wool that lay in loose heaps over their hungry physiques. Their bellies were exposed, and they wore their hair shaved on one side.

One of them spat in Adam's direction while the other stood and pointed. "You're blind!" the woman cried out fervently. "Free yourself from your idols! *Denounce!*" A few curious necks twitched at the disturbance before returning to the entertainment being beamed via satellite to their Loops. Adam quickly escaped down the nearest sidewalk. When he glanced back over his shoulder, the woman had sat back down with her partner in the drool of mist.

He walked ten blocks before inadvertently landing in what he quickly figured was downtown L.A. It bore little in common with the seedy glitz and glamour of the Business District. The once-gleaming skyscrapers had taken their fair share of neglect and now looked dilapidated and confused. Adam peered inside lobby after lobby: lobbies of office buildings, lobbies of hotels, lobbies of banks, lobbies of theaters. They sat eerily empty, their interiors fallen into disuse. Adam couldn't help but feel out of place. He knew he probably looked the part, too.

The concrete jungle gradually dispersed until he passed by a fenced encampment that appeared to have once been a public park. Gusts of music and marijuana drifted by. And other sights, sounds, and smells: an old lady sat stationed just outside the fence, hacking meat off two goats charring over hot coals and stuffing it into grease-stained tortillas; pastel-colored birds with long, pluming tails cooed lightly from the palm trees lining the sidewalk; a gentleman wearing a suit deftly chopped a great variety of fruits and arranged them neatly on top of brilliantly colored sorbets.

A dizzying array of cars yawned along the confoundingly well-kept streets, more in one place than Adam had ever seen before. They were products of assorted bits and scraps from different models; a headlight here, a piston there. Whatever fits in the right places. As a result, no two cars were alike. One driver rolled down his window and shouted at Adam in rapid Spanish. Adam stared back as he drove past.

Amongst these sights was a great deal of destitution. A skinny girl no older than ten sat amongst her belongings in the street, holding her palm out for donations. Her arms and face were deeply tanned by the sun and dotted with bruises. Adam pressed a heavy steel coin into her palm. She looked at the object curiously, turning it in her fingers.

He passed at least ten other children undergoing the same desolation, and Adam's mood turned sour. *This wouldn't happen in Pittsburgh*, he thought angrily before realizing that this was the Chief's voice speaking, not his. He chased away the thought and remembered Miguel and his daughter. *Never neglect disaster, but recognize that it exists everywhere. Sympathies*, Book 2, Passage 14.

The slowly rotating LED barber's pole almost struck him in the face; he had been looking down, minding the uneven gaps in the sidewalk. The placard above the pole read *Sirelis Barbershop*. Adam patted the crumbled envelope in his pocket and walked in the front door to a pleasant *ding!*

The place smelled of hashish and aftershave. A lone barber stood sweeping the floor. He was tall, fat, and dressed in an oddly befitting pairing of track pants and loafers. His neck snapped when he heard the door open. When he saw Adam standing there awkwardly, he smiled and extended his arms, revealing sweat-stained pockets on his body. He wrapped him in a squishy hug, his reeking cologne striking him full-stop. "Water Is Life."

Adam managed a meek *Thanks*, feeling tiny in the giant man's grasp. But at least his words were comforting.

"Have a seat," he said, gesturing Adam to a black leather chair.

"Thank you." Adam sat back in the plush leather chair, somewhat relieved. He eyed his uneven shag in the mirror.

The man suffered a sudden coughing fit and recovered by pounding his fist against his chest. "'Scuse me." He unwrapped a cough drop from his pocket and began sucking on it violently. He swiftly covered Adam in a gown. "I'm Deron, by the way. Nice-to-meet-you. So, we goin' to meet the sparrow?" he asked casually.

"Yes." Adam frowned, unable to help but notice what pronoun he'd elected for. The paper hadn't mentioned the barber would also be in the loop, only that he would make him look presentable for his host.

Deron coughed again (this time away from Adam's ear) and apologized under his breath. A set of clippers buzzed to life, which he flicked with aggressive precision around Adam's ears. He paused to inhale from an electronic pipe in his pocket, which explained the hash odor. He politely blew the smoke behind him before resuming his work.

"How long have you been in business?" Adam asked politely. He was curious how the man remained sober enough to bring sharp objects close to people's necks.

"Goin' on four years now. Business is a-ight. Get lots of locals, kids from the block and such ... nothin' too crazy." He craned his neck and took a swipe at Adam's forehead. "So, Daddy Bill was your grandpa, eh?"

Adam nodded his head lightly. "Yes. I was born in Pittsburgh, though."

"Izzy didn't say nothin' bout that." Deron gripped the back of Adam's chair with one hand and felt his chest as if he were having heart palpitations. "Pittsburgh ... That's some crazy shit. Heard folks livin' underground out there and shit. What's it like?"

"It's easy to get used to what's around you." He changed the subject. "Anything I should know before this meeting? About the sparrow," he clarified, glancing once at the door.

Deron cleared his throat. "I mean ... everyone around here knows the guy. He don't come out like he used to. I know guys out in East LA are always complaining 'bout how he thinks he's hot shit. But, I mean, he's just about running the whole joint now, so what the fuck they expect? He ain't got the *time* to hang no more. He's too big for that." Deron stepped back to inspect his progress. "Dude's a savage though," he muttered.

Adam locked eyes with Deron in the mirror, trying to neglect his half-cut hair. "Like how?"

"Like the fuckin' boogeyman." He laughed at the shift in Adam's face. "Nah. Most people love the guy. I respect the hell outta him. Helped me get a loan to open this place. On God. I don't know what things be like in Pittsburgh, but nothin' comes easy 'round here. Not like people think." Adam nodded lightly so not to earn a gash in his head. He stayed quiet then, thinking about what the meeting might bring.

Deron began to vent about his latest altercation playing pickup, which transitioned to a comprehensive retelling of the Laker dynasty. Adam listened faintly, nodding in agreement when it felt appropriate. He had no perceived wisdom on the purple and gold. "Kobe *Bean* Bryant. Man was unlike anyone our sorry asses'll ever see again. No one hoops like that no more." Just like the ganja, his excitement did not impact the smooth shave he treated him to.

When he determined his work was finished, Deron rubbed/slapped Adam's neck and shoulders with a freshening ointment. A hot towel landed in his lap. He looked at himself in the mirror. He looked good, clean; perhaps even exquisite. Adam stood and went to pay him, but the big man shook his head and pulled Adam into a swift, squishy embrace. "Good luck, Father." Adam thought he might've heard some doubt in his voice. He let the noisy door swing shut behind him and faced the street.

A long, black Mercedes pulled up to the curb within moments of him stepping onto the pavement. It paused momentarily with its silent engine still running before the driver exited and looped around the nose of the car to open the back door for him. "Mr. Martínez is ready for you," the driver said in a bored-sounding voice, gesturing him inside.

Adam blinked. He thanked the driver, shaking away what doubt remained within him, and slid into the back seat.

◆

The Mercedes made quick work of the hills, eventually working its way up an impressively long driveway studded with hydrangeas. The house at the top of the hill was no less impressive than its drive. It was styled after an old Italian or French villa, rectangular with several balconies and windows open to let in the pleasant breeze. Adam's escort, who had been silent throughout the entire trip, simply nodded to him when they'd arrived.

He was greeted before he had the chance to knock by a middle-aged woman with flawless skin. "Bienvenidos," she said, scanning Adam from head to toe. She smiled, revealing a large but attractive gap between her front teeth. "Jus' a minute, honey," the woman purred before turning in the doorframe. "*¡Ay! ¡Visitantes!*" She received no verbal response, which was apparently a sign of affirmation. She held the door open. "Please, come in. Sit, and I will make some coffees."

The living room was tall and white and sparsely dressed in neat and uncomfortable furniture. Adam sat awkwardly on a white leather couch in the frosty living room. An abstract painting of a squid (*Or maybe an octopus?* Adam hypothesized while staring at it) eyeballed him from above a white-tiled mantle. A stove clicked on.

Moments later, the woman came out carrying a tray of coffee and snacks. Adam thanked her and politely nibbled on his biscotti. "So, what brings you to see my husband today?" the woman asked sweetly.

"An introduction," Adam said tersely, folding his leg.

The woman smiled long again at him and blew into her hot tea. "Well, I hope you enjoy his company. My husband is an excellent communicator. It's one of his few good traits." She winked, her lips curling as she blew into her steaming mug. "Do you feel comfortable? Please, I want you to feel at home. This is your home as much as it is ours." Adam took in the room's empty whiteness and scoffed. *More like a blank canvas.*

"Yes. Thank you for your hospitality," he said with a phony smile. "I don't mean to sound short with you, Mrs. ...?"

"No need. Just Carmen," she purred.

"Carmen." Adam took a brave sip from his mug. The brew was deathly sweet and scented with cinnamon. "But it's been a long trip. I'm sure your husband's been waiting."

"Yes, of course. Just a moment." The woman trotted upstairs to communicate with her spouse. Adam clasped his hands between his thighs and let out a loose exhale.

"He's ready to see you now," she announced upon returning. The woman sat back down with her tea in hand and crinkled her eyes at Adam. "Good luck," she said, smiling at him.

The spiraling staircase led to a simple hall ending with a door made entirely of tinted glass. A tall black man in quasi-military garb gave him the nod to approach. He demonstrated a pose and quickly patted Adam down before opening the silent door for him.

The office was dimmed to match the persistent jazz playing over the surround sound. The dual musks of leather and dark chocolate immediately assaulted Adam. Directly in front of him was a wall about two meters wide, centered by a secretary cabinet and a print of *The Fall of Man* hanging above. There were identical archways carved into either side. Adam stepped to the right and entered the greater room, where Juan Carlos Paoli Martínez awaited him. He stood to one side of an ornate desk, jewel-encrusted paw *tapp*ing at its surface.

"Adam," he said simply, raising his arm toward the armchair opposite his. He flapped his arm back down and stood expectantly. His handshake was thin but sturdy. Adam took a seat opposite the sparrow and relaxed his shoulders. "Welcome. You're finally home."

"Thank you." Adam eyed the elongated bowl that fronted the desk warily. It was filled to the brim with identical foil-wrapped chocolates:

tiny, green cubes with a drawing of a hazelnut painted on their exterior. Juan Carlos took notice.

"Please, help yourself." Adam shook his head. The sparrow reached and casually plucked one from the bowl, unwrapping it precisely and popping it into his mouth, where it disappeared with a single *crunch*. He sipped politely from a crystal glass filled with water. "Can I offer you something to drink? I know it's been an *arduous* journey." He placed emphasis on the word, as if it pained him more than it had Adam. Adam shook his head.

"Your wife was more than gracious downstairs."

He waved his hand dismissively. "Yes. Good. Well then, I must ask, what were your first impressions of our beautiful city?"

Adam smiled lightly. It was a natural reaction; his voice was pleasing to the ears, gentle and tinted by a forgotten accent. "Unexpected. I had envisioned chaos by the way we're taught in the East. I knew better, but still ... It's unlike anything I've ever seen. I've never seen a city so spread apart."

The sparrow pouted lightly as if this did not match his desired response. "Yes, this sets us apart from most other towns. It certainly presents its challenges ... It has its benefits too, I suppose."

Adam felt like he'd said something wrong. "I'm sure it does. But diversity can be a strength. We don't emphasize it out East. We try to hide it."

His answer still did not seem to appease him. "*They.* Not we. You're one of us now, Adam." His hands fluttered for a crystalline decanter. He poured two shallow glasses full of liquor. "A toast. To Los Angeles, to the West. To our united future." He slid Adam's glass toward him. "Water Is Life." He stood, and they raised glasses.

"Water Is Life."

♦

"I sent for you for two reasons," Juan Carlos spelled out. Adam listened closely, his eyes focused on the engraved lines in his glass. "I'm sure you already are aware of the first. I recognize the Chief's feelings toward the West. Am I being accurate in saying that the feeling is contentious?"

"Yes." It was only partly true. Although George had no love for the West, he never spoke openly against them either. The propaganda feeds labeling them as poison-worshipping radicals were not even a direct reflection of George's beliefs. He simply understood the value of setting people's sights on an "unknown," an enemy with whom they shared nothing in common.

"Mm." The sparrow set down his glass. "Are you also aware that he plans to mount a campaign against his own government?"

Adam folded his hands in his lap. "There were rumors he was building a secret police. A few board members had noticed some strings being pulled in the budget. We didn't speak about it." The sparrow nodded understandingly. "One of them tracked us through the Subterranean. Me and the fox. She, uh ..." He remembered the fine mist on Isabel's jacket. The canal had been so polluted that the blood seeping from his armor didn't tarnish its color when the two intermixed. "She protected us," Adam finished.

Juan Carlos smiled vaguely. The fox told him news that was otherwise lost to the wind: *The Chief has bought out the Anti-Terror Committee, He's paying MARS Group with his vote, He's building himself an army of IMPs.* "What you and my goddaughter evaded was only the tip of the iceberg."

Goddaughter? Adam hoped he hadn't noticed his ears perk. Either he hadn't, or Juan Carlos didn't care to see. He cleared his throat. "Even before you escaped, he was already planning to launch a coup. The signs are apparent: he's doubled his propaganda efforts in the past twelve months. Support for him has nearly doubled, fittingly enough, while support for the New Colonies has only decreased since. And it is not a secret police he is amassing; it is an army, to be more precise. The troops come from the capital. They lose a man for each man he gains."

"It's power," Adam answered confidently. "He's obsessed with power." *Amongst other things,* he thought privately. Knowing the Chief's concern with his legacy, his true intent may have been for Adam to take lead of the insurrection. *That* would've been a chance to prove himself an apt Chief-in-line, no doubt ...

"So are most men." Juan Carlos smiled sheepishly and sipped from his glass. "We have increased our military presence in the Mississippi Neutrality Zone and beyond in anticipation of an imminent change. But still, Pittsburgh is well beyond our jurisdiction. Our support is numbered there, and our attempts at direct diplomacy thus far have been ignored." The rust-colored light danced in Adam's glass, ice and curves. "It was not suitable for you to live under such conditions," he said, sounding oddly sympathetic.

Adam shook his head, ignoring the last tidbit. "Things will only get worse now that I'm gone." He blinked. "It's not too late, though. If the Colonies hear us out, we could form an alliance and stop the coup before it—"

"Please, Adam. I do not mean to interrupt, but I fear you may not quite understand the second reason to its fullest extent. It alters our position; ours *and* yours. Allow me to explain."

Adam nodded once. "Go ahead."

He did.

"The West is not united. We are a loose conglomeration of sorts— tribes, you might say. Although some may classify me as a figurehead of sorts, in reality, I only represent one such 'tribe' within this conglomeration. I have no delusions of grandeur."

Adam nodded slowly. "I understand. The West is diverse. It's not easy to bring so many people together."

The sparrow nodded in agreement. "For the past decade it has been impossible to organize any bipartisan force to combat the East's antics. But there is one thing the West unanimously treasures; one cause we could unite under. Do you know what that is?"

Adam nodded. "Water Is Life. Bill's founding principle."

"*Father* Bill." The sparrow sipped cautiously from his glass. "Your grandfather was the only thing that kept the Alliance glued together. The Way dissolved after his assassination, and the West with it. Given that he named no successor ... things became uncertain." He set down his glass and stared into Adam's eyes. "Until now," he said, his eyes never breaking. "Father Bill's blood is in you. But what does this mean now, *here*, to us, where we sit? Look at us! A half-warranted leader and an escaped prince; what is our purpose?"

Decisions, selfish, instinctual. Words that seem weightless in the moment. Inconsequential, like an addict's nightly decision to feed their inner demon.

"Our purpose is to change the system," Adam replied. "People are sick of tyranny. They just haven't realized it yet. Nothing will change unless people know *why* I left. If we just show them what it's really like here, they'll see through the lies—"

"Stop saying *left*!" The sparrow stood from his chair. "You left *nothing*, Adam. One does not leave a place that was never home. One can only escape. Your place is here, in the West. You are no longer tied to the East, its people, or its politics." His stare softened. "Tell me your name."

Adam sipped hesitantly from his glass. It tasted like brandy, all sticky caramel and oak. He cleared his throat but couldn't grasp any words. The sparrow spoke for him.

"You are not the last Crombie. That name never belonged to you. You are the Untold. You were born to show us the Way." Juan Carlos looped around his desk and gripped Adam's shoulder. He flinched at his touch. "It's past time you changed your name."

Part III

Man, you don't know how I felt that afternoon when I heard that VOICE and it was my own VOICE.

– Muddy Waters

INTERLUDE

October 28, 2025

Hempstead, Long Island, New York, United States of America

ON OCTOBER 28, the deluge resumed course.

Every chance He could, God sent rain that fell in sheets and filled the streets. It did not deter those with a propensity for danger and invention from attempting to flee the city. A few tried outsmarting the rain in crude floats made of apartment scraps. Only a few did not join the flood.

It has to stop soon, was a common conclusion made by fools and great minds alike. *I mean, it can only rain so much.*

Whispers began to circulate about the flood's impact across the country. *They moved the capital to Atlanta. Fucking Atlanta. That means it'll stay dry there, right?*

You hear about Niagara Falls? Belongs to Lake Erie now. At least that's what my cousin said. He's a waiter up there, so.

Rain, rain, go away, come again some other day.

The rain was indifferent. God was indifferent. It poured on until the sixth day of November.

After the rain left, a ray of cheerful sunshine that seemed to mock the survivors took its place. Few were excited by the sun's sudden reemergence. The rain had already made its mark. The world had become its basin.

Those responsible for keeping track of the death toll lost track of the death toll. The living stopped burying their dead. The flood barred such formalities.

◆

Remember that game we used to play? The one where you bounce the ball and have to catch it before it hits the ground again?

Yeah.

What was it called again?

Tyler snapped awake. "Aaron?" he groaned in the dark. Rain pattered outside the window. He slid his head up and down against the tile just in case his brother was there, but he wasn't. Of course he wasn't. Aaron was dead. Had been. He'd died of a heroin overdose, and Tyler hadn't known.

Tyler succumbed to the pins-and-needles feeling of numbness and slacked against the floor. His eyes were bloated and painful, but he did not care. His jaw felt like someone had sewn it shut with iron thread, but he did not care. A gruesome crust of blood coated his shoulder, and it felt apt to catch fire, but he did not care. His every instinct told him to lie there and die painlessly. Instead, he splayed on his elbow right and inch-wormed his way into his living room, crying out each time his shoulder moved in the slightest. He reached the couch and slugged up its face, and stayed there.

Tyler sweated and shook throughout the night. The rain kept coming. He woke up once to some relief and drank copious amounts of tap water, indifferent to the citywide boil order. He repeatedly tried calling his father's cell. He repeatedly got the same no-answer: *At the tone, please record your message. When you have finished recording, press 1, or hang up for more options.* The rain kept coming. Tyler returned to the couch's saggy embrace.

Pitter-patter. The rain did not stop until the water crashed through his bay window, his studio apartment's lone luxury, and flooded the apartment. The water rose to touch the couch cushions. Tyler did not notice. He saw with eyes blinded.

But fate had more in store for Tyler Haji than death by drowning or exsanguination.

October 29, 2025

A ripple danced on the ceiling. Tyler gaped at the dancing figure, his eyes black marbles set inside yellow-tinted whites. The reflection of water— *Water! Ah, yes.* Water from the Atlantic, summer trips to Monmouth Beach. Vanilla Mister Softees. Boogie boarding with his brother. Stumbling in the wet sand, laughing. Kissing Natalie Martinez on the pier. *Good times.* The ripples swirled and multiplied, a quiet symphony that enveloped his body.

Tyler shuddered. *Cold.* He knew it was cold, but his body was lying to him. He could not feel its sting. How does one know if it's cold when they cannot feel?

Get up, stupid, a voice half his own chimed. It was time to get up. Tyler tried lifting his foot. It didn't obey the command. His bones ached. He was convinced they would snap if he made the slightest movement. *Move, you prick.* Tyler groaned. *What were you thinking, going with her?* the voice mocked. *It's too late. Too late for you, man.*

I know. He decided then to accept death's merciful embrace and let the ripple on the ceiling wash over him. He groaned and clenched his jaw. His jugular bulged, threatening to burst through his skin. The ripple leaned down to grasp him and suddenly adopted a woman's shape. *Allison?* She smiled and swept her hair to the side. "That's not your hair," Tyler mumbled. The woman blew a kiss and turned and walked away, shrinking in size until it escaped the confines of his apartment. "Wait." The woman kept walking until she'd shrunk into an indistinguishable speck of light, joining the rest of the pointless dots on his textured ceiling. *She's gone, man. Gone, baby, gone.* He felt abandoned.

Tyler stared at the ceiling until his vision faded. He spun out of consciousness and into a land called Memoria.

♦

Memoria was windy and covered in sand.

"¿Nadie te dijo que tal son las cosas aquí?"

Tyler shielded his stomach and dry hurled onto the sand. A second foot slammed against his ribs. Tears stung his eyes.

"Stand up, bitch."

Tyler feebly came to his knees, blind and stumbling. A hard push from his rear sent him tumbling down again. He found shelter in the sand and braced himself for another kick. It never came.

"*Coño!*"

His assaulters scrambled in three directions. He waited before looking up and saw their retreating footprints in the sand. Tyler rubbed the grit from his eyes and mouth and stood. He tried to inhale and doubled over in pain, clutching his belly. He began shambling down the beach alone.

He made it a few paces away from the crime scene before a sturdy hand gripped his shoulder. Tyler spun on instinct, fists raised to defend himself if need be. He closed his eyes and waited for a fist to come careening into his nose. Nothing happened. A snickering voice queried him: "What kinda stupid shit ya gots to do to catch an ass beatin' like that?"

Tyler fought the hand on his shoulder and yelped at the pain that stabbed him underneath his ribs. The hand retreated willingly enough. He squinted up at the person who'd confronted him. The man was tall, black, and thin like a rail. His eyes were like hollow sockets, shaded behind thick-rimmed sunglasses. Tyler saw his reflection in them. "I kissed a girl."

"Sounds like you done went and kissed the wrong fuckin' broad. You fuckin' around with somebody else's broad?"

Tyler blinked. "Their sister ..." he managed before he went into a coughing fit.

"Shiiiiyut ... Serves you right." The man laughed and knelt down to meet Tyler's eyes. He offered to bump fists. "All good. I'm just playin' witchu, my man." The man grinned widely. "My man. My fuckin' man!" The sun's glare intensified and glinted off the man's shades. Tyler shielded his eyes.

Memoria was climate-controlled and traditionally furnished.

When he moved his forearm, he was sitting at home, eating dinner, his father chewing aggressively beside him. Tyler stared at his overworked jaw, watching his throat tighten and contract like a bird as he swallowed. He kept on eating, undisturbed by his son's gaze. Tyler looked down at his untouched leathery T-bone.

He turned to his right and saw his mother sipping politely from her wine glass. She set it down and stared glassily at the near-empty bottle serving as the table's centerpiece. Her eyes suddenly sharpened. "Mind yourself, Tyler. Pick up your knife." Tyler moved for his napkin and gasped at the sudden pain in his shoulder. His fork and knife clattered to the floor.

"Goddamnit, Tyler! How many times do I have to—elbows off the table!"

Tyler shrunk into his chair and looked to his father, but he was still chewing. He bent over to pick up his silverware, neglecting the pain reverberating along his side. He returned his knife to its proper place and wiped his nose.

"Tyler," his mother *tsk*ed. Tyler avoided her and looked down at his plate. "Won't you ever learn?"

When he looked up, his mother had changed. She had adopted the high-protruding forehead of the devil. Her nose was severed to reveal two upturned holes. A forked tongue darted between twin pointed fangs, and her eyes gleamed with hellfire.

She dove across the table, grasping for Tyler's throat. Tyler slid from his chair and hid underneath the tablecloth. He clutched his legs to his chest and sobbed, quivering as plates and glassware shattered around him. "YOU COULD'VE STOPPED IT!" the harpy screeched from above. "YOU LEFT ME ALONE! LEFT ME ALL ALONE!" Tyler shut his eyes and hugged himself. His father's feet remained at ease.

Memoria was Tartarus.

When he opened his eyes, he was in utero. A black expanse surrounded him. A phone rang. He couldn't move his arms, but he felt his muscles twitch as if to answer. "Hello?" he heard himself say. No answer came. A faint buzzing noise surrounded him. "Hello?"

A nasally voice rolled toward him, growing louder the closer it came. Tyler looked in its direction; "TWOOOO butterflied pork chops, mashed potatoes with white gravy—hold the veg! Salad with ranch." Tyler tried to speak. "Aye! Have 'em put a little shredded cheese on there for me, will ya?"

The voice warped the space in front of him like a shadowy echocardiogram. Tyler furrowed his brow, the ink twisting like a slow-spinning record. His mouth did not move, but he heard his own voice respond: "Okay. Will that be all, sir?"

"I believe so."

"Name?"

"LUCY!"

"Could you spell that?"

"L-U-C-Y. How else would you spell it?"

"Um, I wasn't sure if it was your first name or last."

"Why's that?"

"It's just—you sounded like a guy, so ..."

"*So?* Why should that matter? Boy, you racist or somethin'?"

"What? No. I've just never met a guy named Lucy."

The blackness compressed like smoke being sucked up through a straw and rolled to the spot where the voice had originated. It warped and spun before taking the form of a huge parrot; it craned its neck and peered down at Tyler with beady eyes. Its beak suddenly snapped open and its oily tongue came at him. Tyler scrunched his eyes and yelped before its jaws snapped shut over his head.

He opened his eyes; the bird's jaws hovered open just above him. Instead of devouring him, the man's voice echoed from within: "Well, I'll be goddamned!"

A huge gong reverberated through the space, tearing ripples through the ink. Tyler tried covering his ears but was paralyzed. The gong sounded again. The noise shook Tyler's brain like he was the brass being struck. He groaned.

The parrot hopped over and dipped its head to gaze at Tyler, its neck twitching. The gong shook him again, louder. Tyler cried out incoherently. The bird spoke: "Time's up! *SQUAWK!*

The gong became a steady vibration beneath his skull. "Stop it! Make it stop!" The bird danced on its creepy bony feet.

"Time up! Time up!"

"Make it stop!"

"Make it stop!" the parrot mocked him, the sound recorded from his cries. *"Stop! Stop!"* Tyler opened his mouth to scream, but the sound did not escape him. Instead, it shook the space around him, as though his thoughts were plugged into some kind of ethereal surround sound. Tyler clenched his eyes. *Wake up,* he thought. *Wake up. Wake up.*

The parrot leaned down, nearly poking Tyler's eye out with its beak. *"Wake up?"* it teased. *Please,* Tyler thought.

An invisible force suddenly dragged him up and away from the darkness. He gasped for air and watched his feet emerge last from the murky pit.

A trickle of water streamed down his forehead as Tyler gasped for air. He was lying on his couch, staring up at his ceiling. There was no bird. His heart pounded. *It's over*, he thought, relieved. He exhaled slowly.

Tyler rolled onto his side and yelped; his apartment was flooded under two feet of water.

A loud voice boomed inside the tiny apartment. This time, Tyler was certain it was real. Tyler twisted and got tripped up in the couch cushions and went tumbling into the freezing water. The voice was identical to the parrot's: "Got *TOO-bo?*"

Tyler splashed about in a panic and kneeled, leaning against the couch's soggy bottom. He wiped his eyes and found a man, not a bird, towering over him. He was grinning at him; *down* at him. He was comically tall, wearing gleaming rimless sunglasses. "*Too-bo?*" he repeated, as if the word made more sense by itself.

Tyler shook his head, puzzled. His teeth chattered. The man's grin stayed, small teeth stained from what appeared to be a years-long dependency on coffee, nicotine, and sugar. "Close call, huh? Yer lucky I happened to be floatin'-a-by!"

Tyler nodded and hugged himself. His shoulders trembled from the cold. He tried to speak, but his throat was unwilling to cooperate. The man bent forward and frowned, leaning on a long wooden pole that resembled an old closet rod. "That don't look good," he muttered, eyeing the crusted-over mess underneath Tyler's ragged t-shirt. "Alright, hold on. I'll go get m'buoy."

M'buoy? Tyler thought to ask, but his tongue would not move.

The man waded toward the bay window and began towing in a rope he had anchored there. Tyler glanced around at what had once been his apartment. The window seemed to sit lower than before, he thought before seeing that the flood was not unique to his apartment. Outside, the water extended into a gray, murky pool that covered all.

"Brooks is the name!" the man hollered from the window. "B-R-O-O-K-S. Spelled like it's said. Got it?"

Tyler swallowed dryly and croaked. "Waaaat—?" The word caught midway in his throat, the second vowel made impossible by his thirst. Still, Brooks seemed to understand. He sucked his teeth and took a bounding step toward Tyler. A thin, vague shape sliced the water where his leg should've moved. *Am I awake?* Tyler questioned. His brain, which screamed for warmth and hydration, suggested otherwise. After another step, Tyler understood the true cause behind the man's seemingly impossible height. He was balancing on top of makeshift stilts of some sort, leaning on the closet rod to balance himself like a human tripod. He wore wader boots so his legs would remain dry where the stilts attached.

Brooks swept his arm dramatically in a circle about the room. "Yes, my friend! Mucho agua! More agua'n we'll need for a long fuckin' time."

He crouched slightly and directed a piece of flotsam toward him. Tyler comprehended and slouched his torso over the floating junk. When he was secure, Brooks gently glided him out the window toward his buoy docked outside.

The green-gray of Queens's newly formed canals dominated Tyler's field of vision. Brooks kept talking in his loud Southern drawl, but his words did not register. The greenness spread until it took hold of Tyler's vision. By the time he remembered to ask him where the water had come from, his face had gone numb. "Good times," Tyler slurred before he lost consciousness.

XIII

THE SECOND man did not stop to introduce himself.

Tyler stumbled through the woods and fought exhaustion until his legs could take him no farther. He found a stream that ran clear enough and kneeled in the mud and drank indifferently, then sat back against a tree and closed his eyes. Before long, he had fallen into a blissful, dreamless sleep.

He awoke to the sun beginning to crest above the horizon. He scratched the wiry hairs covering his crestfallen cheeks. The dawn was gray, foggy, and wet with dew, flora and fauna performing their loud and abrupt post-winter wakening ceremonies. Tyler stood and stretched, grimacing at his knees popping, and ate what remained of the half-spoiled foodstuffs the busker had carried. When he was finished, he began hiking opposite the stream's gentle current.

The stream seemed to begin and end nowhere. It fizzled out at the hill's crest, which was marked by a steep drop-off overlooking a mess of roads below. It was a dead end. Tyler winced at the thought of hiking back down and around. After poking around in the brush, he found a practicable enough path down the cliff that he could maneuver. He minded his steps carefully, the ground damp and loose under his mildewy boots. He breathed a quiet *sigh* of relief when his feet finally met the road.

His footsteps sounded odd to him, boots stamping along the cracked asphalt. He had not touched concrete since their last deployment in the Capital District proper. *You mean your last deployment?* the voice teased him, for he was alone now.

The fog obscured what lay ahead of him. He shivered at the thought of Crunch and Ed's ghosts trailing him in the mist. The sound of his own footsteps echoed along the steep earthen walls that sandwiched the road, trailing him, growing louder, closer—

Get a hold of yourself, Haj. He checked the GeoLoop to distract him from his delusions, cocking his head to favor his good eye. The left had swollen shut and was painful to touch; the music man's good work.

The Loop showed he was due south. He watched it slowly orient west as he continued along the winding path. *The world is your oyster,* he thought grimly. Technology was never a luxury afforded to him as an amphitrooper (which he supposed he technically still was. He had not been discharged him; only his squad mates were). The Colonies and their taxpayers saw little value in equipping their soldiers with equipment beyond basic rifles, boots, and underwear. Despite being dubbed "*The Colonies' single greatest fighting force*" (or so the commercials seeking to inspire young boys to become soldiers claimed), it was an uncommon sight to see an amphitrooper wearing a base-end Loop, much less one equipped with advanced radar technology. Word was that United Tech didn't want their products supporting soldiers who performed "unsavory" deeds. To the best of Tyler's knowledge, most of the high-end models (such as the one he wore now) were reserved for high-ranking officials who never used them in the field and went home every night to their spouse, warm dinner, and goose feather pillows. Meanwhile, troopers toiled with maps and compasses and slept in flea-infested sleeping rolls. The closest they ever got to a warm dinner was the unanimously lauded Beef Stew MRE kit, which, though comparatively better than the others, still resembled dog food at its finest.

He peered down at the glowing gem at his wrist. The fog was growing with the day and had drawn so tight that the screen's hue seemed hazier than before. According to the GPS, the path eventually merged with a still-intact highway that ran north-south from the C.D. to Richmond. According to the GeoLoop's estimations, it was also mostly free of impassable portions, making it possible (in theory if not in practice) to cruise at one's leisure.

Tyler frowned. He could walk, he supposed. Still, being exposed to any sort of traffic, sparse or otherwise, was not ideal for a fugitive. It was not as though he had another choice. Personal vehicles were mostly abandoned after the flood, save in a select few quadrants within the Capital District and George Crombie's bewilderingly manicured underground city. This was due (amongst various other contributing factors) to the lack of a steady gasoline supply, the irreplicable damage to bridges and roadways, and the lack of a workforce to maintain them. The ghastly, forgotten steel shells of those who'd attempted escape from the flood were everywhere, most prominently alongside major roadways. Most of them carried passengers whose flesh had rotted away or been scavenged by roving animals.

It made no difference where he went, he realized as he walked. West and south were all that mattered. West and south, away from Vernon and the Capital District. Away from anything and everything he'd ever known.

BONK

"*SHI—!*" Tyler's boots flitted in the air like he'd been shocked with jumper cables. The sudden noise the GeoLoop emitted was adjoined by an angry, almost *painful* haptic feedback. It'd notified him, in any case.

The screen was flashing from black to red: *MOTION DETECTED.*

Tyler spun his head on a swivel. Nothing stirred except the low-hanging mist flanking the road on either side. He frowned and wondered whether the fog had screwed up its sensors. Regardless of if it had or hadn't, it showed no sign of stopping: *BONK ... BONK.*

"Piece of shit," Tyler muttered. Then he heard a sound that would very much indicate the GeoLoop had not malfunctioned: the *ca-lop* of hooves on pavement. He paused and listened.

The sound was coming toward him.

Tyler searched for a place to hide and quickly realized there *was* nowhere to hide. The fog was the only hiding spot on offer. The bluffs entrapping the road were unscalable, and turning back would only delay the encounter, not avoid it.

He panicked as the sound drew closer. No sooner could he think to run back up the road than he could hear the animal's gruff respire. *It's just a farmer on the road,* he thought reassuringly. The thought did little to comfort him.

Tyler crouched in the fog. He could make out the horse's ominous shape, its dark coat thwarting even the densest of fogs. He could not see its rider—he wondered whether he saw *him.* The horse's trot slowed to a walk. Tyler remained still and held his breath.

"Whoa." The horse stopped. Tyler fought the urge to respire. The fog seemed to stand still in the air. Suddenly, the rider reined his horse to one side. It turned until it faced away from him. Tyler almost breathed a sigh of relief.

As if he had read his thoughts, the rider grunted, "Stay," and dismounted his steed, his feet barely making a noise on the gravel.

And then he could see him.

The fog obscured the rider's face as he approached. Tyler stood and waved cordially. "Hello. Coming from the C.D.?" He would go the casual route; pretend he was someone else, a deserter maybe, or a trooper on his way to Richmond. It wasn't unknown for amphitroopers to travel long distances on foot; Tyler's old unit was far from the only one considered expendable. Plus, none of the Frogs had gotten close enough to him to make out his face, unlike the sad reality forced upon Crunch, Ed, and Brooks—perhaps with the exception of the archer whose face Tyler had bashed in.

But this man was not the archer—his jaw was intact, for starters, and he was not carrying a bow. He carried nothing at all, in fact, other than himself. His fog-lined silhouette was the slim sort, the fog seeming to give before him. He was jockey sized, no larger than Tyler's modest five-foot-nine. He wore gloves over his hands, which he tugged tight on approach for good measure.

"Tough paddling upstream, isn't it?" the Frog said stiffly when he was in plain sight.

Tyler swallowed. The jig was up. He had little else to defend himself with but his hands. He was bigger than the other man, his recent diet of squirrel meat and berries notwithstanding. Still, the Frog's dereliction to carry a weapon himself inspired little confidence. It signaled a propensity for committing violence against others.

"Better than drowning," Tyler said dryly. The thin man nodded understandably.

The GeoLoop chimed in as if to mock him: *BONK—MOTION DETECTED*. Tyler ignored it. This seemed to amuse the Frog. "It'll hurt less if you just came with," he reasoned.

Tyler snorted. "I've been hurt before."

The man sighed apologetically. Then he *leaped* toward him. Tyler's eyes widened, and he crouched in response. What the man lacked in size he made up for in quickness. There was no time to think. Tyler barely avoided the first precise jab. He leaned back in anticipation of the cross that would come next. The cross never came. Instead, the man spun neatly in the gravel and *flew* at him, feet first, launching off the pavement like a frog leaping from a lily pad. Tyler tried to duck, but he was slow by a sizable margin. His lead foot crashed into Tyler's windpipe. He fell almost immediately, clutching at his throat. He rolled on the pavement, trying to catch his breath. It felt as if a tourniquet had been applied to his throat. He heard the man's footsteps come close and tried lashing out to trip him, but all he managed was a feeble fling at his ankles that he skipped over easily.

The Frog sighed as if it pained him more than Tyler to watch him sputter for air on the ground. "Now you'll come with?" he asked presumptuously, reaching down to haul Tyler to his feet. He reached under his belt and bound Tyler's wrists. Tyler made a choking sound.

"Uhcanbee."

"What was that?"

"*Uhcan—!*

"Oh, got it. Well. Don't say I didn't warn you." He squared Tyler by the shoulders almost tenderly and jerked the flat of his palm up precisely into Tyler's jaw. His airway cracked open like a dam breaking. Tyler coughed and breathed in the precious air. "Better," he commented.

The Frog poked Tyler over to his horse and began muttering into his Loop. "Yeah, I got 'im," he said, sounding bored. "Yep. Be there in a jiff." He began adjusting his horse's saddle. "I was aiming for your ribs, you ducking fuck," he muttered as he worked at the straps. He turned toward him and grinned wolfishly. "Time to go, Duck."

Tyler listened only in part to the Frog's smart-ass remarks as he struggled to stay ahorse, his hands cuffed behind his back. It was Brooks's voice he heard as his captor mounted the reins in front of him: '*Member the day I found you?*

Why didn't you just leave me?' Tyler bemoaned.

Interlude

No. 30 Month 9, 0004 P.F.
A day on the lake in the former American South

SOFT MUD transected the lake's murky top, forming isthmuses that either grew or shrunk depending on the season. Allison wiggled her toes in the sticky goop and watched her son stomp off toward the blue-gray water. He waded in up to his knees, squatted, and dipped his arms under the surface. She smiled as he swept his arms up, spraying a miniature torrent of water and mud all over himself.

His smile was most beautiful of all. His smile was that of a child unburdened by pre-flood woes like school shootings and screen addiction. His smile conveyed the joy of living in the moment, free of past pains or future trepidations. It pained her how happy it made her, seeing that smile.

She let Hugo shriek and make a bigger mess of himself until she felt him at her shoulder. She tensed up. She had yet to memorize the sensation of his looming presence, but she thought she might soon. His hands were usually stained by one thing or another, soil or engine grease or dried blood. His fingers were slender and bony, but not in an unpleasant way. They matched his overall personality; a bit rough around the edges, but gentle.

"He looks like he's having fun," Fred commented distantly. He seemed focused on something else entirely.

"He's doing what kids are supposed to do." Allison squeezed his fingers lightly. *Kids are supposed to have fun,* she reminded herself. Up until recently, Hugo had not known *how* to have fun. Fun was considered dangerous in the Colonies. Leaving one's little box for too long was deemed risky behavior; splashing about in *any* body of water (much less a stagnant lake) was practically a death wish. The closest Hugo ever got to having fun in his first four years of life was listening to the bedtime stories his mother told him at night, which was "fun" only in the sense that it provided some escape from the monotonous routine of his existence. Hugo's exposure to the world was mostly limited to the shabby interior of Allison's government-subsidized apartment. That all changed as soon as they went looking.

Fred grunted and slid from her grasp. "We're close. Maybe another two days." He paced lightly in the soft soil.

◆

Allison wanted to believe she had foreseen the doom and despair that awaited her child in the Colonies and had actively sought to remove it from his life. But she knew that was a lie. It was Fred's idea to leave. It was Fred's fault.

They met at one of the hybrid grief/substance abuse counseling groups the government set up after the flood. Attending meetings became the only viable choice for most addicts, as drugs suddenly became much harder to attain following the death/disappearance of approximately thirty percent of the population.

Allison did not begin attending the meetings to quit heroin; she'd done so a full four years prior, for obligatory reasons (i.e., running out). She went with the intent of plugging the void heroin had left in her gut. What exactly with, she was not sure.

Her efforts initially bore no success. More often than not, she left the meetings angry—not with her contemporaries, whom she frequently pitied and occasionally resented, but with herself. How *privileged* of her, she thought, to feel that her life wasn't good enough for her. Surely it was a sign something was wrong with her. Wasn't her sweet Hugo, her shitty studio apartment, and simply being *alive* enough for her? It was surely more than others had—like Carla, who spent most meetings reminiscing aloud on the multi-night, cocaine-fueled bacchanalia she'd attended in better times. *You should be grateful you're even here,* Allison frequently reminded herself. *You should be grateful he's here.* Then she'd look at Hugo, her beautiful baby boy, and for a moment, it would be enough. And then she would go, "Hugo? I love you," and he would pause whatever meandering activity he was doing in the apartment and stare at her. Hugo had scarcely made a sound since he'd grown out of his infancy. Words were out of the question. And she'd ask herself again: *What more do you need?* The vicious cycle drove her mad.

She noticed something odd about Fred immediately. At first glance, he appeared no different from some of the meetings' more strung-out attendees; dark circles under their eyes, gaunt cheekbones, a trademark fidget. What was different about him was his posture. Whereas the others crossed their legs or slouched or nodded off in their chairs, Fred sat perfectly upright. Like the teacher's most prized student, always ready to raise his hand and answer.

Yet he never did. Not once did Fred share his struggle. His only role in the meetings seemed to be to listen and occasionally nod in quiet dismay at some of the others' stories.

Allison pretended not to notice the first time she caught him staring at her. She sat uncomfortably through the rest of the meeting and left with her face flushed. Not once did his eyes waver. His behavior had not changed by the next meeting. Or the next. Or the next.

Allison grew accustomed to his odd, empty stares and eventually began returning them. Her eyes retreated from his halfway through her first attempt. She managed not to move her neck in the next meeting. She gradually worked toward total stillness, focusing first on her eyes, then her hands, then her legs, until eventually, she became inanimate. The two of them would stare at each other motionlessly as the meeting's attendees sniffled and shared stories of dead loved ones or past belligerent behavior. With each session, she became more comfortable in her skin. It became a sort of silent meditation.

◆

She was in the lobby, strapping her mask over her face to brave the allegedly potent fumes that billowed from the flood when she felt a tap on her shoulder. She spun, alarmed, then blinked at the man she'd spent the better part of the past three months staring at. "Hello," Fred said softly, and she met his voice for the first time.

"Hello," Allison replied.

"Are you happy?"

Attendance at the next week's meeting was two short. No one seemed to notice.

◆

"Maybe we could stay here for a while," Allison had mentioned once they reached Chattanooga. "The mountains are so nice ..."

"It's nice." Fred picked at a small patch in his goatee, right under his chin, as he always did when he was weighing something. "But it's not Texas."

That was always his response, in one way or another. All roads led to the same place. Leaving the C.D. wasn't enough. They had to leave behind *everything*, anything tethering them to their old place. The only future that mattered was the next one, Fred pinpointed. He was sick of it. Sick of misery, sick of being surrounded by a government that packaged and sold fear like a drug; so went one of his longer tirades. No, Fred wanted to live amongst the free—the *truly* free. He wouldn't tolerate his life being governed by *any* group, be they men of God or godless or otherwise. Each town they stopped in, they abandoned the next day. *It's not safe here. We can't trust these people.* Freedom, and safety by proxy, lay further south.

The territory still customarily referred to as "Texas" was one of the few places yet to be claimed by East or West. It was a Mecca of sorts for self-determined individuals, or so it appeared in his thoughts.

Allison did not begrudge his decisions. A life on the road was better than her old one, she reminded herself. The farther south they went, the more Hugo began behaving like a normal child, one who loves to play and return love to those who love him. He became more curious, venturing out from the shadow of Allison's leg more often. It felt as though they were escaping a toxic atmosphere. In the city, Hugo was exposed to fear and propaganda on a daily basis. There, fear polluted the air he breathed and the water he drank. Once they were on the road, however, Hugo ate wild greens and stewed jackrabbit (Fred wasn't a hunter, but his time in the Army had made him a decent marksman) and breathed fresh air that blew in from the mountains.

The sex started out of boredom more than anything. Their attraction to one another was based on the pursuit of happiness and not love. It was mutually understood. The relationship was loveless, but altogether functional and necessary. Her only fear was Hugo getting wrapped up in Fred's constant presence. Because one day, whether it was before, after, or when they reached the lawless land of Texas, inevitably, Fred would stop coming around. But he was still young, she reassured herself, and besides, everyone loses something on the road to liberation. His loss would be a father figure, whenever she and Fred did part ways. But what would she lose? That she feared discovering more than anything.

♦

Fred dropped to his rear beside her and picked at his chin. "We should get going," he nudged softly. Allison nodded.

"Just a few more minutes."

Fred patted her leg, not lovingly but courteously. He stood to prepare their things for the road while Allison sat staring at her son's darkening skin. *He doesn't burn,* she thought incredulously. They did not saddle themselves with sunscreen or bug spray or fix-all skin crèmes. They carried only what they needed. She'd never dreamed she'd see her son drenched in sunlight four months ago.

"Hey, Allison?" His voice was gentle up to the very end. "You made sure to turn off the—"

Radio, right? The radio, Allison You stupid, stupid ...

But she hadn't thought that then. At the time, she could only think, *Run.*

There was no gunshot. They didn't *use* guns, because that would make them harbingers of war, according to their interpretation of the Father's doctrine. Bows were somehow different; a bow required skill and discipline on the archer's part. A bow wasn't capable of destruction on a massive scale.

Then what was *this?*

His throat whistled. His lungs expanded and contracted, though only half their air escaped his lips. The rest whistled through the hole the arrow had punched through his windpipe. He gargled and spat up blood, but stayed on two legs. He was calm initially; Fred was always calm.

The initial burst of adrenaline blocking the pain must've worn out, or perhaps he understood what had happened to him. Fred's eyes went wide, and just before he collapsed, she saw fear flash across his face. He lay face down, choking on mud and blood. Despite the terrible whistle emitting from his throat, Allison managed to decipher his last words: *"Go."*

So, she went.

Allison ran toward Hugo, her feet splashing madly in the water, kicking up mud and sand. Hugo suddenly stopped playing. He was staring idly past her toward where Fred lay, watching the three men in white creep out from the treeline, their bows drawn.

She scooped her arms beneath the surface and hugged Hugo to her chest. She splashed awkwardly through the mud, crying, hoping, praying that God or the Father or whoever handled this hellish new reality would take pity on her and her boy and spare them. No one answered her prayers.

The men surrounded her on the mud isthmus and lowered their bows. Two of them were clean-shaven, their faces and their heads. The third had a beard that touched his chest and sheening, brown hair to match. Their uniforms were crisp and laundered, the shade of fresh snow.

The one with the beard signaled his men to stop and called out after her. "Where are you going?"

Allison kept running. She ran until she finally stumbled in the mud, Hugo clinging to her chest. She tried to get up and fell again; the mud was sucking her in like quicksand. "Fred?" Hugo mumbled in Allison's ear. His first words; she never even heard them.

The men hadn't even broken a trot. They'd stayed on dry land, walking along the shore as she ran. Without hesitation, they waded into the muck after her, permanently soiling the bottoms of their uniforms. Allison had sunken to her knees, submitting to the mud's pull. The men stood before her, their shadows draping over her.

"Please," Allison begged, her tears clogging her throat. "Just let us go."

"Why did you run?" the bearded one asked calmly.

"I ..." Tears and mud stung her eyes. *Run. Run Allison, run.* But there was nowhere to go.

They were close enough that Allison could make out their features. The man with the beard squatted down and watched her, calmly, like he was observing a wild animal in its natural habitat. "Do you go seeking the Way?" he asked in a soft, almost angelic voice. She almost heard Fred warning her: *We can't trust these people.*

She decided then. *No.* Fred was dead now. Their dream—no, *his* dream—was out the window. All that mattered was survival. Her son would live. He would grow tall and strong.

Allison looked up at him, her face covered in muck, eyes wild. "We came from the Colonies. We—Fred—he showed me the Way. He wanted us to live in the Father's shadow." Allison took a shaky breath. "Please. We only wish to proselytize."

"Only the Father can show us the Way. Whatever he showed you was a clever ruse, nothing more." The bearded man looked to his partners for counsel. One shrugged. The other shook his head lightly. He turned back to her and smiled placidly. "Fortunately, we are an accepting people. But we must ensure all who join our cause are true of heart and spirit." At that moment, she saw what lay underneath his smile; weakness, indignation, rot. "If this is the case, then say the words."

She could not hold the tears any longer. "I can't." She looked at her son and smiled at him. *Just one last smile.* Hugo looked up at her with the same look of confusion.

The men began chanting. The words were beautiful, but they only spelled death to her:

I have seen the waters of the East, swirling tides filled with fish.

The waters of the North, cold and clear and crystalline.
The South, wide and slow and shallow.
The West, rocks and seafoam ...

Allison did not hear them finish. She listened to the crickets chirp and smelled her baby's hair one last time.

"You are to go back East and never come back again," the bearded one pronounced.

A seal in Allison's chest released. She stood in the muck, her strength suddenly restored, and gathered Hugo in her arms. "Yes." East was good. East was alive. East was her son.

The man smiled toothlessly at her, his thin, awful pink lips creeping beneath his flowing beard. "No." He jutted his finger at her. "Only you. The boy is young. Given time, he may prove himself worthy of the Father's compassion."

Allison's whole body went numb as the men approached and pried her child away from her. She struggled feebly against them, clawing and screaming, hearing but not hearing, seeing but not seeing, feeling but not feeling. Her nail grazed one man's eye, who cursed and hit her on the cheek in return. She did not feel the blow. The one with the long hair frowned at where she kneeled, screaming, sobbing. They left her there in the mud, alone and unable to feel.

Fred's voice rang in her ears as the men escaped with the world's most precious cargo in stow. *Hey, Allison? You made sure to turn off the radio, right?* His voice was always so gentle.

XIV

No. 25 Month 4, 0017 P.F.
Pittsburgh, Appalachia, New American Colonies

TIE-DYE RIVULETS of drool permanently stained Naomi's eggshell blue pillowcase. The stranger she woke up next to was contributing to the pattern. She sighed. *You can't always get what you want.*

She craned her neck and winced to check the time. *05:15.* She always seemed to wake at precise quarter-hour intervals. It might as well have read *00:15*; she was exhausted. But her eyes being open meant it was time to wake. She slid from her bed noiselessly, the still-damp sheet floating neatly where her curvature was. She slipped on her underwear and padded over to the kitchen for some water.

Kyle (or whatever her Caucasian hookup du jour's name was) wrapped his arms softly around her waist. "Come back to bed," he mumbled into her neck.

Naomi smiled uncomfortably and laid her hand atop his wrist, pushing off ever so slightly; the powerful suggestion of a woman's touch. "Make sure the alarm's turned off." His arms disappeared, and he went off to do her bidding, like a good boy.

Naomi sighed and rubbed her eyes. She leaned on the counter and sipped her water. She winced at her Loop's bright blue display. It suddenly came alit, which was abnormal, because her notifications were muted between the hours of 21:00 to 06:30. Unless the sender had marked the message as an emergency.

She reached for the orange prescription bottle on her kitchen counter before reading the message.

◆

Naomi chewed her lip. They'd promised her the officer was amongst their best, handpicked from a select crop of ex-special forces soldiers. He had worked hunting down serial robbers and traffickers on the run, men for whom survival was all that mattered. And he'd been bested, by a *prince*, no less.

"Miss Cieslinski, the Chief will see you now."

"Oh." Naomi stood and smiled graciously. She smoothed the folds of her suit dress and followed the secretary into the office.

The room was a simple quadrant. George Crombie stood staring out a wall made entirely of glass. The view it offered was fantastic: Pittsburgh from its highest point, at the very tip of the Pole. The city's twisting scaffolds stretched out below them. Clothes were hung out to dry on nylon strings, fluttering suggestively in the wind. Children ran between suspended, fenced-in bridges. The shadow of the Pole darkened the scene.

The wall to her left was made up of a grid of computer monitors. Each panel showed a different scene of Pittsburgh, above or below ground. Also displayed: ticking stock prices, news reporters pleading their case, and a recording of an old Cowher-era Super Bowl. The wall to her right was adorned with a portrait of a woman wearing an ornate silk dress. She stood before a backdrop that looked like it'd been plucked out of the Renaissance. A dormant apple orchard stretched out behind her, and a French or perhaps Italian villa overlooked the neat arrangement. Her hair was a comely auburn-red, her eyes downcast and unknowable.

The high-setting afternoon sun flooded in through the ceiling-height window, eliminating any need for artificial light. George Crombie wore a coffee-stained white V-neck and pajamas, his cheeks shaded by three days' worth of scruff. He sighed deeply before turning to acknowledge his guest, forcing a smile across his weathered face. "Thank you for coming all this way, Miss Cieslinski. How was your trip? You came by bore train, I assume?"

She nodded. "I took the new line from the C.D. I believe Mr. Blair oversaw its construction." She glanced nervously outside the penthouse window at the dancing clotheslines; shirts, blouses, and jackets, towels and socks (both worn and new), pants of corduroy and cotton, a child-sized basketball jersey. "I got to see both sides of Pittsburgh today. It's a beautiful city."

"Yes, it can be," said George, turning back to admire his scene. "Please, have a seat." The chair was built from a hard metal that instantly pained the small of Naomi's back. She briefly wondered whether this was intentional. The Chief watched the clothes flutter in the wind before finally meeting her eyes. "Would you like something to drink? Tea? Coffee? I take mine Irish, but I can track down some cream and sugar, if that's your thing," he said with a smirk. Naomi put on a polite smile and squirmed slightly, trying to find comfort in the steel cushion.

"No, thank you. I'm allergic to alcohol, actually."

George grunted. "I suppose we all are. Wake up feeling like shit the next day ..."

"I break out in hives," Naomi clarified.

"Ah." Crombie nodded absentmindedly and took a long sip from his mug. He touched the desk lightly, his eyes scanning the inordinate number of papers spread across it, and exhaled. "Leading has its perks. Paperwork isn't one of them." He collected the papers in a neat stack and promptly threw them into a small trash bin below. "I'm sure you know this from experience."

"Filling out forms can be painful. Computers help, I guess," Naomi said amiably before facing her reason for coming to the small, bright office in the first place: the Chief was due an explanation. She crossed her legs. "I don't mean to be rude or change subjects, Mr. Carne—"

"*George.*"

Naomi's face flushed. "Yes—that's right—I, uh ..." She excused herself lightly. "I came to apologize."

"Not coming to me sooner was rude of you, Naomi. Our business isn't settled yet."

"Yes, but I wanted to apologize for the ..." Naomi fidgeted with her nails. She'd spent most of the loud and jarring train ride contemplating how to address the Chief's son and still found herself floundering for words. "*Fugitive.* In-person," she clarified, reminding herself to lay her palms flat against her lap. George laughed a bit off-puttingly.

"I wouldn't call him *that.* 'Fugitive' implies being hunted, not acting in spite. If that were the case, we'd all be fugitives." Naomi's eyelashes fluttered; she'd carefully done them up with mascara in anticipation of the assemblage. "Perhaps it was a little naïve of you to think a wannabe RoboCop would be capable of apprehending my son. Naïve as he may be, he has not forgotten his tactical training. His teacher saw to that." George bore a painful sigh. "Maybe too well."

"It was inexcusable of us, sir. My men are tracking him as we speak."

"Oh, I'm sure," George chuckled before his melancholy returned. "What's done is done. The last people I thought I trusted have left me. All in reverence of some godforsaken *cult.*" He said the word as if doing so cut him. "So, you came all this way just to apologize to an old man?"

"No—yes, but—"

"Just to show your good faith—I'm impressed. However, I'm afraid I must decline your apology until concessions are made. Do plan on staying a little while. As I mentioned, we have work to do."

We? Naomi bobbed her head. "Chief ... *George*," she corrected herself. "Your reimbursements have been generous since we started working together." Her words only rang half true. MARS Group's monetary reimbursement for its services was not yet said and done, but George's taking of the Anti-Terror Committee was. Their most recent verdict had ruled that the Colonist government could not "*limit, restrict, or thereby discriminate against in any pejorative way a private enterprise's right to contribute to national security efforts*," effectively endorsing MARS Group to expand future IMP recruitment classes as they saw fit—so long as their doing so made the nation more secure, of course. The favorable result was in no small part thanks to the kind donations George made to the Committee's more swayable members' wallets. "But MARS Group delivered you its promise," Naomi said bravely. "We train our IMPs to exact—"

"*But*, Miss Cieslinski, your officers have failed me on all counts. And yes, your compensation has been more than generous, considering the fruits your labor has borne thus far."

Naomi wanted to vanish, to float up and out of the room. But she was no magician or phantom. Instead, she reminded herself how far she'd come. *You are a lioness.* She had recently taken an online seminar on positive visualization. She visualized herself licking her bloody paws after a hunt on the savannah. *You are strong. You are powerful. From waitress to Madame Secretary. Remember that.* She summoned her courage and broadened her chest, a changed person, a grown one, a lioness. Not subject to predation, but formidable, independent, and dangerous to predator and prey alike. "I'm sorry, but were they not trained to your specifications?"

George stared through her. Her braveness dissipated. The lioness within her shriveled and became a field mouse, scurrying from the preying hawk above. "They're fine, apart from the whole being totally fucking useless part ... but I suppose that can't be helped. My greatest concern at this moment is your outstanding debt. You still owe me more men."

Naomi shrunk again. Though the verdict had not been hers to begin with, it'd certainly appeared that way. She'd lost two secretaries in the weeks following the Anti-Terror Committee's ruling. Other employees came to her sporting evidence of death threats made against their families: pictures of spraypainted one-word threats, ominous handwritten letters sent to their home addresses, and even a makeshift bomb that was set on her assistant's doorstep. The bomb successfully detonated. Rather than explode, however, when the clichéd red analog timer on its face expired, a puppet with crossed-out eyes wearing a crude business tie emerged from its crude hatch. Naomi had rebranded his ensuing mental breakdown as a sabbatical. In truth, she did not think the nervous academy graduate would ever quite be the same again.

Naomi was not unincluded in these attempts to will her resignation; she simply did not allow it to affect her. Whatever she absorbed was weight off George's shoulders, she reminded herself. It appeared the gesture was appreciated; she'd had nothing to do with the ununiformed police who came the second week and forcibly cleared out the protesters (most of whom belonged to an ever-intensifying but frequently discredited anarchist movement in the Colonies) outside her office. George's pockets apparently ran deep enough to protect Naomi, even remotely. For better or worse, she was living out of his deep pockets—a discomforting luxury. More discomforting than anything, however, was his discontent with her efforts thus far.

Naomi cleared her throat. "We have over a thousand more IMPs in training at this moment—a few of which are women, actually." George seemed not to notice her distinction. "It's not an automatic process, however."

"Unfortunately, I was not blessed with an aptitude for patience. And I'm not interested in gaining more *troops* for number's sake; I intend to employ their services meaningfully." He carefully analyzed the mat calendar on his desk and spoke without meeting her eyes, murmuring to himself as his eyes sideswiped the days and weeks. "The new bore train channel our mutual friend Mr. Blair just put a wraps on will help transport the sum of my troops to the Capital District. In ..." He tapped a date on the calendar precisely. "Let's say two weeks, I will have a thousand men in the Capital District, armed with state-of-the-art weaponry, which the MARS Group will so generously endow ..." His eyes dragged along the calendar. "A week later—three weeks from today—President Stone will resign, citing concerns over his health. It will be televised, but I'm sure you will get notifications on your Loops too."

"The Continental Congress will turn inwards, citing the new president's incompetence. I'm blanking on our beloved vice president's name; I remember him being a moron when we last met." George nodded as if to reaffirm this to himself. "Inevitably, there will be some chaos in the capital. I'd advise you to book a stay in Pittsburgh around then. It's for your own safety. I'll be reserving some forces to ensure no violence occurs in Pittsburgh. Unfortunately, the District may not fare as well."

Naomi suddenly stood from the steel chair. "If this is a joke, I'd suggest you say so. Otherwise, I'm arresting you for treason."

But he had not yet finished his story.

"After the vice president concedes the presidency, citing 'deep-seated political division' or something along those lines, a referendum to elect a new president will occur. My name will appear first on the ballot. Given I do not suffer some unforeseen political crisis, I will win. Legitimately, I might add; people vote for what they know, and most are already quite familiar with my brand, per se. I can at least count on the vote of any librarian with steady work, what few remain. Anyway, the vote will be natural. In time, the New American Colonies will dissolve, and the New American Society will take its place." George finally looked up from his desk. "Come back six months from now and tell me whether I was joking."

"You're insane."

"Insane?" George pointed a finger at his chest facetiously. "Me? You could argue for it, I suppose, though nowhere near as insane as our enemy to the west. I'll spare you the details—theology was never my best subject—but the Western Alliance vastly outmatches the Colonies in size and strength. I'm told some twenty thousand youths have already volunteered to serve the Father, most of them from San Francisco. *The holy land,*" the Chief added distastefully. "They're organizing a crusade as we sit here and ponder the future."

Twenty thousand? Naomi shuddered. Her scouts in the West hadn't reported on any gathering that large. Or perhaps they were simply no longer inclined to tell her. She could hardly fathom the sway a new Father might have on someone born with Western ties.

George arched his brow at the look of bewilderment on Naomi's face. "Have I said something to offend you?"

"You're ..." *Delusional* was the first word that came to mind, but she hesitated. "You're in over your head."

George sighed painfully. He turned his attention to the children running about on his scaffoldings, their scarves blowing in the wind like colorful banners. "Try telling them that. Those scaffolds will fall if the Alliance lands at our doorstep, that I can assure you. Perhaps rightfully so. We dig holes in the earth and hide in the clouds because we are *afraid* of the world, not because we outsmarted it." The children were called inside by their mother. A dark cloud had begun rolling over the city, and it bore rain. The raindrops coagulating on the cold glass seemed to transfix him. "Fear is what got us into this mess in the first place," he muttered absently.

The silence somehow felt more unbearable than listening to his self-pity. "And you think launching a coup will stop them?"

"The question is the answer."

"I'm sorry?"

"Sometimes, the question is the answer. What other answer would you offer? Who else is privy to the resources necessary to fight this? Our government?" George cocked his neck. Naomi shook her head reluctantly. "I didn't think so." He reached for his mug and drained what remained within. He sat eying the flimsy porcelain bottom. "In any case, we are late to the party. 'The Untold' might *think* he can unite us, but absolute power corrupts absolutely. The Alliance will not reassemble this broken country, nor will we. We are damaged beyond repair. Our youth is shattered by a disaster almost two decades past, one they never even suffered through. Our government uses the same bullshit propaganda it's always used, urging us to avoid each other and water all 'for our health's sake.' They'd rather have us fiddle aimlessly with our Loops than go out and get some goddamn sun. We can't even name the *date* for chrissakes, as if saying what day of what month it is will summon the flood to haunt us again. Small wonder so many are packing their bags ... Hell, if I weren't so goddamned old and cynical, I'd be right behind them." He stared past her, his fingertips tapping each other, alternating like tiny accordions, his eyes not quite registering the room.

The clouds had blocked out the sun, and the room grew dark. There was nothing but the glow from the panel screens to distinguish the lines in George's stress-worn face. "You know the Colonies are my employer," Naomi mentioned, immediately feeling foolish afterward.

If it was a threat, it was a poorly executed one. The Colonies were not the ones clearing protestors from her office, nor whom she scampered to when summoned, like a loyal dog.

"I thought you might say that ..." He cleared his throat melodramatically. "Given the position's upcoming vacancy, United will soon need a new Chief. This is a lucrative opportunity, I assure you, and necessary. We may someday need to bring the fight to the enemy, and, given your, ah, *prior experience*, I suspect you'll find a way to do so. You'll have free rein of my company's resources; God knows we have produced enough Loops to poison all our brains twice over." He stood and reached his hand out. "I don't often reward people so richly after fudging up so badly, Miss Cieslinski."

Naomi neither accepted nor declined his offer, though she knew she would not perform the latter. She remained still, her legs folded one on top of the other. "Say I am to accept."

"Please do."

"What then? What happens ... I mean, *after*..."

"Why, democracy." He laughed at her involuntary reaction. "Do not worry; my stewardship of the Society will only be necessary until the threat in the West is eliminated. Afterwards, I will oversee the transition of power to the people, hence the name. Power is a gospel, not a bible. It is meant to be preached *by* the people, not to them."

"And what about your company?"

"You mean *your* company?" George said with a smile. Naomi shifted uncomfortably. His smile dissipated. "I'm only kidding, of course. I intend to return to my post as soon as the Society is stable enough to govern itself. Though not for much longer, I fear. I'm fucking *old*. I intend to turn over this company to younger, wiser hands." He frowned, rubbing the coarse hairs covering his chin. "All in time ..."

"So, this is a contract position," Naomi said plainly.

George's frown deepened. "Yes, that is accurate. But I see retirement in your near future."

Naomi summoned her courage. *Remember, a lioness.* "I deserve to know then. Is it true what they say about Adam, being the Untold …?"

He need not say anything until later. George's eyes sharpened into flint shards, and Naomi immediately shrank into her chair. All her instincts told her to flee to safety. But there was nowhere to hide. "That's my son you're talking about." The malice in his eyes intensified. "Speaking of lost sons, does the name 'Hugo' mean anything to you?"

Naomi's hands went numb. Her tongue moved in her throat, but her voice did not leave her lips. "Where does your name come from, anyway?" George asked patiently.

"M … my grandparents were Polish, but were born in Germany," Naomi said, the words spilling from her mouth. Her brain and body implored her to stand and bolt from the room, but she remained still, frozen in terror.

George's eyes relaxed just as suddenly as they had become dangerous. "I thought so. My mother was Polish, you know. Well, technically she was a Slav, but then again, we all enjoy styling ourselves as someone we will never quite be." He smiled tiredly. "We have a very busy few months ahead of us, Naomi."

XV

THE FROGS provided Tyler gruel, water, and medical attention as deemed necessary. They observed him mostly from a distance and only paid him any mind sporadically, much like a bored young student eyeing the class pet. His chain-link confines made it convenient to watch for any attempts to escape or harm himself.

His belongings included some ill-fitting spare clothes, a rotating case of bottled water, and a first aid kit, from which he fashioned a sash to wear over his crusted-over eye. They also awarded him half-a-dozen ancient Playboys, which he used as toiletries and nothing else. His meals were mainly composed of boiled grain and leftover pieces of gristly meat, which his jailer claimed was black bear. Sometimes they awarded him dessert in the form of a multivitamin gummy. He ate savagely. At the end of every week, a bucket filled with suds would appear, and he would strip down and wash in front of all to see. It was worth the humiliation, to feel clean.

They called him Duck, which he guessed was conceived by the scout who'd wrangled him back to Vernon. They only ever used it in reference, ignoring him out of basic principle; prisoners were to be disregarded, not chatted up. The only one who addressed him directly was a nameless medic who periodically checked in on him to see how his wounds were healing. The medic cared for him as any other doctor would: always feigning interest, but always professional. He cleaned his eye periodically and drained it of pus and fluid. He applied a soothing ointment to the tender, black-and-yellow bruise that wrapped around his throat. He even addressed the quivering in his hands and began allotting him a small ration of alcohol to avoid catastrophic withdrawal. The medic offered painkillers as well. "It'll make it easier," he promised. He accepted graciously, swallowing the pills alongside the warm vodka he received in one-shot increments. Tyler greatly looked forward to his visits.

The medic reduced his consumption slowly, which made for a miserable time. But it was not the shakes or the sweats that Tyler feared. He was willing to suffer the physiological symptoms of rapid-onset sobriety. The greater obstacle was his memories. *Those* he was afraid of. And sure enough, once the booze was gone, his memories returned to him full-force.

It was apparently against their doctrine to torture Tyler physically, but they eagerly let boredom and isolation do their work. He responded to the Frogs' questions with nothing. Then they would leave him for a day, or two, or sometimes a week. He was never quite sure how much time had passed; it moved at an odd pace with only the sun and lines drawn in the dirt to mark its pass. With no voice to listen to, much less talk to, Tyler's mind resorted to summoning its own voices. And then he felt bad. Very bad.

He was haunted by the same vision: Brooks, Crunch, and Ed floating downstream, their faces submerged, bloated with their own CO_2. The voice rarely changed, and always seemed to mock him: *Fucked that one up, didn't we, Tyler? Look where you've landed us now. How didn't you know this would happen?* Tyler caught himself slipping out little details to his captors, just to undermine the voice. He heard Brooks's disappointment for giving in so easily. *You really that fuckin' soft, Haj? Eh?*

You're dead, Tyler thought. *I'm still here.*

He started to think of his life as a game. It helped his mind turn away from what he'd lost: *Level 1: Get ambushed by a bunch of Frog mercenaries. Level 2: Go for a swim. Eat dinner with a busker. Level 3: Become a POW.* And now, the final boss. *Level 4: Forget.*

No. 7 Month 6, 0008 P.F.

"What the hail's got you so down, Eeyore?" Tyler walked with his chin down, watching his feet troll past layers of garbage. "I think it's that time of the month again. What's your prognosis, Eduardo?"

Ed snickered. "Not looking good at all."

"Thought so. Must be somethin' wrong with 'im." Brooks quickened his pace and tapped Tyler on the shoulder.

All the things stolen by the flood—television remotes, Christmas tree ornaments, disposable chopsticks, toilet seat covers, and all the rest of it—had coalesced and formed a ridge that tracked along the Hudson all the way to the Long Island Sound. Some twenty meters ago, Tyler spotted an old can of Edge shaving gel lying amongst the trash. He spun when he felt Brooks behind him and sprayed the ancient blue goo at him, aiming for his eyes.

"Motherfuck!" Brooks yelled, holding his hand out to shield himself from the stinging gel. Tyler did not let up. Brooks fell backward, sliding down the mountain of garbage ass-first, trying to gain his footing. His efforts only seemed to pull him deeper into the rubbish. Ed bent over and howled.

"Yer gonna fuckin' pay fer that, som'bitch!" Brooks screamed from the ridge's soggy bottom. Tyler smirked. He had noticed that his deep Maryland accent became more pronounced whenever he was embarrassed. He slowly scrambled on his hands and knees up the ridge and rejoined them, scowling and swiping grime from his standard issues. "Least you ain't so miserable now," he grumbled. Tyler sighed in response.

"Let's just get this shit over with."

◆

Ed was far more enthused by the task at hand than his comrades. Tyler couldn't have cared less about the National Environmental Survey's ongoing study on the effects of the flood on land surface temperature. Brooks was equally unenthused, but then again, not a whole lot ever enthused him.

"This block used to be full of laundromats," Ed elucidated. "It was kinda weird, all the same shit, just run by different religious groups; one for the Sikhs, one for the Hindus, one for the Muslims. You get the deal."

"Used to park my food truck right over there—Flatbush and Willoughby."

"Aye, Haj. See that corner up there? That used to be the best dive bar in New York. I used to know this guy named Santino—"

"That's just great, Ed," Tyler spat. Ed took this as a signal to resign from his unofficial tour guide duties.

They crawled along Queens toward the beacon's location. The Letterman had revealed the coordinates to Brooks and Brooks only; he glanced down at his Loop occasionally to confirm their progress. The Letterman trusted Brooks like a son, which was odd, given they were polar opposites. The Letterman was raised in a neighborhood of Chicago named Pullman by a black Muslim father who had once belonged to the Panthers. He fought tooth and nail to ensure his son became nothing short of a lawyer (or so Brooks claimed—the Letterman had never discussed his past with them). Naturally, the Letterman became a joiner before being drafted. Brooks's father had only ever followed two dogmas: that of the Longshoremen's Association and that of the Klan. Naturally, Brooks only dated black women.

Even after the flood's interference, JFK was easy to spot; the air control towers stood out like sore thumbs in the waterlogged cityscape. Though technically Brooks was Tyler and Ed's superior, he mostly refrained from using it as leverage against them. The exception was when they encountered random women at random bars, when they were lucky enough to be stationed in a proper city—in this scenario, Brooks became *Sergeant* Brooks. Tyler humored him on such occasions, if only because he did not mandate that they address him as "Sarge" or otherwise any other time. Rank and order were meaningless to Brooks: "Just do yer fuckin' job" was the closest he ever came to exercising his authority. The moment they came in sight of the beacon, however, Brooks decided to do so.

"That's your cue, Haj." Brooks pointed at a muted, red-lit antenna poking up from the flood's murky depths and smiled devilishly at him, practically daring him to raise a protest. Instead of arguing his case, he hopped down from their slight elevation into the flood, his boots soaking in its impurities.

"Jus' hold down the button on the bottom," Brooks hollered as Tyler distanced himself from them. It was one of the first truly hot days of the year, and the result was a not entirely pleasant rotten fish smell that radiated from the water's surface. Still, Tyler had smelled and waded through worse in his eight years as a trooper.

He held his breath, his waist disrupting the still water until he came within arm's reach of the beacon. He stooped down and plunged his hand beneath the flood, just like Brooks had told him. A cloud of guppies retreated as Tyler invaded their home base.

A plastic baggie filled with oxidated pills buoyed next to him. The pills inside seemed to give off an effervescence that ballooned the bag. He spotted a quick ripple move through the water about thirty yards out and nearly jumped, briefly recalling the days of local news headlines warning beachgoers of tiger and bull shark sightings. He could almost hear the Letterman scorning him: *Get a hold of yourself, Private.* He shook his head and kept walking.

The beacon's blinking red tip transitioned briefly to yellow, and then to solid green. "Job well done," Brooks hollered.

Tyler immediately started back toward his comrades. The ripple remained on his mind. He was unsure whether he should swim wildly back to solid ground or move along at a snail's pace. He opted to wade along at his normal speed.

He was halfway back to solid ground when a ripple identical in shape and size coned toward him. It came less than ten yards in front of him. Tyler did not allow matters to fall to circumstance. He'd left his rifle in drier, safer hands (Ed's), but he reached across his hip and drew his sidearm. He fired three times, about two feet in front of where he'd seen the ripple, each bullet spraying up a glistening geyser.

A fish, perhaps a carp of some sort, splashed away in panic from where the bullets had penetrated the surface. If it'd had pants to shit, it might've. Tyler watched it squiggle away frantically.

A puff of noxious air bobbed to the water's surface. The ripple's instigator followed. It was a corpse of indiscriminate age, rotted beyond the point of recognizability. The only evidence of the person's being were a few leftover strands of long, dark hair. Tyler held his breath and tried to keep from retching. He waded in a wide half-moon around the corpse.

"You good?" Brooks called out to him.

◆

Tyler jerked his flask and scowled because it made him feel sicker yet. "I'm done getting my feet wet for that asshole." He wiped his lips and screwed the cap back on. "Motherfucker's never had to dip a goddamn pinky in the flood."

Brooks frowned lightly. "You that soft?"

"Did you see that shit?"

"Course. Wasn't no thang."

"How about your ass gets in next time then?"

"But you're our Senior Flood Surveyor, Private," Brooks jested. "You've got experience at your belt. You used to mong fish, ain't that right, Haj?"

"*Monger*," Tyler corrected.

"Whatever the fuuuuck."

"Yeah; *whatever*," Tyler grumbled and plugged a cigarette to his lips. "I stopped caring what you assholes think of me a long time ago. *Soft*," he scoffed as he sparked the cigarette. "Shit doesn't matter."

Brooks nudged Ed and snickered. "You hear that? Seems to me that Haj done seen the light. What, you a fuckin' nihilist all a the sudden?" he teased.

"He cares more than he puts on," Ed commented.

"Don't talk about me in the third person." They walked in silence along the ridge, their footsteps pronounced by half-decomposed McDonald's wrappers and Styrofoam.

They came to an unnatural junction, a T-intersection of garbage. If they went straight, they would continue north, snaking along the Hudson to Harlem and beyond. The alternate route was somewhat more perilous, a steady downward slope that seemed ready to collapse in on itself at any moment. Brooks started toward the latter without querying his companions.

Ed skittered behind anxiously. "Why not go back up the Hudson?"

"Gotta haul our asses back to the C.D."

"Which way's that?"

"Straight shot through Jersey." He suddenly stopped his march and whipped his head around. "Either of you got a problem with that?" Ed flinched in response, though his eyes were glued exclusively on Tyler.

Ed answered first. "No. I just thought you guys might want to see my old neighborhood in Manhattan is all," he said, sounding genuinely disappointed. Tyler avoided Brooks's stare and focused on his cigarette instead, cultivating its slow burn between his fingers. Brooks did not look away. No cigarette was worthy of such sustained consideration; Tyler looked up to meet his gaze.

"Jersey's fine," Tyler answered simply.

Brooks spat, Ed swallowed, and Tyler smoked. And off they went.

◆

In those days, it was hard to fill empty space with words. It was far more practical to do so before Ed joined them, as his greatest talent was not shutting up.

But one man can only do so much good (or evil, depending on who you ask) during his time on Earth. Ed could not combat the quiet alone. And so, Brooks took up the custom of singing as they rucked from one place to another. It was not an entirely unpleasant tradition, as Brooks's voice was neither on nor off-key. It carried a blue-collar sort of affability that Tyler could listen to for sensible lengths of time. And though he would never admit it to Brooks's face, his voice comforted him in some small way.

"Who?" Brooks asked, frowning. Ed took this as an opportunity to not shut up.

"Y'know, John, Paul, George, Norm? Man, I used to listen to them all the time. Remember the days when we all carried endless music in our pockets?" Ed reminisced aloud. "Shit—I remember the day Lennon got killed. Guess that dates me," said Ed. Always the expert, Ed. "It's not a Beatles song, by the way. *Originally*, it's by ..."

Brooks was irritated by his unfamiliarity with the subject. "Shut the fuck up, Ed," he grumbled. He stopped singing then, and the quiet resumed.

They marched on in silence, passing by some well-manicured hydrangeas that someone in the area had evidently cared for. They walked along a sidewalk destroyed by water that'd repeatedly filled, frozen, and expanded. Grass poked up through these cracks, a sign of summer. Tyler thought it was beautiful in its own sort of way, one of the more appreciable things about the end of landscaping companies and city ordinances. Part of an old-world beauty that now existed everywhere, one of the few pleasurable sights the flood had wrought.

Tyler looked up from the budding grass and recognized the sidewalk's bell curve around a bus stop. He knew instantly that the sidewalk would then straighten, and there would be a fenced-in yard to the right. In earlier times, there would have been an intimidating but harmless Rottweiler named Darleen panting behind the chain-link, watching school children pass by from the cranny of her doghouse. He knew there had once been a set of overgrown oak trees to provide Darleen shade, and that an ice cream truck had sometimes sat parked around the next corner.

He was the third man in their sequence, and the others did not notice when he stopped to stare at the slanted roof and broken windows of his childhood home at 113 Madison Avenue. The three-paneled window looking out to the street was shattered unevenly like someone had thrown a brick through it. Creeping ivy and moss had invaded their family dining room. The red mahogany table was still there, though the chairs were gone, likely broken apart for kindling or whittled into sharp sticks to scare off enemies. Those were the first few months after the flood.

Tyler stared through the broken window. His mind turned to a family tradition that his father had encouraged every Christmas. Joe Haji only began celebrating the holiday after he met Lori. Tyler always suspected that his enthusiasm for adorning the house with lights and decorations was him compensating for not being treated the same as a child.

Every Christmas, Joe would award his wife and his two sons each a rubber-banded wad containing fifty one-dollar bills. The ante stayed at one. Max bet was two dollars, no matter the game. The games varied from five-card draw to hold 'em to Ship, Captain, Crew. They played cards and occasionally dice and usually succumbed to playing Uno (if Joe Haji allowed it). The flop changed according to the dealer's wishes. Tyler was an exceptionally poor poker player. He would fold even when his cards were in his favor. Aaron was the opposite. *It was me this whole time,* his older brother would tease across the table, splaying out impossible winning hands to cheers and laughter.

The memories were swathed in the scent of fake pine resin and smiles—smiles all around. Tyler, Aaron, and Mr. and Mrs. Haji, all smiles. A proper family. A *good* family.

"You comin' or what, Lil' Hoss?"

Tyler spun to Brooks's voice. "Yeah." He did not turn to look back.

Spring, 0017 P.F.

The vessels only carried eight, but the reinforcements essentially doubled the Frog's existing force. They drifted down noiselessly in canoes off the Potomac, just as Tyler had envisioned before his imprisonment, and his friends were still alive.

Spring's preeminent rain and chill reminded the guards that Tyler might not keep well in his open-air cage. Granted that the manor and other more luxurious living arrangements were occupied, they relocated Tyler to the stable, which, though a marked improvement over his cage, contained no such amenities as fireplaces or furniture. His squadron's (*ex-*squadron, Tyler reminded himself) gear was gone when he arrived, likely in the Frogs' possession.

Tyler made a nest and lived amongst the hay. He continued to be fed on a nightly basis, but no one, not even the medic, came to speak to him. His wounds and other afflictions were cured. The only human life he interacted with was the grunt they sent to bring him his food.

The Frogs did not limit their entertainment for Tyler's sake; they held nightly bonfires, roasted weenies, drank beer, and smoked weed in the middle of the estate's circle drive. Tyler listened to their laughing conversations and felt oddly left out.

One night, his delivery boy did not visit. Tyler waited until well after the sun had disappeared. Still nothing. They held no party that night either. He went to his hay pile, his stomach growling, tired but in no position to fall asleep.

He awoke to the sound of the stable door being jostled open. He peered out from the hay uncomprehendingly as a somewhat sharply dressed soldier broke in. He was towing a mop bucket filled with suds and a plate piled high with pale, steaming meat and potatoes. He left both near the stable's entrance, scowling.

"Someone wants to talk to you in the morning." The soldier sniffed the air. "I expect you'll have this place cleaned up by then."

Tyler peaked out from his nest. "Okay." The soldier scowled at him before turning to leave. Tyler hesitated before calling out after him. "Who?"

The soldier did not turn to address him. "Someone important. Keep that in mind." He shut the barn door, leaving Tyler alone with his boiled breakfast.

XVI

No. 25 Month 4, 0001 P.F.
Pittsburgh, Pennsylvania, United States of America

AUGUST TOOK after the mother she'd never met. Her father's genetics seemed to have skipped a generation. Her eyes were rolling gray clouds and carried a somberness absent from Bill's light hazel ones. She had auburn hair and burned easily, whereas Bill's hair was black and his skin olive. August was short and slight of frame, whereas Bill was tall and broad. August was quick to anger or joy. She accredited this to her grandfather; she realized she had inherited his suddenness after earning two weeks of detention for snapping a boy's finger for calling her Pippi Longstocking. Bill was steady and intentional. Even their last names were different. Wedlock impelled August to abandon her name. Fervor impelled Bill to.

"Adam. Get over here." He pretended not to hear her and grinned at the empty sky below him, his skinny legs dangling past the balcony's ledge. "Adam. *Now.*"

"I'm the king of the world!" he proclaimed. Her heart formed a little bundle in her throat. *Boy.* Her little boy, dangling from a tall cliff. Her own little Humpty Dumpty. *Humpty Dumpty sat on a wall, Humpty Dumpty had a great fall. All the king's horses and all the king's men couldn't put Humpty together again.*

She tried anger. "Get back inside right now!" Adam replied by grasping the rail and leaning out over the edge, grinning. August lurched after him, almost stumbling before catching herself on the doorframe. She exhaled in one deep breath. "Adam. If you don't get up right now, your father's going to be very upset."

That line drew Adam's attention. He twisted away from the ledge and dusted off his shorts, which he wore in spite of the cold, pale day. He was always complaining about having to wear pants—one of the things she loved about her sweet, sweet boy. He crossed his arms and trudged toward the sliding glass door, where August immediately squeezed him tightly. "When I'm Chief, *everyone* will have to listen to me. Just like Dad."

Yes, she thought distantly, the voice distraught to her ears. *One day you'll be king of the world, little prince. Just like your father.* The thought filled her with dread.

♦

The flood and its accompanying virus (or was it the other way around?) made outside interaction risky: school, shopping, errands, and the lot. Their "house" (which bore little in common with the white-paneled suburban boxes of yesteryear) was both their sanctum and their prison. It was on the top floor of the recently finished skyscraper that they simply referred to as "the pole." One could see the entire city sprawled out below from their tall, lonely place. Adam particularly enjoyed watching his father's excavators tunnel out United's latest endeavor, a subterranean economic hub that he alleged would return Pittsburgh to its glory.

Some days felt shorter than others, some longer. The months came and went in a haze. The year had yet to turn over, which August was looking forward to; by the first day of 0002 P.F., her pregnancy would be but a memory, along with her constant nausea and exhaustion. It would also mark one year closer to 9999 P.F., the last year before the newly formed government would have to expand its four-integer timestamp to five. The last era in human history had not surpassed four integers, so the New American Colonies assumed the next would not do so either.

The changing times also marked a shift in motivation behind George's work. Adam did not notice any change. "When's Dad coming home?" Adam had always asked. August initially sought to reason with her son: *Honey, your father's very.* That quieted him—for a time.

Adam quickly took to mocking her, bellowing *"The Chief's busy"* in reply, summoning the most baritone voice he could muster. August's face had resisted smiling initially. She knew she should scold him for such ass-wipish behavior; her grandparents would have. Instead, she felt her giant tummy and tried to recall the last time her husband had spent an uninterrupted night with her and their son.

◆

August put Adam away for a nap and escaped to the balcony to breathe in the fresh air while looking out at her husband's clogged city. The tributaries that'd once cleanly defined Pittsburgh had since become bloated and misshapen, like varicose veins. The flood affected each neighborhood arbitrarily, based on their natural elevations and the rivers' deviations. The lower one lived, the wetter and sicker they got.

August sat, blew on her coffee, and looked down from her high nest. Down below, *way* down below, she imagined her husband busy at work solving his precious Subterranean's endless stream of setbacks. One month it was a drainage issue, the next ventilation. And so on. She did not doubt whether he was actually too busy to visit with his family, both born and in the making. She understood the nonstop stress that helming a business exuded; she'd done it herself, albeit to a much more microscopic degree. Hell, she *admired* her husband's impulse to remain busy at all times. His mind was one of uninterrupted chaos, a nonstop continuum of passion and humor and fury, a busy, busy bee.

Even so, she felt bitter about it in her own selfish way. She felt obligated to feel that way. August loved his busy, wayward mind. She hated what she loved most about it: that it reminded her of hers.

Busy bees. Buzzzz. There were few, if any, of the sort below; people avoided the water and each other in equal measures. The city was quiet and shiny, the sun glinting off its muddy new canals and drowned concrete. August gulped down her caffeine. It made her nauseous now and again, but her caffeine dependency necessitated the occasional yackery.

Bzzzz!

The angry noise came seemingly from nowhere. August spun and yelped like a proper lady, spilling coffee on her slippers. She shielded her belly out of instinct, though it was not necessary. A laptop-size scouting drone hovered behind her, casually scanning her with its flashing red camera. It sat still and stared back at August like a tenured neighborhood raccoon.

The drone lowered until it hovered an inch or so off the ground. August feared it might sprout spider legs and crawl onto her. It did not; rather, it made a grinding noise and abandoned its load, a small gray box that fell neatly on the ground. The drone then lost interest in her and flew up and away like a bat out of hell, rotors chopping the air violently. She turned and watched the thing swoop down from their home's balcony, maneuvering the shifting winds like a mother bird returning to its hatchlings.

The smooth metallic gift fit in her hand and was about the size of an espresso mug. It was a small figurine of a stag, nose, tail, and antlers all forged from one piece of shiny nickel. She turned it over and discovered a small latch on its underbelly. She popped it open curiously; a tiny paper scroll lay inside the small compartment.

August looked over her shoulder before unfurling the message—a silly movement, she realized, given the altitude. The author's handwriting was half print, half cursive:

Hello. It's been a while. A lot has changed. I'll be in town on the 26. If you like, we can meet at the Museum of Natural History. There's a lot to say.
Your loving father,
Bill

August crumpled the note to throw it over the edge of the balcony. The little paper ball was about to leave her fist and tumble a hundred stories into the flood below when the sliding door opened behind her. Her son stood quiet, rubbing his eyes. "Can I watch TV?" he muttered, sleep still in his voice.

August swallowed and tried to erase the stress from her face. "Sure." Adam tottered back inside.

She toyed with the note in her hand before she stuffed it into the hem of her bulging yoga pants. She closed her eyes and counted to five.

◆

It came to be that time of day. Her days had become slow, intentional things since the flood: wake, coffee, breakfast, pretend to homeschool for about an hour before inevitably surrendering to "new math" and its puzzling stress load and August's inability to provide serious instruction. They'd inevitably shift to some other indoor recreation, like putting together some confection together or playing games.

Adam came to recognize that at around 15:00 (the government had implemented military time alongside its new calendar), his mother would grow too tired to entertain any more asinine behavior. He usually spent the time before Abdul showed up for night school drawing or reading. After came dinner and bed at 21:00 sharp, which was before his father came home.

At precisely 15:14, August lay down on the couch to rest. She watched Adam briefly contemplate the fridge's contents before selecting his favored snack of chocolate milk and a banana and escaping to his room. She closed her eyes before her nap hit her and brainstormed ways to convince George that a field trip to his family museum was safe and necessary.

◆

Their arguments were rarely loud but were often left unfinished. Both August and her husband were overtly conscious of how confrontation might impact their sons' development; the boys needed to grow steadily and become *robust* men, just like their father. August used this same point to help aid her argument.

In a year free of flood and Tubo, Adam would have been exposed to a myriad of extracurriculars: sports outings, after-school clubs, *school*, and field trips to places including, but not limited to: the Crombie Museum of Art. The Crombie Free Library. And the Crombie Museum of Natural History.

Missing out on such things was bad for his development, August reasoned; therefore, it was bad for George too. "It's *your* fucking museum, George. Make it happen. He needs to get out, or else he'll wind up being scared of *everything*. Not just you."

August knew her husband's natural response to criticism; he had an uncanny knack for proving his dissenters wrong. George left the argument without finishing it, grumbling they would "talk about it later," which August was not sure how he would make time for. George's work (i.e., his life) began at 4:00 AM sharp, so they would have to discuss the museum issue sometime before then. Maybe they would share a dream about their conversation, and that way they would come to a conclusion.

August woke up to get sick at precisely 5:55 AM, a recent development in her pregnancy. She went to make coffee and found one of her husband's handwritten instructions waiting on the kitchen table:

Called this morning. You have a private exhibition from 12-5. Abdul's coming with. Pack a lunch. I love you.

No. 26 Month 5, 0001 P.F.

Abdul was silent on the drive through Pittsburgh's formerly bustling downtown. George had seen fitting their SUV with a lift kit, off-road tires, and a snorkel in order to traverse the flood's diminishing but still substantial depth. He navigated the confusing labyrinth of roads with a stone mask etched over his face. August copied his silence while Adam buzzed excitedly in the back seat.

They were the only visitors allowed inside for the afternoon, just as her husband had promised. They passed through the same large bay doors that the Crombie Museum of Natural History used to accept its (literally) mammoth-sized artifacts. A meager-chested museum worker wearing a mask politely greeted them. "The tour starts in ten minutes," he informed the dark vehicle, its external mics picking up his voice and sending it to the SUV's sound system. Abdul flashed the brights to signal he understood and idled forward. They parked beside the entrance.

They rejected a guide to curate their tour. Instead, they let Adam's curiosity lead the way, which inevitably took them everywhere. The museum's trappings included a practice excavation site where they took turns dusting off fake dinosaur bones from undiscovered plots in the earth. Also on display: a plethora of full-scale diagrams of prehistoric beasts, a gallery of primitive weapons used by prehistoric man, a fully stocked self-service fro-yo kiosk, and an entire exhibit dedicated to the ecology of the Sahara. Each discovery newly overjoyed Adam, his eyes set to burst with curiosity—one of the things she loved about her sweet, sweet boy.

August chewed at her lip, supporting her waist while following Adam's lead. She tried to copy his enthusiasm for the subject material, but her stomach would not abandon its uncomfortable bloated feeling. The symptom was not brought on by her pregnancy. Something else was troubling her—something far more consequential. She wasn't sure whether Abdul could detect it. He seemed altogether too distracted by his duty to preside over her and her sons.

Abdul eventually recused himself from his duty when his Loop (a prototype from United's newest subsidiary, United Technologies) alerted him of some pressing matter that demanded discussion with the Chief's other security personnel. He removed his laptop from his pack and set up in the museum's vacant gift shop while August and Adam continued exploring.

The hour approached 16:00 and the only box yet to be checked was a forty-five-minute walking cinematic experience titled *Age of the Colossus: The Jurassic Period.* The sliding theater formed a disjointed circle that wrapped around the museum's perimeter. They entered at its southern mouth. August unenthusiastically put on the AR headset designed to enhance her experience and in all likelihood give her a headache.

The quality of the displays far exceeded her expectations. She mirrored her son's amazement as they left their flooded reality and were dropped into a safari set in the Jurassic age. Giant, feathered creatures sniffed at them as they progressed along the seemingly alive corridor. A narrator with a compelling British accent enriched each visual splendor via their attached headphones:

Our lives today are luxurious compared to those of our primordial ancestors. We are free to browse grocery store aisles and purchase whatever we may be craving on a particular day: fruits, vegetables, meat, dairy. Men are omnivores, flexible consumers; as such, we have mastered how to manipulate our natural world.

Their headsets cut to moving images of grocery shoppers swathed in white, looking down and smiling at their prepackaged selections before placing them happily in their carts.

Today's humans are far less connected to the environment than ever before. We no longer must hunt for our food or clean our clothes in a stream. Today's economy revolves around a globalized system governed by such puzzling principles as "law" and "morality." During the Jurassic period, however, such conveniences did not exist.

The scene swiftly changed. Time rewound in million-times speed; humanity blinked from existence and was replaced by massive, roving creatures.

Moreover, our species did not yet exist. As you will learn today, life in the Jurassic period bore nothing in common with the life we enjoy today. Our Earth, its ecology, its environment, even our continents—all of it was once different. The scene rushed outward, portraying Earth as it was, with Pangaea as its chief landmass.

The narrator continued, although the man's speech could not stand up to the sights that surrounded them. They fell deeper into their alternating states of disorientation, terror, and joy with each new scene. Some colossi gazed down at them sort of sadly with their cattle eyes, whereas their predatorial counterparts watched with eyes deprived of morality. Both species were subject to a simultaneously lawless and orderly system in which only *live* or *die* mattered, the narrator explained in his glib English accent as August stared, perplexed by the gentle giants. Through her elation, fear, and confusion, August felt at peace. She let her son's fingers leave hers. Adam wandered farther ahead to take in more sights.

Her father's ghost had mostly gone from her mind when he spoke her name. August shrieked and spun; her headset went tumbling to the floor. The land before time dissipated. She was back to standing on the theater's ugly metal rolling pavement, surrounded by nonsensical moving screens, which synched with the AR's display. The first thing she saw was Adam craning his neck about the corridor with his goggles and headphones attached, totally unaware of time and space.

And then she met her father.

She tried to distinguish the man's face in the theater's shifting light; it contorted his features into weird, jagged edges. Each time the light moved, she recognized a new (or old—it was all new to her) feature: his smooth cheek, gulched by a fresh scar; his hazel eyes reflecting the theater's monochromatic light; his chin, nearly identical to Adam's. She scanned his face for a long time as they rolled gently along the metal walkway. "I'm sorry," he said softly.

Bill stroked her cheek, then her belly. His voice was at once the same and the opposite of what she had imagined.

◆

The final twenty-six minutes of *Age of the Colossus* were captivating enough to keep Adam's attention from shifting for even a moment. August spent the entirety of those twenty-six minutes confused. Her father, who allegedly stood before her, did not. The man she encountered had no relation to her father. Perhaps an odd, distorted version of him, fine. But not *him*. Not Bill Milo. Not how her grandfather described him.

This man had confounding eyes and called himself *Edenson*. All he could seem to focus on initially was August's appearance. "You grew up to look just like your mother." August did not react because she had never seen her mother. Not in memory or in pictures or otherwise.

The man digressed and spoke of distant things. He detailed his journey since he woke up in a hospital in Germany. It ended in exaltation. "We can go back to the way things were; how things should've been." He told her more, though none of it she grasped: Water's lifesaving grace, how a man in some distant garden had shown him the way to find happiness, their need to reunite under one leader, a patriarch figure whose power was untold. His eyes were incapable of staying in one place, darting from her eyes to her stomach to Adam and back to her, yet they still felt prescient. His shifting stare had a chilling effect that made her want to escape the ring-shaped theater.

She touched his arm at one point, to see if he was warm. "Where have you been?" she breathed. "Where were you ...?" His skin felt unnaturally warm against hers.

"Searching," the man replied.

Interlude

July 6, 2024
Death

JOHN'S TOMATOES grew faster than he could pick or eat them. It didn't bother him. It was the smell he was after.

John! his mother would shout from the balcony while managing the clothesline. *Bring me something from the garden.* She didn't have to specify *what*; John eagerly returned with an armful of ripe, red fruit, their grassy smell covering his shirt. *We ate them like apples back then.*

He had good days and bad days. On good days, he remembered the right things at the right times. On bad days, he remembered everything at the same time. The memories came at their own chaotic rhythm. *Dad, look!* It's 1980; Bill grins and holds up a fish by the lip. He has buckteeth. *Hey, Milo! Here's how you cook a pie.* It's 1964; a man handles a rumbled pack of aluminum over a blast furnace with a pair of tongs. Sometimes there were no voices, just sensations. It's 1942; a soccer ball slaps into his foot. His brain responds in alarm, looking for a teammate to pass to. It's 1976: his Volvo 240 bumbles forward, responding to his foot on the pedal with no hesitancy. He doesn't know where he's going. It's 1996: his granddaughter hugs him, her tiny arms barely reaching his waist. He doesn't know who she is.

"Mr. Milo? Are you okay?"

And he was back, sitting in a plastic lawn chair and admiring the tomato vines, and it was a good day. "Yes, sweetheart. Just enjoying the good air." Teresa took good care of John, and he did his best to do the same for her. It was harder on his bad days, but he tried nonetheless. She smiled, her eyes crinkling, and went inside to start dinner.

A fly landed on John's nose. He scrunched his cheek, and it retreated and landed again. John rose shakily from his chair and went to walk amongst the giant vines, feeling Teresa's protective gaze from the kitchen window. *To hell with her*, he thought. To hell with caution; he wanted to cover himself in the tomatoes' green smell and pretend he was still young.

The rough leaves greeted him like an old friend. It was cool and dusty and secret underneath. He reached the end of the first row, scooped a bucket from the ground, and began plucking the drooping fruit from their vines, the ripe ones that his mother liked. His hands were cracked and blemished, but the tomatoes were that way too, and it was soothing.

When the bucket was half-full, he retreated to the shade and sat. It was warm but not humid at all. The air was clean; Carolina's cleanest, according to the elder-care spokesperson. "*Mediterranean climate*," John scoffed aloud.

John sniffed the air and determined that fish was for dinner. Teresa was a good cook when she stuck to her roots. At first, she'd insisted on making the stuff they'd taught her at the school where ladies learn how to take care of old people: meatloaf, soup, mush. Anything chewable. When John asked if she enjoyed cooking, she quickly replied, *Yes*. But the apprehension in her voice hinted at a different reality. Then John began regaling his mother's cooking out loud, and Teresa suddenly could not contain herself. She talked a bit excitedly and a bit sadly about her grandmother's cooking. John slowly smooth-talked his way into ditching the nursing home fare for Teresa's grandmother's cocina. His diet had made a marked improvement ever since. He figured she still took it light on the seasoning and whatnot, given her duty to his health. But he had ditched the bland chewables in favor of something with a bit of soul to it, and that was what mattered.

He stared at the tomatoes for a very long time. A spoon fell to the floor somewhere in the kitchen and went unnoticed as John gazed at the stacked canopies. A child was running amongst the vines, his feet crunching in the dirt. He'd seen the boy's face before but could not match a name to it. John frowned. He knew a piece of him lived somewhere inside the boy—where or what part of him, he wasn't sure.

The child emerged from the vines. It was just half a face, the other half suddenly obscured by his mother's hip. "Mommy," the boy murmured. He wasn't old enough to know much more than that word.

"Pa, I have to go," said the mother.

"What's your name?" John chuckled, ignoring her.

"Pa ..."

A man in a suit and gleaming leather shoes suddenly emerged from the vines, his stiff heels somehow clicking in the thin grass. John balled his fists. "Fucking Kaiser," he growled.

The woman sighed and looked at her husband. "It's just the shoes." She pet her son's hair. "Let's just go."

Oh no, a tiny remote voice inside John's head screamed. He was having a bad day now. His arms trembled, and his neck flopped back meekly. His head hit the lawn chair, and he sat there, staring at the sun.

Dad. John knew the voice. It was his son. His son. His son ...

"*Bill!*" John screamed thinly. He looked up to the heavens and beyond. "Tell me where you are!" Bill did not reply, for he could not. He was not there. Hadn't been for years.

The neurons in John's brain fired aimlessly. He saw splashes of color. Clips of memories assaulted his prefrontal cortex, some clearer than others. A house on fire; gently laying an Otis Redding record in his brand-new player; a finicky car battery jumpstarting, followed by cheers. It's 1946; his brother leans out past the rail of a ship, smiling. He asks John how long he thought until they arrived. *Soon*, he hears himself say.

John's tongue lolled aimlessly in his mouth and settled between his molars. His chest heaved once, twice, then quit. By the time Teresa came outside to announce dinner, John was dead. An ambulance came screaming but left quiet.

"Any relatives?" asked one of the paramedics, casually sipping his coffee.

Teresa shook her head slowly. "I think a daughter. I don't think they speak much."

◆

John was buried in a small cemetery beside his wife. His funeral was well attended by friends and family. There was only one key absence.

Tears were shed and condolences said, but underneath it all, there was quiet relief. For all men shrivel and eventually die, and then are mostly forgotten.

And yet, the vines grew long after John was gone.

Part IV

He had, they said, tasted in succession all the apples of the tree of knowledge, and, whether from hunger or disgust, had ended by tasting the forbidden fruit.
– Victor Hugo

XVII

April 30, 2043
Canyon's End Military Base, California, Western Alliance

THE SCREEN refreshed with an audible *tick* reminiscent of an old projector transitioning slides:

Are you hateful?

"No."

Who is your best friend?

"Don't have one."

Who was your last best friend?

"Never had one."

Who was your last best friend?

"My mother."

What do you fear most?

"Personality tests."

What do you fear most?

"Quiet expectation."

How many men have you killed?

"None."

If given a choice, would you save an enemy or let them perish?

"It depends."

If given a choice, would you save an enemy or let them perish?

"Save them."

What's more important: unity or trust?

"Trust. Trust leads to unity."

What did you want to be growing up?

"An artist."

Have you ever wanted to kill a man?

"No."

Have you ever wanted to kill a man?

"Yes."

Would you kill if it meant saving a friend?

"Yes. I think."

What is your first name?

"Adam."

What is your last name?

The machine repeated itself.

"Edenson."

Thank you for your participation. Goodbye.

Dr. Hsu knocked before entering. "That's all, Father."

Adam nodded. "Has Aldridge cleared us to sail yet?"

"I believe so. I'll check with him—"

"No, don't. I was meaning to speak with him, anyway. Where can I find him?"

The doctor frowned. "I would check the main cockpit. Take the stairway, the one next door, up to the main deck and—"

"Thank you." Adam began walking away briskly.

Hsu saluted dutifully. "Water Is Life."

Adam strolled through the fluorescent-lit tunnels of Canyon's End, nodding at the privates and cadets who saluted him as he passed. Two grunts fiddling with a bunch of wires saw him coming and abandoned their work. One of them inadvertently shocked themselves as the wires grazed him; he stood at full attention until Adam dismissed them with a nod. "Keep up the good work," he grunted as he walked past. The men waited until after Adam turned the corner to relax their shoulders.

Adam enlisted the day before he left Los Angeles. They'd made the decision on the basis it would bring him closer to his troops; in other words, to make him seem *normal*. A Father to all, just like Bill. The strategy seemed to have worked to a tee. Few soldiers saw his enlistment for what it was: false advertising. Though his advisors insisted otherwise, Adam was dubious whether San Franciscans would react with the same instant shock and awe. He somehow doubted it, given that it was the one place Father Bill had ever called home. He often explained his penchant for the city in *Sympathies*: *The buildings are stacked one atop the other like towers of cards. The streets and bridges and parks are all constructed against impossible odds, the rolling hills a constant reminder that nothing comes easy. It is a city under constant siege, the ocean and mountains never releasing their tight grip. It is a city unlike any other. I guess I'll call it home.*

Surely, they would label Adam an imposter. They'd had their Father—why embrace another?

Adam found the captain more or less where Hsu predicted. He was pacing in the hall outside the cockpit when Adam arrived, gnawing passively on a black-enameled pencil while his eyes focused on a chart in his hands. "Captain." He jumped when Adam announced himself, scattering his papers and pens all over the floor. Adam bent over to help him clean up while he apologized emphatically. When the mess was gathered, the captain stood tall and saluted him.

"It's an honor, Father."

"The honor's mine. Are we set to sail?"

"Yes, Father. Here—I've laid out our itinerary."

Two sailors co-captaining the giant vessel excused themselves when he and the captain entered the cockpit. "We'll drop anchor about three miles out from San Francisco. From there, you will be escorted by nauticycle."

Adam frowned. "I've never ridden one."

The captain nodded fervently, as if this were something he'd long mulled over. "I'm afraid it's too dangerous to maneuver the *Coronado* so far inland. The water tends to shift along the bay. A symptom of ocean warming, I'm told. If a different convoy would make you more comfortable, I can have that arranged."

Adam patted the old soldier on the shoulder. "Easy. I wasn't getting on you. I'll be fine." The captain looked down and smiled nervously.

"No—it's just a bit overwhelming is all. I am to be a part of history ..." Adam could see tears sparkling in his eyes. "Water Is Life," he choked, bowing deeply.

◆

The *Coronado* departed on schedule at 7:00 AM and arrived by the same virtue at 3:00 PM. Adam spent the afternoon perched on the ship's deck with his journal as his only company. His so-called contemporaries tended to avoid him out of respect, fear, veneration, or perhaps a mixture of the three. Adam was happy to listen to the ocean hiss and foam alone.

San Francisco was hard to call a city. It was more akin to a labyrinth, its hedges replaced with canals. Rising sea levels had made the cityscape lopsided; in some places, the tops of old high-rises stood parallel with the roofs of newly built homes.

There was not a cloud in sight to impede their view of the Golden Gate Bridge. Adam was spellbound; how could such a miraculous thing be made for no other reason than to encourage people to go and to come? The bridge grew larger in Adam's field of vision until the salt-foam sizzle at the *Coronado*'s rear suddenly quit.

As they prepared to drop anchor, Capt. Aldridge emerged from his cockpit in the company of three fresh-faced sailors. "Father, allow me to introduce your escorts." The squad formed a line and stiffened at attention.

Adam pocketed his hands. "Thank you for your help today. You can call me Adam." He extended his arm to the first soldier, who hesitated in his chin-high posture before shaking his hand wearily. "Just show me the ropes. I'll do my best not to drag you back."

"At ease," ordered the captain. They nodded graciously and took turns greeting him. Two other soldiers strained with lowering the nauticycles into the ocean.

The sailors turned and saluted the captain (Adam included) and began boarding the cycles. Adam wobbled as he adjusted to the ocean's rock and sway, aided by two small stabilizers strapped to either side of his cycle. Adam started the quiet engine as they'd instructed him and felt a gentle churning in the sea beneath him.

They opened at a slow pace so Adam could spend some time acquainting himself with his machine. The ocean reacted wildly to his movements at first, splashing up the nose of his cycle and soaking his torso. After some trial and error, Adam learned to work with the waves rather than try to fight them. His guides gradually accelerated until their pace suited both Adam's novice and their lead-man's concern for staying on schedule.

The whip of the wind rushing past them was deafening. They communicated mostly by signal, but each man wore an earpiece that could offer live feedback to their comrades upon saying a command phrase. Their CO, a gray-haired lieutenant named Simpson, paused once to turn back toward his comrades and point toward the city. "The bridge is our best shot. The other canals are too tricky to cross during a swell. There's debris at either side, so we'll shoot straight up the center." He looked toward Adam. "Mayor Cho has security arranged portside, so you'll have nothing to worry about when we arrive, Father.

The crowds should be mild." Adam nodded and boosted two thumbs up. Simpson turned and revved his motor, and they kept on.

The bridge became magnificently large as they approached. Its size was somewhat distorted compared to the photos Adam had seen; waves crashed over where the abutments had once projected from the sea. Simpson slowed down ahead of the sunset-colored behemoth and steered them into a diamond formation, with Adam at its center.

Simpson's promise of a modest welcome was misled. The crowd had outgrown the bridge's platform and was forced to spill out to the cliffs on either side. It was a wonder the thing had not yet collapsed. Some had pitched tents and camped, likely days ahead of the event. Some watched them approach with binoculars; others closed their eyes and muttered prayers. Some sat in wheelchairs, others propped on each other's shoulders. Some reached out to him, others held up signs with messages ranging from *Welcome Home, Father!* to IS THIS REAL LIFE? All were restless.

Adam heard their clamor over their engines. They shuffled excitedly, gossiping and theorizing until a woman on the bridge pointed Adam out from the convoy. "*It's him!* The one with the training wheels!" Her claim spread quickly, and the crowd erupted, shoving each other away for a glimpse at the Untold.

"Is it him?"

"He looks way shorter than Father Bill."

"Father! Show me the Way!"

A wall of fluttering hands appeared; some merely waved, while others yearned for him as if they could reel him with fishing line. Adam watched, amazed.

"We have to pass, *now*," Simpson buzzed in Adam's ear, returning him to the present. They whirred their engines and aimed beneath the bridge in a staggered line, Adam following second. As they crossed, the crowd's weight shifted from one edge of the bridge to the other, following Adam with their eyes and feet, reaching out, drawing him in. Adam slowed down.

Adam veered left from the formation and quit his engine. He bobbed up and down on the choppy waves, exasperated by the bridge's massive steel beams. "*Zephyr.*" His visor beeped in response to the command phrase. "Stop here." Adam removed his visor and waved to the crowd. They celebrated in near ecstasy.

"*We have to keep moving!*" Simpson shouted over the waves, removing his earpiece.

"Relax. They won't bite," said Adam, grinning like a fool. His escorts removed their helmets and waved cautiously alongside him. The crowd's clamoring intensified.

Adam pointed at a staircase carved into the nearest cliff. His eyes lit as he surveyed the crowd that waited above. "Can you get me up there?"

Simpson guided himself toward Adam and clipped onto his cycle, connecting the two so they bobbed in unison. "Father, that would impose a serious security risk. The rocks are slick going up, and you never know who in the crowd might try something."

"They're gonna follow us to Oakland either way. Might as well get to know them." Simpson frowned, but offered no further protest.

Simpson maneuvered the party to a landing point on the bridge's northern end. The midshipmen disembarked their cycles and left Adam waiting. The crowd migrated to the cliffside to be amongst the first to see the Untold up close, in person.

Simpson guided the other men up the rocks from below. They landed on a small vista and ushered the crowd away so Adam could ascend. Simpson waited at the water's edge until they'd formed a wide enough security blanket for Adam. He offered him his hand, and they slowly progressed up the salt-sprayed rocks until their rubber feet touched solid ground. The crowd hushed when Adam landed. They poked their heads above and beneath the lieutenants' outstretched arms. Some pointed cameras. The air felt stiff, so Adam broke it. "Thank you for the warm welcome; I'm flattered."

They cried out for him. His escorts resisted the force until Adam placed his hand on Simpson's shoulder. "Keep going with the others. I'll meet you across the bay." Before he could protest, Adam stepped into the crowd.

The crowd parted before him and weaved together to form a mass behind him, human souls strung together and moving as one. Adam came to the feet of the stone steps leading up to the bridge's walkway. More men, women, and children awaited him above. They saw him and cheered, a mob so dense they nearly piled on top of each other.

Looking at Adam, they saw themselves. They saw life. Looking at him, they saw the future. They were a collective then, unbound, unbroken, one people under one leader: one Father.

Adam climbed. His people followed.

XVIII

IN THE evening, Tyler set about cleaning the stable as best he could. He rearranged the stacks of hay that had been put there decades before, before the flood made tourism a luxury intangible to most. He swept the thin carpet of dust and dirt covering the floor into one of the stables, then covered it with more hay. He stripped nude and upended the suds his jailer had given him over his head. He scrubbed himself meagerly with his fingernails, rinsing himself with his limited drinking water. When there was little else that could be done, he lay on his side and waited to see if he would fall asleep.

Tyler detected the scent of fresh coffee before the door even cracked open. He had learned to eat with his nose, so he had feasted on hot dogs and s'mores for some two months. Coffee was a new smell to him, and it aroused some deep and perhaps primal impulse inside him. He could've sworn he could smell a smoking Chesterfield alongside it, though this was likely contributed by his brain's correlation of the two.

The door opened, and the morning light revealed the dust motes he breathed. Tyler did not see his guest until the door shut and the light returned to its normal haze. The man was tall and handsome in his own way. He was bald and clean-shaven with dark, scruffy eyebrows. He was tan, though Tyler couldn't discern whether this was a product of the sun or his pigment. He yawned into the tray of coffee he was carrying. "Good morning." His voice was tinged with the remains of an abandoned accent.

Tyler scratched his mangy beard. It had crept down his neck toward his chest. "Good morning," he replied throatily. He eased into one of the patches of hay he'd set up like chairs in an office and pointed to the one opposite him. "I figured we could sit." The man nodded and sat, crossing his legs while pouring himself a coffee. He watched Tyler stare hungrily at the black liquid as he poured and smiled. He poured a second cup.

"Cream? Sugar?" he asked lightly.

Bourbon. "Sugar." Tyler blinked. "Please." The man neatly sifted two spoonfuls of sugar into his drink, stirred, and handed it to him. Tyler instantly put the mug to his lips and burned his tongue indifferently. He went back for more. The man stirred cream into his own and set down the silver platter.

"My name is Abdul. I'm very pleased to meet you, Mr. ...?"

Tyler nodded and tipped back his mug eagerly. A slosh of grounds stuck to his tongue. "Just Tyler."

Abdul nodded. "I thought this morning we might speak about your future with us, Tyler," Abdul said gently, appearing very comfortable in his hay chair. He set down his cup and watched him intently. "Have you ever heard what life is like in the West, Tyler?"

"Dry," Tyler grunted.

Abdul laughed. It was a lighthearted sound. "So you say. That's what I used to think as well." He looked Tyler up and down. "Something tells me that your feet aren't dry so very often."

"I do what I have to."

Abdul sipped his coffee and smiled sheepishly. "I'm relieved to hear this." He reached down for the carafe and refilled Tyler's mug. "How have my men treated you so far?" he asked. Tyler allowed his mug to cool this time.

"Could use some company ... but a prisoner can't have everything, can he?"

Abdul nodded. "Not in the traditional sense, no. That would go against the rules." His eyes narrowed. "Tell me where you are from, Tyler."

Tyler frowned. He didn't like bringing back those memories—any memories, but specifically those he'd practiced forgetting. "Long Island. Close to the city. You?"

"I am not from here," Abdul confessed.

Tyler smirked. "Everyone's from somewhere."

For a moment, Abdul's body language changed. His eyes sharpened into threatening shards and he stiffened somewhat. Tyler noted a tautness in his forearms that had not been there seconds before. He could tell that his hands were familiar with violence; his movements carried a certain precision. He sensed that if he were to pounce on him now, he would not come out victorious.

His anger dissipated just as suddenly as it had appeared, and he shook his head and was at ease again. "I lived in Pittsburgh for many years."

"Never heard of a Frog from Pittsburgh."

"No, it is uncommon. But if I have learned anything, it is that people learn to adapt to their environments in unexpected ways." He abandoned his mug and leaned closer to him. "They tell me you almost killed one of my men." *And you killed two of mine*, Tyler thought. "His name is Alex. He's only nineteen, still just a boy. The doctor says he's very lucky to be alive. In any case, he'll suffer irreversible brain damage." Abdul rubbed his hands together. "Do you know what it's like to lose a child?"

"Can't say I do. Never had one."

"It is a hell that brings a man to the brink of destruction. It causes a man to question his faith. But that is a trap set by the devil himself.

God commits no errors. To say otherwise is blasphemy." Without blinking, Abdul reached into his pocket and unveiled the GeoLoop they had confiscated from him upon his arrival. "Do you know whom this belongs to?" he asked.

"I took it from someone who didn't need it," he said plainly.

"I see." He eyed its gleaming edge. "It is a remarkable piece of equipment, to be sure. With it, one can travel to whatever destination they please. Without it, one is limited to what they can see. You made the sensible choice in claiming it as your own, correct?" Tyler made no move to answer, yet Abdul smiled regardless. "Yes, I would agree. But you only saw the benefit; remarkable as it may be, it is the only reason our scouts were able to track you down. There is a trade-off in everything, you see. Nothing is wholly righteous. Only the truth is; God's truth." Abdul laid the equipment gingerly across his thigh. "But some evils are necessary. The Loop's owner was in your way, just as Alex was. This I can understand. War is not fun. You and I know that quite well. We do not enjoy taking part in it; only monsters do. But war is often *necessary*. And the war mind is different from the regular mind. You must be ready to use it when necessary. If you silence this voice, you die. You know this just as well as I do. Your predicament attests to it. You've not shaved in two months and you're covered in fleas and ticks, but that doesn't bother you because you're just doing what's necessary to survive. You are playing the long game. What is the saying, 'In it for the long haul'? Yes; few are capable of thinking in such ways. I do not take such men for granted." Abdul cleared his throat. "What do you know about our cause, Tyler?"

Tyler grunted. "That you're all part of the same cult."

"Ah." Abdul's smile returned. He seemed to take great joy in responding to Tyler's criticisms. "Most of the things you have heard about the West—'Frogs,' as you say—are false. But this you already knew. The things we supposedly believe in—'Water Is Life,' 'it is in us all'—it is all nonsense. They are just distractions from what's really happening."

He paused, waiting for Tyler to say something. "And what's that?" he asked dryly. Abdul's eyes lit up.

"Before the flood, before the virus, before steel and technology and pharmaceuticals, before *all* these things, people used to go out and simply *be*. They were not obligated to brag to each other about their status. They enjoyed each other's company. They enjoyed life. There weren't all these, eh ..." He crinkled his nose in overt disgust at the GeoLoop. "*Distractions.*" Tyler couldn't help but nod in agreement. He remembered those times; movie-hopping with his friends. Smoking his first joint. Weekends at the pier. *Good times. Innocent times.* "I want you to help me eliminate these extra things: selfishness, vanity, frustration." He leaned forward and grasped Tyler's shoulder— *The closer,* Tyler thought bitterly. "Our only hope for peace is if one man succeeds; one Father."

The stable was quiet. Tyler made no move to reply until the silence became too deafening to ignore. "I don't care about your Father," he rasped. "And I don't care about the distractions. I think they're fine."

"Ah, yes. You are a wise man. Tell me something: Do you pray?" Tyler shook his head. "No?" Abdul asked, smiling ever so slightly. "You're telling me you never think to yourself, 'Please God, let this be so'?" Tyler shook his head, yet Abdul continued as if he'd nodded. "Of course. It is only natural. Tell me: Has God ever answered your prayers?" The silence was almost cutting. "*No,*" Abdul concluded. "But that does not mean it is not your duty to serve God's will."

A laughing thing took hold of him. The laughs emerged from Tyler's belly, working their way up through his chest until he was wheezing in front of Abdul. He coughed feebly. "*Fuck* God. I don't believe in fairy tales." He kept laughing. Abdul shifted in his chair, uncomfortable, and sighed.

"God embraces true believers and skeptics. What you believe in is irrelevant. God has called upon us to serve a greater good."

"And what would that be?" Tyler asked, bemused.

"To make the world whole again." Tyler's laughs slowed until they subsided. "There. Does that align with your god?"

"I told you, I don't believe—"

"You do not believe in a unified world?" Tyler was quiet. "It is not for us to question powers greater than us. Define it however you like. What do you truly miss? Is it fine goods, or the right to toil away at a screen? Or is it something simpler? Normalcy, perhaps? Be as it may. I do not need you to believe in or care for our new Father; I only need that you *respect* him. He alone has the power to make us whole again." His eyes wandered, gazing past Tyler to the stable's dust-ridden corners. "The change has already begun. Many follow the Way in secret, and even more are readying themselves to make the journey west. Even floodlings have begun to realize the futility of living in fear. Not even your government can stop this change, no matter how much they try."

Tyler stared at his placid expression and shook his head. He forced himself to remember where and who he was. "Why are you keeping me ... I'm not ..." He did not know how to convey himself. Abdul tapped his head.

"You are a soldier. You do whatever is necessary to survive. And, in this case, a soldier is precisely the type of person I need; someone who will do what is necessary."

"Last I saw, you have plenty of good soldiers on your side."

"They do not know what you and I know."

Tyler looked at him quizzically. "What is it exactly that you want from me?"

Abdul smiled. "To kill George Crombie."

He said the words with such an utter lack of gravity that Tyler could not help but bark out a short laugh. "Why the fuck would I do that?" He wanted to throw his coffee in his face and storm out the barn door. He'd cross the river and take the same path he'd escaped down the first time. He'd walk south first, then west a bit, then south some more. He'd cross into Mexico and keep going. He'd hurry through Central America before shipping across to South America. He'd stop in Brazil, or maybe Argentina, and stay there and just *exist*; an early retirement. Or maybe not; maybe he would head north until he met the Arctic, then canoe over to Asia. He'd pause to take in Russia (what was left of it, at least), then go find himself in Asia. Where he went was irrelevant; only that he went. He'd walk, disappear, and walk, seeing but not caring until he faded from existence.

But his legs did not move. He stayed put, and instead of laughing, he frowned.

"Because it is necessary," Abdul finally said. He offered his palm out to him and waited.

Tyler stared into his empty mug, grinding away at his teeth. After some time, he asked, "What's in it for me?"

"Purpose. Unity. Normalcy. All things you crave. Or am I wrong?"

Tyler could not help but nod slowly in agreement. *Good times.* He remembered those times; he *wanted* to remember them. Tyler eyed Abdul's waiting palm. *Fuck it.*

He shook the man's hand. "But I'm not doing it for God's sake."

"You may serve whichever god you please. But know that yours has designed the same plan for us as mine," Abdul said quietly. "Only He knows our true purpose."

Interlude

October 14, 2021
Puebla, México

ALEJANDRO KNOCKED on the chapel door. A man replied almost instantaneously: "Who is it?"

"I'm here to see Mr. Blue," said Alejandro. The fixer had told him to ask for Mr. Blue.

"That's not what I asked."

"A fox who dances." The fixer's other piece of wisdom.

There was a pause as the doorman considered his answer. "One moment."

Alejandro checked to make sure his daughter was behaving. She was lying on a park bench where he'd told her to wait, gazing at the starlit alpine sky. *If anyone comes by, just tell them your father's inside. Okay, Papa.*

Though she had yet to turn eight, Isabela had already lived two lives. Though Alejandro protected her as best he could, she was still maturing at a shocking rate, a product of her environment. The last three months on the road had seemingly affected him more than it did her. He'd tried at first to ease her into the unease: *We're going for a ride in a truck today. Does that sound okay?* He didn't mention the ride being twelve hours of heat and humidity and bumps, packed like cattle in the back of a pickup truck with fifteen other crossers and jugs of gasoline bouncing at their feet. He didn't need to mention that; Isabela had outgrown her fear. In a week, the tears had dried, and she turned into the silent child he knew now. She no longer asked for her mother, either. He was jealous of her in that regard.

The door opened quickly. "Mr. Blue's ready for you now." The man was bald and heavily tattooed. He told Alejandro to spread his arms and legs, then ran his scribbled hands up and down his arms, legs, and torso. He nodded toward the chapel's arched entryway when he was done. "After you." Alejandro lingered by the door.

"Can my daughter come inside? It's very cold."

The doorman shook his head regretfully. "I'll keep an eye on her." He sounded sincere. Alejandro nodded and stepped into the chapel.

The church had appeared simple from the outside—white mortar, heavy oak doors, and a square roof with a wooden cross at its top. That all changed as soon as he entered the altar. The pews faced a cavernous, arched opening decorated with crosses, iconography and scenes from antiquity. The altar itself was carved from mahogany and painted with red poinsettias.

Mr. Blue sat alone in the chapel's front pew. He slid from the bench when he heard Alejandro enter and watched him walk down the aisle. He wore a silk suit with no tie and his hair slicked back. In his chest pocket was a folded handkerchief dotted with red poinsettias that matched the altar.

Alejandro offered his hand and suddenly felt aware of his comparatively poor appearance. He'd purchased new clothing for himself and Isabela since they'd arrived in Puebla, and they'd spent the night prior in a hotel room where they enjoyed warm showers, a luxury they had not experienced since leaving home. He would've been far more comfortable in his white coat, *Alejandro Arroyo Aguayo, Cardiólogo* stitched on the chest pocket. Instead, he wore a secondhand denim jacket. His doctoring days were well past him.

Mr. Blue shook Alejandro's hand firmly and introduced himself. "Welcome. No need for silly nicknames anymore—you can call me Juan

Carlos. Please, sit." He gestured to the bench. Juan Carlos watched Alejandro take in the altar, his eyes fleeting. Alejandro rubbed his hands in between his knees.

"My daughter is waiting for me outside and it's very cold, so please forgive me for my abruptness. The fixer said you could fly us to the States with new identification cards."

"I take no offense." Juan Carlos scratched his cheek. "Whatever the fool told you is true. I know people in the right places to make such things happen. But my services are not cheap. I assume you already know this." Alejandro nodded, though in the back of his mind he was calculating how much cash they would have left once—*if*—they landed in America.

"Will I get a work visa? Or will we become citizens?"

Juan Carlos shook his head. "No. You'll have to work for someone who agrees to take you in. They'll pay you cash. This is not a problem in the United States, as you likely know. The gringos reserve manual labor for those who look like us. Are you a skilled worker, if I may ask?"

Yes. I am a doctor, Alejandro thought bitterly. But he restrained himself. That was his old life. And besides, he did not want the man guessing how much money he had saved. "Yes. I'm a carpenter. I also speak English."

Juan Carlos nodded. "Good. And how about cooking? Cutting trees? Stuff like that?" Alejandro shook his head slowly. "Finding work won't be a problem, just as long as you don't mind getting your hands dirty ... or get a job as a carpenter. There's always help needed in the construction—"

"I'll find work," Alejandro said abruptly. "Where will we land? Who will take care of us?"

Juan Carlos rubbed his chin. "New York, Chicago, Denver, Los Angeles ... I can arrange for any of these locations. Once you arrive in the States however, you will be out of my jurisdiction. This is strictly a matter of transport. I cannot risk exposing myself beyond the border. For this reason, it's good to have friends or family waiting for you, wherever you decide."

Alejandro nodded. "I have a cousin in Seattle. I haven't spoken with him yet." He glanced warily at the altar before averting his eyes to his hands. "Will we be safe? I mean, once we land? I've heard things ..." It was hard to discern the truth from the lies on the road, and not having someone he could rely on only made matters worse. "Those guys running crossers in the desert? They say ICE is hunting down Latinos *everywhere*. Even in Los Angeles ..."

Juan Carlos scoffed. "Nobody's safe in America. Not unless you suddenly lose your pigment." The trafficker seemed bemused by this. "But as I mentioned, you will be out of my jurisdiction."

Alejandro did not flinch. A conditional life in America was better than one in Venezuela. "How much—for everything."

"Ten each." He watched Alejandro's eyes for any hesitancy. "Or, pay two and walk," he suggested. Alejandro wetted his tongue.

"I can pay half my daughter's fare now, as a down payment. The rest tomorrow, or the day after. You will have it before the flight leaves." Alejandro took out the cash bundled in his jacket—money he had earned legitimately, tributes for his work saving lives. Now it only felt *dirty* to him. He presented it to his trafficker.

Juan Carlos squeezed the paper wad to judge its thickness and slipped it into his pocket. "The only flight for Seattle this week leaves tomorrow afternoon. If you plan on joining her, you'll have to hurry and wire the funds."

Alejandro nodded. "May I make a phone call?"

"Of course."

As Alejandro rose from the pew, the door cracked open. It was the bald man, with Isabela clutching his arm.

"What did I tell you? Only clients are allowed inside."

"I'm sorry, boss. She was out there alone in the cold, so I ..."

Juan Carlos looked down at the little girl and cocked his head ever-so-slightly. Her eyes were dark and narrow and matched her sharp eyebrows. Her hair was black as midnight, waved and long, reaching down her back. Alejandro noticed his curiosity and clenched his jaw.

Isabela released Clemente's tattooed paw and sat in the pew opposite her father. "I got cold, Papa."

Alejandro reached over the aisle and squeezed his daughter's hand. "That's okay, my love. I was just about to come back. How would you like to sleep in a hotel again tonight?" Isabela looked uncertainly at the dark-haired man standing, watching her.

"Is your daughter baptized?" Juan Carlos asked suddenly. Alejandro regarded him scrupulously.

"No. Her mother and I ... We were not very religious."

Juan Carlos knelt to meet Isabela's eyes. "How would you like to be baptized today, princess?"

"What does that mean?"

"It means you are one of God's children. It's a mark of protection from God. It means that he loves you. Good things will come to you. And, for the rest of your life, you will have a godfather that protects you."

Isabela turned to her father, excitement in her eyes. "Papa? Can I?"

Alejandro looked at his daughter, and then at Juan Carlos. He felt the wad of money bulging against his front pocket.

"Anything you want, my love."

◆

Alejandro watched as oil and water dribbled down his daughter's forehead. The ceremony's minister (doubling as godfather) uttered God's name and let the moisture drip from Isabela's hair, gingerly keeping the oil from her eyes. After the rite, Juan Carlos knelt before her, removed one of the jeweled rings from his fingers, and folded Isabela's tiny hand over it. Alejandro's anger stirred. He reached down to smack Isabela's hand away. He stopped himself as he thought through the repercussions of offending the trafficker.

"No matter where you go now, your godfather will be with you," Juan Carlos whispered. "Just as long as you wear this. Can you remember that?" Isabela bobbed her head. She played idly with the ring, rolling it around in her hand. Juan Carlos kissed the crown of her head and turned to shake Alejandro's hand and congratulate him. Alejandro shook back limply.

Juan Carlos lent Alejandro his satellite phone to make his call; the buttons became slick with the oil from his daughter's baptism. Alejandro's cousin was older than him by some eight years and had gone through the legal immigration process ten years prior. He chased the American Dream by picking grapes up and down California before eventually gaining an apprenticeship as a vintner. He saved enough money to bring the rest of his family from Venezuela and now rented a few precious acres in Tacoma, where he cultivated his own grapes.

Though years had passed since they last spoke, Alejandro could tell his cousin was drunk. "*Hello?*" he answered too loudly. The phone showed it was 12:50AM in Puebla.

"Jesús?"

"Hello? Who is this?"

"Jesús," Alejandro repeated. "It's me, Alejandro. María Josefa's son."

There were scratching noises at the other end. "God, I was wondering why you hadn't called! Jito, are you good? How's Alba—"

"I need your help, cousin," Alejandro interjected.

"Of course." Alejandro smiled. He'd always wished Jesús had stayed longer in Venezuela. "Anything for you, cousin. Tell me."

He explained everything, leaving out the least savory parts. He explained where he was and how he'd gotten there. He avoided mentioning his wife. He finished by telling him that Isabela would arrive at Terminal 2 at SEA the following evening. Jesús listened carefully, wheezing a bit on the line's opposite end. Juan Carlos listened from a distance.

"Listen," said Alejandro. He tried to keep his voice level. "You've never met or seen my daughter. You have your own family to take care of. I'm asking you as a favor, not an obligation. But she is the most precious thing in the world to me. I promise, if you do this kindness for me, I'll be indebted to you for the rest of my time."

"To hell with your debts. My God ... You're family, Jito," Jesús said simply. He called for his wife. "*Lorena! Wake up!*"

"Thank you," Alejandro started. Jesús kept yelling on his end. The line shuffled, and Jesús's wife took the phone.

"Jito—our home is yours. We'll be waiting at the airport for Isabela tomorrow, okay? You just work on getting you and Alba's asses over here."

◆

In the morning, Alejandro took his daughter to the local market to shop for a present. In truth, he wanted to buy her something to remind her of him while they were apart. More pertinent to the business at hand, he had to retrieve the rest of the money for Isabela's fare. He noticed Juan Carlos's ring dangling from her neck as they meandered along the corridor of vendors. It angered him. He would call Jesús and have him confiscate it once she landed.

He told Isabela to wait at a stand where a kindly old woman was carefully rolling colorful candies in wax paper. The woman smiled with her gums at Isabela and asked for her name. Isabela smiled bashfully. "Look how beautiful you are," the old woman crooned. She winked at Alejandro before goading Isabela to see her wares.

Alejandro left her to bond with the little old lady and headed towards the brick alleyway where they had slept intermittently over the past week. He ducked beneath the brick archway that'd shielded them from the elements just a few nights prior and patted the alley's back wall until his hand struck a wobbly brick. He removed the brick and patted around inside the space he'd made. He retrieved the second wad of cash, alongside a small .32 he'd purchased from their fixer in Guatemala. He returned to Isabela and thanked the old woman, dropping some money into her palm before leaving with Isabela's hand in his own.

Alejandro led his daughter down the aisle of merchants, feeling the creases of her palm against his. "Tell me when you see something you like," said Alejandro. She nodded, toying with the heavy band dangling from her neck.

♦

The SUV was to depart from the chapel at 3:00 PM. Alejandro showed up with his daughter a half hour early and explained that she would be staying with her aunt and uncle for a while; *without* him. "It's our next adventure," Alejandro hyper-explained. Isabela sobbed and wrung her arms around her father's neck. She demanded he join her, which pained him more than anything. He promised it would only be a few weeks.

The bald doorman Clemente set down Isabela's neat-packed suitcase against the curb. Isabela and Alejandro sat holding each other on the rough pavement until a black Escalade rolled up quietly. Isabela was half-asleep by then. The sudden change had overwhelmed her.

The driver put Isabela's suitcase in the trunk. Juan Carlos was notably absent; he'd left immediately after collecting the last of Alejandro's life savings, shaking his hand grimly before being shuttled away in a dark sedan. It was not a goodbye; that Alejandro felt sure of.

Alejandro gently lifted Isabela into the back seat, clipped her seatbelt over her, and kissed her forehead. He whispered how excited her aunt and uncle were to meet her. Isabela nodded dreamily, a stuffed animal of a smiling bull propped loosely in her grasp.

Clemente began outlining Isabela's itinerary as soon as he'd shut the door. He explained that an elderly woman, who was completely unaware of the operation or its illegality, would pose as Isabela's grandmother and act as her sponsor. "Don't worry about little Isabela. She'll be safe with Doña Antigua." He showed Alejandro Isabela's false documents before handing them off to the driver, who pocketed them to later give to the Doña.

The driver pulled away as quietly as he'd come, only now he had the most precious cargo in the world in stow. Alejandro's face was stone as he watched them depart. He decided his face would not change until he earned the money to join his daughter.

The SUV turned onto a busy intersection and disappeared. Alejandro followed Clemente into the chapel to discover how he would earn his own fare.

◆

The driver picked up instantly. "Yes, boss."

"The girl is still with you?"

"Yes, boss."

"No complaints?"

"Yes, boss."

"Good," Juan Carlos purred. "Make sure Doña Antigua takes good care of her. I want my goddaughter to feel comfortable. And make sure she knows where to go from LAX. Understood?"

"It's taken care of." The driver lowered his voice so not to disturb the sleeping child in the back seat. "What about the other girls? You want me to make sure they're fed?"

Juan Carlos pinched his sinuses. "Leave the whores to the Chinese. I want you to ensure that my goddaughter doesn't get mixed in with the other cargo. Is that understood?" He practiced his English momentarily. "*You make sure.* Understood?"

"Yes, boss." Juan Carlos flipped the phone shut without another word.

His office was still for a moment until there was a knock at his door. Juan Carlos sighed and rubbed his forehead before permitting his visitor. "Yes." The door opened. It was Clemente. He stood in the doorframe, rubbing his knuckles.

"The job's almost done."

"'Almost'?"

"I mean ... It's in the cellar still. Steve's still not here with the truck."

"Let me see then." Clemente hesitated. "Now!" He nodded in haste. Juan Carlos uncapped a crystalline decanter levying a dark fluid and poured himself a glass before he stood to leave.

The staircase was molded from the same concrete as the chapel's stained floor. Juan Carlos stepped down cautiously. A splash of brandy dripped onto one of the steps.

Alejandro lay in the basement's corner, his hands and feet zip-tied together. He heard the approaching footsteps and struggled blindly, moaning beneath the rag stuffed in his mouth. Juan Carlos dropped to a squat in the room's center and observed him. He sipped from his glass.

"Don't make a mess of it," he instructed Clemente simply. Alejandro screamed upon hearing his voice. Juan Carlos stood to leave but stopped midway to the stairs. Alejandro lay helpless, choking on his tears, his sobs reduced to muffled groans. Juan Carlos approached him and knelt beside him.

"*Calm,*" he commanded before slipping the rag from Alejandro's eyes. He looked up at him desperately through one eye. The other had been reduced to a swollen pulp; Clemente's doing.

"You listening?" Alejandro inhaled loudly through his nose and nodded. "Your daughter's safe. You deserve to know that much," Juan Carlos said. Alejandro's breathing slowed. "You are very blessed. She's a special girl." Juan Carlos remembered the girl's eyes. That severe look, both light and dark, soft and intense.

Alejandro's eye shifted. Juan Carlos flinched; he had grown accustomed to violent suffering. But he recoiled at the pleading look conveyed by that one eye.

Then Alejandro began screaming like an animal, banging his head against the floor. Juan Carlos heard new footsteps entering the chapel; the rest of the crew. He stood and turned to Clemente.

"Be quiet about it. And leave no mess."

◆

Juan Carlos woke up feeling refreshed. He had slept well, comforted by the thought of his goddaughter finally being introduced to a stable environment. The Doña would take her straight to the ranch in Santa Barbara, where she would see and smell the ocean for the first time without a cloud of fear hanging over her. She would hear the waves crash without having to worry about such things as poverty, war, or starvation. Terrible, nasty things. The thought was reassuring. The father had not been capable of granting her such luxuries. He was the thing holding her down. *He* was the problem, a problem she'd inherited. His insistence on raising her had only led to her suffering. Had he simply allowed a loving Mexican family to adopt her (*or even gringo*, Juan Carlos conceded) at birth, she never would have been victim to the same suffering. But he had been too vain. He'd let emotion cloud his judgment. Now that he was gone, so was the problem. Isabela was free. Juan Carlos had solved that. He had done a good thing.

He had a mind to join her once his business in Puebla was taken care of. He expected the payment from the Chinese to arrive come morning, assuming the girls arrived on time and healthy. Though the second condition seemed to matter very little to the Triad, Juan Carlos insisted on taking care of his cargo. He was righteous in that way.

Later, he was scheduled to meet with the municipal president to discuss plans to refurbish The Star of Puebla, the city's massive Ferris wheel that attracted tourists from other states. Juan Carlos expected the mayor to ask him to provide the labor at a reduced cost, which he would agree to, so long as the president let him continue operating his business as he wished.

His last errand was not precarious by any means, but he wanted it to stay that way, so his oversight was necessary. Their quarterly shipment from Brazil had to be packaged, secured, and shipped before federal agents could retrace the cargo. It was not a difficult operation; the Brazilian girls came forth willingly enough, desperate for a life which, although not luxurious by any means, was preferable to dying young in the favelas. The Americans mostly turned their cheeks, so long as the Brazilians included some of their pure white powder with the girls.

Still, like most deliveries, the delivery carried the risk of being hijacked or falling into the wrong hands. Though Juan Carlos trusted Clemente to see the job through on his own, still, he could never be too sure. If his father had taught him anything growing up, it was that leaving the family business unattended for even a day could destroy it. He was a pasta maker, of course, but the principle applied to trafficking just as it did to macaroni. *A house can only fall if it's left to.* His father had lived and died on that mountain, working day-in, day-out through cough and cold, broken bones, and hangovers until cancer finally proved worthy enough to kill him. Juan Carlos copied his behavior as tribute; he never left his business unattended for more than a couple days at a time.

Clemente knocked. Juan Carlos permitted him, expecting him to be carrying a briefcase filled with clean money. His hands were empty. When Juan Carlos heard his voice, he understood immediately something was wrong.

"Boss ..."

Juan Carlos squinted at him. "Say it."

"It's the girl," he said, his hands folded at his waist. He forced himself to look up. He would face repercussions if he did not meet his godfather's eyes. "Your cousin, Angela. She says the girl never showed up at the airport. She wasn't on the plane, she says."

"What?" Juan Carlos's eyes pierced Clemente's center, who'd spent the entire night awake trying to track down the girl. His neck jerked. "Where the fuck is Doña Antigua?"

"Angela says she wasn't on the plane either, boss." Clemente had no solutions left to offer.

"Bring me the phone," Juan Carlos gripped the edge of his desk with his left hand. "*Now!*"

◆

"*I'm sorry, Carlito, but I'm telling you—*"

"Don't call me that." A vein at his temple threatened to rupture. "Goddamnit ... did you call the airport office?"

"*What office?*"

"*Useless!*" Juan Carlos hung up snappily. He closed his eyes and kneaded his forehead. "Call Airport Police and demand that they find out where she is. *Isabela Rodríguez Aguayo.*"

Clemente dialed the number meekly. "Yes, I'm calling on behalf of Juan Carlos Paoli Martínez. Yes, that's correct." He cupped the speaker. "She's transferring me to the boss." Juan Carlos waggled his fingers. Clemente handed him the phone obediently.

"*Yes?*"

"Who am I speaking to?" Juan Carlos asked urgently.

"*Mr. Paoli? This is Alejandro Gomez, from the Attorney General of the Republic. Please, tell me how I can help you.*"

"My niece," Juan Carlos croaked. "She was scheduled to arrive in Los Angeles yesterday, and, well, apparently she wasn't on board the plane."

"*I am deeply regretful for this situation, Mr. Paoli. I assure you, this will be my office's top priority until we locate your niece. May I ask for her name, please?*"

"Isabela Rodríguez Aguayo. She is my goddaughter as well. I'll be adopting her soon, as a matter of fact."

"*Congratulations, sir. I will call this line directly as soon as she is located. Please allow me thirty minutes, no more.*"

Juan Carlos seethed but managed to hold his tongue. "Of course." He clicked the phone shut.

"I need you to call the municipal president," Juan Carlos instructed Clemente. "Tell him I have to reschedule due to a family emergency. And see to the fucking Brazilians."

Gomez called back eighteen minutes later. Within forty-five minutes of the second call, Juan Carlos was shaking Gomez's hand and boarding a private jet at Puebla International Airport.

◆

"*Sir, you can't begin to understand how regretful I am of this situation,*" Gomez shouted uselessly over the jet's twin engines. "*Our agents are addressing the situation as we speak.*" Juan Carlos read his lips and shook his head from the top of the airstair as it closed.

His lawyer, Berbel, a thin, white-haired man who always wore the same thick-rimmed glasses, awaited on board in one of the small aircraft's plush leather chairs. He stood to embrace his client before ushering him to the seat opposite him. Juan Carlos accepted a vase of liquor placed in his hand as Berbel began explaining Isabela's situation.

His words did not fully register with Juan Carlos as the plane skipped taxi and took to the sky. He sipped his brandy and tried to calm his nerves. Privately, he was lamenting his business. He had left it in strange hands, put it at risk of injury. He could almost feel his father's shame.

◆

Their driver greeted the Border Patrol agent confined inside the dusty security vestibule and presented their IDs, plus an official letter from the Mexican Attorney General. Their meager rental car rolled by the checkpoint and joined the rows of employee vehicles parked neatly outside of the prison.

The desert wind whipped at Juan Carlos's suit as he left the car. His lawyer pinched his glasses in place as they unlatched the desert facility's main entrance, bringing in the dust and wind alongside them.

An American wearing a campaign hat approached them in the entryway, holding out his hand as if he were meeting them for a round of golf. "I'm terribly sorry for the misunderstanding, Mr. Paoli," the man said in a vicious Texan accent. Juan Carlos's fingers twitched at his side as Berbel spoke for him.

"My client and I are here to locate his niece. We don't wish for any renumeration." Berbel dismissed him with a nod, and they walked swiftly down the hallway. The Texan trailed them, apologizing animatedly.

A sign pointed them to a set of gym doors with a laminated sheet of paper Scotch-taped onto it. The sign read DET. CENTER 1. Juan Carlos swung open the doors and passed through a corridor with a transparent security booth built into its right side.

The warehouse was about the size of a soccer pitch and was bordered by black-and-yellow striped tape. A mess of Border Patrol agents lazed about with rifles in their arms. The most easily identified sound was that of crying children. Their half hazard cages were composed of chain link fencing topped by a single line of razor wire. Each cage was fifteen feet tall and was segmented by a meter-wide corridor that the guards used to access them. A laminated sign in Helvetica font labeled each one: LOT A, LOT B, and so on. Inside, dark-skinned Latino men in faded and poor matching clothes sat or stood or squatted, packed in so close it was a wonder they could breathe. LOT C contained a similar proportion of women, similarly dressed and colored. A separate area marked MEDICAL sat just outside of the maze. Its floor was dotted with colorful tape to mark where cheap gurneys should go, upon which adults and children lay on their sides, moaning and shivering. A single doctor in a white coat and surgical mask tended to each patient.

The children's voices came from a separate cage spanning the entire length of the facility's back wall. This was designated LOT D.

Juan Carlos placed his hands on his hips and exhaled. Berbel's eyes darted repeatedly from one sight to the next, as if his brain had to reaffirm each visual signal. The double doors through which they'd come opened behind them. It was the Texan, accompanied by a fat man wearing sunglasses in the same trooper's uniform. He wore a forest-green baseball cap with CBP monogramed on its crest.

"Hola, ca-ba-yeros. Mah name's Deputy Patrol Agent Betancourt." He offered a pudgy hand. Juan Carlos ignored the offer and sucked his teeth. "I see there's been a, uh, mix-up with one of your relatives here. Now look, we run a pretty tight ship here, as you can see, but give us just a second to locate your daughter. Is that okay? *To-do bien?*"

Juan Carlos ignored the fat man and instead walked with Berbel toward LOT D. The children were congregated by the fence. Their eyes tracked their small entourage as they passed by the cage.

Juan Carlos crossed the cage's yellow tape border and slowly tracked its perimeter with his eyes. Some older boys held their hands out through the fence, mocking them in Spanish. The younger children sat crisscrossed behind them, some playing aimlessly with makeshift toys while others lay sleeplessly under thermal blankets resembling sheets of aluminum foil. Juan Carlos's hands trembled with rage.

He found the peculiar set of eyes he was looking for in the cage's far right corner. Isabela was wearing the same cotton shorts and loose T-shirt with a cartoon character printed on it as she was when she departed. One of her knees was bruised. Her sharp, dark eyes were not fixated on Juan Carlos but on a horned stuffed animal perched in her lap.

Juan Carlos's immediate instinct was to rush over and stick his arms through the cage and embrace her. Instead, he swallowed and nudged his partner. Berbel gained the deputy's attention and pointed towards Isabela.

"That one?" The deputy frowned at Isabel, his chin doubling toward his chest. Juan Carlos and Berbel nodded in unison. "Hmph. She's got contraband on hand. I'll have to report that."

"Keep the fucking doll," Juan Carlos interrupted.

◆

"Where's my papa?" Isabela asked sleepily. Juan Carlos leaned back to cushion her weight, her legs wrapped around his torso.

"He's here, in your heart. You might not see him right now. But he'll never leave you." He patted her on the back. "*Inside* you, little one." Isabela briefly removed one of her skinny arms from Juan Carlos's neck and felt her chest. Juan Carlos opened the car door and laid Isabela in the back seat before sliding in and shutting the door behind them.

The car dribbled along the desert highway amidst waves of heat and tumbleweeds until they arrived at the small municipal airport. Isabela fell asleep on the journey, her feet curled up beside his lap. She opened her eyes abruptly when they stopped and sat up, staring at the small jet that awaited them. She clamored into his arms before the airstair opened before them. Juan Carlos ascended first, with Isabela's arms wrapped tight around him.

He sat down with Isabela still clung to his chest. He felt tears dampening his pressed shirt and noticed there were no cries escaping her. "Did they treat you alright, my love?"

"They told me my papa was gone," Isabela murmured, her voice muffled by Juan Carlos's shirt.

"Ah, but I already told you. He's with you now."

"But where? He's not in my heart. Or else I'd know."

"You can't see him. It's his soul that's inside you. He will always be with you." Isabela nudged from his chest and looked up at him, her eyes sharp and bold.

"¿Cómo lo sabes, Padrino?"

"Because he told me before he left, my love." Juan Carlos felt the ring dangling from her neck pressing into his chest. He kissed the crown of her head and translated his thoughts into English. "From now on, we are going to be happy." Isabela gazed up at him, perplexed.

XIX

ISABEL LIFTED the hood of her jacket and sauntered alongside her compatriots. *No; you're not one of them,* she quietly reminded herself.

They would go south first, following I-79 until they were well out of the Chief's sight. His patrols neglected to oversee the southern passage; their utmost concern was detecting infidels escaping *west,* not south.

A few walkers had wisely packed parkas amongst what select belongings they could carry with them. The rest had either decided against carrying the additional burden or were not privy to such luxuries. The wise flaunted their coats now, while the shrewder folk leered at them enviously.

A woman belonging to the coatless group found comfort in Isabel's shadow. She wore sunglasses to shield the droplets from her eyes, even though the sky was gray with clouds. "What's your group?" she asked, trying to mask the fear behind her voice and sound upbeat.

"D," Isabel replied. "You?"

"Really? Me too." The woman loosened in her shoulders and veered closer to Isabel. She shrugged away, but she seemed not to take notice. "What made you decide to leave?"

"What else?" she scoffed. The woman looked hurt. *Half of these people are leaving just for the sake of it,* she thought to herself. Isabel sighed. "To see the new Father. I've practiced in secret for many years now."

"Really? Oh." The woman stared down at her feet. Her hiking boots were caked in mud. *She's probably terrified to be out in the rain,* Isabel thought. *All of them.* "I've heard the stories. About Father Bill, I mean. It all sounds ..."

"Too good to be true?"

"No—yes, but ..."

"It's natural to think that way. But the Father is capable of things that normal people only see in dreams. The Way is just one of his miracles."

"But doesn't the Way belong to us all?" the woman responded quickly. She blushed immediately after, her hand covering her mouth like she was abashed to have spoken her mind.

"You're right," she said, smirking. "It's just as much ours as it is his."

The woman smiled. Isabel saw that she was quite young; not quite a floodling, but close enough. Close enough not to remember dryness. "What's your name?"

"Yana."

"I'm Sharla," the woman replied, even though Isabel had not asked. "Hey ... do you think the Untold be as ... *good* as Father Bill was?"

"Yes." *Maybe yes. Maybe not. Either way, he's necessary.* "He'll do more good than harm."

The apprehension on the walker's face lessened somewhat. She smiled despite the soggy mess the rain had made of them. "That's good."

Isabel apologized before wishing the woman luck. She fell behind to watch her caravan from the rear. She much preferred to observe her operation from the inside, boots-on-the-ground. It was a privilege that the packs she herded were not privy to her identity. Her migrants paid and arranged their passage through one of her agents, most of whom were unaware of her true identity. All spoke of "the fox who dances" in hushed tones.

Eight of her men protected the caravan. They carried spotting scopes and compound bows, as was standard for Alliance men, though most opted to arm themselves with rifles as well. They scanned the horizon while the others guided the migrants themselves, like herding dogs corralling sheep to pasture. *No. Not sheep,* Isabel thought. *More like rabbits trying to make it to summer. Running from their predators: lions, tigers, and bears ...*

◆

The caravan was about fifty strong—or weak, depending on one's preferred nomenclature. Most were young and eager to absolve themselves of the eastern paradox and create new lives for themselves. Some dragged their children behind them while others shuffled alongside their parents, matching their slow, arthritic pace.

Clemente knew their exodus cost more than what the eye could behold. The price was far greater than sleep-ridden eyes and gimpy thighs. They bought freedom and received nooses. They paid for their fares in advance, even though they were only guaranteed safe passage across the Mississippi. After that, they would suffer what they must.

It shocked him to see how eager people were to forgo their old lives given the promise of a new one. Some traveled alone, towing their most meaningful possessions on their backs. Others carried more sensitive cargo, like multiple generations of relatives. *All in the name of a bad fortune teller,* Clemente thought sourly. He had no love for any "Father" but his own. Yet people seemed to adore this man without ever having met him. That was just their conviction, he supposed. For him, a man's convictions were the product of his worth, not the other way around. *Let the weak suffer what they must,* he thought; *that* was worthwhile.

His focus shifted from the procession to the dark-haired girl calmly observing it at its rear. No one gave her a second look. She was dressed conspicuously in budget sports apparel that coincided with much of the group. As far as the others were concerned, she was a fellow dreamer, walking for a new life. He was the only one privy to the fact that she alone was responsible for the operation. Even if she revealed her identity then, no one would believe it, walker or flanker. A fox can't herd a flock of anything. They hunt alone and avoid exposing themselves at any cost. They rarely considered the fox's true cleverness. The fox knows that the best camouflage is often the plainest. The fox knows to speak in many tongues. It whispers in the bear's ear and tells it when to charge, and befriends the deer who knows all the best paths.

But the sparrow who watches from the trees sees and knows all.

He developed a subtle limp and gradually fell back to the procession's rear. He dipped his chin and pulled his patterned bucket hat down over his ears. "How long's the walk?" he asked the dark-haired girl, wincing at his leg and adding a convincing yinzer inflection to his voice.

Isabel answered in a second-generation voice, the sort of voice that willfully adopts certain cues from their parents' native Spanish. The voice sounded practiced to him, but then again, he'd been taught how to detect such things. "Six days. They say it's the starting and the ending that's hardest. Once you're in it, it's like nothing."

Clemente chuckled and dropped the Pittsburgher accent, the slouch, and the limp. "I'll do my best to keep up, nieta." Isabel's neck jerked to Clemente's smiling face, towering above her. He laughed heartily at the surprised look on her face.

"Quiet," she hissed. He quit laughing, but the smile still lingered. "What are you doing here?"

"Just business, little one," he said in Spanish. "The sparrow's business." He frowned then, and Isabel felt a lump form in her throat.

The sparrow had not been subtle with his orders, nor with his manner of evoking them. "She is to drop her assignment and personally escort him to the Chief's quarters. If a few caravanners have to disappear to ensure that happens, well ... as they say." Clemente did not need reminding: *The strong do what they can. The weak suffer what they must.*

Clemente stopped walking suddenly. "No point in walking anymore." He waved his hand toward the men flanking the caravan. "There's been a change of plans. You're going back to Pittsburgh. Something important."

Isabel gritted her teeth and gestured toward her flock of refugees; they were *hers*, hers to escort and care for. "How am I supposed to do that? They paid in advance. I can't just send everyone back to their hovels ..."

"Better they pay before than after. Besides, you'll find others." He looked at her with what could have been sympathy or bemusement. "It's not up to you to decide. You know better than that." He wiped the rain from his eyes and cursed. "Fucking Christ. I don't know why you do this shit, anyways."

"Because if I didn't, no one else would," Isabel growled. She nudged her head at the slow-moving mass of humans. A child was crying somewhere in its midst. "And it *is* up to me to decide. I made them a promise."

"Then go, if it's them you give a shit about. But you know the message that'll send." Isabel glowered. "Quit pouting. We do what's best for us, which is whatever the fuck the sparrow says. You know better than that."

Isabel scoffed. "Well, guess what? I don't see no sparrows around."

"That really what you think?" Clemente chuckled. He reached into his coat pocket and pulled out a walkie-talkie. He squinted into the rain before raising the device to his lips. By the time Isabel translated his words, it was already too late. "Hombres: ya es la hora. Hazles limpios."

There was a brief pause before the handset came alive: "Ya está."

It's already done.

Isabel craned her neck in the same direction as Clemente. She watched the man she'd once considered hers put down his walkie-talkie and reach for his rifle. The others copied his action. "No!" Isabel cried out just before they opened fire.

They did them clean, as promised. There were few cries of terror or sorrow or agony or otherwise. The bodies lay strewn about the muddy field after they were finished, inconsequentially, like remnants of a fall harvest. Some were spared by the initial barrage. They tried to run, but the sentries were good marksmen, and so they did not suffer much longer. It was quiet once they had finished, save for the rain's slow patter.

Clemente half-hugged his niece. "We do what we must now, so that one day we won't."

XX

No. 17 Month 5, 0017 P.F.
Pittsburgh (Subterranean), Appalachia, New American Colonies

TYLER GAZED at the city's twinkling scaffolds in awe. He'd never imagined they would be so vibrant. They seemed to glow with an almost ethereal light that was surely intentional. He wondered whether the people up there were happy.

He gazed up at the scaffolds and felt ashamed. For better or worse, the man who'd built them would be dead soon. He wondered whether the people up there would still be happy afterward.

◆

The Frogs' stern policy of isolation suddenly shifted after he agreed to take their assignment. Tyler was pampered from the moment he shook Abdul's hand to the moment he set out on his journey. He showered under running water for the first time in months. The feeling of water flowing freely over his head was incomparable to the limited pleasure of suds in a bucket. His diet suddenly upgraded from boiled oddities to fruits bursting with ripeness and choice cuts of meat. One night's menu was braised venison shank with wild asparagus sautéed in butter, another pork shoulder steak with potatoes baked in the ash of their campfire. He was even allowed to have a beer on occasion—*cold* beer, a pleasure denied to most since the flood made mass distribution, ice making, and bar ownership far less feasible careers to choose than before. Luxuries aside, they still denied him a razor to shave off his scraggly beard, fearing he would rather escape via suicide than join their cause. Their fears were warranted, he supposed, for each rich meal he enjoyed in the days leading up to his departure felt oddly akin to a death row inmate's last request.

SkyRail was a revelation to him. He'd expected a wet and plodding trip on horseback, carefully fording the flood basins that lay between the C.D. and Pittsburgh. Instead, he got plush bucket seats and vibrant air conditioning. He hadn't been on a train since he was a kid, when his father took him and his brother on an Amtrak to see his cousins in Detroit. The lines were considered outdated *then,* while America was still well and thriving. He vividly remembered eating his first and last tuna salad sandwich on one such trip. SkyRail was caviar, by comparison—which they indeed served, though not sandwiched between white bread.

SkyRail held a firm grasp over rapid, long-distance travel, and its exuberant cost prevented most (aside from those who came from extraordinary means) from seeing other parts of their divided nation. Fares were high in large part due to SkyRail's requisite bribing. They had to pay off the various city and state authorities whose borders they crossed, who, being shrewdly aware that the trains mostly carried well-to-do passengers and fine goods, demanded a steep price. As a result, it was not unknown for transit officials to wear fine furs and know the intricacies of fine wines. The rest of the company's revenues went toward maintaining its lines—a significant undertaking on its own.

Travel-hungry citizens verboten such luxurious modes of transport had to make do with what they had. Most simply stuffed the bulk of their belongings into makeshift trailers towed by old engines or horses. Clothes and family heirlooms, pets and pantry remnants, water jugs and leather baseball mitts. They went into it knowing (and fearing) that traveling so far away from home was as assertive an act as any. Once you left, there was no going back. And yet, few reached their destinations. A broken axle or impassible portion would inevitably halt their sad caravans, and they resorted to thrusting up improvised homes at the site of their journey's premature demise. The lessons stuck with them for the rest of their lives, and few risked venturing out again.

Tyler imagined the people slowly making their way west on foot or on horseback as the sheeny glass-and-chrome bullet sped through the hills he'd once rucked. The notion of people leaving their homes to join Bill's successor had captured Tyler's attention. *Even floodlings have begun to realize the futility of living in fear,* Abdul had claimed. *That* point had stuck with him; he remembered Crunch and his wariness of anything even remotely tinged by the flood's decay. Most floodlings' perceptions of the known world were limited to a ten-mile radius around where they were born, and that's where they tended to stay. The world was a big and ugly oyster, they were told, full of monsters and plague (or so their parents, who were all survivors and by nature more cautious, were convinced). As an amphitrooper, Crunch had been the black sheep of the bunch. But even then, he was relegated to following orders. His life was controlled in that way—predetermined, regular, and therefore safe.

Abdul saw Tyler off before he boarded the exceedingly large train in the C.D. There, he informed Tyler he would not be working alone; he was to rendezvous with a fixer, someone who did not belong to his ragtag militia. "Be as it may, there are individuals asides from us who would sooner see the Chief dead than alive," he'd explained. When Tyler probed him on the logistics of the operation itself, he responded with shockingly few details: "Your fixer will see that you are well equipped."

And so Tyler departed with no weaponry whatsoever to aid him in his steep undertaking. The last thing he told Abdul before the train slowly accelerated down-track was that he expected a parade to be thrown in his honor upon return. That'd awarded him a thin-lipped smile.

The plushy two-hour trip did nothing to ease the discomfort in Tyler's mind. Nor did it mask the uncertainty of throwing a fixer into the mix; he'd sooner work alone than with a stranger. They'd marked his fixer's location on the GeoLoop (which they allowed him to reclaim for his own sake; more likely for their mission's sake, he figured), represented by a ping that refreshed every few seconds. He frowned at the glowing blue dot as the scenery outside his window blurred past.

The moment the train stationed, he promised himself he would do what was best for *him*, and no one else.

◆

The scaffolds reflected against the glass facades of the city's abandoned downtown. Tyler knew the true city, the one in question, awaited him below, not above. The office-goers and skyscraper tenants had not disappeared; they had simply moved.

Tyler checked the GeoLoop. It sat just below a raised bump on his forearm. The medic back at Vernon hadn't bothered with local anesthetics while chipping him. Abdul had sat through the simple, mostly painless operation. He'd been apologetic: "Please don't take this personally. It's for your protection just as much as ours." Tyler wasn't offended—he would've done the same were he in their position. And besides, he had no say in the matter—at least, not anymore. His freedom had gone right down the toilet the moment he shook Abdul's hand. He could've simply rejected his offer and lived in the horse stable until the Frogs inevitably left to pursue some other interest.

But he hadn't. He wouldn't; the *what-ifs* floating through his mind were invalid, because he *knew* he could never refuse the prospect of returning the world to normalcy. He missed normal things. He missed those days of blind innocence: summer break, top-40 music, windows down, cliff diving, and underage drinking. So, he shook the man's hand. He'd shake away, do whatever they told him, just so long as he got to see a fucking firework show again someday.

Tyler started jogging. The city aboveground was eerily devoid of any other humans, except those at work or asleep in the scaffolds above. He checked the GeoLoop. The ping representing his fixer was closer than he expected, albeit underground. It showed a distance of fewer than two miles. His stride lengthened.

He was out of breath when he spotted an illuminated sign announcing the nearest Subterranean entrance:

FORBES STREET GATE: 1/4 Mile
Lines: Blair/Mellon

Tyler followed the signage and rushed into the first elevator that serviced the station. When it landed, Tyler deposited a crumpled-up hundred into an eTicket booth, then scanned it to pass the metal turnstile.

Tyler boarded the first bore train to arrive and sat near the door with his face turned downwards. The train filled quickly with passengers. Tyler didn't pay them any mind. He stared at the ping as the train jostled along, listening to the robotic female voice announce each station. At the third stop, she dictated *DOWNTOWN—STRIP.* Tyler stood to exit, noting the two dots on the GeoLoop's digital face nearly touching.

He stepped through the train's sliding doors and joined his fellow passengers. They made their way to a large steel platform and milled about restlessly on its galvanized floor, checking Loops and sighing exasperatedly.

The platform's sensors detected when it was at occupancy, and four panels of glass ascended from each side, caging the restless commuters in like cattle. Tyler's knees jerked as the platform began suddenly descending—slowly at first, then faster, strings of LED lights guiding their passage. He watched the walls of the shaft whizz past until the platform braked and settled, and the cavernous vertical tunnel was but a square hole looming above. The glass panels opened, allowing the herd to exit. Tyler let the other passengers mill past him before stepping off.

A massive stone gate preceded by rows of turnstiles stood directly in front of him. Tyler glanced to his rear and beheld rows of shops illuminated by bright neon signs, each trying to outdo the other in their capitalist aspirations. Tyler stood facing the gate, the crowd parting around him, most heading toward the gate while others were lured in by the brilliant commercial facade. He checked the GeoLoop. The cursor representing him pointed directly toward his fixer.

A gathering of lavishly undressed Roman demigods reclining alongside their paramours was carved into the gate's ornate crest. The encased statuettes regarded Tyler with cold and demeaning stares. He shuddered at their eyes—he could *feel* the Chief watching him. His periphery senses were sure of it, but a remote voice lodged somewhere in his brain urged him on: *Get movin', Haj.* He shoved his hands into his pockets and merged with the swarm of suit and skirt-clad wasps, trying to convince himself these were just his delusions acting out.

◆

Isabel sipped her coffee. It was mediocre, a good thing. *Nothing better than a good shitty cup of java,* she thought wryly. The white mug, like every white mug at Tobin's, was embossed with the diner's namesake: *Tobin's ... Open Lights-On or Off!*

Tobin's day crowd was mostly of the professional sort: dressed-down work-from-home company men and dressed-up bureaucrats from the Leistung Building. Their omnipresent yawns and trademark table setting gave them away: laptop/tablet, coffee, side dish, napkin. Their orders had to accommodate their workspace and go well with coffee; hence, Tobin's sold more bagels, oatmeal, and egg sandwiches than it had any right to.

Tobin's twenty-four-hour availability made it a natural hangout for night creatures who preferred to socialize after lights-out. Blurry photographs of celebrities who'd landed there by accident or in sincere need of a greasy late-night meal littered the banister splitting the diner in half. It was a place one could show up to hammered or sober, alone or with a small army. Eat or not eat, tip or stiff. Do as you wish; just know the House Rules.

The House Rules are as follows:

1. Order coffee. Help keep it fresh. Drink it or don't.

2. No carryout. Don't ask.

3. Cash only.

Isabel arrived at Tobin's the first hours of what the diners surrounding her considered day No. 17 of Month 5, though she much preferred her calendar to theirs. She sat at her usual table, a round two-top cornered by two small booths, and drank her usual: coffee, black, and water, no ice.

She could see the front door from where she sat, and her booth provided an excellent view of the TV mounted above the banister. A familiar-looking news anchor whose name Isabel had forgotten was elaborating on the screen. The solo line cook manning the grill abandoned his spatula for the screen's remote and leaned out the window pass to turn up the volume.

The anchor sat in front of a studio set showing Earth as seen from space at night. Her face was indifferent, though her eyes conveyed an angst that all the makeup and visual effects artists in the world could not obscure.

To our viewers, tonight we honor President Christopher Stone, who formally announced his retirement approximately two hours ago. President Stone has been open about his battle with dementia, and today will be his last day in office.

The news anchor gazed at the camera for an elongated moment, just as the show's producers had instructed her. The dining room was silent, save the dribble of fresh coffee spewing from the machine. She cleared her throat, wiped away a faux tear, and muttered a soft *Excuse me* before resuming.

Our great Colonies endured many prosperous and challenging years under President Stone's leadership. Former vice president Mendez, who assumed the presidency just moments ago, has assured the rest of the country that he is ready to take on the president's mantle. In a statement recorded from the White House, the new president promised that national security will remain his administration's top priority. He also laid out plans to address mounting tensions in the West:

> *The people at the core of this country are stronger than you can imagine. Only by standing together can we overcome this increasingly tumultuous era. To reiterate the precedent set by President Stone, my administration will not tolerate the recent violent challenges to our democracy. Rioting and treason will be treated and prosecuted as such. Only together will we defeat this sudden dark reality. Only as one will we succeed. One America; one Colonies.*

Thank you for watching us during these unprecedented times. We'll be right back.

The screen shifted to a commercial for paraben-free deodorant. Isabel stared into her lukewarm coffee and scratched the table indifferently. No one else in the diner reacted.

Her Loop buzzing called her attention. She answered not with a greeting but with silence.

"Hola, ahijada," her godfather hummed. His voice always managed to make Isabel sit up straight. Her hair caught static against the vinyl booth. "Are you at the place?"

"Yes," said Isabel, sipping her coffee, her eyes scanning the dining room. "Still nothing."

"Soon, they tell me." Isabel nodded. She had learned not to take her godfather's uncanny forewarnings for granted long ago.

"I hope he fits the bill," she said coolly.

"He would not have been selected if he did not."

Isabel cleared her throat. She would have mentioned Adam by name were it not for the frenzy the name might register amongst the diner's other customers, who, rest assured, were eavesdropping. "How's your visitor?" she asked instead.

"Good. But no longer here; he's made it his mind to follow in his grandfather's footsteps and call San Francisco home."

"That's ..." Isabel wasn't sure whether to sound content or dissatisfied with the news. "Noteworthy."

"Yes, very noteworthy," Juan Carlos muttered. In an instant, his voice shifted. She recognized this voice: now she was speaking with the sparrow. "Listen to me: you are to go the long way. You will escort the asset to the estate and no further." His sharp tone signaled it was not up to debate. "Be careful. And remember: no one is to leave the Chief's home alive. *Him* included."

Isabel said nothing. If she was going to plead her case, it must be then, she decided. She lowered her voice. "All the more reason to let me handle this instead."

"No." She almost shrank into the booth, despite the great distance standing between them. "You are too important. To us, and to me."

The line *click*ed. He did not offer any parting wishes; her godfather had called, and the sparrow had spoken.

Isabel rubbed her temples, listening vaguely to the old-timey crooning playing over the tinny speakers. The owner insisted on playing nothing but old blues over the stereo, which also discouraged obnoxious teenagers from flocking there for hand-dipped milkshakes. The music matched Tobin's ease, its lack of a dress code. As she listened, the music became soothing, a sort of blanket for her brain. She leaned into the corner of her booth and closed her eyes.

Her one chocolate chip pancake arriving interrupted her impromptu meditation. She sighed, slathering butter on top of it before cutting it into eights. She forked a piece into her mouth and washed it down with more fresh-filled, semi-stale coffee. The diner's quick-moving busboy began unrolling black window covers behind the counter; in order for Tobin's to stay open during lights-out, they had to blanket the windows with thick black canvases that prevented inside light from spilling out onto the streets. The only way to leave or enter Tobin's after lights-out was by night cab. Fortunately, Isabel had a driver she could rely on, an old friend of her godfather's ... who was, in reality, indebted to him for helping him out of some unsavory situation. To the best of her recollection, the debt had originated from some smuggled abalone that Juan Carlos had convinced the powers-that-be to turn a blind eye to. The favor itself was unimportant. What mattered was that *he* had done the man a favor, and a favor from the sparrow could only be returned with dutiful service.

◆

Tyler gazed up at the dimming neon sign projecting out onto the street. The measly-looking diner was purportedly open *Lights-On or Off!* Tyler checked the ping again to make sure he was in the right place. He was.

He rolled back his shoulders and walked inside, unsure of whom—or what—to expect.

♦

Isabel straightened at the sound of the front door opening and closing with a *hiss.* She frowned at the man who entered. He was a short, scraggly thing with hungry raccoon eyes and shaggy hair in need of help. He looked both old and young, his posture bent like an old man's, his face fresh and unblemished. Isabel met halfway and guessed late thirties.

The man stood awkwardly at the door, turning his head about the dining room. His eye—his left—was bruised and swollen near shut. The other darted about the diner, scanning each table carefully. He skipped Isabel, who lay hidden behind the partitioned wall.

Isabel eyed him a moment longer before returning to her midnight breakfast. The asset was supposed to be a former amphitrooper stationed in the Capital District. He (or she) would be nimble, trained, sturdy, and presumably have their vision undeterred. She quickly branded the man as just another bum flocking to Tobin's at night for water and the occasional free meal.

The reporter's voice had returned to the TV's crappy internal speakers. Isabel looked up to see what else was happening in their small world. Instead of the TV, she found the man staring down at her, like some ugly doll.

"May I help you?"

"Thought I'd join you," Tyler said dryly.

Isabel's waitress came to check on her. Her least favorite part of her job was dealing with vagrants and truck drivers, the two sorts of men who tended to harass young women dining alone. She leaned visibly between Isabel and the stranger. "Can I get y'all anything?" she asked, her tone semi-sweet. Tyler nodded.

"Do you have a bar?"

The waitress glared at him. "We're not licensed for that sort of thing, sweetheart."

"I'll have coffee, then." The waitress looked to Isabel first to confirm. She nodded.

"Room for sugar?"

"Please."

The waitress snorted and waddled over to the BUNN burner as Tyler took the seat next to Isabel and watched the meaningless banter on the television before the waitress returned, coffee in hand. He dumped five seconds' worth of sugar into his mug, then sipped loudly. "So, you're here to clean up my mess," the man presumed.

Isabel chewed a bite of pancake and swallowed. *Like it or not, it's him*, Isabel thought grimly. "I almost mistook you for someone else," she said cautiously.

"That's kinda what I was going for."

"Didn't go for it enough." She lowered her voice. "George found you out pretty quick. You took a platform down, didn't you? Yeah—not the brightest move. If it weren't for this ..." She tapped her Loop. "You'd be alone in a dark room with an IMP right about now." She forked a triangular strip of pancake and examined it.

Tyler fumed. *Go. Start over,* his instincts screamed at him. Before he could stand up and go, Isabel barked at him. "You won't last a minute out there alone. You've had more help than you think. The West is not only to our west."

At once, as if calibrated to the same network, the diner's customers and employees turned and craned their necks toward Tyler. They scanned him from top to bottom, their eyeballs lolling in their sockets. Tyler froze.

"Water Is Life," they echoed as one.

Tyler returned their gaze for a moment. Doubt clouded his vision. *Go ahead, run. You'll still remember. Nothing will change.* He lowered his eyes and sat down reluctantly. The occupants went back to their side plates and to their workstations. His leg bounced nervously. "Abdul said you'd have the tools. For the job."

"I've taken care of my end of the bargain," she chimed, skidding her half-finished, congealing plate away with a *sigh*. "My name's Alexandra, for what it's worth," she said, neglecting to offer her hand.

"Tyler," he rasped. It still pained him to talk or eat, his throat painted with yellowy bruises. Isabel pretended not to notice.

The news channel had switched over to helicopter footage of the C.D. The Capitol sparkled intensely in the footage:

We now turn to a protest gone awry at the Capitol Building. Mayor Burwell has ordered all residents to stay home until further notice, citing public health concerns over stagnant flood pools in the area. There were reports of gunfire and bottles being thrown at police, who dispersed the crowd with crowd control tactics, including rubber bullets. Sources say the violence stemmed from a peaceful protest gone awry. Event organizers have since claimed the riot was spurred by government agents concealed within the crowd, despite video footage of the same leaders calling for "freedom or death." This all comes just hours after President Stone's resignation this afternoon ...

"Strange times," Tyler muttered.

"When weren't they?" She studied him and frowned. "Eat something. It might be a while before you can again." The busboy hooked the last sheet of black canvas over the windows. She glanced at her Loop anxiously; still plenty of time before lights-on, but better not to leave anything up to chance. She began tapping her foot impatiently.

The waitress returned, ticket pad in hand. She looked at Tyler expectantly. He wrinkled his nose; the thought of food was sickening, so Isabel ordered for him: "Four eggs scrambled, hashbrowns and wheat." The waitress nodded and went to turn in the order, her pad still blank.

The waitress brought Tyler a tall glass of water before his food arrived. He discovered his state of dehydration and drank four glasses, the latter three sans ice. Isabel watched him eat while the time on her Loop ticked. Tyler scarfed down his food without pausing to taste it. He sopped up the last bit of diner grease with a half-slice of toast and set his fork down. The water and the meal were much needed.

Isabel quickly downed the last of her coffee and stood to leave. Tyler noted her state of dress: black jeans, black hoodie, and matching boots; dressed for the night.

Tyler pushed his plate away and searched for the waitress as Isabel made out the front door. He found her chatting with the short-order cook behind the window pass. He handed her a flat hundred-dollar bill before rushing out after her. The waitress watched him go, perplexed, before scrunching the cash into an untidy ball and shoving it into her apron.

A yellow cab sat waiting outside, its undercarriage illuminated by white-blue LEDs. Tyler climbed into the back seat. The scent of Royal Pine immediately assaulted him. "We're off our mark," Isabel snapped from the passenger seat.

Tyler frowned. "Sorry?"

Isabel scowled and gave directions in a foreign tongue to the driver. The driver gave a word of confirmation, eying Tyler in the rearview mirror all the while with shifty eyes set above a surgical mask. They started off at an unpleasant, lurching pace that never seemed to idle.

A small screen occupied by constant interactive ads projected the news in the back seat. Tyler opted to watch the Subterranean pass by instead as they bumped along. The city was asleep for all intents and purposes, swathed in the cool shades of night. The city seemed to depend on the lights like flowers do spring rain—were they to ever fail them, citizens would be left in a perpetual dusk, their eyes shrunken like bats. The thought made the already-grim scene somehow grimmer.

They jerked to a stop in front of a tall and rectangular brick building. It'd been built separate from any neighboring structure, and its bright red front door was easy to spot even during lights-out. Isabel said something to the driver, who bowed his head and said nothing. She didn't bother paying him before stepping out onto the street, which Tyler frowned at, though the man seemed none the worse for it. In fact, he quietly thanked Tyler as he exited the vehicle. Tyler waved as the cab made a U-ie, its headlights fading away in the same direction from which they'd come.

Tyler followed Isabel toward the home's rear, squinting to distinguish her dark shape from the rest of the artificial night. He rounded the house's edge after her and found himself on a shoddy patio that stood open to the vast concrete lots surrounding them. Isabel was kneeling on the ground, patting the cool stone tiles one at a time. "Don't move." She carefully lifted a pallet-sized concrete tile from the patio and lugged it away until she was content with the size of the impromptu manhole. She reached inside and felt for the ladder's topmost rung before casually dropping inside. The *clank* of her thick-heeled boots meeting each rung signaled her descent. Tyler knelt and cautiously took a step down into the chute after her. "Hey." He looked below him, trying to discern her dark shape from the darkness. "Cover it."

Tyler nodded, though he doubted Isabel could discern the gesture. He climbed down further before nudging the tile back into its spot, drowning out the Subterranean's twilight afterglow.

◆

The heat intensified the further they descended into the Subterranean's contracted arteries. Tyler ignored his heavy breathing and focused on the rungs, ensuring his sweaty hands did not fail him. Each step was more fraught with peril than the last as they slowly lowered into the earth's core. Tyler breathed a sigh of relief when he heard Isabel reach the pit's floor below him.

Isabel turned on her Loop to brighten the pit's bottom before he landed. Tyler copied. Their lights revealed a strange tunnel up ahead. The tunnel was barely tall enough to crouch under. He had to fold his knees and stoop his neck to navigate the tunnel, Isabel only slightly less-so. It was just wide enough for one set of shoulders to shuffle through at a time. Tyler edged along, favoring his right side—his good side, ever since the music man had a say in the matter. The dried tears and pus had ceased, but the damaged organ was still swollen shut. At one stop along the plush train ride west, he'd gotten up to use his car's cozy restroom and teased his bruised eye open. He'd winced at the pain but saw his reflection momentarily before his fingers retreated—a reassuring sign.

Tyler watched the mineral in the walls change as they moved along, his right eye his guide. The sediment was mostly gray slate, occasionally interrupted by veins of hard red clay. "Who did this?" he wondered aloud, spinning his neck to judge the tunnel's circumference.

"A miner in one of United's last coal operations in Appalachia. The dust got him. United gave him his severance package—insurance, 401k, everything. After he signed an NDA, of course." Isabel spat. "Guy's lungs were toast, so they moved him and his family down to the Subterranean. Said the air would be cleaner."

"So he made this?"

"No. They found it out back one day. Some doomsday prepper, probably. Guess he didn't think Crombie dug deep enough. Hold on," she warned, edging past a steaming pipe ahead of them.

Tyler's mind began to wander, which caused him to panic. His mind was capable of taking him to dark places. He intervened the silence before his mind swept him away. "What do you hope to get out of all this?" he asked calmly.

"Peace. An honest government that provides. One that will bring rich and poor onto the same playing field. One that puts the truth to light."

"Who's 'us'?" Tyler probed.

"America."

"Oh." *She's probably not old enough to remember America,* Tyler thought. "What do you have against Crombie?" Isabel snorted.

"He feeds people lies."

And what have you been fed? Tyler thought. "People sort of admire him," he said quietly. "When I was a kid, the Crombie Foundation built a movie theater in my neighborhood in Jersey—part of New York Metro now. They let kids in for free during the week." It was the first time he'd thought of the Hudson-Crombie Theater in some twenty-odd years. The enduring vivacity of the memory shocked him: the old-school outdoor ticket booth, the plush, velvety chairs, the eternally sticky floors. "We even got free tickets for every B we got on our report cards. It was fun, I guess ..." He broke away from the memory. "What will killing him accomplish?"

"Everything. The system will have to change. The patriarchy ..."

"Do you really think that whoever takes his place is going to be that much better?" Tyler probed. He was not sure whether he was lecturing her or himself.

"Yes," Isabel avowed. "We'll finally have a genuine leader. One who gives back to the people." Her voice changed. "What are *you* getting out of this, if you don't mind me asking? If George Crombie's such a righteous man, then why the fuck are you here?"

"I just want things to be normal again," Tyler said quietly.

Isabel scoffed. "This will be the first time things have *ever* been normal."

Tyler was grateful for the darkness then, to mask the sudden sense of rage he felt. *She doesn't know,* he thought cruelly. *She's too young to remember normal.* How could someone miss what they had never known?

But when were things ever normal? a proud and vengeful voice hissed at him. *What is it that you miss? Watching your mom get trashed every day, week after week, and you doing nothing? Was it watching the world fall apart and doing nothing but get drunk? Or maybe it was watching your friends getting killed and doing absolutely nothing. Pardon me, you did do something—you ran.*

"*Shut up,*" Tyler growled under his breath. Isabel either hadn't heard or couldn't be bothered. He shook his head at the voice and focused instead on following.

◆

They finished the journey in silence before they finally spotted the tunnel's end. They turned off their Loops at Isabel's behest. The darkness that swallowed them immediately after was like drowning in ink. "This is it," she whispered. "I'll get you as close as I can, but after that, you'll be on your own."

"Right."

The tunnel transitioned to an impossibly cramped dirt corridor at the tunnel's end, making the Earth's crust all the more threatening. They snaked upward on their hands and knees until they felt the ceiling begin to grow in height above them. Eventually, Tyler was able to come to his knees, then walk with his shoulders hunched.

Isabel stopped abruptly when they could go no further. Tyler grazed her arm with his outstretched hand. She flinched. "Light?" Tyler asked softly. Isabel shook her head, her hair bouncing in his face.

He activated the GeoLoop despite her objection, revealing the crawlspace momentarily.

Their only exit lay directly above them and was covered by heavy wooden floorboards. Tyler pressed gently on the rough chop with his fingertips. He moved the first plank to the side and repeated the process until he'd formed a big enough hole for his torso to fit through. A lesser darkness beckoned them.

They pulled themselves through the hole one after the other and stood in the cellar, tasting the fresh-to-them air. It was tinged with the funky smells of vinegar and wine.

Isabel ascended the concrete staircase leading up and out of the cellar. Tyler hesitated before following her up the steps, his mind racing at what lay above. The cellar door swung open gently.

The purplish sky lit up their irises the moment they exited the basement. It seemed unusually high in contrast, almost as if it were being emitted from a projector. He looked down, perplexed.

They had stepped out onto a recently cut path of lush grass. It was not the artificial turf that covered the lawns of well-to-do Undergrounders, but proper grass, green-smelling and wet with dew. A sudden sense of calmness washed over Tyler.

The verdant smell of unripe tomatoes crept up on him and almost made him sneeze. He saw several rows of the vines planted neatly in a small garden next to the shed. A few square planting boxes were dug next to them, where heads of lettuce and broccoli poked up, practically begging to be eaten. A picturesque, rolling pasture extended behind him, stretching as far as the eye could see. The hills were set beneath a Technicolor sky, acre upon acre of dizzyingly verdant grass. Tyler was simultaneously confused and awestruck by how such a magnificent landscape could exist so far below the surface.

A steel box that looked like a surrealist artist's rendition of what a home might be in the distant future overlooked the garden. It was featureless and unlit on the exterior, with scarcely a window to grant its inhabitants a view of the magnificent valley beyond its doorstep. Tyler looked at it and shivered.

"It's all fake." Isabel craned her neck up at the house, the purple clouds blowing softly overhead west. She began marching up the hill toward the house, seeming to have forgotten her past vows.

Tyler hustled after her and hissed for her attention. "Where the hell are we?" he asked urgently. She ignored him until she had finished her uphill march. She reached the hill's crest, reached under the loop of her jeans, and pulled out the small handgun once destined for Tyler's grip. Tyler finally emerged over the hill, panting. "Wait—"

She spun on her heel and sneered at him. "Stay out of this." She held the gun at her side, her finger already clasping the trigger.

Tyler shook his head. "Listen to me." He reached toward her cautiously, like a zookeeper holding a lioness at bay. She flinched back, raising the barrel of the gun to his chest.

"Last warning," she said emptily.

Tyler stared past Isabel and felt the same sudden calm that'd come over him upon stepping out into the valley. *When were things ever normal?*

This time, he acknowledged the voice. He finally knew whose it was. *It was me this whole time,* he said gently.

Tyler lowered his hands. "Alexandra; listen to me. I understand now." He nudged his head toward the spectacular artificial scenery. "All of this is *fake.* It has to stop." He spread his fingers and swallowed. "Let me do it."

She hesitated, aiming the handgun at him a moment longer before placing the tacky grip in Tyler's hand. Her eyes moved to the ground in shame.

"Thank you." Without hesitation, Tyler lifted the barrel to his chin. He kept his eyes open, vaguely aware of the cold steel against his skin, and fixed his gaze past Isabel's shoulder, avoiding her eyes.

Sorry, Tyler thought before squeezing the trigger. He'd expected the voice to reply somehow, but it had abandoned him. No one was listening.

He never learned the woman's real name.

◆

The stars pulsated in the purple night sky. They seemed to dance, growing brighter and dimmer, waning and reappearing. Teasing her, mocking her.

Isabel stared at the black pool of blood growing thick beneath him. She shook her head slowly and forced her eyes to the sky, away from the cruel person sprawled on the grass below her. She forced her mind to indifference and stared at the stars. Their tails stretched into white streaks, growing tails until they dissipated, leaving her in total darkness.

When she finally looked down, she felt different; stronger. She plucked the gun from where it'd spun from the cruel person's grasp before touching the house's enameled shell.

The house's lone entrance was a thin, knobless contour embedded in its exterior. Isabel lay the flat of her palm against it and pushed softly. It gave to her touch.

Interlude

May 28, 2032
Rest

WE SCAR *this world as we pass through it. The world scars us in return. These scars are not ugly. They are lessons, like bruises earned in playground scuffles.*

Too often we jetty through this thing we've named life without reflecting on our temporariness. Someday I will be gone, as will you all be. Only a dry, smog-ridden Earth shall remain.

This begs the question: What was the point of leaving those scars to begin with? Is there a point to this game? What is there to life when the universe has deemed us so small?

Bill sighed and abandoned his journal to make his morning medicine: lazy, machine-brewed java plus Kentucky's finest. He checked his inbox, which blissfully contained only one new message from *Torrez, Jon.* He did more emailing than writing these days.

Writing had become an arduous thing since the crisis commenced. Bill spent most of his time of late wading in lakes or rivers, administering Rites as more and more migrants arrived at the pearly gates of San Francisco.

The majority came from the once-moderate populations of the Great Plains and South. They came for him, or at least for the idea of him: *Hope, opportunity, peace, and love.* They came in droves, exhausted by the East's staunch rebuttal of the pandemic having ended.

Bill did his best to preserve what they came for. He embraced his new people and delivered their Rites himself, as was his duty. It helped ease their pain. But it also pained *him* to ingest their suffering. Bill's notebook was only growing emptier, thinned by torn-out pages.

He sipped his coffee and returned his pen to the page. *What is life without its simple pleasures? A walk around the block, a beautifully codependent conversation over a cigarette, a seat at the bar, a burger, a cold beer. Left alone. These are essential human rights, are they not? Mankind loses half its population yet continues to make these pleasures available. The fruits of our labor, our labor of existing. Is everything worth nothing?*

It was near sundown. The great oaks reflected in the garden's shoddy koi pond. Bill breathed heavily. He no longer felt comfortable sitting there. The ambient noise of fountains trickling, bugs buzzing, ducks quacking—it was unbearable. The ambient sounds reminded him that there were no more human conversations to be had; at the very least, none involving him. Any interactions he had now were to show loyalty—nothing more, nothing less. His partners, in love and in conversation, were mere shells of real human beings—bewildered fanatics who saw him as their savior. Bill only ever received praise. His wisdom was preordained.

Wake up, make coffee, and stare at blank pieces of paper. Get mildly drunk. Go to the river and dunk heads. Feed, fuck, and sleep. Do it all over again. Pray for a swift end.

His followers had yet to notice any real change in his regularly scheduled programming—or if they had, they simply neglected to mention it. Bill's original awe-inspiring delivery was gone. They had desecrated the Way, replaced it with a toxic mishmash of technology and anxiety. His teachings—whether sourced from *Sympathies*, his daily addresses, or public Rites—were once the subject of debate for modern philosophers, besides being read or listened to daily in nearly every household west of Denver. Now they were *hashtags*, regurgitated by mindless teenagers who could not discern fantasy from reality. The Way was once revolutionary; the Belle Époque, Delta blues, French New Wave, Woodstock. Now it was *content*, edited down until they deemed it consumable. It was spineless, gutless, and bland—not unlike instant mash.

Bill had an editing team—pardon—a *Social Engagement* team. The message they produced was irrelevant. It simply had to garner enough Likes, Shares, Tags, and, most important of all, Revenue. They continually fed his young followers rice. They habitually went for seconds.

Adopting the Way had once been a decision made for the community, the *ummah*. Now it was as selfish a choice as any. Bill was often an unwilling participant in strange photo ops conducted by mere children, posing for pictures while friends snapped away with their silent electronic shutters. Receiving one's Rite became something to brag about—like a PR stunt, only the person was not famous and had done nothing special in particular. The days of shared listening to the Father's complete, unabridged teachings followed by intense and self-evaluating philosophical debate were by and gone. *Feed 'em rice.*

In a previous era, he might have fallen back on his own independence. Not even that was attainable anymore, having his freedom. His every need was catered to by an army of doves, white-garbed initiates of the Way who'd dedicated their lives to its propagation. They'd sprung into existence without his express consent or benefaction. One moment he was folding his own laundry, leading a small but quickly multiplying congregation. The next he was surrounded by his doves and a harem of glassy-eyed women.

It was his fault. He knew that. He'd let the change occur. He'd changed, and they'd watched. Actually, he *enjoyed* it. The rice had tasted pretty good actually, up to the sixteenth consecutive protein-deficient day.

Bill sipped his coffee.

Is misery a byproduct of fame, or is it the opposite? Maybe we are drawn to misery, like flies to honey. If we are the bees, then who is our keeper?

The bee's knees.

Jon and Kyle Torrez, Alejandra and Israel, Al Steersman. Once his followers, his friends. Now they went about styling themselves as self-made luminaries. "New Disciples" was the moniker they'd coined, and each of them now commanded a small fandom. They rarely bothered to visit him anymore unless it was to discuss some "spiritual" matter that they could later deploy for their own benefit. Even Lorena had succumbed to the temptation of fame; the simple cloth blouses and T-shirts she'd dressed in when Bill first met her were since replaced by designer jeans and clattering gold hoop earrings. She avoided mentioning the past, the humble origins from which they'd come. Her dead son-in-law seemed forgotten to her; in fact, she rarely went to see her own grandson. It was hard work, enjoying your own luxury.

Bill's congregation had reorganized to include priests, actors, even military generals who commanded the Alliance's suddenly established Preventative Security Corps ("They're just there for our safety," Jon Torrez countered after Bill questioned what good generals were to a society that condemned all war). CEOs nagged him to make exclusive appearances at networking events, and politicians were desperate for his blessing.

A pop-up in the corner of his ceaselessly annoying tablet disrupted him. *Reminder: Rites tomorrow. 7:00 AM @ Green Marina.* As if he didn't already know. He wanted to declare the tablet's usefulness by throwing it off the roof of his mission-style home/prison.

"Hello, Father."

Bill jumped. Mary's voice had one tone. Bill regarded Mary with the same pity most caring people afford to helpless, needful things. She was a devout follower of the Way. If the religion was her tree, Bill was the fruit it bore. She was one of few individuals so blessed as to touch Father Bill without strict permission, and perhaps be touched by him. He might even deem her worthy of spreading his seed. *One day*, she promised herself.

Bill sighed and set down his pen. "Good morning, Mary." The curve of her breasts showed through her white, see-through shawl. She came to Bill and straddled his thigh with her usual blind reverence. His graying hair and creased cheeks seemed exasperated in the aura of her youth.

"How's your writing going, Father?"

"It's going, Mary. Thanks for asking."

Mary sucked her lip. He was feeling unwell. She leaned her hips forward. "Can I help, Father ...?"

Bill glanced down at his journal. He admired the heat of beautiful women just as much as that of whiskey. He found Mary and the others *cold*, like spoiled leftovers.

Bill blew into his make-believe coffee. "That's all right. Go back to sleep, Mary."

She sauntered off. Tears stung her eyes, but she knew they were a result of her own impudence. She would go sleep. *Yes, sleep.* She could do that; if He could be Him, then the least she could manage was sleep. She opened a sliding door to a canopied bedroom and buried her face in down. Perhaps Father Bill would be less busy later.

Bill filled his empty mug with one ingredient and reorganized. He had to write ... The writing had him. *Which one? Which one, which one, which one?*

Why don't you just nuke it? Burn it all down. Water Is Death. "Danger! Water ahead!" Turns out, it's poison. Sorry for the confusion.

Bill tore the page from his notebook and crumpled it and frowned. He sat back in his cheap metal chair and thought of the day it had all started, at the end of a hike, reclining against a piece of sandstone in Colorado. The old man had told him to plant a seed. He wondered what he would think now of the tree that had grown from it. He hoped he wouldn't be disappointed. After all, he was rich now.

Bill sighed and reached to down the rest of the fiery liquor. Just before he grasped the mug's handle, however, a rare thing happened. He dropped the mug intentionally and watched the liquid that had remained trickle along the paved stone, the broken ceramic shards diverging course here and there. A smile slowly crept across his face.

Ideas had become rare things as of late until they'd disappeared almost entirely. But this one came to him like a spirit and was transformative, the sort of idea that haunts you until you act on it.

A prophet could only change so much. Only in death could real change occur—martyrdom.

Bill picked up his pen and wrote for the first time in what felt like years:

A clock ticking is a scary thing.

◆

Jon twisted his pinky ring. It was the third in a succession, from middle to ring to pinky finger. The digit was slightly more red than the others. He would have to have it refitted soon; his hands had lost their old deftness. His chest and belly were once flush; the latter now pooched over his belt.

He had recently become a reoccurring guest on Alliance News Network. He was on a name-to-name basis with the producers back in LA. They traded viral clips of dogs and cats doing doggy-cat shenanigans. As a New Disciple (as the *Chronicle* had labeled him and the other OGs from El Paso), he mainly appeared on urgent

BREAKING NEWS stories, though he occasionally delivered his hot takes on other news-related content. He said what they told him to and lived well as a result—though not as well as he *should* have.

Jon Torrez began as the tech arm of Bill's original small flock in the desert. He recorded, edited, and shared audio that was heard by millions. It didn't matter that he never appeared on-mic. He was an integral part of the experience.

For a time, Jon was spiritually motivated. He believed in Bill and his Way just like the others. Bill Edenson was magnetic. His nightly bouts of spoken word were entrancing. Jon often became so dismayed by Bill's rhythmic incantations that he neglected to monitor his audio for long stretches. It made no difference; Bill would simply abandon the mic Jon had manufactured for him and use his raw voice instead, even as the crowds and venues grew increasingly larger. Bill was infectious. He infected Jon, for better and for worse. Bill was the talent. Jon, the support.

Jealousy kept Bill's Way from cementing itself into Jon's heart as it did to the others. He felt he was Bill's peer rather than devotee. It was Jon who ran the show, after all, Jon who handled all the budgeting and producing and marketing solutions, Jon who ran his errands, Jon who was always available at a moment's notice.

Ultimately, it was Bill that people crossed mountains, rivers, and in a select few cases, *oceans* to see, not Jon. And Jon recognized this, for better and for worse. The same maxim that is attributed to rock stars and famous actors applied to Bill: women wanted him, and men wanted to be him. Jon hated that he did not receive the same reverence. He hated it, but he did not envy Bill. Bill was too large to envy. Only a disillusioned man would do so, for to envy God is to commit blasphemy.

◆

Jon Torrez slept in, despite knowing that his most recent interview with Wendy Wu was airing that morning. He was not interested in seeing his face on TV for the umpteenth time; he had other business to tend to.

The Father had acted with unusual restraint since proclaiming the Eastern government "*infidels to science*" for their assertion that ALIN-12 was an ongoing threat. Bill's choice words had only exasperated the already peaked westbound migration. Eastern urbanites had begun packing their bags (or sometimes not) west in defiance of their government. The Colonist president's reaction to the drooping population: *We will confront the anti-science, virus-denying socialists to our west with sweeping new sanctions and embargoes. The New American government will not condone threats to public health or verbal acts of terrorism.*

If the Father had a plan to pause the influx, he had yet to unveil it. The inward flow had gotten so heavy that new migrants were being processed in encampment shelters in the forest. Publicly available images of the fenced-in, thrown-together facilities worried Jon, not out of concern for the migrants' well-being but for his political reputation. Yet Bill insisted that they welcome all his children. They needed him. They needed the Way.

Jon did not want or need them. They could destroy him. Jon refused to be destroyed, after all he'd done for him. He would address the situation as necessary, Father be damned.

He'd already convened with Commander Stahl, one of the few Vietnam vets still-kicking and not sedated by their age. If he could solve trip mines in the jungle, surely he could handle a few extra people in need of housing or, better yet, deporting. But even the commander expressed his doubts. "There's just not enough space. The cities are too crowded, and the desert ain't gonna help no one. It might be time to expand our borders; go west of the Mississippi."

"Do you think Bill would be up for that?" Jon asked, fighting to stifle his excitement. He could practically see himself in his Florida condo, once the territory was theirs.

Stahl grunted. "Depends. Risk and reward. Adding territory right now's a risk, considering how riled up they are out east ... They might not take well to us expanding. And they're not to be messed with; not until we've got people in the right places, anyway." He could almost detect Jon's disappointment from the opposite end of the line. "Sorry, kid. That's all I got."

But the seed was planted. He could hear the seagulls cawing outside his condo. The West Coast and inland desert could not accommodate the population influx. Expansion was inevitable. And why stop short of the Mississippi? Who's to say Illinois, Kentucky, the mining towns in Virginia, and beyond *shouldn't* belong to them? The Father already had plenty of admirers there. It was just a matter of increasing their presence there. No, *commanding* their presence. Jon doubted Bill would advocate for such an expansion. But he would try. He would try, and he would finally confront him. He would demand what he deserved. He deserved to be rewarded for his hard work. Work, work, work. Work was life, and he'd spent his in undying support of Bill. He made him rich, worshipped. There wasn't a block in San Francisco free of his presence; bars and restaurants named in his honor, salvation-hungry worshippers leading street processions, taggers who incorporated the Father's luminescence into their artwork. Bill's voice rose above all, emitting from apartment windows, in bars, coffee shops, on vinyl. *Hear* Bill, *see* Bill, *feel* Bill, *pray* Bill, Bill, Bill, Bill, Bill, Bill. His voice was Jon's creation. Without him, it would have traveled only as far as he could shout. Why didn't they know? It was *him*; Bill too, he supposed, but also *him*.

Jon kept these assertions to himself. He would not reveal his discontent. Instead, he would solve it.

◆

Jon climbed awkwardly into the back of the red Jeep parked at the curb. It was a rideshare; he couldn't afford such luxuries as drivers or police escorts (*For now*, duly noted). Jon cleared his mind of its inventions to focus on the task at hand.

He arrived a half hour early to their meeting. Tucked beneath his arm was a box wrapped in lilac-colored tissue paper. Inside was a vintage absinthe fountain, a measure of his good faith. The Father was a noted fanatic of premodern inventions, tools, and gadgets considered revolutionary for their times. His compound was densely ornamented with old radios, relics from annihilated cultures, wineskins, daggers, pottery from the Levant, and beyond.

The security guard monitoring the front gate recognized Jon's face from that morning's *Wake Up!* segment and permitted him entry. Jon exited the Jeep at the top of the small circle drive and was greeted by a perfectly proportioned, smiling woman dressed in flowy white pants and a wide-neck T-shirt. "Hello, Mr. Torrez," she pronounced through a thin smile. "The Father is inside, resting."

The woman was dazzling. She stared at Jon, weirdly absent, and his face turned red as he returned her gaze. He knew her purpose and envied it. He was never rewarded a beautiful woman, even after all he'd done. Jon tugged at his belt loops and smiled sheepishly. "Thanks. You can call me Jon, though."

He received a vacant stare from the woman's eyes. Jon quickly excused himself and hurried through the arched entryway. The woman shrank away and disappeared.

Bill valued simplicity above all, which was apparent in his home's size and design. Plain, neutral-colored floors and walls, accompanied by comfortable Southwestern fabric furnishings. It contained no ornate chandeliers, no precious paintings bought at auctions, no custom cabinetry. Only the occasional premodern gadget: an antique French press, a framed collection of chopsticks from different cultures, a cup for sipping yerba maté. The only bedroom aside from Bill's had been converted into a place to store junk; old vinyl records, assorted tools, bottled water, and dust-covered hunting equipment.

The house possessed some hidden extravagancies. It was practically a fortress, humming imperceptibly with advanced technologies. The builders saw that it was outfitted with the most advanced security, as well as a top-of-the-line air filtration system and wiring for future retrofitting. On these grounds, Bill's wish for simplicity was ignored.

The only luxurious addition Bill himself made to the home's design was its audio system. To say they delivered upon his wish for hi-fi sound would be an understatement. A keying piano could suddenly envelop the space, so gentle it seemed to dance inside one's ears. Within seconds, the walls would shake, threatening to succumb to the whiny power of an old punk rock record. Then, as if the chaos had never occurred, a fiddle or ukulele or bongos would take over the space. Jon felt like he was interrupting some private concert whenever he visited, which was rare. At that moment, Bob Dylan was orating nasally over the speakers.

The foyer was separated from the dining room by a short partition. A sturdy wooden dining table dominated the room where Bill ate, drank, and conducted business in the winter months. Bill was not sitting there.

The table overlooked a wide sliding door that provided direct access to the gardens. A stone pathway traced from the screen door and intersected off toward hidden fountains and flower beds. A folding table and chair were propped up in the garden's center. Bill often sat there while he wrote and drank coffee, usually nodding to some secret music that only he heard. Bill was not sitting there either. A sparkling object caught Jon's eye; upon further examination, he saw fragments of broken porcelain by the chair's legs.

The house extended to the dining room's left, where a kitchen and breakfast bar sat, both rarely used. On the right was a short corridor that led into an unknown space. Jon announced himself over the loud music. "Bill? It's Jon. I thought we could catch up before our meeting. I brought you something."

His only reply came from Mr. Dylan. The dark corridor challenged Jon into its unknown. Bill might've been inside, conducting one of his strange meditations. Or perhaps an intense orgy of sorts was underway; the girl in the driveway was only one of the soulless mistresses who faded in and out of Bill's compound like ghosts. *But no one for me,* Jon reflected bitterly. After all he'd done.

Jon shook the thought from his head and walked down the hall.

"I brought you something," Jon said, again to no response. To the hall's left was an open archway emitting soft, natural light. Jon rapped on the wall. "Bill?"

"*The West is not free.*"

Jon jumped. His voice had come from behind him. He spun to face the kitchen, "Shit, I didn't even see you."

Bill was not in the kitchen, however. He heard his voice again, this time coming from above him: "*It is scary. We are scared.*" The music had stopped. Jon finally realized Bill was not addressing him directly, but via the speakers. A light ambient fuzz interceded with his voice. "*We are cowards.*" Jon poked his neck through the archway.

He dropped the boxed antique and shielded his eyes with his elbow until he felt the fluid rise in the back of his throat. When the feeling ceased, he turned back and hesitantly confronted the atrocity in the room. He staggered inside doggedly, as if Bill possessed some secret gravity that dragged him against his wishes. He did not feel his hands clutching at his hair. "*Fuck,* Bill ..."

Bill's feet did not sway or move otherwise. He hung perfectly upright from his bedroom's ceiling fan, motionless, like a rope swing on a windless afternoon. The homemade noose—a purple martial arts belt—had slipped to the underside of his chin. His teeth had clamped down on his tongue as a result; half-dried blood caked his mouth down to his chin, a grotesque expression frozen over his face. Jon's eyes fluttered up and down Bill's stature before his soliloquy resumed:

"We became cowards the moment we declared our beliefs would lead to a better future. By worshipping Water, we were only trying to escape from our present. It was the only way we could redefine the drought's impact on us. Water is the fountain of youth that we throw all our fears into. As a result, we've villainized our contemporaries in the East, who rather than hide from their fear bask in its glory. It makes no difference. Fear motivates us both. They merely treat the flood as what it was to them—bringer of death—and we judge them for that. I regret this sentiment. I am a hypocrite. The Way does not create equality or community. It only divides." Bill paused to drink something. Jon's eyes flashed over to the lone empty glass sitting on Bill's desk, beside the mic where he had recorded the monologue. He knew what it would smell of.

"I, Bill Edenson, formerly known as Father of the West, hereby denounce the Western Alliance, for we are a cancerous growth on this land. Water does not bring life. We do—we, us, the people."

The track paused for some time. Jon scrunched his eyes. Bill's voice returned:

"Many of you will be devastated to learn about my death. Hell, I'm tired of painting pretty pictures; many of you will be devastated to learn about my suicide. You may feel lost or abandoned. I understand your pain, for I have felt it for quite some time now. I have touched your hearts and your loneliness, and worked to realize your wish for a better world. I have failed. I tried fighting your loneliness, and it has broken

me. I am the great divider ... Fear me. 'Now I am become death.' Do not forgive me. Forgo me. This pain has poisoned my heart."

Bill stood from the microphone. The gentle slide of him slipping the belt around his neck was almost indiscernible; *almost.* He spoke his last words away from the microphone: *"August, I'm sorry."* Then, suddenly, the *zip* and *snap* as the belt became taut. Choking, struggling. Then it was quiet.

The tape clicked to its end. There was a pause before it began replaying from the beginning. Jon wanted to clasp his hands over his ears until he spotted a piece of paper lying face down on the desk. His heart skipped a beat. He rushed over to analyze the note, veering wide to avoid Bill's swelling gray feet. Jon gingerly flipped the paper over with his fingernails.

Dear Jon,

No doubt you are surprised (or more apt "shocked") to find me this way. I apologize for any long-term trauma my death may cause you.

It feels antiquated writing a suicide note. Melodramatic ... I hope you never have to experience this for yourself. But as the time to commit the act approaches, writing a note becomes more and more appealing. It seems like the polite thing to do. So, here goes nothing.

As Father and Shepherd of the Way, my dying wish is to dissolve the Alliance. Our self-declared righteousness has only made us more divided. I am to blame for the Eastern government's tyranny. The blood they've shed is on my hands.

I recently came to the realization that if I am to remain alive, only bloodshed will occur. A jihad has formed around me. Look at this "home"; I am surrounded by white-clothed radicals, willing to sacrifice their lives for what began as a simple message: "To fear Water is to fear life. To live in fear is to live in denial." I was simply repeating what I was told. I was told that water brought life, and I assumed it to be true. Water feeds trees, carves rocks, and lessens our thirst. I believed every word of it, and I was wrong. Though I am by no means innocent, nor am I excusing my actions. Someone must hold me accountable. So, here we are.

Only as a martyr of change may I correct this foul disease I have helped spread. I am determined to do so; I am determined that you will help me do so, Jon. You have seen my religious fervor firsthand. I've chosen you for this mission because you are one of few to have abstained from this fervor. I believe you may know the secret to resisting it.

It is not too late to reunite this continent. We will not achieve unity by declaring war on each other's ideas, however. To unite, we must first learn to accept.

The East has long styled me as their villain, which my followers cite as good reason to dismiss them. No more. The West must learn to live in shame and confusion. Its Father must disgrace it. Know that this is a necessary phase. I must go so that you all may grow. My only fear is that misguided actors will see an opportunity in my death and sustain the Way for their own benefit. You must stop them, Jon. Not alone, but with support.

Which explains the recording you are likely hearing now. There are dozens like it, approximately eight hours' worth of audio, which can be found in an encrypted file on that wretched tablet. These are my last set of teachings. Rather than "Sympathies" however, they are Confessions; evidence of my guilt and of this movement's unforeseen and evil consequences. Share these Confessions with the world. Make them free and accessible to all. Let them become unanimously listened to. The world must remember Bill Edenson as a liar and manipulator. Bring the West to its knees so that it may become whole again. Tell those who came to go back to their homes. All of this is necessary if we are ever to reunite.

The tablet also contains the identity of my sole heir, whom I have failed for some time now. I trust you to decode its contents and deliver this message to them, in the hopes that they will learn to avoid copying my mistakes. This is my dying wish.

A clock ticking is a scary thing. I hope you never have to learn for yourself.

Jon heard footsteps coming down the hall. "Bill?" a woman's voice asked softly. Jon bit his tongue. It was the dead-eyed woman, the concubine.

He panicked. His hand clamped down on the suicide note and crumpled it. He spun to face the girl just as her drugged irises lifted to greet Bill's corpse. Jon saw a sign of life in the creature's eyes for the first time. She dropped the tray of refreshments and stood in horror with her arms still perpendicular. Her whole body began to tremble. He heard her breath quicken as she stared at Bill's neck.

After all I've done.

The girl's legs quivered before they decided whether to flee or shut down. She retreated clumsily, sobbing as though she were running through a sludgy dream, a monster chasing after her. Jon was the monster. She yelled and tugged loosely on the locked screen door to escape from the horror in the bedroom. The glass reverberated; Jon's momentum carried his shoulder into the back of her neck. Her head deflected against the reinforced glass, and she slid into a loose pile on the hardwood floor.

Jon fell on top of her. "*Quiet*," he seethed. Mary struggled feebly under his weight and whimpered, then wheezed until he no longer heard her breathing, and when he looked down, he saw his hands tightening around her throat. "Don't," he sputtered. His face turned red, and his hearing steeped until he could no longer hear Bill repeating his farewell: *I understand your pain, for I have felt it for quite some time now. I have touched your hearts and your loneliness, and worked to realize your wish for a better world ...*

Jon stood up quickly from the body. He went to touch it and jerked his hand away. He began hyperventilating.

A sheening square object in the kitchenette caught his eye. Jon hurried over to the tablet and scooped it up. He clutched it to his flabby belly and panicked. "Confessions" had the power to ruin Bill's legacy. And Bill's legacy was Jon's foundation; Jon was *his* Disciple, not vice versa. Sans Father, he was ... What? An ex-confidant to a disgraced leader? Or worse: *Nothing.* Jon was not prepared to become a Nothing. Not after all he'd done, in Bill's name.

Maybe this was a hidden blessing. No one had to know about Bill's suicide; his death could just as well be framed an accident. A sudden hemorrhage. Took the wrong medicine, choked on a chicken bone. All he would have to do is untie him (the thought of which stirred his stomach again) and frame the death as an accident. Scatter some pills, pour out some booze. It wouldn't have been that far from the truth, anyway.

My only fear is that misguided actors will see an opportunity in my death and sustain the Way for their own benefit.

Jon stared at the tablet before snapping it over his knee.

There was a knock on the front door. Jon inhaled sharply and stuffed the broken technology beneath his silk vest before hurrying over to the front entrance. He was not sure whether to look nervous or tranquil when he answered.

It was one of Bill's doves, a male. He looked at him tranquilly with his hands grasped together. His head was shaved. He stepped up on his tippy toes to glance past Jon's shoulder. "Just checking in, Mr. Torrez. Are you and the Father still visiting?" Jon frowned and sidestepped to block his vision. The man sniffed the air faintly, as if he could detect Jon's nervous body odor.

"Uh," he said stupidly. Jon swallowed. He hadn't prepared his lines. His face had turned two shades whiter. The dove's eyebrows arched in alert.

"Mr. Torrez?"

Jon was sweating. "I—I don't know where Bill is."

"Well, he must be *somewhere* inside. He's not in the garden." The man shouldered past him.

His eyes widened immediately at the kitchen's mess. "I didn't know what to do," Jon stammered.

The dove sucked through his teeth and lamented that he could not immediately summon one of his brothers for assistance; Loops were strictly forbidden amongst their brotherhood. "Is anyone else inside?" Jon shook his head.

"No. This is how things were when I got here."

He led the dove around the banister wall over to the big table with the view of the garden. The dead concubine lay propped up against the door's edge, where Jon had squeezed the life from her. The dove scanned the body almost factually and frowned. He stood rubbing his forehead until he'd thought the situation through. "Where is the Father?" he asked urgently.

Jon swallowed and pointed down the hall toward Bill's bedroom. "In there." The dove took a high-arched stance and stalked over with his hands raised. Jon's heart quickened. He turned to the kitchen, quietly slid a nine-inch blade from Bill's wooden knife block, and plodded down the hall in his misfitting Oxfords.

The dove stood, watching the Father sway ever so slightly. He did not drop to his knees to lament his loss. Instead, he bade a silent farewell and went to apprehend the visitor. Later he would inform the authorities and—

Jon cried shrilly and thrust the chef's knife into the dove's belly. It slid in shockingly, and the man did little but grunt while Jon shuddered and stepped away, leaving the knife stuck in place. The dove looked down somewhat tranquilly at the blade's insertion point above his groin and watched his white clothes begin to turn red. Jon watched the man's placid expression as he yanked the blade from his gut in one swift motion, gasping lightly as the point slid out from him. He gripped the blade and plugged his insides with his other hand.

Jon stepped backward to run and disappear before he was apprehended and burned at the stake, or worse. As he turned, his foot caught on the carpet's slightly raised edge; his knees hit the floor. He heard the knife slice the air behind him as he scrambled to his feet, and felt its sharp edge slash across his back. Jon yelped as he fell again to the floor.

The dove let his insides hang from his belly and grasped Jon by the collar. Jon tasted blood before he realized what had occurred. The dove had forced the knife vertically into Jon's neck. He gargled momentarily, his eyes locked in terror before the dove released his grasp on him. He choked feebly on the floor and was quiet within moments.

The dove clogged both hands over his insides and stepped over Jon and down the hall. He swung open the front door and bellied up on the patio. One of his companions found him there. He called for help immediately, but the blaring ambulance came too late. He comforted his brother through death. The dove's last thought was how wonderful it would be to greet the Father and Mary and Jon Torrez, too, in the afterlife.

♦

The investigators came dressed identically in navy-blue jackets, the same three-letter acronym splayed in yellow across their backs. They looked identical, befitted with surgical masks and clipboards.

Clemente adjusted his mask over his face and leaned over the "fat one." He made sure none of his would-be associates were watching and withdrew the broken tablet from the inside of his silk vest. He unlatched his EMT kit and stowed the halved tablet inside. He removed a white sheet and covered the body before quickly gathering his things.

Clemente went to pay his respects before leaving. He briefly lamented the scene inside Bill's bedroom and signed the cross. He nodded at his false peers as he made out the tape-marked front door, walking at a leisurely pace with the EMT kit at his side.

XXI

May 17, 2043

San Francisco, California, Western Alliance

FEW PEOPLE from outside of the neighborhood knew about Frank's Delicatessen. This was a blessing for the owner, whom good help had avoided for years. Frank's was always remarkably well stocked. An array of imported cheeses populated the glass display case, and various cured meats hung down from the ceiling like meaty stalagmites. Steel baker's racks lined the walls, stocked with pickles, sweet peppers, and various other accoutrements.

Frank's was owned by a burly, scowling man named, of all things, Bjork. Bjork handled the daily duties of slicing, chopping, and interacting with customers himself. Most people from the neighborhood called Bjork Frank, because the sign out front told them so. Bjork didn't bother correcting them, partly because he didn't care, partly because he was afraid they might be put off by the fact he was not Italian.

Bjork stood behind the counter, slicing tomatoes, scowling. His eyes turned up from his work at the door opening. He instantly recognized the kid from the neighborhood. He knew his stepmom, Angie. That was a lie. He did not know her by name—he only knew her by the way her jeans hugged her ass.

"Welcome to Frank's," Bjork grumbled. The big man wiped his stained hands on the front of his double-folded apron and tapped on his UniPOS system. "What do you want?"

"Could I have the Italian combo?" Sam asked, feeling stupid immediately afterward. *Why do you always sound like you're asking for permission?*

Bjork grunted. "That all?"

"No thanks ... Oh, no mayo, please," he added. Sam loved mayonnaise, but a *Men's Health* article he'd read that morning titled "Cut Out These Nine Foods and Get Shredded!" had deemed it an empty source of calories.

Bjork took Sam's money and began assembling his hoagie, his meaty hands slicing open the roll horizontally and deftly plucking different ingredients from their plastic vessels. Sam waited with his hands glued to his pockets, eyeing the unique blends of pork hanging from the ceiling. His Loop claimed his attention suddenly. "Fuckin' kids these days," Bjork sighed out loud without Sam's realizing.

"Ey!"

Sam jumped and looked up from his Loop. "Huh?"

"Are you even listening?"

"What? Sorry."

Bjork grunted. "You goin' to the rally?" The kid shrugged.

Bjork sighed. Rather than repeat himself, he sliced the sandwich in half and slid it into an unmarked brown bag. "Thanks, Frank," Sam muttered, peeking inside the bag as he left.

Bjork leaned onto the counter and kneaded his forehead. He decided to start another pot of coffee before the lunch rush started.

◆

Sam sat alone, watching stick-limbed grungers frivolously swing in and out of the skate park's small halfpipe. They barely registered his existence. Sam had learned that the best way to be left alone was by wearing headphones. Most people simply assumed you couldn't hear them when you did. One didn't even have to play music—just plug in and eavesdrop.

Sam looked down at his half-eaten sandwich and saw his belly bulging over his cargo shorts. He scowled and threw the rest aside.

Sam's last two years of high school were a living hell. He was shorter, fatter, and timider back then. "Samwise the Brave" was the best insult his worst bully, a sneering trust-fund baby named Skyler Zoz, could come up with. The bullying extended after school, usually at the skate park. His repertoire included (but was not limited to) body shaming, teasing him over girls, punching, pinching, pushing, and recording his reactions to all those things. Sam often wound up crying and going home, which only made matters worse. *"Mister Frodo! Wait!"* Zoz would call after him.

A simple phishing scam was enough to hack into Zoz's WeChat account. Sam disguised the URL slug, *The Easy Trick Most Guys Don't Know To Make Her Finish Every Time!* When Zoz clicked to conduct his research, Sam instantly gained access to Zoz's WeChat profile, email, photo gallery, and text vault, which—and this was critical—also included the nude pics that he and his ironically gothic girlfriend traded.

Sam posted the choicest photo from his gallery—a nude he had snapped in his parents' bedroom mirror, captioned *cum get it*—on Zoz's own account. He uploaded the rest to a WeChat account entitled *zozbangs*. Sam sat at the park afterward to watch Zoz check his Loop when he got the first text reacting to the photos. Inexplicably, he did not show up at school the next day. No one saw Zoz at the park for about a year after. They made fun of him during his absence.

Sam picked his early sandwich up off the pavement.

When he was finished, Sam took out his notepad and began making lazy swirls with his pen. He chewed his lip and searched for something to draw. A goateed high school burnout named Taylor was dropping into the huge concrete bowl that was the park's main attraction. Sam doodled a gawky skater in Taylor's image, looking down nervously at the drop. He recreated the park's inverted dome beneath the skater's toes in one swoop, extending its exit down past the page of his sketchbook, a trailing tunnel into hell. Sam propped on his elbow and massaged his hand, then went about drawing demons in the tunnel. He drew Satan at the tunnel's end, laughing. He introduced a speech bubble by the antichrist's furled horns: *DROP INTO MY HELL-PIPE OR <u>BURN!!!!</u>*

Time seemed to compress as Sam drew aimlessly. When he looked up from his notebook, he saw that the park had emptied around him, leaving him alone in the concrete playground. Sam stood, wincing at the soreness in his rear, and unplugged his earbuds.

Loud music echoed around a nearby street corner, the sound growing louder as it grew closer. Sam dug his fingers through the park's chain-link fencing and peered out at the commotion.

A military buggy rounded the corner, straying into the opposite lane. A large subwoofer was strapped to its rear, booming vintage hip-hop. Inside were three soldiers: one driving, one shotgunning a beer shotgun, and another singing drunkenly from the back seat. The small truck swerved from side to side as the men cheered and hurled obscenities at each other.

The man riding shotgun spotted Sam peering out through the fence and nudged his driver on the arm. He nodded and smiled. The buggy skidded to a halt by the fence, its engine puttering. The passenger honked the horn over his friend's forearm, grinning. Sam's stomach fluttered.

"Hey, kid!"

Sam let go of the fence and took his earbuds out of his pocket. He scooped up his sketchpad and plugged them into his ears again, making for the park's opposite entryway.

"*Hey!*"

Sam pretended not to hear. He noticed the shoestring on his left sneaker had come loose but neglected to tie it. The engine kicked back into gear, and the men veered around the block and disappeared. Sam sighed, relieved to have avoided human contact.

His hands went clammy as the screech of tires echoed off the block. The buggy emerged from one street over and came roaring toward the park's lone entrance—and exit. Sam stopped in his tracks.

The driver mashed the brakes, and the jeep jolted to a halt. The drunkard riding in the back peered up from his seat, his aviator sunglasses crooked on his face. He waved his beer in the air almost threateningly. "Headed to the rally?" Sam shook his head.

"Need a ride?"

Sam shook his head.

"Wanna beer?"

Sam shook his head.

The man huffed. "You in that big a hurry to get back to the banana stand?" The driver, a skinny black man, choked on his cigarette.

"No," Sam replied quietly.

"Then what the fuck are you waiting for?" Sam looked down at his sketchpad. "Not every day you get to see the Untold, kid."

Sam stared at the buggy before dropping to his knees to tie his shoe, his sketchbook fluttering from his hands. He left it where it landed and climbed into the backseat to cheers.

◆

The fresh-faced soldier riding shotgun spun in his seat and offered his hand. Sam smelled brown liquor on his breath. "Name's Steve. Call me Benton, though. Ya dig?"

Sam nodded and shook Benton-Steve's hand uncomfortably. "Sam." He wiped his hand against his shorts after.

"Sam-I-Am," the driver crooned.

The drunk one riding in the back with Sam cracked open a fresh beer and forced it into his hand. "You twenty-one?" he asked sarcastically. He had an overgrown mustache and smelled like BO. He grabbed Sam by the shoulder and leaned into him. "You better fuckin' be." Sam pulled away and spilled beer onto his lap. The man laughed airily. "I'm just fuckin' around. Welcome to the revolution." He offered his hand. "Atkins."

"Lemons," added the driver with a wave of his finger.

Sam smiled nervously and fidgeted with the can. Benton cracked open a brew of his own and cranked up the music. Atkins bumped Sam's can and swallowed his, rolling his eyes back in his head. Sam took a polite sip. Atkins flicked the edge of Sam's beer into his mouth. It spilled down his chin, but he managed a smile. He accepted a healthier next dose.

"Sammy, tell me what it is you do for a living," asked Benton from the front seat.

"I work in tech. Mostly just programming Loops and stuff ..."

"How good are you?" Lemons asked in the rearview mirror.

"Pretty good. I mean, I'm okay."

"How long to crack standard encryption on a United device?"

Sam looked at him uncertainly. "Are you joking?"

Lemons grunted. "Ain't no joke, young buck. Nine rounds, 192 bits."

"I dunno ... fourteen hours?"

Atkins and Benton looked to Lemons to interpret. He puffed his cigarette and nodded lightly. "Ain't bad."

"Computers, eh?" Atkins muttered. "What, we talkin', like, hacker-type shit?"

Sam smiled and rubbed his neck. A fresh beer landed in his lap. "No, not really. Just normal stuff. Some coding. Setting up cloud networks, CRM, managing email servers ... graphic design ..." Atkins looked disappointed.

"Well," Sam began, eager to unveil his side exploits—the "hacker-type shit." But Atkins had already moved on.

"Well, you're in luck, kid. Now's the time for change, my friend!" He slung his arm around Sam's shoulder. "There's work to be done! We need young whippersnappers like you to join the fight! The good fight!"

Benton lifted his arms above his head and began convulsing in the front seat. "Praise the Way! Praise the Father! Hold on jus' a sec—by God, I can feel 'im! I can feel 'im in my soul! Wait—nah, that's just my butt plug." Lemons cackled. Atkins burped. Empties *clank*ed into each other around their feet.

Sam smiled nervously, picking his fingernails. He'd once asked his stepmom, Angie, why people in the West cared so much about the Father. The excitement had always confused him. "You wouldn't understand," she'd said, her eyes going teary. "It's not your fault. You just had to be around back then ..."

"Cigarette?" Lemons took his hands off the wheel and flicked open a fresh pack of Newports. "Company benefits."

"No, thanks." Lemons sparked one anyway, giving it a friendly puff before handing it back to him, the burnt end smoking. Sam put the filter to his lips and sucked on it like a straw. The smoke came out in a mass and made him cough and bend his head out the door to spit. Lemons chuckled, tapping his knuckles against the buggy's thin steering wheel.

They bumped and wiggled through the empty streets in synchrony with the random but unequivocally loud playlist. Unlike Los Angeles, San Francisco was not a car town. Walking was local practice. Sam quickly got accustomed to it after they moved. Still, his stepmom forbade him from ever walking across the bridge to Oakland. "There's nothing but thugs and homeless people over there, sweetheart," Angie asserted whenever he mentioned venturing out to the Chabot Center or going to see the A's play. And now he was alone, headed toward the Bay Bridge (though technically not on foot, he'd be sure to mention if Angie found out somehow), half-drunk and smiling.

They cruised along the bridge for what felt like hours, their pace halted by the diverse crowd of San Franciscans making their pilgrimage across the bay. Young couples and families and hippies and a few odd women wearing leather and furs teetered along the sidewalks to either side of the jeep. They became silhouettes against the westward sun, shirts and shorts stuck to their sweat-soaked skin. A hunched-over old woman leaned forward on her cane and passed their idling vehicle. "Water be with you, sista!" Benton shouted at her. The old woman looked back and blew him a kiss; he caught it and stowed it in his crotch, grinning foolishly.

Sam looked back and saw San Francisco proper behind him, a midget in the distance. *This is what Oakland's like,* he thought incredulously. By then, the men in the buggy were too exhausted from the sun and the beer in their bellies to celebrate anything. Sam was wide awake.

The streets were too full to gun it in the buggy, so he hopped out and walked alongside it, the blood returning to his legs. He surveyed the parade surrounding him and blinked. He suddenly realized he was a part of something big. Something *very* big—much bigger than him sitting alone in the park eavesdropping on high schoolers.

The farther inland they delved, the more the crowd grew. Entire neighborhoods joined in as they came closer to their destination,

Oakland residents who'd coordinated to see the Untold together. The crowd gradually ran its course and had to split in two, one branching east and the other south.

Sam looked dubiously at the mob's participants, mostly his age or younger. A trio of girls who couldn't have been out of high school walked together, huddled over their Loops and violently gossiping over their contemporaries' latest WeChat posts. Most of them hadn't even been alive while Bill Edenson still was, Sam realized. Surely, WeChat was flooding with selfies of teenagers posed at the march right about now, biceps poking out from tank tops or cleavage in vogue, each one trying to out-Like the next.

And then Sam frowned. He'd realized that he was part of the same demographic. He had barely been alive while Bill still was, and still he had not been old enough to remember much less comprehend his message. Sam defended his own participation; he hadn't planned on coming out to the event, which made it different, he reasoned. And he wasn't bragging about it either—though he could have, and ought to, he thought. Sam hopped back into the buggy, feeling some regret for leaving his natural habitat to begin with.

Lemons lolled his neck against the headrest, letting the buggy roll along with his foot riding the brake. He steered in line with the group due east. Atkins snored soundly in the back seat. Benton sat on high alert, carefully gutting an unlit cigarette and stuffing white crumbs into the tip. He sparked it and inhaled. The smoke smelled vulgar. He turned and looked at Sam oddly, his head wobbling ever so slightly. "How many of these assholes you think left their kids home alone tonight?"

"I dunno," Sam mumbled. Benton's eyes twitched manically.

"Kid ... Do you *ever* have fun?"

"M-hm."

Benton bit his tongue and turned his attention to tying Atkins's bootlaces together.

◆

The House of Water had been a cathedral in earlier times. One could make out faint traces of old crosses and symbols on its exterior. They'd been smudged from existence as soon as the Father came and took on the role Jesus and his disciples had once occupied. Nevertheless, the old Catholic markings had survived. One just had to look hard enough to spot them—and to have reason to look in the first place.

The cherished building underwent various stages of decrepitude in the years following the Father's death. For nigh on a year, it served as an altar of sorts. People left flowers, candles, and sometimes teddy bears as tribute—none of which were things Bill was known to care for especially. After the reality of his death set in, the House—where Bill had delivered his weekly addresses, administered Rites, and even taught youth swimming lessons—fell into disuse. Its shiny, enameled exterior gradually became dull. A colony of ducks invaded the lake it overlooked, the water still from the sudden lack of baptisms. At the peak of its desertedness, fiends who snorted and/or injected a myriad of substances moved in, and the former place of worship became a place of emotional escape. Perhaps they felt ashamed continuously committing self-harm on such hallowed grounds, or perhaps their product migrated and they followed. Regardless, after they left, the building went dark for some years.

In the weeks leading up to the New Father's first public rally, the House's old spirit was revived. A crew of blank-faced men in blank clothing came and restored its bygone glory, scrubbing away years of neglect and turmoil and unbranded stains. They resurfaced the plaza next, erecting two brand-new exterior fountains in a matter of days: one dedicated to Father Bill and the other to his heir, their future, the

Untold. They installed dual jumbotrons on either side of the House's lakeside amphitheater and wired speakers around the length of the shore.

They funneled Sam and his adopted regiment into the latter of two groups upon arrival. A small throng of men clad in white diverted the heavy flow of human traffic under one of two separate and massive banners that read, *CIVILIANS THIS WAY*, and *MILITARY THIS WAY.* A private waving an orange stick instructed Lemons to park their booze-ridden buggy in a separate lot reserved for military vehicles.

Lemons parked and cut the engine. He reached down and threw a badgeless military jacket into Sam's lap. "Welcome to the cause, Sam-I-Am." Sam nodded and shrugged the jacket on over his sweat-stained T-shirt.

They joined the military portion, restless men and women with tight abs and short-cropped hair. Sam shrugged uncomfortably in his thick camouflage jacket. The soldiers (Lemons and his brigade included) were outfitted like hippy hoplites, sporting bandanas and rolled sleeves to combat the wet heat. They began to shed layers of clothing as the audience grew and the spaces between them shrank.

The civilian side enjoyed protection from the sweltering humidity beneath a grid of massive tents, where fans and misters worked around the clock to cool them. Young men sacrificed themselves from the shade so damsels and old folks could enjoy the Shangri-la mist. Only the elderly and disabled (of which there were a surprising amount) remained seated; otherwise, the banquet chairs were pushed aside to accommodate more bodies.

Overlooking them all was a raised, shaded pavilion populated by the local aristocracy and their confrères. Some bought their tickets with their influence, others outright with cash. Still more weaseled their way in with promises of future political favors, while others used their charm to win dates with older, wealthier bourgeoise. A vast array of species could be found within this cohort: the proud, borderline arrogant lion, the gluttonous pig, and the quietly ruthless sparrow, to name a few.

The segregation naturally pitted the two lower ends of the trichotomy against one another. At one point some privates strutted over to the civilian sides to teach a lesson to some mouthy teenage boys. An officer's presence quickly diffused the situation. Another young and severely drunk private tried to climb the steps to the House, perhaps to speak at the podium, or perhaps to take a nap. Three men in white drabs appeared seemingly from nowhere and swarmed him. The private yelled and managed to wriggle free momentarily. He popped up at the front of the military assembly and shot up his arms like a rock star. A few laughs and cheers trickled amongst the crowd. They quickly grew disinterested as the men in drabs dragged him away, kicking as they went.

No one questioned whether Sam belonged with the enlisted folk. There were some younger and even gawkier boys on the military side, actual enlistees. But their minds were hardened, made that way by training and duty, whereas Sam was nervous and already fantasizing about being alone again. The sheltered feeling that goes hand in hand with loneliness awaited him. Alone, where it was just him and his screen. Alone, where there were no variables other than os and is. Alone, where things were under *control, his* control.

"Check it out, man," said Atkins, interrupting Sam's daydream. He jammed his finger at a woman barreling through the crowd toward them. Sam's face flushed red.

"Sammy!" the woman shouted.

Sam almost knocked heads with his stepmother. Her eyes were adorned with glistening blue makeup. "Angie?" She sniffed the air when Sam spoke.

"Have you been drinking?"

"Huh? No, I'm fine."

"Why didn't you say anything about coming?" she asked, looking at Sam with a mix of pride and shock.

"It was kind of a last-second thing." He concentrated on Angie's feet for a moment. She was shoeless, her toes cracked and blistered. "Angie?"

"Yes, Sam."

"Why are you here?"

She blinked gaudily. "To see the Untold, of course. Your father would have been here too. You know, we met at one of Father Bill's rallies."

As Sam thought of how to respond, the crowd became exceptionally restless. The ambient music that had been playing on the loudspeakers died. A familiar-sounding voice (belonging to Dolf Wagner, chief correspondent for Alliance News Network and frequent spokesman for rheumatoid arthritis medication) boomed over the mic. "Ladies and gentlemen, please rise for the reading of the Founding Principle."

The crowd whispered excitedly before the voice returned. Dolf himself led the incantation: "Do not fear water. Water is the basis of all life." The crowd joined instantly, tens of thousands of voices repeating the lines, Angie's amongst them. Sam only knew to listen:

I have seen the waters of the East, swirling tides filled with fish.

The waters of the North, cold and clear and crystalline.

The South, wide and slow and shallow.

The West, rocks and seafoam.

Everywhere there is water. The desert flower. The sprawling city.

It is in us all.

Without water, there is no life.

To fear water is to fear life. To live in fear is to live in denial.
We deny fear. We choose life. We choose the Way.
Water Is Life.

The air was calm. Then, slowly at first, people began to sit; in chairs, on the ground, in each other's laps. Legs crossed, legs sprawled, legs kicked out to one side. Spindly runner's legs, legs in wheelchairs, tiny child legs mushed together, pretzel-style. Legs in denim, legs in camouflage, smooth-shaven legs. They sat, squatted, and kneeled. They waited.

◆

Adam did not ask to be crowned.

Its band was inscribed with a cornucopia of fruit trees—oranges, apples and pears, peaches, figs, and apricots. A halo of constellations overlooked them, the stars represented by tiny winking gemstones. Rather than end in jutting points, the crown sloped up in gentle, breaking waves. Dazzling opal gems were set just below each wave's crest. Some sparkled with the polychrome radiance of diamonds, while others gleamed with unfathomable darkness.

Despite its delicateness, the crown sat unnaturally heavy atop his head. A mistake had been made during its manufacturing, and a loose bit somewhere within rattled whenever Adam moved his head. As far as he could tell, only he was attuned to the maddening jingle; otherwise, his subjects pretended not to hear.

Adam frowned at the mirror. His eyes left the gilded monstrosity set atop his brow for a moment to observe the freshly formed lines on his face. Though he had yet to break into his thirties, his face told a different tale. He looked thinner than he had when he left Pittsburgh, even after the months he'd spent worrying over his escape. He seemed to have aged decades in a matter of weeks. His hair had been trimmed, combed, and styled to suit his audience. Though he certainly looked the king's part, underneath was a different story. His hair felt dry and brittle to the touch and seemed a shade lighter than its normal jet black. *Heavy wears the crown*, he thought grimly.

"Father." The voice was gentle, trying to soothe him, but it only achieved the opposite. Adam sat up stiffly. It was Darlene, the teary-eyed bespectacled woman who'd coached him on how to stand and move his hands in front of a crowd of thousands. "I think it's time," she said, smiling assuredly and clutching a clipboard to her chest.

◆

There was a hush in the crowd as a man dressed in a dazzling suit the shade of snow walked out onto the House steps. Some gasped involuntarily. Then came the whispers. Sam tried clearing his throat. He choked and let out a quiet sob.

The Father looked from left to right. He was shorter than Sam had envisioned. His shoulders were relaxed, but he stood leaning forward, as if he was prepared to jump out into the crowd and disappear in its midst. He was handsome, with sunken cheeks and dark hair that met his ears. His crown shone a distinct shade of spun gold. Its brilliant gems glimmered in what remained of the light of day.

He finally broke the silence. "Thank you for coming out in this heat. I wish I could meet you all face-to-face, but ... Well, I guess that's why you all came."

Tens of thousands of disciples both old and new cried out to their savior.

Adam paced the stage like a restless stand-up. He came to the House's quartz staircase and settled there. "We've all been told that Father Bill, my grandfather, was a great man. While I can't say I ever met him, I imagine he was. My grandfather did not come here with any specific agenda. He didn't come to give speeches or perform Rites. We all consider him a holy figure now, like Jesus after the crucifixion. But things were different back then. He had a life before ... all this. Things were *simpler.*" Heads in the crowd began searching for someone to help interpret the Father's speech. "I'm sorry. A lot of you might not know who Jesus was ..."

A woman from the back of the civilian crowd cried out to him: *"Father, please! I love you! Show me the Way!"* The crowd reacted unanimously with hoots and whistles. Adam's eyes flicked toward the source of the noise before he continued.

"I'm not sure why Bill decided to stay here. I didn't know him; not personally, at least. I'm not from here, as you may have noticed ..." Adam stood quiet for a moment. He looked down at his feet and listened as his followers jostled amongst themselves. "I'm not sure enough of you realize how different life is where I come from. In the East, at least in Pittsburgh, they tell children terrifying stories about the West. They teach us that you all—we—are fanatics. That we have forsaken science. That we worship water that's poisoned. I'm sure you're all familiar with the term *Frog.*" The crowd visibly flinched. "We know these are lies."

"That's right!" shouted an elderly man from beneath the civilian tent.

Adam shook his head lightly and paced the length of the stage. "But lies exist all around us. Everywhere I've gone on this tour—Los Angeles, Portland, Seattle—I've spoken with people like you; soldiers, farmers, bankers, and everyone in between. *You* are the West. Not the Alliance, its politicians, or its celebrities. All the people I've spoken with are good, honest folks, just like every last one of you. But, along the way, they all told me different versions of the same story. One woman asked if I was relieved to finally come home. I asked her what she meant by 'home.' She told me, 'Well, there's no freedom out East. Out East, only the rich get to live. Out East, Water isn't sacred; it's feared.' So I asked her next, 'How do you know all this? Have you seen it for yourself?' 'Of course not,' she replied."

"All over the West, I heard the same story repeated. What does that say about us?"

Eyes darted confusedly at one another, seeking clarity. A young soldier nudged Sam on the shoulder. "Is this how he always talks?" Sam shrugged.

"It means that we are lying to ourselves. Many of you came from the East, looking for salvation. Did you find it?" Adam gestured toward the aristocracy perched high above the rest of the crowd. "There are your 'saviors'—I include myself with them. Do we truly seem any better than you?" Adam cried. "The commoner, the housewife, the student? Those of you who *walked* here?"

Juan Carlos Paolo Martínez smiled to himself as the crowd shifted its focus. *You can't deny he has guts*, he conceded, the condensation from his brandy glass dripping onto his shoes.

Adam waited for them to answer with a resounding *No!* that never came. The loose stone in his crown *clink*ed softly. He blinked and continued. "Of course not. We are all each other's equal. East, West—it does not matter. No, not everyone lives on equal footing *there*. But not everyone is equal *here*, either. We cannot vilify the East, because we are them, and they are us."

The crowd began talking amongst themselves anxiously. When was the Untold going to profess the Way's holy power? He was not supposed to speak in conjecture. They came all this way to celebrate their new Father. Instead, they'd gotten ... this?

Adam swallowed. He'd envisioned his people hailing him as a hero. Instead, he felt like a villain, knowing that he alone was responsible for dismantling their faith. "This whole time, I've been trying to figure out how to be Bill Edenson ... but I was wrong. Father Bill was a *liar*." The crowd gasped. "Those of you who came West looking for salvation, know that you were deceived. There is no set Way to life." Every instinct in Adam told him to go along with the crowd's eerie quiet. But he forced himself to continue. "Bill Edenson knew that too. But he lied. And he kept up with it, because he was a coward."

For a time, the silence was louder than rolling thunder.

The crowd erupted. Sam lost his footing and fell as the crowd swirled and breathed.

"Liar!"

"Traitor!"

"Murderer! You killed Father Bill!"

Someone hurled a bottle at the stage, which inspired a barrage of other objects. Most fell short, but a few didn't and bounced off a previously undetectable translucent shield protecting Adam. This only angered the crowd further.

Sam stumbled to his feet, ducking to avoid the rocks flying overhead, landing with *thunk*s against the stage barrier. He came across a lost set of keys and lobbed them meagerly alongside the other projectiles, hoping he wouldn't be mistaken as an Untold defender.

The turmoil brought on a swift change to the military side's comportment. The first row of soldiers stood in unison and turned to face the crowd. They brandished their weapons and held them tight against their chests, which inspired more objects and insults. Angie chucked a half-empty beer bottle lying nearby.

Adam stood onstage with his hands held out as if to parry the attacks. *"Stop! Listen to me!"* he appeared to shout, but his microphone had been cut.

◆

Empathy is the greatest weakness one can have, Juan Carlos lamented as Clemente escorted him away from the podium. His actor and politician co-panelists had excused themselves from the chaos before him. He'd delayed his retreat just in case Adam suddenly saw the error of his ways and re-embraced his role. He had failed to do so, and now the clock was ticking.

A ring of security quickly formed a canopy around him in the event any wayward bottles or shoes directed toward Adam incidentally came flying his way. Clemente leaned close to him as they strutted away. *"Our man is in position,"* he whispered hoarsely in Spanish. *"Just say the word."*

Juan Carlos need not do more than nod his head.

◆

The soldiers abandoned their loyalties and joined the civilians in attacking Adam. They spilled onto the stage, and the Father vanished from sight momentarily.

Sam fought to keep his footing in the swirling mass. Fireworks exploded off in the distance, perhaps a miscued celebration. A wayward elbow came suddenly flying into his breastplate, knocking the wind out of him. He clutched his stomach, gasping for breath.

Suddenly, the crowd grew still. The House was silent. Then Sam heard his stepmother scream, breaking the silence.

Sam felt his chest and frowned. He was sitting down, though he was unsure how he landed there. A dark red circle had sprouted from his chest. He tried covering the stain, out of embarrassment more than anything; *Nice going, Sam.* Blood gushed between his fingers, and his eyes went wide. He searched the crowd for his new friends, Lemons, Atkins, Benton. But they were gone.

The crowd parted around him. He held his chest, trying to breathe and gargling blood instead, which only made him more afraid. He was vaguely aware of Angie sobbing at his side, her eyes hiding behind her palms. Sam took in the strange faces surrounding him. He didn't detect any sorrow on their faces. If anything, they seemed curious.

"Don't you see?"

Then it was the Untold who stood over him. Silent tears streamed down his cheeks. Sam blinked at the multicolored light being filtered through his crown. He wanted to apologize. He felt like he was hurting him.

Adam bent down and picked up Sam as though he were a small child. A red circle stained the floor where he lay. The crowd spaced out to allow Adam to move toward the lake.

"Don't you all see?"

Rows of fanatics garbed in white combed through the crowd. Sam gazed past Adam's chin, watching the sky darken. Men and police sirens screamed in the distance, but no one gave it any thought. Their only concern was Adam.

Adam stepped over the stone retaining wall separating the lake from the pavilion. A splash of water grazed Sam's cheek as Adam dropped to his knees and gently lowered him into the water, the wiry muscles in his back and shoulders straining at the effort.

Sam did not feel wet or cold. The water rippled outward and clouded with his blood. Adam's face blocked the setting sun, and the solar crown he wore was more beautiful than anything Sam had ever seen. When he looked into his veiled eyes, he felt like he belonged.

Adam scooped warm water into Sam's hair. He wiped his face, smoothing out his eyebrows as a mother does to her child. Rust-tinged water came streaming between his fingers. "I'm sorry." He was crying. "You're doing great." *Don't be upset. I'm okay now,* Sam wanted to tell him. But he could not speak.

Sam's eyes tracked a moving piece of Adam's hair before they settled and turned still.

Adam wiped his tears away and carried the boy back to the bank. He laid him gently atop the retaining wall. Blood continued to seep from the hole in his chest, muddying the water below. The crowd did not seem to notice. Adam folded the boy's arms over his chest and raised his head above his chin, then straightened his legs and crossed his feet over each another. He swept his hair back to show his forehead and gently folded his eyes shut.

Adam looked up from the boy's body, adjusted his crown, and recoiled ever so slightly. His devotees had formed a line. He saw the shimmer in their eyes, a foul, blind devotion, and knew instantly to fear it. He did not linger on any one face too long. To do so was to greet an entire nation.

They patiently awaited his blessing.

The first baptisee wore vibrant blue makeup around her eyes. She was crying, the tears running cyan blue down her cheeks. The woman came to the boy's side and gently kissed him. Then she stepped over the wall and joined Adam in the lake. She grasped his hand and placed it over her breast. When his fingers grazed her collarbone, she shuddered and fell. Adam caught her before her knees touched the lake's shallow cement bottom.

The woman gazed at him like a deity and joined her palms together. "Father?" she asked. "Take my pain away. Show me the Way."

He dipped his hand in the Water and wet her hair.

Epilogue

September 19, 2025

Manhattan (Lower East Side), New York City

"DOES THIS product meet your expectations, chef?"

Sarcastic prick. Anthony wrinkled his nose and closed the lid over the pristine hamachi. "This will do." He tapped his foot anxiously "Anything else?"

"I do not believe so, Chef."

"I only deal in absolutes. Was that a 'Yes, that'll be all, Chef?'"

Abdul smiled without the faintest hint of contempt. He would not let this man's boorish behavior ruin his weekend with his son. "Yes, that will be all, Chef Anthony," he pronounced neatly, Anthony sneering at him all the while. "I will see you next week then. Goodbye." Abdul stooped his head and slipped out the receiving door. His heart soared as he approached his rust-stained delivery van. He knew that his son eagerly awaited him in the passenger seat.

He had asked some months ago for Abdul to come to El Paso to attend Career Day, where mothers and fathers in finance and firefighting and food service showcased their work to a classroom of third graders. *Papa has to work in New York,* he'd told him, already aware that neither brother Ferraro would ever allow such a thing; orders were taken on Mondays and Thursdays, and deliveries went out on Tuesdays and Fridays. Wednesdays and the weekends were the time for such follies (or *minchiata,* as the brothers Ferraro took to calling it). Anything not having to do with fish on those four sacred days was *minchiata* in the brothers' eyes—Career Day included.

Abdul vowed to take his son with him on the job the next time he visited instead. *You will be my right-hand man,* he had promised him over the phone. Surely the brothers Ferraro would allow that. "Long as your shit gets done." This was the youngest Ferraro brother, Nico's favorite way to answer requests from his employees.

Abdul slammed the finicky driver's side door shut and patted his son on the shoulder. "Ready?" His hair had grown past his neck. It suited his almond-shaped eyes. He loved those eyes more than anything.

He grinned that toothy grin that Abdul loved so much and opened his mouth to speak. He moved his elbow to his mouth and coughed instead.

Once the fit subsided, he nodded eagerly and croaked, *"Yes, Papa."* Abdul put the gear in R and backed out of the alley, smiling as only a rich man could.